zosia wand

trust me

First published in 2017 by Head of Zeus Ltd

9 7 5 3 1 2 4 6 8

A catalogue record for this book is available from the British Library.

ISBN (HB): 9781786692290
ISBN (XTPB): 9781786692306
ISBN (E): 9781786692283

Typeset by Divaddict Publishing Solutions Ltd

Printed and bound in Great Britain by CPI Group (UK) Ltd, Croydon CR0 4YY

Head of Zeus Ltd
First Floor East
5–8 Hardwick Street
London EC1R 4RG

WWW.HEADOFZEUS.COM

With love to Simon, for making it possible, and Jemima and Nadia for making it matter.

This book is dedicated to the community of Ulverston, my home.

Chapter 1

Sam sees it first. I'm oblivious to what's about to happen, resting against the wooden lip of the hull with my head tilted up as the sun licks my face. Coniston Water. The English Lake District. A glorious spring day, sharp as a shard of glass. We're gliding up the lake, the boat following a comfortable melody, and I'm finally beginning to relax.

I'm a city girl; sailing is an alien activity. In my former life, people who sailed inhabited a different world. I glimpsed them in foreign, sun-kissed marinas as they descended from dazzling white yachts in their deck shoes, designer jeans turned up at the ankle and pastel-coloured jumpers draped across their shoulders. I was the one walking past in search of a cheap hostel, interrail card in my pocket, back sweaty from the rucksack dragging on my shoulders. When the boys first mentioned sailing I'd foolishly imagined gin and tonics in iced glasses and careless laughter over meals in restaurants too exclusive to display their prices, but this is Coniston in March, not La Rochelle in August.

I knew it would be different, just not quite this different. This boat isn't a yacht. Apparently it's an Enterprise, thirteen feet long, though it feels much smaller with the three of us on board. It doesn't gleam white; it's wooden with worn varnish and bits that need replacing and the sails are the colour of dried blood, but it is pretty in its own *Swallows and Amazons* way. Sam is winding a piece of rope into neat coils, the tendons in his forearms shifting beneath his flesh as he works. He's not been still since we pulled up in the car park with the boat on the trailer behind us. The two of them jumped out and set to in a rhythm of activity I've never witnessed before. Jonty, solid, established and weathered by the world, Sam, his younger, slender echo, unhitching and lifting, pulling and manoeuvring to the pebbled shore, then clipping and unclipping, more lifting and pushing into the water, shoving and wading and climbing and beckoning and reaching and stretching, and me, hovering behind with the chill damp rising up my calves, waiting to be told what to do. Sam holding out his hand, helping me in. The unsteadiness of the boat beneath me. Allowing myself to be told. Sit there. Hold this. Mind your head. Do what I say and everything will be fine.

Sam has been sailing since he could walk, more or less, like Jonty before him, though he rarely goes out these days. The two of them have a language they share; words, and commands which mean nothing to me but result in flurries of activity. Ready about! Bearing away! Lee ho! (Lee ho? Seriously?) Sheets to the wind, I guess, and tacking and gybing and something close hauled. These snaps and barks leave me jumpy and impotent while Sam flits from here to there, knotting and unknotting, looping and threading and shifting his weight from one side to the other. I'm completely at his mercy, but he's patient, smiling, kind. Jonty is steering from the back of the boat, his eyes flicking up to check the sails, which flap and thump above us like the wings of an angry bird. Sam works quickly, methodically, concentrating, eyes squinting, forehead lined. He's competent. Masculine and adult. No longer a boy. I like watching him. The graceful sweep of his limbs, these strong, confident movements. Jonty lets him take the helm and he rests his hand on what I now know is the tiller, which somehow steers us. His faded blue T-shirt is billowing below his buoyancy aid, offering glimpses of a taut stomach above the waistband of the shorts I teased him about this morning. Feeling the cling of damp denim against my flesh, I can see the sense now.

This is Sam's environment: the lake, the mountains, the wind. He could be one of those beautiful young men from that other world, gliding into a continental marina, ready to disembark for an evening of cocktails with a pretty girl.

It was Sam who suggested we take the boat out today, swallowing the last of his tea and taking the stairs two at a time to gather the kit. I grabbed the coolbag and threw in anything that might lend itself to a picnic, because I knew once we got to the lake we'd be here until sundown. Days like this can be rare. We might be lucky and have weeks of sun right through spring and summer, but that's the thing about Cumbria, you can never predict the weather. If the sun is out and it's at all possible, everyone drops what they're doing and heads for the lake. The weather forces even the most reticent to be spontaneous because it rains a lot in the Lake District. I knew that before I moved here and I wasn't looking forward to it, but what I didn't know is what happens when the clouds part and the sun breaks through. It's like someone has picked up a paintbrush and splattered the world with colour. Indigo lake reflecting the sky, mountains of lavender and mauve, grey blue slate. Today the first early buds are appearing on fragile branches; in a matter of weeks there will be green on green added to this palette, khaki through to lime, the purple hum of bluebells between. Our slice of paradise.

Sam's body stiffens. He straightens up. I follow his gaze. Ahead of us the sky looks darker. There's a menacing grey cast across everything.

Jonty laughs. 'We'll be fine!' But he's on his feet, taking the tiller from Sam, preparing for something.

The shining mirror of the lake has shattered, offering a broken reflection of the sky. The surface of the water is changing in texture, becoming rougher, matt. I shiver, suddenly chilled. 'What's happening?'

Sam is focused on Jonty. 'We should reef, Dad. That wind from the valley is strong.'

Jonty laughs. He's in his element, the wind on his face, his body alert, but Sam is nervous.

'We should reef the sails while we're still calm.'

'We'll be fine.'

I can hear the familiar edge to his voice and ask, 'What's reefing?' to distract them from one another.

Sam explains. 'We reduce the sail. It gives a smaller surface area and makes it easier to cope with the wind.'

'Reefing's for wimps!' Jonty fixes his eyes ahead. 'Let's show you some proper sailing!'

My gut clenches. I want to say something, but I'm in a foreign place, without the experience or the words.

Sam gives me a reassuring nod, but he looks worried. 'Just do what I say.'

I take comfort from the fact that there are other boats

braving the wind, and half a dozen windsurfers riding the gusts like giant butterflies flexing their wings, but as we get closer I notice the boats ahead of us are leaning over, their masts conspicuously tilting away from the wind. They seem to be lowering their sails. I look back at Sam.

'It's all right. He knows the lake. If it gets too much we'll turn around.' But I can hear the anxiety in his voice. He guides me down to the front end. 'We need to distribute our weight evenly across the boat.'

Stumbling, I fall against him as we pitch to and fro. He lowers me on to the bench along one side and sits opposite. Goosebumps pepper my arms, my hands are trembling. As the boat shifts this way and that, Sam leans back and then forward, following the rhythm, using his body to steady us.

'What's happening?' I'm trying to understand. To prepare.

'The air flow is more turbulent up this end of the lake. It's disturbed by the landscape as it rolls over Torver Common – the contours of the ground, buildings, trees.' Water sprays over the side of the boat as we pitch alarmingly to one side. Cold seeps through the seat of my jeans. Sam leans back to compensate and has to shout over the rush of the wind. 'The further up the lake it goes, the more agitated it gets.'

'Should I rock backwards and forwards like you?'

He shakes his head, leaning towards me, but Jonty barks, 'Sit still! I'll keep the boat steady.'

'I'm just—'

'I know how to sail a boat!'

Sam does as he's told, but his body is tense and I can see he's angry. A sudden gust of wind hits us and the boat tips towards his side, the water rising behind him. He shifts instinctively, but Jonty bellows, 'Sit still!' and Sam stops, the boat leaning dangerously towards the water. I want to grab him before he topples back, he's inches from the surface of the lake. He compensates by leaning forward, lending his weight to me, his upper body almost in my lap, and I'm momentarily reassured to have him so close, but then we're smacked by another gust of wind and pushed so far down that water sluices over the side. I feel a cold flush across my feet, my ankles. Another great wash follows, a long tongue unfurling and spewing water, flooding the far corner. The lake has become an angry, living thing, an enormous gulping mouth, determined to swallow us up.

Everything changes in that instant. The mass of murky water and debris sloshing about adds to the weight on Sam's side. I'm now raised quite high and Sam is low, so low and getting lower and lower. The water behind him is rising and slowly, almost inevitably, as if it was always meant to happen this way, the edge of the boat dips right down and slides in. I scream. Sam slips back and is slurped up, floating in his buoyancy aid out into the great gaping mouth of the lake.

I'm tipped forward and crack my forehead on the boom; there's a terrible pain as I too slide in, the cold creeping up under my clothes, chilling my flesh, claiming me. The boat lurches over on to its side and the sail, the great wing of a wounded bird, descends over Sam, landing with a rippling thud on the surface of the lake, covering him entirely. Jonty is in the water, clutching at a long tail of rope. I grab the boom and lift myself up, as high as I can and shout to Sam, but he's trapped. I can see his outline kicking and struggling beneath the blood-coloured fabric of the sail, and then it stops abruptly.

I scream, 'Sam!' Jonty drops the rope and swims, long, strong strokes slicing the water, along the length of the mast. Faster! Faster! How long will Sam be able to breathe under there? I try and push myself up higher to look, but the boom sinks beneath me, I can feel the boat behind me shifting and then I see Sam's head pop up some distance from the sail and he waves. Relieved, I drop back down to rest my aching arms, but he shouts, 'Lizzie! Look out!' and I'm aware of a looming dark, the hull closing in on me like a clam shell, Sam's voice shouting, 'Hold on! Stay calm!' and I trust him, though my heart is punching into my throat and the dark that's descending, slowly, is like a dreadful omen, as the vast shell comes down over my head, blocking out the wind, the sky, the light and creating a trembling cave on the surface of the lake.

I'm alone. Trapped in the watery quiet. Dark. Chill. Without Sam or Jonty all I can do is float in this foreign place, my heart banging against my ribs. How did this happen? Moments ago we were sunlit and laughing, surrounded by colour and beauty. I shudder. I'm struggling to breathe, no idea what might be in the water beneath me, what might happen next. I instinctively tense every muscle in my body, hardening myself against imaginary razor-sharp teeth.

'Lizzie!' It's Jonty. He sounds miles away, as if he's shouting to me from the shore. 'Lizzie, are you OK?'

'Yes! Yes, I'm all right. What do I do?'

Sam's voice. Closer. 'Stay there! I'll get you.'

I feel him before I see him, a giant fish splitting the water, propelling himself under the rim of the boat, his sleek dark head rising, surfacing in front of me. He's gasping, shaking his hair from his face, blinking, grinning. 'You OK?'

I'm awed by this water creature he's become. I've never seen him like this before. Elemental. Heroic. The quiet settles around the two of us in our little water cave.

He asks, 'You're OK to swim?' I nod. 'You'll need to dive

under the boat and up out the other side. I'll follow you.' Another nod. My words have been sucked out of me.

Jonty's voice is closer now, through the wood that separates us. 'Are you OK?'

'She's fine.' Sam grins at me, exposing his even teeth. 'This is how we'll do it. You take a deep breath, OK?' He waits for me to nod. 'I'll need to weigh you down, because of your buoyancy aid. Hold your breath and I'll push you under the lip of the boat and you'll pop out the other side.' Another smile, but I don't want to go. I want to stay here in this stillness with him. He reads my mind. 'Dad will be there.' He swims around behind me, his voice in my ear. 'Ready?'

'Ready.'

He pushes hard on my back and I sink a little into the water, but not low enough. He pushes harder and I reach for the edge of the boat to try and grip, push my head beneath the surface, my eyes clenched tight, but I can't get any further down. I come up gulping for air, feeling desperate. Useless. 'Sorry.'

Jonty calls out. 'What's going on?'

Sam grabs at the strap of his buoyancy aid, feeling for the clasp. I try and stop him. 'Don't take it off!'

'I have to get lower into the water.'

Jonty's voice, anxious, shouts, 'What's going on?'

'He's taking off his buoyancy aid!'

Sam insists, 'I have to. I can't get low enough. I'll be all right.'

We wait for an answer. Permission. Since we set out Jonty has been the captain. He hesitates. Eventually a reluctant 'All right.'

'No!' I can't let Sam do this. It isn't safe.

He persists, 'I'm a strong swimmer and I'm staying close to the boat.'

Jonty shouts, 'Make sure you bring the buoyancy aid with you.'

'OK.' He's already wriggling free, attaching the strap to his arm as instructed, and he positions himself behind me again. 'Ready?'

He climbs on to me, like a child looking for a piggyback, much heavier this time, and I sink down just low enough to wriggle under the rim and up towards the light, to Jonty, his face crumpled with worry, his eyes, those dark, dark eyes, searching, checking me over. Relief. Relief and guilt and delight, as he hugs me to him and plants his mouth on mine.

Sam pops up a little distance from us, his buoyancy aid bobbing about in the water beside him. 'Get that on!' Jonty barks and Sam, rolling his eyes, does as he's told.

The boat is a great turtle, bouncing beside us while Jonty shouts instructions to Sam. We still have to get back to shore and my jaw is tense, my teeth clattering wildly. As I look to Sam, to see what I should do, he turns and freezes suddenly, his eyes fixed on something beyond me. I cringe in panic at whatever disaster is coming next, unable to look.

'Can I help?'

Rotating clumsily in the water, I see a woman in a slick black wetsuit on a surfboard, blonde hair pulled in a tight ponytail, perfect bone structure.

Jonty grins. 'Where did *you* come from?'

She raises an eyebrow. 'I was watching you from the other side of the lake.' She's clearly amused.

'Yeah, well, these boats are a bit harder to control than that thing,' he says, nodding at the windsurfer.

'You should have reefed.'

I look over at Sam, expecting him to be laughing, to say, 'I told you so,' but he's swimming away from us, around the hull.

Jonty ignores the comment and says, 'We need to stay with the boat, but if you could take Lizzie into shore, that would help.'

Me? On a surfboard?

Jonty feels inside the interior pocket of his lifejacket and passes her the car keys. 'We're parked at Brown Howe.' Much to Jonty's amusement, she unzips the top of her wetsuit and slips the keys into her cleavage. She takes her time zipping it back up, enjoying the moment as much as Jonty. We are all mesmerised, watching her lower herself into a crouch and slide gracefully into the water.

Holding her board steady, she tells me to drape myself over the end. I assume we're going to paddle side by side, kicking our way across to the shore, and I grip the far edge, but she shakes her head. 'Further over. Get your belly on to the board, so your weight is evenly distributed over each side.'

I wriggle inelegantly forward, my sodden jeans making my legs clumsy. She climbs back on, wobbling to and fro a little, getting her balance and adjusting the sail. She is tall and lithe and Amazonian in her posture and I am a useless deadweight as we take off across the water.

From my position I can't see much more than the surface of the lake and we reach the shore in what seems like seconds. She removes the keys as I struggle to my feet and holds them out to me. They're warm from her body. I'm beginning to shiver. 'You need to get to the car and get yourself as warm as possible. Do you have a jumper with you or a coat?'

'I think there's a couple of dog blankets in the car.'

'Get your wet things off and wrap yourself in them. Find anything you've got. Those two will be a while yet; they'll need to right the boat and bring it in. If you're still shivering, turn the engine on and get the heater going for a bit.'

'Will they be all right?'

She laughs. 'They'll be fine. It'll teach them not to show off in future.'

'What about the boat?'

'The boat will dry out and survive to sail another day.'

'Not with me in it.'

She laughs again and she's still laughing as she gets back on to the windsurfer and makes her way down the lake, away from the turtle bobbing about on the water.

The blankets are itchy and smell of damp dog, but after a quick blast of the heater they help get my body back up to temperature and I lower the car seat and allow myself to drift off while I wait. It's getting dark by the time they've brought the boat in, de-rigged it and got it back on the trailer and they're both dripping, cold and desperate to get home. As we make our way along the narrow road that skirts the lake edge I ask about the windsurfer.

'Do you know who she was?'

Jonty shakes his head.

I turn around to look at Sam in the back seat. He says, 'No,' as if the question is ridiculous and turns away, his face burning. I've embarrassed him. The windsurfer's wetsuit hugged her slim frame and accentuated every curve, but it was more than that, it was the way she carried herself, her posture, her confidence. She did look pretty sexy.

'I didn't ask her name,' I say, feeling bad. 'I'd like to thank her properly.'

'I'm sure we'll bump into her again,' Jonty says. 'Can't avoid it in a place like this.'

'Is that wishful thinking?'

He chuckles.

Sam is quiet. 'You OK?' I turn to look at him again.

'Fine,' he says, irritably, eyes fixed on the lake.

Chapter 2

Our little episode in the water leaves me with a rotten cold I struggle to shake off. By Friday I'm working at home with a hot-water bottle in my lap, my paperwork spread out across the floor and a cup of hot lemon and ginger steaming beside me, which is why I'm the one to take the call. Jonty doesn't answer his mobile, so I throw on some clothes and head out to Sam's school.

Tarnside High School is a grand Victorian construction crowning the hill, with gleaming glass additions and a magnificent view over the town and surrounding countryside. My city comprehensive was a mess of ageing concrete boxes and flimsy prefabs. All this space and light and possibility, does Sam notice it? Or is it only the off-comers like me, washing up here, who can appreciate the beauty of this place?

I sit down in Mr Wright's cramped office. Through the window behind him I can see the muddle of slate roofs and cobbled streets, the greys and blues punctuated by an occasional ice-cream-coloured façade. I still can't believe I'm living in this absurdly pretty place. Cumbria? The Lake District? This wasn't on my radar. I grew up in suburban south London in a pebble-dashed semi like the fifty or more others in our street and the street beyond that and the one beyond that. Two bedrooms and a box room, with a strip of garden divided from the neighbours by a panelled fence. Streets upon streets of people who had nothing to do with each other. No market square, no festivals or market days, no sheep, lakes or fells, no geese flurrying on to the tarn as the sun goes down.

'I was hoping to speak to a parent.' Mr Wright looks me up and down with a frown. I should have thought this through before I rushed up here. Chosen a different T-shirt at least. I don't think Mr Wright appreciates the message, *This Is What A Feminist Looks Like*, scrawled across my chest.

Mr Wright is head of sixth form. He's a proper grown-up, in a suit and tie, and he's not impressed. He needs to speak to a parent. Jonty is the parent, but he's not answering his phone. His job as South Lakeland's arts officer involves a lot of face-to-face meetings, which he generally tries to arrange in his favourite cafés. He usually answers his phone quite promptly; this silence is unlike him.

I'm not an adequate substitute for Jonty. It's not what I'm wearing that's the issue. I could be dressed in a stylish suit or a frumpy knee-length skirt and cardigan and it probably wouldn't make a lot of difference. What's bothering Mr Wright is the fact that I could easily pass for Sam's sister. We're an odd sort of family.

Judging by the explosion of files across his desk, managing paperwork is not one of Mr Wright's skills. He picks up a pen and starts to twirl it in his fingers. I feel sorry for the man; he appears beleaguered and I'm not helping the situation. He doesn't know who I am in relation to Sam but isn't quite brave enough to ask. He knows me. His wife, Eve, is my boss. She runs the community park where I work and he's met me at events, though he's obviously not connected me to Sam, or Jonty. Out of his suit he's different, more natural. Rusty hair and freckled skin. His broad face is stern now, but I've seen the softness when he looks at Eve. He's young for a head of year. He and Eve are a bit of a power couple. No kids, though Eve's told me they'd like them; it just doesn't seem to be happening.

I don't know what to say. I'm not Sam's mother, but I live with his dad. Sam's been with us two years and we're muddling along. It works pretty well. It's difficult for me to define the nature of our relationship; there is no word for what I am. I'm not married to his father, I'm not an aunt, nor an older sister, no blood relation. The school forms say 'parent or guardian' but guardian sounds dusty and formal. If I was Jonty's wife I would probably be Sam's stepmother, but I'm not, I'm simply Sam's dad's girlfriend. This sounds trivial and my relationship with Sam is not trivial. It was a bit of a shock to suddenly find myself responsible for two children, but I rose to the challenge.

There are so many things I'm not – mother, sister, friend – but in some way I'm all of these things to the gentle seventeen-year-old boy we're here to discuss. Mr Wright is waiting for clarification. I look him straight in the eye. 'Sam's dad is at work and not currently answering his phone.' I bite the bullet and make a choice. 'I'm Sam's stepmother.'

Mr Wright's eyebrow flickers, but I hold his gaze. Damn him. I've earned that title. The school want to talk to a responsible adult? I'm a responsible adult. Mr Wright may not remember, but I've been to the school in this capacity before, when Sam was first considering the sixth form here. Nell, Sam's younger sister, was still living with us then. Both kids had moved in at the end of January that year, when their mum had to go over to Ireland to take care of their nanna after her stroke. The timing couldn't have been worse. Nell was in the last year of primary school and Sam was taking his GCSEs, so they moved in with their dad. And me. Not exactly part of the plan, but we got through it and Nell went to join her mum once the summer term was over. Sam, however, decided he wanted to stay, with us, in Tarnside and go to sixth form here rather than Ireland. Last time I was in this building, Jonty was doing the grown-up parent bit, with me sort of hovering supportively in the background, but I was part of that and dressed appropriately that time. I remember the Nicole Farhi jacket, a charity-shop find, but Mr Wright wouldn't have known that.

'You are responsible for Sam?'

'Yes. Well, as far as anyone can be responsible for a boy of his age.' A deep line sinks between Mr Wright's Fuzzy Felt eyebrows and I make a mental note to cut the jokes. Responsibility isn't something I usually have any trouble with; I've been behaving like a responsible adult since I was a young child – somebody had to – but there's something about being back in a school, dressed in this T-shirt and what I now realise is Sam's hoodie, that's put me on the back foot. I have a similar hoodie in a darker grey. Sam's taller than me but still quite slight, so the fit is more or less the same and this was hanging on the back of the chair. I glance at the clock. My proposal needs to be in to the Arts Council by five. I reassure myself that I'm almost done. In truth I could send it through now, but I was hoping to double-check the supporting documents first. Maybe Sam's behind with some homework? Or they need to discuss his uni application? But if it was as simple as that we could have talked on the phone. 'What's happened?'

'Do you know where Sam is?'

I wonder if I've heard the question right. 'He's here – I mean, not here exactly, but somewhere here. At school.'

He shakes his head. 'We haven't seen Sam all week.'

This isn't possible. Sam went to school this morning. He slung his rucksack over his shoulder and sloped out of the front door with a 'Catch you later!' like he always does. Like he has done every day this week, and the weeks before that.

'I don't understand.'

'As far as you were aware, he was in school?' I nod. 'Is it possible that he's been revising at home? Or the library?'

Has Sam said something about this and I haven't registered? He was revising at home over half-term. He borrowed my battered copy of *Macbeth* with all the scribbled notes in the margin so he could reference another Shakespeare play in his arguments. I was at the office most days, but we did grab lunch together and there was clear evidence of his school work spread out across the kitchen table. The recycling bin was overflowing with newspapers he was reading for some assignment and I remember spilling coffee on his history textbook. He has a desk in his room, but if the house is empty, Sam likes to stay near the fridge and the kettle. It's perfectly possible he's revising somewhere. He'll have a plan of some kind; Sam's very clear about what he wants to achieve.

Life is frantic at this time of year, with funding applications to get in before the end of April, Easter events in the park, St George's Day looming and then, just a week later, the Flag Festival. As the town's festivals coordinator I'm responsible for all these events and I'm struggling to keep on top of it, if I'm honest. Eve's priorities are revenue funding, sponsorship, contracts and staffing; she needs me to work independently and I don't want to let her down. Since Nell joined her mum in Ireland, I've not bothered so much with the domestic stuff. Sam's old enough to take care of himself pretty much. Or so I thought.

I picture Sam at the breakfast table, scooping cereal into his mouth, bowl in one hand, spoon in the other, one eye on the clock. Did he mention the library? I remember taking an apple out of the fruit bowl, one of the green ones he likes, and throwing it to him, 'For break,' and he caught it and dropped it into his rucksack. I assumed he was going to school; he said nothing to correct me.

'Maybe he is at the library. I mean, as long as he's revising, that's what's important at the moment, isn't it?'

'This is a school, not a drop-in centre. We are still teaching. If he has chosen to revise somewhere else, we would need to be informed and I'm not sure we would necessarily approve.'

If only Jonty was here, he would know what to do. Should I be saying something to defend Sam? What do good parents do in a situation like this? I have no idea. The very thought of my mother entering the school premises and embarrassing me was enough to keep me on the straight and narrow. My family life remained firmly locked behind our front door.

Behind Mr Wright, through the window, I look across the playing fields to the town nestled at the bottom of the hill. Nothing very bad can happen in a place as pretty as this. Tarnside reminds me of Sunday-night TV programmes from my childhood: small-town stories, a vicar, a local bobby, a district nurse, all moving through a soft-focus world with no city drugs or blades, where even the murders are cosy and neatly solved. Sam loves this place. He came back from Ireland to go to this school. So where the hell is he?

Mr Wright taps his pen against the table repeatedly. He says, 'Anything going on at home?'

That question! How dare this man suggest there is anything wrong in Sam's home! Sam has Jonty. He has me. He has a clear routine, food in the fridge, bills paid and a home he can take for granted. Calm. Order. Welcome. He is taken care of, loved, listened to. There is nothing wrong in Sam's home; I've made sure of that.

So why is he skipping school?

A thought pops into my head. Silly. It was nothing. I probably imagined it. A look. Nothing else. I was singing along to the radio in the kitchen one night, weeks ago, I'd forgotten all about it until now. I was wiping down the surfaces, getting ready to go to bed. I didn't know Sam was there. When I glanced up he was watching me. Looking at me. And there was something about that look. Something different. Something more adult. I don't know. Whatever it was, it's got nothing to do with school. I need to focus.

Mr Wright is waiting. His face is not judgemental but concerned. He and Eve are off-comers like me, though they've been here longer. Mr Wright is also Neil Wright, distracted, overworked husband to Eve, who's struggling to conceive a child. He knows things aren't always straightforward.

I get out my phone. 'I'll try calling Sam now.'

I'm relieved when it goes straight to voicemail, having no idea what I'd say if Sam answered. It's three o'clock; he'll be back at the cottage soon, pretending he's been at school all day. 'I'll speak to him this evening,' I say, trying to sound in control.

'He's a good student.' Mr Wright smiles suddenly, his face transformed and I'm relieved. He likes Sam. All the staff like Sam. He works hard, he's respectful, he gets along with people. It wasn't always like this. I'm proud of him. If I'm allowed to be proud. Proud to be connected to him. 'This isn't like him,' says Mr Wright, looking at me as if I might provide an answer. He thinks it's something to do with me and Jonty. Why does everyone assume we can't make this work? They know nothing about us, about the way we are together. 'Sam has a bright future ahead of him. There's no reason for him not to do very well indeed...' Mr Wright pauses. There's a but coming. He stops himself. 'I would hate...' He looks at me. 'He's worked so hard.'

We've worked so hard. I remember the angry fifteen-year-old who arrived with his little sister, looking me up and down, lip curled, glancing at his father with contempt and then back at me. 'He hasn't told you?' And Jonty standing with his eyes closed, wishing the whole thing away. *I've* worked hard. Swallowing my anger, gritting my teeth, looking at it from Sam's point of view. Patience, patience, patience. Talking to Jonty, encouraging Sam, cajoling the two of them to do things together, building that relationship. I thought we'd cracked it. Sam has been doing well. Everything has been going well.

Sam avoids confrontation. When he's disturbed by something or upset, he withdraws. I know this boy. I've earned his trust and he's blossomed with us. What's happened? Could it be something to do with Jonty? They don't talk much, but that's always been the case: two testosterone-fuelled men fighting to be the alpha male; I assumed this was just part of adolescence. Sam's been fine with me.

Why hasn't he talked to me?

Chapter 3

I call Jonty as I leave the school. Still no answer and Sam's phone goes straight to voicemail again. I look at my watch. It's not half past three yet. If he's at the library he'll have the phone switched off. I could go straight there and confront him. I feel a sudden need to see him, to be close to him, to be reassured that all is well. My logical head is telling me to relax, he'll be home soon, as he has been every day this week, but a dark shape has formed at the edge of my thoughts and clings on.

Tarnside library takes up the ground floor of the old manor house in the community park. They regularly host events for us and support our projects with linked reading initiatives and displays. A quick scan of the reference section and the four desks that are tucked between the bookshelves shows me that Sam's not here. Jean, a smiling librarian with a shock of spiky pewter hair tells me she hasn't seem Sam all week. So where has he been? I take a deep breath and try to steady my heartbeat. Wherever it is, he'll be on his way home now. I'll talk to him there.

Tarnside is a market town which serves the surrounding villages between Windermere and Coniston. It's survived partly due to the industry that has built up in Barrow-in-Furness, but also as a result of its position along the Cumbria Way. Jonty was part of the millennium initiative that saw the future in tourism and developed the notion of a festival town, which eventually led to my job being created. He and Eve worked on the funding application together, though I suspect Eve did all the work; Jonty's more of an ideas man.

Fell Rise stretches up from the centre of town towards Coniston. The street is a hotchpotch of grand and modest houses, villas and cottages, two and three storey. Some are separated by narrow ginnels that lead into secret courtyards, but for the most part they butt up alongside one another, fronting the pavement directly or with steps up to the front door. Jonty's cottage is a raspberry-coloured slice, sandwiched between its midnight-blue twin on one side and an imposing, whitewashed, double-fronted house that straddles the ginnel leading to the shared access lane the runs behind the back yards. I can hear the familiar sound of Loopy, Jonty's black and tan lurcher, yapping at me through the front window as I approach. Sam will be home soon and everything will be explained. I try and concentrate on the poetry festival that forms the basis of my funding application. Tarnside hosts about ten festivals a year with new ones starting up all the time and I'm employed on a part-time basis to support them and ensure they run smoothly. The poetry festival is something I'm planning for the quiet winter weeks in February next year. There's something about Tarnside that's always embraced arts and culture. I read somewhere that there were once seven theatres on this street; the whitewashed house next door might well have been one of them.

Loopy scuttles and slides along the tiled hall to greet me. Crooked ears and espresso eyes comfort me. She is oblivious to worry. Jonty always has a treat in his pocket for her; I never do, but she remains hopeful. Sam's bike key isn't on the hooks in the hall. We keep the bikes out the back, which means taking them through the ginnel and back down the shared path. It's quite common for him to forget to hang up the key. It's been through the washing machine several times and is often the cause of a last-minute panic in the mornings. I call out, 'Hello? Anyone home?' but there's no answer. I open the back door, which we tend to leave unlocked, and step out into the yard. Loopy thrusts past me, growling and barking, leaping up at the gate that leads to the access lane. Next door's cat is probably sniffing around out there. There are just two bikes leaning against one another under the narrow plastic roof Jonty fixed to the wall to shield them from the rain. Sam is either still out with his bike or he's left it somewhere.

Upstairs, I check his room, just in case, picturing him sitting at the makeshift desk under the rear window with his headphones on, oblivious to my presence. He's not there. Several lined sheets of notes litter the desk, Sam's tight script straining to the right, as if the words are rushing from his brain quicker than his hand can keep up with them; there's also yesterday's newspaper and a revision guide to Shakespeare's tragedies. I stand looking at the single bed, duvet discarded on the floor. Loopy licks at an upturned cereal bowl. Tea-splattered mugs and dirty tumblers clutter the bookshelf and windowsill. The battered, reconditioned laptop Jonty bought him for Christmas, usually left abandoned on the floor, isn't there. The blind is half down and I instinctively go over and roll it up to let in the sun. Where is he?

I leave Loopy upstairs, basking in a splash of sunshine and make my way down the narrow staircase, calling Jonty's number again, but no joy. I need to get back to the computer, but it's like an itch I have to scratch. What if Sam's in trouble somewhere? I look at the clock. It's almost four. He's usually home by now.

When I return to the kitchen, the door is open. I'm sure I closed it. I step back into the living room, in case Sam's slipped in and spread out across the sofa, though I know this is impossible; I would have seen him when I walked through. I go back out into the yard, followed by Loopy, whose hackles are up as she sniffs suspiciously. The gate is ajar. Loopy slips out and sniffs up and down the path, but there's no one there.

Filling the kettle in an attempt to tame my increasingly wild mind with domesticity, I try to think rationally. The latch on the gate is loose. Loopy probably dislodged it when she smelt the cat and jumped up. I'm being paranoid, imagining intruders when the issue is Sam. There is no obvious reason for him to be skipping school. He particularly wanted to go to Tarnside High School and his end-of-year report was excellent. He's predicted good grades in his A levels and he's got an offer from Newcastle. He's applied to do English, to keep his options open a little longer, but he's more or less decided he'd like to be a journalist eventually. I try and comfort myself with the thought that he will have been revising somewhere. It isn't the work that's the problem, it's the place. I realise that we didn't actually

Whenever I speak to her I can't help but feel lighter, younger. Living with a man old enough to be my father, surrounded by middle-aged and older people, can make me forget that I'm still pretty young myself. 'Lizzie, listen! Pack your bikini and sun cream. Miranda's organising a weekend house party at her parents' place!'

'Majorca?'

'Yes!'

I've seen photos of Miranda's parents' villa. She complains that it's not near the beach (too expensive, even for Miranda's banker father), but who needs a beach when you've got a pool and a veranda with spectacular views of the hills? I can almost feel the sun on my skin as I picture it. The winters in Cumbria are long and grey and by March I'm longing for a burst of sunshine. This would be perfect. To have a weekend pleasing myself, not worrying about anyone or anything else. I could slip away for a couple of days at a push. 'When?'

'April 22nd to 25th.' I'm dropped back to reality like a stone sinking into the tarn. 'Lizzie? It's OK if you can't get the Monday off. I'm flying back in at silly o'clock on Monday morning—'

'It's no good.'

'Are you sure? Sam and Jonty will be fine. They'll want you to go.'

'It's not that.' Damn! 'The 23rd is St George's Day. I have to be here. I've got a big event on.' The disappointment is overwhelming. I want to cry.

'Oh, Lizzie, love! Could someone else cover for you?' But she knows it doesn't work like that. If I'm not here, the event won't happen. I briefly consider asking Eve, but it wouldn't be fair.

Clare lets me go, promising to arrange something for us another time. I hang up and listen to the hum of the fridge and Loopy's gentle snores and think of the evening unfolding in front of me: the confrontation with Sam, the inevitable mediation between him and Jonty. If I was in London I'd meet up with Clare and go to a gallery, or see if there was an installation or performance going on somewhere to distract me, but there's no one here I can do that with. Jonty's friends all have responsibilities and routines. I have no friends my own age in Tarnside; they're still living in the cities they discovered when they went to university, or travelling the world. They won't come back until they're starting families of their own, which for most people is in their early thirties. I'm a bit of a quirk at twenty-seven with someone else's teenage son to take care of.

It's now gone five o'clock. I'm beginning to envisage accidents, the screech of brakes on tarmac, Sam's body in the road. I know this is ridiculous, but I can sense something's wrong. He's been different. I thought it was the pressure of A levels, being in the upper sixth. One minute he's his usual easy self and then he's distant or agitated. When I've asked him what's up, he's changed the subject, shoving whatever was bothering him aside. I haven't pried, because he's seventeen, he's entitled to his privacy, and yet... maybe I should have pushed a little harder. What if he's in trouble?

That look. I don't want to think about the way he was looking at me. Not Sam. Not my Sam. We're not like that. I'm sure it didn't mean anything. It was just the once, and I might have misinterpreted it. I can't even say what it was exactly. He's a teenage boy, I'm not that much older; he's bound to be curious, processing stuff. He'll be home soon. I'll talk to him then.

I force myself to get back to my laptop, but I can't concentrate on the documents. Deciding the check I did briefly this morning will have to do, I attach them as they are and press Send.

The key in the lock. Finally! Loopy throws herself down the hall and I run after her, but it's not Sam. Jonty slams in, yanking the strap of his battered leather bag over his head and throwing it on the floor.

'What's wrong?' He doesn't answer me straight away and I find myself wishing I hadn't asked, because all I can think about right now is Sam. 'Did you get my messages? Why haven't you been answering your phone?' And before he can say anything, I blurt, 'Sam's missing!'

Jonty's dark brows pull together. 'What are you talking about?' He looks at his watch and back at me and I know I sound like I'm losing it, but I've got this awful feeling and I'm about to explain, to tell Jonty about Mr Wright and the school and this sense of foreboding that I can't escape, when I see Sam's outline through the glass of the front door. I push past and throw it open. Sam is standing there, dressed in his uniform, bag over his shoulder, as if it's any ordinary day.

I shriek, 'Where have you been?'

He takes a step back, the same frown, the same dark brows as his dad. He glances at Jonty, then back at me and gives a shrug. 'The library.' And then, 'Why are you wearing my hoodie?'

I look at Jonty. His face, usually all soft lines collapsing into a smile, is flat, hard. He looks old and exhausted.

I feel bitter cold bile in my throat. 'What is it?'

'Apparently, I'm redundant.'

Chapter 4

Sam disappears over the brow of the hill ahead of me. He's got a very expensive bike with a dazzling array of gears, but even if I had a better bike I wouldn't be able to keep pace with him. This was my idea, though I'm having second thoughts now.

Jonty's redundancy is a shock. I knew it was coming; when the council cut the arts budget I suggested he start fundraising for projects and develop his post to make it more viable, but he wouldn't listen. Jonty's fifty-three years old; he doesn't want to reinvent himself. It was only a matter of time, but even I didn't think it would be this abrupt. The consequences are going to be difficult. He has no mortgage, which helps, and he'll have a redundancy pay-out of some kind, and a pension, and I have a steady income, but Jonty loved that job, the role he had in the creative and cultural life of the area, the status that gave him in this community. He won't find another like it locally. At his age he'll struggle to find anything. This may be it. Retirement. The word sounds old and dusty and doesn't fit with the Jonty I know and love. He won't take this well.

It's one of those bright, blue Saturdays in late March that Cumbria can sometimes deliver, like an unexpected gift. I thought it might help, after yesterday's events, if we all headed out to Coniston. I haven't mentioned my meeting with Mr Wright to Sam or Jonty yet. All Jonty wanted to do last night was drown his sorrows and Sam disappeared to his room. I thought about following him, but I didn't want to risk Jonty overhearing. It'll be easier to talk when we're outside, with the view to focus on. I persuaded Jonty to take the boat out, so, with a bit of luck and a reasonable wind, he'll be sailing up the lake right now, which will put him in a much better mood for later. We've booked a table for dinner at the pub. My plan is to talk to Sam before we all meet and then decide how to approach things with Jonty.

It's surprisingly warm in the sun. Too hot when you're pedalling uphill. I should have suggested something easier. We could have driven to Coniston village and sat on the deck of the Bluebird Café in the sunshine, watching the ducks, or taken the launch across the lake to the café at Brantwood with its spectacular view. Sweat dribbles between my breasts and down the centre of my back. My legs are like jelly, but then the road flattens out and I'm able to relax a little and enjoy the patchwork fields and twisting narrow lanes. Sam turns on to the winding road that skirts the east side of the lake and I follow, through Nibthwaite with its whitewashed houses, the jolly postbox embedded in the dry-stone wall and the old barn that has yet to be converted into a fancy new home by someone with cash from the city. I catch the first glimpse of the lake. At this end Coniston is wilder, reed-filled and straggly. The water shimmers in the sunshine like a promise.

Sam has stopped and is waiting for me beneath the shade of a tree which shoulders the road. I approach, all too aware that my face is probably the colour of an overripe tomato and my T-shirt stained with unbecoming damp patches.

He shakes his hair back from his eyes. He hasn't had it cut for months. It hangs in thick chestnut waves that if stretched straight would reach his shoulders. Girls would kill for hair like Sam's; he barely gives it a thought. He holds out a water bottle. I balance the bike between trembling legs and swig.

'You OK?' He looks concerned, which makes me feel all the more pathetic.

'I'm fine. Just bloody unfit.' I return the bottle.

'You're all right,' he says, tipping his head back to drink. His Adam's apple bounces up and down as he swallows. I would like to pour the remains of the water over my sweaty head right now, but we'll need it later. 'You ready?' he asks, hooking the bottle back into place against the frame of the bike, nodding towards the road that curls in and out along the lake edge.

I don't need to ask where we're going to stop. There's a particular cove Jonty introduced me to on our first date. He's been coming to this same spot since he was Sam's age, and brought his own children when they were still in nappies. It involves walking from the road through the woodland, skirting the lake shore and climbing over a small headland. My knees are quivering and I'm sticky with sweat as I dismount. Pulling off our hoodies and tying them around our waists, we leave the bikes where the path peters out and make our way up the small hill carpeted with low green bushes. Soon the ground here will be peppered with wild bilberries. It's cooler beneath the trees but could easily pass for a mild summer's day. I wish I'd thought to throw the swimming costumes and wetsuits into the pannier, but I never expected it to be so warm. To reach the cove we have to scramble down a steep drop. Sam pauses on the stony beach at the bottom. The water winks sunlight. I like watching him here, part of this landscape that's shaped him. He looks out across the lake, topping up something inside himself. I'm glad we did this. It feels good to be back where we've spent such happy times, seeing Sam so relaxed.

A short distance from us is Wild Cat Island. I don't know if that's its real name or the fictional one. I have never read *Swallows and Amazons*. Jonty was astonished, when we first met, to discover that I'd never heard of the book, but I don't come from the sort of home that offered children's classics at bedtime. He insisted on reading it to me, a chapter a night before we turned out the light, my head resting on his chest, listening to the rumble of his voice as I drifted off to sleep. We never did finish it.

From here I can see a canoe pulled up on the beach facing us. People often row over to the island for picnics. Sam and I swam out there last summer, lay on the rocks to catch our breath and swam back again.

This is Jonty's favourite lake. He grew up on the shore of Windermere – quite literally, his garden went right down to the lake – but Coniston has his heart. This lake requires more effort. There are only one or two places offering lakeside catering, and the public car park at Brown Howe offers toilet facilities, but you have to take your own picnic. For the most part, if you want to get down to the water's edge, you have to be prepared to walk. Meandering paths through woodland lead to tiny pebbled beaches and hidden coves. The only place to launch officially is from Coniston Boating Centre or the sailing club. There is a boathouse at

Chimneys, Jonty's family home on Windermere, where his mother still lives, but he would rather store his boat in a Tarnside garage and tow it to Coniston on a trailer. He describes Coniston as the locals' lake while Windermere is a day-tripper magnet. While I know a lot of this attitude is to do with issues relating to his childhood, I think he has a point; I like the simplicity of Coniston.

We scan the lake for his distinctive red sails, but he must still be up at the north end. Anticipating my worry, Sam says, 'It's calmer today; he won't have the chance to take stupid risks.'

The water will be freezing, but right now what I want to do more than anything is plunge straight in. As if he's read my mind, Sam drops his rucksack on the stones and pulls his T-shirt over his head. I'd love to do the same and, not for the first time in my life, I wish I had a flat chest instead of these EE-cup breasts, currently firmly encased in a very expensive moulded bra, without which they'd bounce painfully against my rib cage. If I get this bra wet it will soak up water like a sponge and dribble unattractively through my T-shirt, which won't look too good in the pub later on. Sam is now pulling off his socks and trousers. He'll swim in his underpants and simply go commando this evening. Oh, to be a teenage boy right now.

He glances at me, his eyes a dare.

I hesitate. That's my mistake. He knows he can persuade me now. I suppose I could squeeze the water out of my bra and hope for the best. I've got a hoodie with me which I can wear in the pub if all else fails.

'I won't look,' he says.

I could leave my T-shirt on and just wear the hoodie over

my bra when I get out. That would work. The water glitters at me. My neck and back itch with sweat.

I undo my belt. Sam turns away discreetly as I step out of my jeans and before I can change my mind, wincing, I run across the pebbles into the water, in my knickers and T-shirt, shrieking as the splashes sting my belly and the small of my back. Sam thunders through the water, laughing. My legs are numb. It takes several weeks of sunshine to warm the lake, but the cove is sheltered and shallow, so it's not as bad as it could be. I throw myself forwards, gasping.

Our squawks and hoots of laughter bounce across the surface of the water. We won't be able to stand this for long. I'm already turning back to shore, sufficiently cooled and exhilarated, when I see the canoe, gliding and tilting across the lake, a little distance from us. The canoeist is sleek and fit, sensibly dressed in a wetsuit. A man in his late thirties or early forties. He slows down, holding his paddle in front of him, openly staring. I glance down. My wet T-shirt is entirely transparent, accentuating the outline of my breasts and cleavage. I can't see the expression on his face, but I can feel it like a burn. I instinctively sink lower into the water. The man is familiar, I've seen him in Tarnside, walking with his young son to the primary school near our street. His wife sometimes comes to the park with a younger child in a buggy. I seem to remember he's a policeman, not the uniformed sort but higher up than that. I think he's part of Jonty's cycling group; about a dozen of them head out once a week together.

Cold though the water is, I feel a hot flush of shame, though we're doing nothing wrong. I turn my back to him and make my way to the shore where I grab my hoodie and press it up against me, glancing back. I'm starting to shiver now, goosebumps on my flesh. He hasn't moved. I can see what it must look like. I'm more covered than I would be in a swimming costume, but I realise now that there's something about underwear that's more intimate, and wet underwear is positively erotic. I look like something from a top-shelf magazine. The shivers are turning into shudders. Canoe Man looks across at Sam, splashing about, trying to keep warm, and then back at me. Raising the paddle, he pierces the water and glides around the headland, out of sight.

Sam waits discreetly for me to dress before he joins me on the beach. I wring out my T-shirt and throw it to him. 'Here, use this,' I say, turning away to allow him to remove his pants and get his jeans on. When I hear him fiddling with the clasp on his belt I turn back round. 'Did you see that man?'

He shakes his hair and droplets of water spark the air. 'What man?'

'In the canoe.'

'What about him?'

'He was watching us.'

Sam shrugs, drops to the ground and throws himself back, arms spread wide, giving himself up to the sun. He couldn't care less. Why should I be worried? If someone wants to misinterpret what's going on, good luck to them. We have nothing to hide.

It's a pleasure to watch Sam so at ease. He's young, fit and happy and has the world in his hand. It feels good to be around that kind of energy. I spend too much time with people Jonty's age. There's a lot I like about that: the experience they've had, the stories they tell, the confidence; there's none of that showing off or having to prove themselves, but sometimes I need something more.

Sam is perfectly still apart from the rise and fall of his chest. His eyes are closed. He looks utterly content and at peace with the world. And yet this is the boy who's been leaving the house every morning pretending to go to school and not turning up. This is the boy who's been living a lie for the last week.

I wince back up the stony beach in my bare feet to my bag and take out the two low-alcohol lagers I packed as a treat. The bottles are still cool. Sam sits up as I approach him. 'I forgot the bottle-opener.'

He gives me that look, which is all Jonty, takes the bottle, searches for a stone and nudges off the cap, and for a moment I allow myself to imagine Jonty here, in this place, a younger Jonty than I've ever known. Tall and dark and a little gauche, his middle-aged certainty, that self-assurance that first drew me to him, still to be earned. There is a kind of grief in this, for me. A sense of loss, though that younger Jonty was never mine to lose.

We sit, side by side, chins resting on our knees, staring out at the lake. My body is alert, tingling on the outside and glowing inside. This is better than any fancy spa: clean air, sunshine, fresh water. A boat with white sails slowly zigzags across the lake towards Coniston village. There isn't much wind at all. I picture Jonty, frustrated by the pace.

Sam's not looking at the lake but picking at the label on the bottle, peeling it back. The muscle in his cheek is working and he has that air about him that I've noticed recently. Something's chewing at him again. He turns to face me and there's an intensity about him, unsettling, as if he's peeling back layers to reach me. Maybe this was what I saw last time and I misunderstood. It was so fleeting; he'd turned and left before I could register what was going on.

'What is it, Sam?'

He drops his head down, nudging the stones with his finger. I can sense him turning the words around, trying to find a way. Instinctively I reach across and lift the curtain of hair to see his eyes and at that moment the canoe reappears from around the headland. I can see the man looking at me, at Sam, at the beers. He's close enough now for me to see his smirk, as if he's understood something and he's agreeing to be complicit.

As I pull back, face on fire, waiting for him to disappear around the next headland, I catch sight of Jonty's red sails. We don't have long.

'Where did you go yesterday?' Sam twitches, as if I've startled him out of something. I can feel him weighing up what I've said, how much I know. I don't want this to be a power game. 'Mr Wright says you haven't been in school all week.'

'Is this why we're here?' His face is pinched with hurt.

I say, 'No. It's a beautiful day. I wanted to make the most of it,' meaning every word and hoping he believes me. He turns back to the lake. That muscle near his cheekbone working away. I carry on. 'He's nice, Mr Wright. Decent.' Sam says nothing. 'He's worried about you. I'm worried about you.' I place a hand on his forearm. 'What's going on?'

He shrugs me off, all awkward angles, an echo of the agitated boy that arrived two years ago. 'I *am* revising. You don't have to worry.' He takes a swig of beer and looks back out across the lake. 'I'll go back on Monday.'

Jonty's boat plaits the surface of the water as it comes towards us. 'You can talk to me, Sam. If there's anything I can do?'

He sighs, his whole body easing, letting something go.

'No. It's nothing. Stupid. I should have said. I just wanted a bit of space. It doesn't matter. I'll go back.'

Jonty waves from the boat. He's moving towards us quite quickly now. We've run out of time; there's no point in pushing this any further.

Sam says, 'Don't say anything to him. Please. I'll sort it.'

Jonty's busy lowering the sail, the sun a huge orange ball behind him, lending the world a mellow glow. I should tell him. I believe Sam when he says he's been working, but the truanting niggles at me. Sam is not a rule breaker. Why didn't he talk to us about this? It's not like Jonty would object to him studying at home.

Except he hasn't been at home. 'Where *have* you been working?'

He arranges stones in little piles. Blue, silver, pink, grey. 'The boathouse.'

Pip's boathouse. Of course.

Jonty shouts for Sam to come and help him bring the boat in. Sam stands, glancing back at me, his face a question.

I should talk to Jonty about this, because something's wrong, Sam isn't normally deceitful, but I don't want to spoil a lovely evening and Sam clearly doesn't want Jonty to know. I need him to trust me. If he trusts me, he's more likely to confide in me. 'I won't say anything.'

Chapter 5

It's now Monday and I drive out to Windermere to see Pip in the hope that she'll shed some light on what's troubling Sam. He knows he could have talked to us about wanting to study away from school. We would have listened. We could have arranged for him to study at home, or at the library, or even at Pip's, if that's what he'd have preferred. Why did he feel the need to lie?

Pip is completing her yoga routine in the garden so I pause inside the gate. It's cooler today, but I'm sheltered in a patch of sunlight and happy to wait. She sees me and gives a nod of recognition. It's a pleasure to watch her fluid rolling and reaching, the lake a cool blue pool behind her.

Pip is Jonty's mother. Not 'Mum' or 'Mother' to Jonty, not 'Grandma' or 'Granny' to Sam and Nell, simply 'Pip' to everyone who knows her. She has lived in this house since she and Richard first discovered the place, standing empty and in need of attention on the shore of Windermere, back in the early seventies. It has to be seen to be believed. I fell in love with Chimneys the first time Jonty brought me here. He gave me no warning. He's always been a little embarrassed by his family home, not wanting to be seen as one of the privileged set. We turned off the lake road, up the tree-lined drive and it appeared before us like something from a story. My mouth was literally hanging open. In estate agent's language it would be described as a stunning, highly desirable, luxurious, detached property, but what I saw was vast windows, enticingly irregular shapes and the imposing elephant-leg chimneys that give the house its name. Inside were high ceilings, panels of light falling across oak and slate floors, a house crammed with hidden spaces, cupboards, attics, snugs and window seats. Places to escape to and read or dream. Every window provides a perfectly framed view of the lake in one direction, the abundant garden in the other. Jonty's parents were squatters to begin with, the owners living temporarily in Spain. As he tells it, a letter arrived one day from a solicitor, offering them Chimneys for a modest sum. Apparently the owners had died in a car crash. They had no children and their grieving parents wanted to sort things out with the minimum of fuss. You couldn't make it up. But it's a story he tells with bitterness, viewing what happened later as some sort of retribution. In Jonty's eyes, luck has to be paid for.

I didn't tell him I was coming here this morning. His relationship with his mother was never good after she sent him to boarding school as a teenager, but his father's death and the history of this house only make it worse. They see one another regularly, but their communication involves landmines that need to be navigated carefully.

Pip is a formidable woman. Her age is a carefully guarded secret, but she must be in her late seventies at least, though you wouldn't know it to look at her. She has been practising yoga since her hippy days, when she was younger than I am now, and it shows. Her posture is perfect; straight as an ironing board, long neck, chin at just the right level. There's a melody in the way she moves and Sam has inherited her natural grace. She commands any room she enters. Handsome rather than pretty, she's a thoroughbred with her glossy hair, now white but still thick and long, good teeth and bright eyes.

She was a mother in the sixties and seventies, part of a bohemian crowd, educated, questioning, prepared to break the rules and with strong views. A trained teacher, she has worked, on and off, in the education system, raging against government agendas that fail to allow for spontaneity and insist on the unnecessary testing and placing of children in inappropriate boxes. Jonty was one of five and they were all home-educated until secondary school. They went to a state-run school in Windermere from the age of eleven, but Jonty, who admits he was a wild teenager, was sent to a boarding school at thirteen. He was there for three years before transferring to Tarnside High School for sixth form. He has never forgiven his parents, particularly his mother. Pip stands by her decision. I've heard the arguments unfold over countless Sunday lunches. It's like a magnet in the room, waiting to pull them in. Jonty gets hot and passionate, but Pip remains cool and firm. He was uncontrollable. She could not cope. Boarding school was the right choice. She insists Jonty's life is far more stable and happy than it would have been had they not taken this action. Jonty believes he would have buckled down in the end and maybe he's right. I don't know. No one can.

I like Pip, but I am slightly intimidated by her. She is

honest, brutally so. The first time we met was for afternoon tea. Pip is a woman who lives in a world of light lunches and afternoon teas, which infuriates Jonty, who likes to remind her she was born in Salford. 'Good grief!' she said as Jonty and I walked into the room. 'What on earth are you doing with a man old enough to be your father?'

Jonty had prepared me in the car on the way over. 'She speaks her mind,' he'd said, so I'd been expecting some direct questions, but not quite as direct as this. I decided to brazen it out and told her he was really good in bed. I'm still not sure what her real reaction to this was. She guffawed with laughter, but her eyes tracked me for the rest of that afternoon. I thought she was suspicious of my motives, protective of her son, but now I think she was just trying to work me out. I had to prove myself to her. I wanted to prove myself. I hope I have; I can never be sure with Pip. She's a very difficult woman to read. You can feel her assessing you, but she gives nothing away. She has a Masters in psychology, which she completed a couple of years ago, and she did talk about studying for a PhD, but Jonty rather cruelly told her he couldn't see the point of spending all that money at her age, and I think she took that to heart. She reads lots of books and has mentioned various tutorials she's accessed online, but I think she'd enjoy something more rigorously academic. She shouldn't have to justify it to Jonty. He sees qualifications as a means to an end, but for Pip it's all about the pleasure of learning.

I'd like to be like Pip when I'm old: an hour of yoga every day, some studying, a light lunch, a bit of charity work and afternoon tea with friends, evenings spent curled up with a book in front of the fire. This is a privileged world I've only ever witnessed from the outside or in novels. There was a time when I condemned this sort of injustice and trivialised the people involved, but Pip has worked hard to create this place. Yes, she had a bit of luck, but they lived in a house they couldn't afford to renovate for decades, patching up the leaks, living frugally, camping out in different rooms to try and keep warm. There was no central heating or insulation, no fitted kitchen or carpets. None of that could happen until Richard died, which was years after the children had left home. She used the money from his life insurance to finally renovate the house properly. In her eyes, this was the sensible thing to do, investing in the family legacy. She's enjoyed restoring Chimneys to her former glory (Pip talks about the house as female, like a friend, a lifetime companion) and she doesn't hide the fact that she delights in living in luxury after years of making do, but Jonty sees it as a betrayal. He can't bear to see his mother enjoying what he regards as the proceeds of his father's death. Richard died unexpectedly, in a car accident, ironically, something that continues to haunt Jonty.

Pip has never been idle in the lap of luxury. For years she ran a Steiner nursery in the house, but it became too exhausting and she had to admit she was too old to carry on. She still teaches illiterate adults to read and supports several charities. She doesn't make a fuss about it, but what she does makes a difference. She's helped me with my fundraising, introducing me to people important enough to make financial decisions. I've come to respect her and I like to think she respects me. She continues to talk quite openly about the age gap between me and Jonty. I think she still believes our relationship is temporary, which hurts. I wish she had more faith in me. She's perfectly warm and welcoming, but this assumption leaves me feeling more of a visitor than a member of the family. She is always encouraging me to put myself first and I appreciate that she's fighting my corner, but I'm happy with Jonty. When the kids arrived everything changed. She keeps reminding me, 'They are his responsibility,' but it isn't as simple as that. During those early weeks, when they were settling in, she suggested I move in with her, but, tempting though that was at times, Jonty would never have forgiven me, and the kids needed me.

She completes her routine with an elegant salute to the sun. 'Darling!' Kissing me on both cheeks, floating towards the house, beckoning for me to follow, slipping out of her flip-flops in the doorway. I pull off my muddy Converse, leaving them outside the French windows, and look up to see her facing me, green eyes alert. 'To what do I owe this pleasure?'

'I thought I'd drop by for a catch-up.'

She raises an eyebrow. 'Lizzie, dearest, you do not drop by. Everything you do is part of a tightly managed to-do list. You are here for a reason, so you might as well tell me what it is while I make us a coffee.'

She assumes I'm drinking coffee. She has a stove-top espresso maker. It's a ritual, the coffee making. It takes time. She doesn't offer tea. Coffee with warmed milk, and sugar if I need it. And she will have cake. Pip always has cake and always eats cake, though where she puts it is beyond me; there is not an ounce of excess flesh on her body.

I follow her into the kitchen as I'm expected to do. 'I've come to talk about Sam.'

'Ah.'

I wait, but she offers nothing more, measuring the coffee meticulously with a china scoop. It seems I'm the one who has to explain myself. 'Apparently Sam wasn't in school last week. As far as I knew he was going in. He took a packed lunch, he was dressed in his uniform, he left the house at the right time, but he didn't go to school.' She says nothing, placing the pot on the hot plate of the Aga, gliding over to the dresser and selecting two porcelain cups and saucers and placing them on a tray, along with a sugar bowl, a milk jug and two cake plates. I keep prompting, 'He told me he was at the library, but I know that's not true.' She takes her time, pouring milk into a red enamel pan. Pip doesn't trust microwaves.

Eventually she turns to face me. 'I would think the pertinent question would be why he felt it necessary to escape school?'

She's right, but I need to get to the bottom of what's going on here first and I'm not going to let her distract me. 'I wondered if you had any idea where he might have been going?'

She sighs. 'Darling, you clearly know the answer to that question, which is the reason for your unexpected visit.' She takes an Emma Bridgewater cake tin down from the shelf. She has matching mugs hanging from the plate rack on the wall, a gift from me that I've never seen her use. Two slices of Victoria sponge with fresh raspberries and cream. Tiny cake forks.

'Is he here now?' I ask.

She shakes her head. 'It appears we have been rumbled.'

'Is he in school?'

'I presume he must be. I haven't seen him this morning.' The coffee pot starts to gurgle. She lifts it off.

'I was called into the school on Friday, by the head of year.'

'*You* were?'

'They phoned the house. Jonty was at work.'

'Sam is Jonty's responsibility.'

'Jonty wasn't available.'

She looks at me carefully. 'Did they ask to see you immediately?'

'Well, no. I just...' I give up. She's right; I didn't have to go. 'I should have waited.'

Her face softens. 'I am not chastising but protecting you, my dear. You do understand that? The more responsibility you take, the less Jonty does. Let's sit in the sunshine.' She pours the milk into the jug and hands me the tray. I carry it out to the sitting room. 'Inside, I think. It's a little nippy out there for sitting still.'

I place the tray down and perch on the creamy sofa, aware of the mud splatters around the hem of my jeans. Pip pours. The fingers of her right hand are bent into awkward shapes. Her arthritis is getting worse, but she shows no sign of the pain she must be in. The thick gold band of her wedding ring, her only jewellery, sinks into the flesh beneath the swollen joint. She's been a widow for nearly thirty years. Jonty has told me that he expected her to fall apart after his father died, they'd always been so close, but it was like she turned a page and began writing a new chapter. He still finds it difficult to come to terms with this, but I have to admire the woman; she refused to quietly shrink into grief, and chose instead to create an independent life. Jonty sees this as a betrayal of his father; I think it shows courage.

I ask, 'Has Sam said anything to you about why he's not going to school?'

'He told me he needed somewhere quiet to revise and asked if he could use the boathouse.'

'And you didn't think to tell me?'

'He asked me not to.'

'Why not?' I sound peevish.

She watches me carefully, as if she's about to say something and decides against it. She's his grandmother, she doesn't have to answer to me. 'I suspect he didn't want to have to explain himself. I was a little sceptical at first but agreed to a trial. I checked on him once or twice to make sure he wasn't on one of those tablet things, shooting people, but to his credit he was working very hard. Textbooks, notes. He is driven, that boy. He wants to succeed and I'm sure he will, whether or not he goes in to school.'

'They are still teaching. He is still under obligation to attend.'

'But if he can work better here?' A slow smile. She's on familiar territory.

'It doesn't work like that. What happens if his grades are borderline and Newcastle have to reconsider their offer? How's it going to look if he's got weeks of absence?'

'I'm sure they won't look at that. Besides, it's in the school's interests not to broadcast it, but if they do, he can explain. It's impressive that he has taken matters into his own hands. He has shown self-motivation, problem-solving skills, excellent initiative for a journalist. It's to be admired.'

I'm not interested in a political debate about education right now; I'm worried about Sam. 'Do you think there's something wrong? Not with his academic work but something else. Something more personal?'

She sips her coffee. There's something she wants to say, but she's measuring it for size. I wait. She puts the cup back in the saucer and places both on the table. Her voice is low. 'Be careful, darling.'

I try to read her expression, but there are no clues there. 'What do you mean?'

'You are a lovely young woman. You are talented, ambitious and hard-working; I can see why Jonty was drawn to you, but you know how I feel about that. I believe he is being selfish. I encourage you to be selfish too.'

'I love Jonty.'

'I know you do. And I know he loves you, very much. But this in itself is not enough.'

I don't want to hear this. I know Pip thinks she's on my side, but she doesn't know everything and what goes on between me and Jonty is none of her business. 'We were talking about Sam.'

'We are.' She looks at me intently in a way that makes me want to squirm. 'Sam…' She pauses, taking a breath, selecting her words. 'You do realise he's in love with you, don't you?'

Chapter 6

Work is busy in the run-up to the Easter weekend and I throw myself into it.

Pip's announcement has been exploding over and over in my head like an unwelcome firework, too harsh, too loud. Sam? In love with me? It's ludicrous. I refuse to think about it. Obviously there was something going on at school and he needed to escape to study. If it was something to do with the way he feels about me, he would have moved in with Pip and be avoiding me altogether, which he isn't doing. Things are fine at home. School was the problem, but he seems to be managing that now. I've made time to check in with Mr Wright every day this week. He's reassured me that Sam has been attending school regularly again and he's agreed to email me directly next term if there are any further absences. I don't want to bother Jonty with this. Hopefully it will all settle down and he need never know.

The family activities I've scheduled in the park on Good Friday and Saturday have attracted a lot of last-minute interest and I don't want to turn anyone away. Eve was apologetic about leaving me to manage without her help, but she and Neil – Mr Wright (it doesn't feel right calling him Neil) – are off to Prague. I told her not to feel bad, she's owed more time off than she'll ever recover and I don't want to add to the pressure. The timing of the trip isn't ideal, but I think it's been planned around her cycle. It seems so unfair that a couple so decent and successful can't start a family when they would make such brilliant parents, while my mother couldn't be bothered with the two she had, and even Jonty and I are muddling through trying to patch something resembling a family together for Sam.

I spend Wednesday cleaning out the garden room, which functions as an equipment store and brew room for the volunteers. This will give us an additional space in which to run workshops, alongside those in the room above the coach house, though it will mean that I'll need help. Normally I'd ask Sam to come in, but after the conversation with Pip I hesitate. She gave me this pitying look after she'd delivered her announcement and it was all I could do not to get up and walk out. Pip has this romanticised view of love, all passion and drama and epic emotions. She's had her fair share of affairs, while Richard was alive and since his death, about which she's open and unapologetic, but her view of love is just one aspect of something I see as much richer and more complex. For Pip, love is passionate embraces on a beach as the sun sets or flirtations over cocktails and angst-ridden trysts. Her extra-marital affairs were brief, from what I gather, and her reconciliations with Richard all part of the excitement. I've no doubt Richard was doing his fair share of exploring during the ongoing drama, but as I only have Jonty's version of events I can't be sure; Jonty won't say a word against his father. Pip's current relationships are still clouded in mystery. I've suspected her lovers to be married, but this may not be the case. I think she enjoys implying things are more dramatic than they really are.

Love isn't always silver bows and sparklers, sometimes it's plain brown paper and string. Love is what you do, the actions you take for someone else, when their happiness is essential to your own. It's the accommodating and compromising and making things work. It's sacrifice and commitment. This is how I love Jonty. And Sam and Nell are part of that.

I asked her, 'Has Sam spoken to you about this?'

'Of course not. I'm not sure if he even realises it himself yet. But you need to be careful.'

'I am careful! I would never, never…' I couldn't find the words.

She reached over and placed her hand on mind. 'I know that. I'm not making accusations. If it had not been for you, I would have had to step in and take responsibility for my grandchildren. I shall be honest, I had no desire to do so. I have brought up five of my own and I am too old for all that teenage rebellion.' She sat back, watching me carefully. 'Sam can cope with a schoolboy crush. He'll grow out of it. It's you I'm concerned for. It is never easy when the boundaries are blurred. You and he could be siblings, but you are not. He is, in some ways, a younger version of Jonty.' She paused, allowing this to hit the mark. 'It's difficult.' Another pause. 'Messy.'

'What has this got to do with school?'

She shrugged, picking up her cup and saucer and taking a sip of coffee. 'Perhaps Sam needs a bolthole at this moment in time, somewhere to escape everything and focus simply on his studies? I don't know. Have you spoken to Jonty?' I told her Jonty had enough on his plate and she raised an eyebrow, waiting. It wasn't my news to share, but what could I do? When she said, 'Tell me,' there was strength in those words. A gathering of resources. I can well imagine many moments over the years where she's issued this instruction to one of her children, possibly her husband. In those two words she was offering to share the burden, assuring me that she could take it. So I told her about the redundancy. Jonty would be furious if he knew, but Pip is discreet. 'I shall wait for him to tell me himself,' she said, her eyes reading me. 'First the children,' she said, wearily, 'and now this.' Pip thinks I shouldn't have to take on Jonty's 'middle-age baggage', but I don't see it like that. I love Sam and Nell. I wouldn't have things any other way. Jonty and I will be fine. Pip might like to think she knows everything, but she doesn't.

She's invited us for lunch on Easter Sunday. Jonty doesn't want to go, but with Eve away and so much going on at work, Pip's lovely house, even with the landmines involved, was too enticing. I accepted and told Jonty we couldn't wriggle out of it without appearing rude. And she'll be able to see for herself that there's no problem between me and Sam.

I call Fi to see if she can help with the workshops over the weekend. She's supported me before and could probably manage a group on her own. There's a bit of extra cash in the budget and I know she could do with the money. Delighted to help, she agrees to meet me at the park in the morning and stay for as long as she's needed.

I come home sticky and drained, greeted by the sound of Sam playing his guitar along to a CD in his bedroom. Jonty has gone sailing and won't be back for a while yet and I'm relieved; his glooming presence is difficult to accommodate in this small space. Hopefully the lake and a good breeze will ease his mood. I've persuaded him to wait until after Easter to get his CV together and plan a strategy and he didn't argue. I've no idea what that strategy is going to be, but that's a problem for another day.

I run myself a bath to the sound of Sam's music. He obviously hasn't heard me come in, but I'm glad of some quiet time and decide to catch up with him later. Jonty's bath is beautiful, a proper freestanding tub with claw feet that shine like silver. The underside is painted a deep iridescent turquoise that makes me think of mermaids. It's the original bathtub, though it was boxed in when he bought the cottage. Memories of the vast enamel tub in his childhood home, chipped and stained, prompted him to restore it, spending more than it would have cost to replace. I once used this story to try and get him to understand Pip's motivation for renovating Chimneys, but he didn't want to hear it. I lean back against the smooth enamel lip and slide down, easing my head under, feeling the water creep up around my ears and hairline, giving myself up to the blissful weightlessness.

With my ears submerged, I don't hear Sam. I open my eyes to see him looking down at me. It takes a moment for me to register. I lurch up into a sitting position, curling my body away, my face to the wall, expecting him to back out, but he doesn't move. Glancing over my shoulder, I see he's still looking at me. Bath bubbles slide down my arm and plop into the water. He is properly looking at my body, taking it in.

Pip's voice. *Be careful.*

I'm reminded of the fifteen-year-old boy standing at the bottom of the stairs that first day, looking me up and down.

Something about that expression – assessing me – and something more.

'Get out of here!'

'You don't have to hide.'

'I'm not hiding, I just don't want you staring at me. Stop it!'

'You weren't bothered before.'

'What are you talking about?' But as I ask the question an alarm starts to clang in my head and Canoe Man leers in my memory.

Sam keeps his eyes fixed on mine. A spotlight in my face, an interrogation. Stupid! Stupid! I should never have gone in that bloody lake. 'You were coming on to me.'

My knees are trembling, my voice is a thin string of spittle. 'I need you to leave now.'

He doesn't move immediately, but something shifts and in that instant it's Sam again, my Sam, familiar, face burning, 'Sorry, sorry!' as he rushes out.

Chapter 7

I sit in the tepid bathwater, shivering. I have no idea how long I've been here, numbed, stunned.

Downstairs, Loopy throws herself at the back door, barking wildly. I open the window and look down into the yard. The gate bangs in the wind. That damned latch!

I reach for the towel and rub at my flesh until it burns, but the trembling continues. My knees feel weak, as if I'm drunk. I wish I was drunk. I wish my senses were dulled, my brain slow, but I'm on red alert, Sam's face vivid in my immediate memory.

I push open the door. The hall is silent. Sam's door is shut. Normally I would walk through the house in my towel without hesitating and if Sam came out and saw me he'd discreetly look away. Is that wrong? Have I suggested something in the way I've behaved?

Loopy races through the house to the front door and throws herself at it. I go to the top of the stairs and look down, but there is no shape visible through the glass. Now she's at the window, growling. I wait for a knock, but there's no one there. Probably just someone walking past. That's the problem when there's no garden or forecourt dividing the house from the street; people literally walk right past the front window. I don't want to hang about any longer in case Sam appears, so I leave Loopy growling and hurry down the short stretch of hall to the master bedroom, slamming the door behind me.

I'm dressed and making myself a hot drink when I hear Jonty's car pull up outside. Normally I would put my pyjamas on after a bath and collapse on the sofa, but I felt compelled to get properly dressed. Jeans, a loose, high-necked jumper.

You do realise he's in love with you?

But it wasn't love I saw in Sam's face as he looked at me just now. Love is compassionate, gentle and kind; this was more visceral. I don't know what to do. I could pretend it never happened or I could have it out with him, but I don't know who I'm dealing with. The Sam I know, the Sam who's blossomed in this house over the last two years, is thoughtful and a little shy; he'd be mortified by what just happened. But the Sam I saw looking at me in the bathroom was someone else. Someone more knowing.

Maybe it is just curiosity. I remember the lake, my wet T-shirt, the look on Canoe Man's face. Maybe I've suggested that this kind of behaviour is now appropriate.

Jonty shoves his way through the front door, dropping his gear in the hall. He's damp, flushed and grinning, buoyed by the wind and the lake, talking about the weather, someone he hooked up with, but I'm not listening, I'm thinking of Sam and what Jonty would say if he heard what happened, what he'd do and I'm trying not to think of it, I'm trying to listen to what he's saying as he slips his arms around my waist and kisses my neck and I know that he wants to take me upstairs and I know that's what we both need right now, but I can't, I can't give myself up to this, I can't let go because Sam's face, that look, is imprinted on my brain, and my body is alert to him, I can feel him through the fabric of this house, sense him in the room above my head, and I have to escape.

I wriggle free, making excuses, inventing a meeting. 'One of the volunteers that's helping out at the park this weekend, I said I'd go for a quick drink.' And he doesn't question it, because why would he? Jonty and I don't lie to one another, we've nothing to hide. He trusts me.

If I told Jonty about the lake, he'd laugh. I can see his face falling into those familiar folds. He'd think it was nothing, a funny moment. He'd make a comment about the cold water and me being daft, and Canoe Man being a lucky bastard to get a glimpse of a great pair of breasts; he wouldn't read any more into it than that, but if I told him what happened with Sam in the bathroom, that's not so simple.

Jonty takes himself off upstairs, pretending to be more dejected than he really is. 'Well, if you don't want me, I'll have to go play with myself in the shower,' and I am so grateful for his uncomplicated good humour at this moment. I'm right not to tell him. I will talk to Sam. I'll deal with this.

***

The pub is busy and cramped. Tarnside has at least one pub on every street, in some cases two or three. They've each got their own atmosphere. I like The Crown because it's small, but that doesn't stop them cramming a band in there. Pressed shoulder to shoulder, you can't drink alone, even if you turn

up by yourself, and there's always someone you recognise. Tonight Pam, the landlady, is singing, accompanied on guitar by the guy who runs the pet stall on the market. His Alsatian sits patiently nearby, quietly attentive. Pam's got a lovely voice. I wish I could sing. I enjoy live music but when I open my own mouth what comes out is nothing like what I intended; I have to make do with humming and tapping my foot. Jonty tries to be supportive – he believes everyone can sing, they just need to find the right range – but I see him wincing, he can't help himself. Sam thinks it's funny. My Sam, not Sam from the bathroom tonight, but I don't want to think about that. I order a glass of white wine.

'Large or small?'

Before I can answer a female voice behind me says, 'Large. Make that two.' I turn around. It's the windsurfer from the lake. She looks completely different with her hair down and made up; a perfectly presented model with a smooth curtain of blonde highlights. Sophisticated. Sexy. She grins, showing a line of neat white teeth rimmed by skilfully painted lips. 'My treat.' She hesitates. 'Unless you're meeting someone?'

I shake my head, delighted to have some company my own age. 'No. No, that would be great, but let me. It's the least I can do to thank you.' She accepts with a gracious nod.

There doesn't seem to be anywhere to sit, but she leads me to the window seat and persuades the old boys to shuffle up and let us squeeze on to the end near the fireplace. We're far enough away from the music to be able to talk if we pull in close. She smells of strawberries. Her face is immaculate. I can see now that she's wearing foundation, but it's obviously expensive and applied with skill. Her eyelids are painted a peachy nude with a little shimmer and lined in dark blue/black, her dense lashes can't be natural, though they look it.

Her face is a work of art. I only wear make-up if I'm going out somewhere special, and then it's only a bit of eyeliner. I can't be bothered with mascara because I can never wash it off properly and the dark residue collects under my eyes for days afterwards.

She sees me looking and raises an eyebrow, but in an amused way. I apologise for staring. 'Your make-up is amazing.' I hope I haven't offended her, but she laughs.

'Thank you.'

'I'm Lizzie. I'm sorry, but I don't…' I can't remember if she told me her name at the lake.

'Rebecca.' She raises her glass and smiles at me, and that smile lights a dusty corner inside me. She wants to be my friend and it's like I'm ten years old again and standing in the playground waiting to be picked for the team. Rebecca, the golden girl, sparkling as if she's been superimposed on our simple world, has chosen me.

We listen to the music for a while. It's all covers of songs from a different era, but Pam's voice is sweet and Pet Stall Man plays well. Rebecca leans in and whispers loudly in my ear, 'I'll get another round,' and she's up on her feet before I can say anything. I haven't finished my first glass and I told Jonty I was just popping out for a quick drink, but I don't want to go home and face him or Sam tonight. How long has it been since I went for a drink with someone my own age? Rebecca is dazzling and she's chosen me. I send a text telling Jonty not to wait up.

It turns out we have a lot in common. She's a freelance creative like me. 'A writer,' she says brightly, which surprises me. I'm not sure why, something to do with how polished she is. I don't expect an artist of any kind to look so conventional, I guess, but that's just my daft prejudice.

'What sort of writing?'

'Short plays. Performance poetry.'

I'm impressed. 'You manage to make a living?'

'I do the occasional feature for magazines and teach a bit to make ends meet.' She tilts her head to one side in a question.

I try to explain. 'I thought you were too glamorous to be a writer. Magazines make sense.' I giggle, aware of how stupid I sound. 'For some reason I think journalists can be more glamorous than other writers.' I've blown it. She'll see I'm not cool now, that she's made a mistake, but she smiles and nods, as if she's making a note of this and doesn't seem offended. We talk about how difficult it is to balance a creative life with earning a living. She asks me about my job, the festivals. She's new to the town and eager to know about the arts scene and I hear myself talking a lot, and laughing and sharing things I haven't shared with anyone, not because they're intimate or embarrassing in any way but simply because there's no one here that would be interested. Rebecca is interested.

'So, is Sam your partner?'

'Sam?' Why would she think that? She's looking at me, expectantly. 'No. Not Sam.' I wasn't aware that I'd mentioned Sam specifically. She gives me a slow, conspiratorial smile. I shake my head. 'No. Jonty. Jonty's my partner.'

'Really?' she grins, arching her eyebrow. 'Seems to me that Sam's your man. He's the one you've mentioned about a hundred times in the last half an hour.'

'Sam is Jonty's son.'

'Oh.' She puts her hand up to her mouth. 'Oops. Sorry.'

She drinks up quickly and plants her empty glass down on the table. I don't want to leave it like this. I can't keep pace with her, but she's insisted on paying for the last two rounds so the onus is on me to go to the bar. I return with two more glasses and explain that Sam is, to all intents and purposes, my stepson, but I'm starting to feel a bit woozy and the more I talk the more I sound like I'm trying to justify something. I'm relieved when she cuts across me and says, 'You should let me do your face.' Dragging her oversized handbag on to her lap, she pulls out an enormous make-up purse. 'I'm really good.' She leans forward and squints at me. 'You have amazing eyes.'

I do? My eyes are brown, a good size, but nothing special. Before I can argue she's steered me into the toilets and perched our glasses on the shelf under the mirror. Her make-up purse has exploded across the sink counter with pencils and brushes sitting in pools of water. She doesn't seem to care. 'Seriously? You carry all this stuff around with you?'

She shakes her head at my reflection like an exasperated schoolteacher, her eyes drooping a little as she steadies herself against the counter. 'A girl has to be prepared for every eventuality.' Her words slide up against each other. We're both pissed. It's a long time since I've been this silly. She holds up a small brush. 'So, shall I?'

'Go for it.'

She hesitates, glances around, frowning, then drops the brush and pushes her way back out into the pub, returning a moment later dragging a chair in behind her. 'Here, park your butt on this.'

'What if someone needs the loo?'

Tearing off a piece of toilet paper, she takes an eyeliner and writes *Toilet blocked. Use Gents*, then shuts it in the door jamb.

I let her do her worst. I'm quite enjoying the attention. I can't remember the last time someone spent so much time this close to my face. Even when Jonty and I kiss, we move on within minutes and he usually closes his eyes. Rebecca is examining, powdering, combing and painting for what feels like quarter of an hour or more. I can smell the citrusy scent of the wine on her breath, see the pores in her skin, the faint blonde moustache on her upper lip. She has gold flecks in the irises of her eyes.

'Lips!' I purse my mouth into an exaggerated kiss and collapse into giggles. She frowns. 'Hush! Keep still.' I can't stop giggling. I want to see what she's done, but as I try to get up she shoves me back down. 'No! Not until I've finished!' I do as I'm told. She draws a careful line around my lips and colours them in with a brush. For someone who's had a bit too much to drink she has a pretty steady hand. It tickles. The whole experience is slightly erotic and a little unnerving and I'm aware that if it wasn't for the alcohol I'd probably feel too self-conscious to let her continue.

She steps back and appraises me. Frowns. Picks up the eyeliner and touches something up, steps back again and finally nods. Approval. 'Take a look.'

I stand up and turn to the mirror, expecting some gross exaggeration of myself, smudged and pathetic, but that is not what I see. The woman looking back at me is stunning. I have to blink and shake my head, to see my reflection do the same, simply to check that it's really me. It is me. An enhanced, heightened, beautified version of the woman I usually am. I expected to be appalled. I expected to want to wipe it off immediately, but this is incredible. This feels delicious.

Rebecca is grinning at me. 'See?' I am Cinderella. I turn my head, gather my hair and pull it back from my face. 'We need to do something about that next,' Rebecca says. 'A good cut and maybe a bit of colour. Plum would be nice.'

Plum hair? Me? But this woman in the mirror? Yes, her hair could be plum. I came into this toilet looking like someone who could advertise milk; all windswept and natural and radiating good health, straight off the fell. But this woman looking back at me has nothing to do with milk or fells. She is glamour and cities and seduction. She is enticing. Rebecca retrieves our wine and hands me my glass. 'To the new you!'

Chapter 8

I gulp cold water straight from the tap. In the mirror a smudged, distorted face rises to meet me. Ugh. So much for glamour. It's three in the morning. I've woken with a pounding headache and a mouth like cracked leather. I have no one but myself to blame. Was I embarrassing? Images of my mother shove their way into my head, eyes rolling as she tried to focus, staggering, belching, oblivious. I do not want to be that woman. I shouldn't have bought that last glass of wine. They were large glasses. I don't usually drink and if I do, it's one or two small glasses in an evening. I should have ordered a soft drink. I can remember talking, a lot, but not the detail. I do remember talking about school, the way the cool girls made me feel. Oh God! I talked to Rebecca about that! Cool Rebecca, who was probably one of those girls. Mortified, I try and remember exactly what I said, but all I can recall is going on and on. I talked about Sam. I kept trying to persuade her there's nothing going on between us and whinging about how difficult it is to find anyone under thirty to be with. I must have bored her to death! She will have been listening to that self-indulgent drivel and thought: pathetic. I shake my head at my reflection and take another gulp from the tap.

Jonty was fast asleep when I got back, so he never got to see my seductive twin, but Rebecca has given me a list of the products she used and with a bit of practice I might be able to reproduce her work, or a more subtle version of it next time Jonty takes me for a night out. I did make some attempt to remove the paint before I crashed into bed, but there are still dark smears beneath my eyes from the mascara, which was thick and sticky as tar. Rebecca told me she has false lashes done at a salon in town every three weeks. The effect is stunning, but I can't maintain a façade like that on a day-to-day basis and Jonty and Sam would just laugh at me. Looking at my sorry reflection in the glass, I decide that glamming up for a night out is fun and I'll definitely make more of an effort from now on, but Lizzie the festivals organiser needs a more down-to-earth look. I will, however, book myself in for a haircut. I hold a clump of split ends up to the light. Rebecca was right. I can't remember the last time my hair was trimmed. I tip some more cleanser on to a cotton-wool pad and get to work removing the tar.

Rebecca calls me at ten. 'How's your head?' I'm stupidly relieved to hear her voice. I can't have been that bad if she's calling me this morning. I answer her question with a groan. Jonty brought me coffee in bed at seven, took one look at me and drew the blind back down again, telling me to sleep it off. He's gone to do some work on his boat. A friend of Pip's has offered him some barn space while he sands down the hull and gives it a new coat of varnish. It's an ideal distraction from the redundancy.

'Do you have to work today?' Rebecca is as fizzy as a glass of Prosecco. She can clearly take her alcohol better than I can.

I hesitate. 'I was planning on going in, but I am working tomorrow and Saturday…'

'It's Easter weekend! You *so* need today off.' She wants to meet me. She listened to my drunken whining last night and she still likes me. I'm a teenager again, hoping to get in with the in-crowd – hell, any crowd. 'Meet me in an hour for strong coffee and brunch at The Barn and bring your credit card.'

'How much are you planning to eat?'

'Loads, but brunch is on me. The credit card is for your new wardrobe. Put on some nice underwear, we're going shopping.'

I'm not sure what she means by nice underwear. I never really think much about underwear, apart from making sure my bras are the right cup size and the straps don't dig into my shoulders. Why is it important? I guess it's because I'll be trying things on, but that's in private, isn't it? Or does she envisage one of those awful communal changing rooms? Do they still have those? I quite like the idea that someone with style is going to take me shopping. It will be fun and I don't have to buy anything. I look at my watch. It's too late to go to Manchester. Lancaster is a forty-five-minute train journey; it will be early afternoon by the time we get there, which will give us two or three hours before the shops close. I dig out my whitest bra and take a pair of knickers from a new M&S multipack I bought a few weeks ago.

The Barn is exactly what it suggests, an old cattle barn which has been gutted and turned into a very simple and stylish café. It opened a year ago and took a while to get going. It's not like anything else in Tarnside. The guy who owns it is a Mancunian who's moved to the area. He's kept the cavernous interior plain: high ceiling, exposed beams, concrete and brickwork. The bar is stainless steel, the tables and chairs simple plywood and metal, suggesting a work canteen, with industrial light-fittings and odd bits of rusty farm machinery displayed like works of art. I love The Barn. Jonty wanted to dismiss it as a city off-comer's idea of style, but couldn't. It's simply too classy for that. The guy has invested money in this project and Tarnside residents appreciate that; the strong flat whites in little glasses, the fabulous cakes and European sandwiches, the dazzling choice of breads.

I'm meeting a friend at The Barn! A friend my own age. A glamorous, charming young woman. My friend, not Jonty's, not Sam's, but someone of my own. Rebecca is waiting for me at a table in the corner, two glasses of freshly squeezed orange juice in front of her. She looks clean and fresh, in a blue and white striped Breton T-shirt and faded jeans. Her hair is pulled back in a loose ponytail, her skin is almost make-up free. I feel grubby beside her, running my fingers through my hair, lifting the oily strands from my scalp, wishing I'd washed it before I came out. We order sourdough toast with smoked salmon and scrambled eggs, which is quite possibly the best thing I've ever tasted, and my fragile body sings with appreciation.

Rebecca calls in the bill before I've finished my last mouthful and hurries me out on to the street. I assume she's aiming for a specific train, but she heads in the opposite direction. 'Where are we going?'

'We'll start with Linen and Silk.'

Linen and Silk is an exclusive Tarnside boutique I have only ever ventured into once. It's where the rich women from the villages shop. The owner is thin as a lolly stick and has huge hair, all copper and gold highlights tonged into immaculate waves, that makes her head look too big for her body. I've never seen her smile. When I dared cross the threshold of her shop, she looked me up and down in a way that told me quite clearly that I did not belong. I took a quick look at a few items on the hangers and the astronomical price tags attached, aware of her eyes boring into my back, and got out of there as quickly as I could. 'I don't know if that's really the sort of shop—'

'Rubbish!' Rebecca grabs me by the arm. 'They have some great stuff and there's a sale on.' I let her lead. With Rebecca I feel a little braver. She looks the part, and the way she strides in, doing a quick scan of what's on display, as if the whole shop was designed simply for her convenience, is liberating. Lollipop smiles, she actually smiles! At Rebecca, not me, and it's not a real smile but one of those stretch-your-lips-sideways painful kind of smiles. Still, it's more than I've ever managed to get out of her. I hover behind Rebecca as she moves along the rails assessing the stock like an inspector. Having satisfied herself with what's on offer she heads for the sale rail. 'Let's start here,' she says and begins to sift through items at an impressive rate, plucking various garments and holding them aloft as if waiting for a hook to appear. I realise that these things are for me and I'm about to step forward and take them from her when Lollipop emerges from behind the counter and says, 'Would you like me to hang those in the changing room for you?'

Rebecca doesn't even look at her. 'Lovely. Thank you.'

I stand in front of the mirror in my bra and knickers and stare at the items hanging in front of me. I would never have picked up any of these things. There are strappy little tops that I couldn't possibly wear with my huge boobs, an extravagant skirt which I think is actually a net petticoat and entirely transparent, cropped leggings which will make my legs look even shorter than they are, a fitted dress and a variety of complicated tops that I don't know how to put on. And the colours! I usually wear white and navy blue, which go with everything, sometimes a dark pink, but nothing fussy, nothing that can't be combined with a jumper. It's cold in Cumbria. These clothes aren't for me. What am I doing here?

Rebecca plucks aside the curtain and takes a step back. 'Bloody hell! Where did you get that underwear?'

'What's wrong with it?'

'Never mind. Why aren't you trying things on?' She takes the cropped leggings from the hanger and hands them to me. 'Come on, start with these.'

'They're too short.'

'They're meant to be.'

'I don't look good in cropped trousers.'

'These aren't trousers and you won't see them.' She unclips the net petticoat from the hanger and holds it out. 'They're to go underneath this. Hurry up! I can't wait to see you in it. Try it with the smoky-grey camisole.'

'I can't…'

'There's no such word as can't. Just put it on and we'll talk then.'

I do as I'm told. I don't want an argument in front of Lollipop and I might as well give it a go. If I look ridiculous we can at least have a giggle about it.

But I don't look ridiculous. The leggings are comfortable

and a perfect fit. When I put the petticoat on I expect it to flare out and make me look like a rain cloud, but actually it drapes quite gently over the hips and flares out towards the hemline, which is below my knees and finishes just an inch or so above the end of the leggings. It looks pretty and a little quirky, which I like, but the thick straps of my bra ruin the strappy top. Rebecca yanks the curtain aside and steps back to take a look. She nods approvingly. 'Good. That's very good.'

I pluck at the bra strap and pull a face in the mirror.

'Don't worry about that. We'll get you a decent bra to go underneath it.'

'It's no good. Any bra that fits me will have thick straps.'

She shrugs, undeterred. 'It doesn't matter if the straps are pretty. We'll find something.' And I know she will. Rebecca has a way of getting what she wants. Lollipop is positively fawning. She's been rummaging through the rails and is waiting, patiently, for Rebecca to notice her offerings. The clothes she's presenting are all sludge colours. I shake my head, but Rebecca pounces on several items, exclaiming, 'Ooh, yes. That's perfect. And this. Yes, thank you.'

'I don't like the colours.'

'These are your colours.'

I wrinkle my nose. 'Really? Murky brown and dirty green?'

She affects a camp voice. 'Caramel and lichen, darling. Trust me, this is the perfect palette for you.' She holds up the green blouse to my face and my grimace falls away because she's right. This colour complements my skin tone and brings out my eyes. She tries the brown and this time my hair is accentuated. Why haven't I worked this out for myself before? I have a degree in fine art, I work with colour. Why have I never spent time in front of a mirror playing like this?

Rebecca takes me to the fancy underwear shop and we do manage to find a bra in my cup size with pretty lace straps that will be visible beneath the camisole. Rebecca and the shop assistant assure me it will look great if I choose a contrasting colour and persuade me to go for fuchsia pink, but the matching thong is a step too far. I agree to the alternative Brazilian-style knickers, which barely cover my buttocks but are at least a little more modest. I spend more money than I have ever spent on clothes in a year in just two shops. I'm physically trembling. I feel almost afraid, but I want to do it. It feels reckless, decadent, impulsive, all the things I rarely allow myself to be. And I have at least supported two local businesses, even if one of them belongs to Lollipop.

Rebecca takes me to the wine bar for a celebratory drink. I insist on paying. 'I don't know how to thank you.'

'You don't have to thank me. It's been great to get out and just have a giggle with someone. I've been so bored since I got here. I mean, everyone's really nice and all that, but…'

I realise, suddenly, that it's different for her. I have Jonty and Sam, a family, but she's on her own. If I sometimes feel lonely here, how must it be for her? 'Where do your family live? Do you have any brothers or sisters?'

She shakes her head. 'Only child.' And she leans in and adds, 'Which is why I need a good girlfriend!'

Rebecca wants to be my friend! I know it's pathetic, I know the reason she's choosing me is that there really isn't anyone else, but I still can't help feeling delighted.

'Have you enjoyed yourself?'

'It's been fun. Thanks.'

She shrugs. 'You need a bit of fun.'

I feel myself blinking back tears. When did I stop having fun? I used to have fun. I used to *be* fun.

She says, 'It must be hard, being responsible for a teenager when you're not much older yourself.'

I nod and feel something unfolding inside me. 'I don't really have any friends my own age here. Jonty's crowd are lovely, but they're all a generation older than me and sometimes...' I stop. I don't want to criticise Jonty and his friends. They're good people and I'm fond of them. They've been kind to me, welcoming me into their world; I don't want to seem ungrateful.

'Well, you have me now!' Rebecca says brightly, beaming like an air hostess. She has focused all her energy on me today. I noticed she didn't try anything on herself. All that attention. All that care. It's a long time since I felt like this. Clare is hundreds of miles away and my life is so different from hers now.

'We'll have to organise a night out, so I can wear some of this stuff.' It will be my treat. I'll have to think of somewhere impressive that Rebecca won't have been.

'Ah!' She winks. 'That's all organised.'

'Where are we going?'

'Not me. You and Jonty. He's taking you to dinner tonight, so we need to get back to your place.'

'Jonty?'

'He called.' She glances at my phone and pulls an apologetic face. 'While you were in the loo.' She answered my phone? 'I saw his name come up.' She gives a little shrug, her eyes scanning me anxiously. 'I hope you don't mind, but I couldn't resist grabbing the opportunity.' I don't know what to say. 'Eight o'clock,' she says, smiling. 'So there's plenty of time for you to get ready.' She brandishes her bulging make-up purse. 'I have my little bag of tricks with me.' She's trying so hard. It was a nice thought. 'I've told him to keep

Sam out of the house for a couple of hours so you can get ready in peace.' No one has ever done anything like this for me before. I'm the one who organises, who pays attention, who makes the gestures. Jonty has taken me out, of course, and he likes to be extravagant when he does, but he would never think to plan such a surprise. I thank her and she grins, delighted.

***

By the time Rebecca has finished and I'm dressed in my fuchsia-pink bra with the camisole and leggings and petticoat, I look and feel amazing. I have a pair of suede ballerina pumps in smoky grey that brush up well. Rebecca suggests that a jewel on the front would look good and I remember a pair of vintage clip-on earrings I found at a car boot that I thought might be useful for the Christmas workshops at the park. They instantly transform a plain pump into an evening shoe. She pulls my hair up into a loose bun, quite high, and then teases a few waves free to create an elegantly dishevelled look. The make-up is a bit dramatic. I make a mental note not to rub my eyes.

Rebecca leaves before Jonty and Sam return. I hug her and can't thank her enough, but she insists it's all been great fun for her too and promises to take me with her next time she heads to Manchester to check out the summer collections. A whole new social life is opening out in front of me.

I hear Jonty and Sam approaching, their voices a low rumble as they pass the window. Waiting nervously in the living room, twirling in front of the mirror, this way and that, I'm still not sure if I can quite carry it off. I look like a model. Me, Lizzie, who is always dressed practically, ready for any eventuality, windswept and flushed. Tonight I am a mannequin. Tonight I am glamorous, seductive. Young.

They bundle in, their sweatshirts, jeans and hair covered in a fine layer of golden dust; Sam must have gone with his dad to work on the boat.

Jonty sees me first and does a double take, straightening up to have a proper look.

'You like?' I tip my head coquettishly to one side.

He gives a low whistle. 'Rebecca did good.'

Sam's head jerks up. I wait for the shock to shift into a smile. His face turns crimson. I hold my breath. Pip's voice, *Be careful*, and I remember the bathroom, his eyes on me, and I think, too late, that I shouldn't have done this, that I shouldn't be standing here parading myself in front of him. Jonty is one thing, but Sam… 'What's going on?' he snaps.

'A bit much?' I feel myself shrinking.

'Rebecca?'

'The windsurfer. From the lake, the day we capsized. I met her at the pub. She's given me a makeover.' I look at Jonty for support. Maybe it is too much. Have I made a fool of myself?

Jonty grins and gives Sam a shove in the ribs. 'Ignore him. He's just jealous!'

But Sam squirms away from him and looks me up and down in a way that makes me feel dirty. This isn't fair. Why shouldn't I dress up? I can look sexy. I'm his dad's girlfriend, not his. It's not my fault I'm young. I've a right to feel pretty and have a bit of fun.

Jonty rubs his hands together, hamming it up. 'Well, I'd better go and get myself spruced up. Don't want to let the side down!' He takes the stairs two at a time. I'm left facing Sam. He turns away and walks past me into the kitchen, stopping in front of the washing machine and pulling off his hoodie and T-shirt in one move, exposing the smooth bumps of his spine. I look away. The vegetables I was going to roast for tea are on the kitchen counter. Sam will be eating alone if Jonty and I are out.

He's facing me. I can see the outline of his ribs, the smoky pink of his nipples. I try to focus on his eyes. 'You can come with us if you like?'

He gives a derisive snort. 'You're all right. Not my thing really.' As he passes, on his way back to the stairs, he pauses alongside me. For a moment we are shoulder to shoulder, me facing in one direction and him the other. I'm acutely aware of his body. I think I feel something, but I'm not sure; the softest stroke of my bare arm. I picture Sam's fingers, so light, barely skimming the hairs, not even touching the skin. Or is that me, my body sensitive to the slightest impression? He moves off and I'm frozen, the hairs on my flesh standing on end. I imagined it. He walked past, his arm probably just brushed me. I'm becoming paranoid. If I carry on like this my relationship with Sam, this innocent, beautiful thing we've built between us, will collapse.

'There's some lasagne in the fridge if you get hungry.'

'I'll probably go out.' Usually he'd say where he's going and who with, what time we should expect him home, but he offers none of this. Pausing on the stairs, he looks down at me, his expression reminding me of the moment in the bathroom. 'Don't wait up.' He's suggesting Jonty and I will want to fall straight into bed when we get in and he doesn't want to be here when that happens. And maybe that's fair enough. Maybe, at seventeen, he's got to accept that his dad and I have sex. We are grown-ups. And so is he, almost.

Chapter 9

Jonty and I had a magical night. He enjoys an occasion and can really play the part. He came downstairs in his dark blue suit with a white crumpled linen shirt that looked just perfect. He has style, Jonty. He doesn't dress like other men his age, but he doesn't try to look like someone twenty years younger either. His skin tans quickly and he always looks like he's just come back from a holiday. People assume he's younger than he is, and I forget the age gap between us. I don't associate him with my mum's generation, even though his friends are that age; Jonty is a perpetual twenty-something. It's not just his colouring, which is naturally dark, but his demeanour: easy, happy to go with the flow; he knows how to enjoy himself. We used to have fun, Jonty and I. Since the kids arrived, the fun has fizzled out and we need to get it back. I'm the problem. Jonty hasn't changed, but I have. Ironically, it's me who's become middle-aged, but I intend to do something about that now.

Sam wasn't home when we got back and I was glad,

because nothing was going to stop Jonty, and I knew I wouldn't be able to relax if I was aware of Sam in his room. We fell into the house and didn't even bother to make it to the bedroom. Just like it used to be.

I hear the door when Sam finally comes in and squint at the digital clock on Jonty's side of the bed. It's three seventeen. Where can he have been until this time? There's a run-down nightclub in the basement of one of the pubs in town, but I can't imagine that would be his sort of place. He might have gone back to a friend's house, but he's never done that before. Fi may have been with him. She might be able to shed some light on what's going on. I roll over and try to get back to sleep, pulling the pillow over my head to drown out Jonty's soft snores.

In the morning I'm up and out before seven. I like arriving at the park while the rest of the town are still in their beds. I relish the stillness, the sense of expectancy. It's Good Friday, so the town is sleeping in, but in a few hours this tranquillity will be churned up by families with children and dogs, picnics unfolded, footballs and softballs, tinfoil and Tupperware, blankets and cardigans and shawls, wobbly toddlers, doting grandparents, kids on the zip wire, teenagers slipping out of sight into the woodland. For now, though, all is still as I sip my coffee and look out across the water.

The tarn glitters in the early sunlight. I remember Jonty choking on his beer when I referred to it as a pond. In my defence, I was thinking of the pond in Hyde Park, not a garden pond, but to mention that would not have helped the situation. I was two years out of art school, not just an off-comer but a southerner. Jonty needed an artist to create a series of sculptures. The clue was in the name of the town, of course, but I didn't know what a tarn was back then, so didn't make the connection. It was my first big project and I was working with a team of teenagers who, once we got over the initial feigned indifference and sarcasm over my accent, were enthusiastic and imaginative. One of the girls had an older sister, working in the shipyard who taught me to weld and we worked with willow and scrap metal and created bizarre woodland creatures that you stumble on as you follow the nature trail or enjoy a picnic. We had a day out at Grizedale Forest for inspiration and I know I'm biased but our sculptures could easily hold their own there. They've rusted into the landscape now; a permanent reminder of how I came to be here.

Tarnside Manor was bequeathed to the community by the resident lord over a hundred years ago, along with the vast garden which reaches down to the water's edge. It's all a bit make-do-and-mend, but the profits from the coach house café pay me a small salary to manage the team of volunteers who take care of the garden, now a public park, which tops up the wage I earn for the festivals work. I'm proud to be part of this project, proud to live in a town where community initiatives are supported in this way. I feel like the modern-day equivalent of a kitchen maid at the original manor house, serving the multi-generational family, earning my place.

I didn't sleep well last night. I'm uneasy about the change in Sam and what that might mean for our relationship. I wish Pip hadn't said anything. She meant well. I know she was thinking of me, but she's started a niggle in my head that won't go away.

Fi isn't due in until ten. If I set out the materials for the family workshops (egg painting and miniature raft making) and get the room ready, she and I can grab a coffee and talk before people start arriving. I'll buy her a bacon butty in the café; knowing the way things are for her at home, she'll appreciate something to eat.

On the opposite side of the tarn the land rises into a steep hill, at the top of which stands the high school. I look at the elegant Victorian windows, the grey Lakeland stone, the new glass extension and I try to imagine Sam, currently sound asleep at home, moving through those spaces from lesson to lesson on an ordinary school day, the people he encounters, how he is with them, how they are with him. He's tall, and one of the eldest navigating those corridors, and he holds himself straight, so he'd be visible above the crowd. And he's dark, like Jonty, though Jonty is turning silver at the temples and around his ears. The girls notice Sam, I've seen them dig one another in the ribs and giggle as they pass him in town, pink flushes in their cheeks, but he's unaware of the effect he has. Boys acknowledge him, still measuring him up. He tells me he's not part of the popular crowd, though he's not unpopular and he's OK with this. He's never been one to give his allegiance to any particular group; he glides through, doing as he pleases. Or so I thought. Who was he with last night? It's not like him not to tell me.

I focus on the view to still my mind. To the right of the tarn are open fields where sheep graze, soon to be joined by young cattle. To the left is the town. At this end, close to the park, are the larger houses with views over the water. A few have gardens that stretch down to the shore. Further up and spreading out west is the town itself, with its church and market square. A train, a single blue carriage, like a child's toy, makes its way along the railway that stretches from Lancaster to Barrow and into Tarnside's pretty Victorian station.

A solitary figure comes down the street towards the

park, shoulders hunched, hands in pockets. I recognise Fi's blue hair, the purple Doc Martens. She has her eyes down, looking at the ground ahead of her. Sam is still in bed and won't emerge for several hours, the café isn't open yet and she won't be expecting me to be here. I wonder how long she's been up, if she's slept at all.

As she sees me approach, she wipes a hand across her face and sniffs. I pretend that there's nothing unusual about her being here at this time and ask if she fancies a coffee. She nods, offering a feeble smile. She knows I won't ask questions.

'Do you want to wait here or come with me?'

'I'll wait,' she says, grabbing the opportunity to compose herself. I leave her sitting on the wooden bench dedicated to Margaret Thwaite, the housekeeper at the manor who oversaw the bequest after Lord Whatever His Name Was died. A formidable woman, she was quite probably the visionary behind her employer's bequest and remained as manager of the park into her seventies. Passionately committed to the people of Tarnside and the long-term success of the park, she's the one the community remember. A hard act to follow. Eve told me she likes to sit on that bench sometimes, when it all gets a bit overwhelming, and seek Margaret's advice. Margaret remained chair of the board after she retired and Eve got to know her well. I never met her, but I've seen photographs and heard stories. I sit on her bench too sometimes and imagine her beside me, telling me what to do. I know it sounds mad, but it's a way of taking a step back and seeing things from a different perspective. Her imaginary, no-nonsense voice in my head calms me.

I take my time in the kitchen, to allow Fi some privacy. Maybe Margaret Thwaite will comfort her too. I recognise something in Fi, as the children of alcoholics often do. The lack of sleep, the exaggerated sense of responsibility, the need to avoid conflict, to make things right, the low level of anxiety that hums continually through our veins like an electrical current, waiting for the next explosion. I know she can sense my empathy, but we don't talk about it; that would require painful explanations and betrayals. In order to function in the normal world we must lock that chaos out of sight. Here we are different people. When Fi goes home she becomes someone else. It was like that for me once.

She wraps her hands around the mug and stares out across the tarn. We sit in silence. Fi has no one. Her older siblings have all fled and she is dealing with the chaos, day in, day out, alone. This was the situation I left my brother with when I went to art school. Danny was thirteen. I knew I was abandoning him, but I'd delayed going for a year already and I had to get away. I hoped that by living a different life I could show him it was possible. He came to stay with me at weekends whenever he could escape, and I was back every holiday, but it was hard for him. He's not as tough as me and he's had to cope alone. He's at uni now, on a year out in Australia. He managed to wangle himself paid work-experience in Perth doing something mathematical I don't understand, but he's about as far away as he can get from our mother, which is exactly what he needs. I get an email now and then, but mostly he's enjoying his freedom and I'm letting him get on with it and trying not to miss him too much.

I snatch glances, checking for bruises; I've seen Fi's mother in dark glasses on cloudy days, counting out her change with trembling hands, but so far Fi appears to have escaped the physical violence. I could go to the police, but it would feel like an intrusion and I know her mother has refused help in the past. I don't know Fi's family. It's none of my business. She's still technically a child and she's vulnerable, but she is managing the situation and she has an escape plan. As soon as she's completed her A levels she'll take up the live-in job I've set up for her as a holiday rep at the caravan park in France where I worked after my A levels. This is her ticket out. In the meantime I offer the quiet support I can and I watch. I can be here for Fi in a way I couldn't be for Danny. She has only two more months to go and she'll be free.

'Were you out last night?' I ask, waiting to hear of teenage hijinks that will put my mind at rest. There are dark shadows under her eyes. She looks surprised. 'You didn't meet up with Sam?'

'No. Why?'

'He was out pretty late. I just wondered.'

She looks wounded and I feel bad for suggesting that something was going on that didn't include her. I hope I haven't put my foot in it. But if Sam wasn't with her, who was he with until that time? And where?

Fi stifles a yawn. I'm guessing she hasn't slept much. I have tentatively suggested she can stay with us any time that's convenient, but she's never taken me up on that offer. She would rather sneak into the office and sleep on the floor than admit to anything going on at home.

'Shall we boil some eggs and start setting up?'

She nods, loosens her shoulders. Shaking off the chaos of her domestic life, embracing the world beyond, like the survivor she needs to be.

Sam is home when I get in and has no plans to go out. Jonty cooks a pasta dish from a recipe in the Sunday supplement and we eat it on our knees in front of the TV. Later, when Sam and I are washing up, I ask him what time he got in.

'About midnight.'

I hesitate. I'd expected him to come clean, to laugh and say it was really late and explain where he'd been. 'Who were you with?'

He shrugs. 'Some mates from school.'

But if that was true, I'm sure Fi would have been invited. I know he's lying, but why?

On Saturday there are even more people than we expected. It's not really warm enough to sit outside, so lots of families have taken cover in the café and sent the kids upstairs to see what's going on. One of the mothers is a former volunteer, a primary-school teacher on maternity leave with her second child. Seeing me struggle with the number of children wanting to take part, she leaves the baby with her mother-in-law and gives me a hand, which means I can pop across to the garden room to check on Fi.

I hover in the doorway for a moment, watching Fi help a dark-haired girl of about Nell's age finish her raft. Their heads are bent close. Fi's voice is gentle, kind, a series of suggestions rather than commands. She's patient. Was I patient like that with Nell? I remember suggesting we bake fairy cakes once, because I thought that was the sort of thing you did with kids. I'm no baker and I was trying to double the quantities so Nell could take the cakes to school for her class. She didn't ask me to do that, I put it on myself, and I forgot to double the eggs, which meant the cakes were a disaster. The whole process was stressful and unpleasant and poor Nell couldn't wait to escape. Did I snap at her? It was the cakes I was mad at. I wasn't concentrating but already thinking about what I had to do next. I did a lot of that with Nell; didn't pay enough attention, didn't make the most of being with her while I could. Five months. She arrived in the bleak slush of January and was gone before the summer had really begun.

We're running low on materials, but Fi has the great idea to commandeer a couple of kids who have completed their rafts to go through the park and collect bits and pieces while we break for lunch. She and I head for the woodland to pick up extra twigs and moss. I'm still thinking about Nell and Sam. He must miss his sister. Sam's mum, Kay, is living in the family home she inherited from her parents and has picked up with her childhood sweetheart. She's promised to fly over with Nell for St George's Day. I've booked the two of them into the newly refurbished rooms above The Red Lion. Nell will love the walk-in shower and widescreen TV she can watch from her bed. We'd hoped they could come at Easter, when they might have had a bit longer, but Easter is a big family event in Ireland and Kay felt she needed to be there. We shall have to make the best of a couple of days.

'You're great with the kids,' I tell Fi as we move between the trees, eyes fixed on the ground. 'Does Sam ever talk about Nell with you?'

'Yeah.' She stoops to gather a handful of leaves. 'I've chatted to her a couple of times on Skype. They're always on the phone. We're going to meet up when she comes over.'

'Do you think he misses her?'

She shrugs. 'A bit, I guess.' It doesn't sound like that's the issue.

I wonder what Fi knows about the truanting. 'Has Sam spoken to you about that time he was off?'

She frowns. 'When he had that bug thing?'

So he hasn't told her. If he was going to confide in anyone it would be Fi. I'm surprised. She wouldn't necessarily tell me, of course, she'd be careful not to betray him, but this response feels genuine. 'Is there anything bothering him at school, do you know?'

She shrugs. 'There is someone…' She hesitates, glancing at me, as if she's making her mind up what to say. I wait, but she starts walking again, scanning the ground, avoiding my eyes. 'From his old school… Oh! Wow!' She stops suddenly and bends down to tug a huge patch of moss from a stone. It's obvious she's regretting having said anything. The moss lifts like a blanket and drapes in her hand. 'This is great!' Rolling it carefully, she places it in the hessian bag over her shoulder, but she can sense I'm waiting for her to tell me more. Her eyes meet mine. She sighs. 'She's all friendly with Sam, but it's a bit, I don't know, embarrassing.' She sounds peeved. More than that. She sounds jealous.

I've never considered Fi to be anything other than a good friend of Sam's, but that's naïve of me. I know he doesn't see her as more, but that doesn't mean it's the same for her. I should have been more sympathetic. I should have realised. Fi is like one of the lads, the girl everyone feels safe with, the one they include and confide in and trust, because they don't fancy her, because she isn't obviously pretty or girly or seeking their adoration. They assume she doesn't feel the same as other girls feel, that she doesn't long to be admired or cherished in the same way. She'll dissemble and pretend this is the way she wants it to be, because that's safer than risking ridicule. She's a laugh, but that doesn't make her less of a girl at heart. She still has the same feelings, the same need to be loved. I know this. Of course I do, I was that girl, and it's such a lonely place to be. I can imagine just how she feels right now. If I was Fi's age and friends with Sam, I would be hopelessly in love with him. I can feel her pain. He's so beautiful and gentle and that attention that he gives her, without thinking, that comes so naturally to him, will only feed her hope. She'll be battling with herself, interpreting things to mean more than they do and then chastising herself for being so foolish. The pain of it! I wish I could tell her she's beautiful. She is, in a different, quirky sort of way. I would like to tell her that someone will see this when the time is right, and she will be loved, but I can't say that; she'd be mortified.

'Is Sam coming today?' she asks, trying to sound casual, but now I've realised, I can hear the need in that question.

'Jonty and Sam are coming at four, when we launch the rafts. They're going to stay and clean up with me when everyone's gone.'

'I can help with that.'

She doesn't want to go home. I remember how that felt. With all her siblings having escaped, there is no one she needs to return to protect. 'That would be great.' I give her a hug. 'Fancy fish and chips at ours after?'

She beams with gratitude and relief. I decide not to ask any more questions. I can find out about this girl from Sam.

The rafts are a huge success. Jonty and Sam arrive in time for the ceremony and help with the launching. The participating families from both days gather at the shore. There are close to a hundred people. I never expected it to be so popular. Next year I'll have to look at recruiting more staff. The local tree surgeon has agreed to judge, choosing First, Second and

Third, and adding another category, Most Creative, to allow for a raft which will never float but requires some recognition for the ambition behind it. A scruffy five-year-old walks away delighted but determined to get it on the water despite our warnings. He wails when it sinks, and his mother has to wade out in an attempt to placate him and rescue the wreck. There are more than thirty rafts in total, decorated with woodland flowers, ribbons and beads, bobbing about while their creators stand at the tarn edge clutching their bits of string. We stand, Jonty, Sam, Fi and I, an odd, makeshift family, watching the fruits of the day float in the evening sun.

Sam's phone buzzes with a text, shattering the moment. He fumbles in the pocket of his hoodie, checks the screen, frowns and puts the phone away without responding. I try to catch his eye to check everything is OK, but he turns away.

Some time later, while Fi and I pack up the workshop materials, Jonty volunteers to go to the chippy and takes our orders. 'Where's Sam?'

I remember him saying he was going to do a last trawl for rubbish and I wander out to look. He's at the far end of the park, standing beneath the old oak tree talking into his phone. He's too far away for me to see much, but there's an urgency and tension in his posture. He turns and kicks the bulging bin liner at his feet, spilling plastic cups, paper and other rubbish across the grass. I hang back and wait until he's collected up most of it before approaching.

'Your dad's off to the chippy. What do you want?'

His phone buzzes. He ignores it.

I tell him, 'Fi's coming home with us,' hoping this will bring him back.

He bites his lip. 'I've got to go.'

'Now? Where?'

He hesitates. 'I'm meeting someone.'

This will be the girl Fi mentioned. This must be who he was with on Thursday night. Was he arguing with her? 'What about Fi?'

'I didn't know she was coming back.'

This is true. It's not unreasonable for him to have plans of his own. Sam hasn't had a girlfriend in all the time I've known him. Jonty teases him about it sometimes, which is cruel. I've wondered if there might be a problem of some kind, a bad experience in the past, but maybe it's just that he's shy and hasn't been ready for it until now. Poor Fi. But it's his choice and it's not my place to play Cupid here. 'It's a bit awkward, Sam. Why didn't you say something before?'

'I didn't know until just now, all right!'

He's upset. I don't want to make things more difficult for him. He should be able to slip off to make it up with this girl. It will be good for him to have a girlfriend; his life is too centred on revision and helping me out. If he's got a girlfriend, his crush, if Pip's right, will be forgotten and he and I can get back to how we were.

'Is it a girl?' I smile, inviting a confidence, but he blushes scarlet and turns away. 'Sorry.' I feel rebuked, though he hasn't said anything. It's his silence, this closed door, that stings. He used to tell me things. It hurts to be excluded. 'Don't worry.' I give him a little shove. 'Go. I'll sort it.' I watch him walk away, but he's not exactly skipping along and I can sense something, an uneasiness that has been crouched, lingering quietly for a while now, growing darker.

Chapter 10

Sam gets home before midnight this time, but he's very drunk. Jonty and I are in bed. I hear him groping his way up the stairs and banging against the doorframe as he stumbles into the toilet. He hasn't come home in this state since he was fifteen and Jonty was phoned by a furious parent who demanded he drive straight over and collect him from a party. He was still in that angry phase. I know he drinks, but I'm fairly confident he manages it sensibly these days. Maybe he was nervous with this girl and trying to impress. I wonder how well that worked. I want to get up and check he's OK, but he'll probably be embarrassed and I don't want to disturb Jonty, who's snoring beside me, blissfully ignorant.

In the morning, I suggest we let Sam sleep in. Neither of us have bothered with Easter eggs, but I have a chocolate rabbit for Sam and a bag of his favourite sweets. Jonty is in a chirpy mood and heats croissants in the oven. We sit in the living room with yesterday's paper, Jonty reading the review while I flick through the magazine.

The phone rings. The caller ID tells me it's international and I guess it's probably Kay calling from Ireland. I let Jonty answer so they can have a moment to talk about the kids, not that Jonty says anything much. I wonder if I should tell Kay about the truanting, but what can she do from that distance? And it seems to have settled down anyway. There's no point in worrying her. Sam is working hard, he's going to do well and I can hardly tell her if I haven't mentioned it to Jonty.

Jonty mouths for me to fetch Sam. His voice shifts a gear when he talks to Nell. I wonder what she's saying to him as he listens and laughs and if she'll ask to speak to me.

I knock on Sam's door. 'Your mum's on the phone!' Not waiting for an answer, I slip straight downstairs again. 'Is Nell still there? Can I talk to her?'

Jonty says his farewells and hands me the receiver. Her voice is full of giggles. She thanks me for the chocolate and tells me all about grandpa's old Labrador finding and eating most of the mini-eggs Kay had distributed around the garden. Her voice echoes through the room like a memory. I wish I could picture the garden, the house she's living in. I wish I could be there with her, just for a moment. Smell her. Strawberry and vanilla, shampoo and lip balm. Feel her hand slip into mine. Watch her cartwheel across the grass, uninhibited. Happy. Sam chats with his mum and Nell most nights through his laptop. I can't get used to communicating this way; the delayed response and the lack of proper eye-contact are disconcerting, and with Nell, particularly, I find it painful to see her jerky image in another life. I'd rather talk over the phone or email. She types funny, disjointed messages: *How are you? Is it raining in Cumbria? In Ireland it rains a lot. Is Loopy still playing with the squeaky donkey?*

(The squeak has been removed, but the pink toy, now rather smelly, remains a favourite.)

Sam appears in boxers and a threadbare T-shirt I'm sure I threw out weeks ago. He smells musty and sour and his eyes look bruised. I say my goodbyes to Nell reluctantly. He takes the phone and disappears straight back upstairs. I wish, briefly, that it was Nell living with us. Nell is so uncomplicated, spilling out what she's thinking and feeling, so easy to love.

After ten minutes or so I hear the shower. When Sam reappears his hair is damp and he's wearing a clean T-shirt and jeans, but he looks spent. I ask if he's OK.

'Fine.'

Jonty glances up and raises an eyebrow. 'Heavy night?' Chuckling, he returns to the paper.

Was it nerves that made Sam drink so much? I hope he's behaved himself. But he would never treat a girl badly, he's not that sort of boy. I watch him take a pint glass from the kitchen cupboard and fill it from the tap. I keep a packet of headache pills by the kettle. From where I'm sitting I can see him break out two from the foil and swallow them, drinking the entire pint of water in one go. My own stomach is clenching and churning for some reason. I remember his vomiting the night before, which brings bile to the back of my throat and I have to grip the arms of the chair, forcing myself to swallow. What is this? A sympathy hangover?

I wonder if the date didn't go according to plan. Maybe he didn't manage to win her over. I wish I could talk to him, but all his signals tell me to back off. I hope this isn't the way it's going to be from now on, I don't know if I could stand that.

***

Jonty grumbled about going to Pip's for Easter Sunday lunch, but I think he's as glad as I am not to have to think about entertaining. Pip greets us at the door, dressed in a dove-grey silk dress and silver ballet pumps. We're all in jeans. I did put on a floaty top and I've done my make-up following a pared-down version of Rebecca's instructions, but I should have worn smart shoes instead of my Converse. Next to Pip I feel dowdy and embarrassed that I didn't remind the boys to make more of an effort, but she doesn't seem to notice and ushers us all into the sitting room.

'Sam, darling, would you be a dear and prepare us all a gin and tonic?' She waves towards the tray on the side table where a decanter, ice bucket and glasses are all ready. There's even a small wooden board and a knife to slice the lemon. Jonty rolls his eyes. He finds all this pretentious and Pip knows it, which is partly why she does it. I'm sure she never drank gin from a decanter when Richard was alive.

Sam sets to work. There are four glasses on the tray. Pip smiles at him. 'Would you like to join us?' Sam glances at Jonty, who shrugs. He looks at me. What do I know? Pip seems to think it's OK. Maybe a little hair-of-the-dog might be a good idea. He measures the gin carefully. His hands tremble. I slice the lemon and show him how much tonic to add, reminding him I prefer it without lemon. He distributes the drinks to Pip and Jonty, but as I reach for mine he tells me to wait and slips into the kitchen. He's back a few moments later with a strawberry, which he pierces with the knife and slides over the rim of the glass. It's a lovely gesture, but I am painfully aware of Pip watching, taking it all in. I hate to think what she'd say if she saw the chocolates he presented to me when he finally got up this morning. Gift-wrapped, expensive ones from Booths that we were once offered at a tasting when we stopped off on the way back from school to buy an emergency tea. He remembered how much I like them. Damn Pip and her warped suspicions.

Jonty sinks into the sofa and picks up a magazine, flicking through it as if he's in the doctor's waiting room. I wish he could relax in this house.

Pip is a good cook and an advocate of locally produced, simple, organic food. We have a slow-roasted leg of Herdwick lamb, with potatoes and cabbage she tells me she bought from the kitchen garden at the park, a gesture she knows I'll appreciate. There's cauliflower cheese, a childhood favourite of Jonty's, which he pretends he doesn't remember, but Pip scoffs at this and serves him a double portion. Opening a bottle of red wine, she pours it into a long-stemmed glass and passes it to me. 'Jonty can drive. You relax and enjoy yourself.'

Jonty stretches and yawns. 'Sam can drive.'

Pip turns to Sam. 'Really? Have you passed your test, darling?'

Jonty answers for him. 'He's got a provisional licence. He can drive if we're in the car.'

'Not if you are not fit to drive yourself.' She pours herself a glass.

'I'll be fine. I'm not planning to get plastered.'

'You will drive, Jonty. Sam, would you like a drop?'

Sam shakes his head. 'No, thanks.'

She pours Jonty a small glass and removes the bottle from the table. 'Jonty, darling, would you carve?' Pip knows just how to handle her son. As Jonty regresses to his teenage self, she reverts to firm parent. And she knows how to distract him. He's in his element at the head of the table and loves to carve. His irritation over the wine is forgotten as the lamb slides from the bone, perfectly cooked.

Sam asks for a small portion and quietly picks at the food on his plate. Jonty watches from across the table. 'Feeling a bit queasy?' Sam ignores him. 'Where were you last night?'

'Out.'

'Out where?'

'Town.'

'Who with?'

'None of your business.'

'Hey!' Jonty straightens up. 'Less of the attitude.'

Pip raises her glass. 'Leave him in peace, Jonty. He's feeling a little the worse for wear. You of all people should understand.'

'What's that supposed to mean?'

She smiles at him. I catch Sam's eye across the table. Here we go.

'Alcohol is a difficult thing to manage. We can all make mistakes.' She offers me mint sauce. I feel Jonty tense beside me. I put a hand on his leg. I can almost hear him counting, one, two, three... and the moment passes.

For dessert we eat Cartmel Sticky Toffee Pudding. Pip apologises for not having prepared something herself. 'But I see no point when we have this produced on the doorstep. Sold at Harrods in London, don't you know.'

'And apparently a favourite of Madonna's,' Jonty adds, as if we haven't heard this before. Sam looks at me and rolls his eyes. He almost smiles.

After lunch we clear the table together. Pip will not allow

me to help load the dishwasher but shoos me back into the living room and suggests a game of Monopoly. She has a cupboard overflowing with board games: an ancient box of Scrabble with several letters missing, a tatty Cluedo, but also more recent games she and her friends have discovered. There's a group who come regularly to play. 'I find it keeps the brain alert,' she says. This is a woman who can turn any problem into a reason for pleasure. I pull out the ancient Snakes and Ladders, the disintegrating box held together with thick layers of Sellotape, and remember Nell fixing it one winter Sunday afternoon, pulling length after length of sticky tape off the dispenser and ripping it across the jagged teeth with relish. It had been wet and windy and Jonty and Sam had gone sailing, but it was too cold for us to stand on the shore and watch, so Pip had lit the fire and suggested 'us girls play a game', kneeling on the Herdwick rug and spreading out the board. I wish Nell was with us now. It was always easier in this house when she was here. She was my bridge into the family. Her uncomplicated, unconditional affection provided a certainty for me. She held my hand, curled up next to me on the sofa, led me into all the quiet spaces and closed rooms I would never otherwise have seen. The library with all those books and the polished oak step to reach the top shelves; the pantry with its pots and pans, rusting enamel buckets, colanders and bowls; the back attic where we rummaged through Pip's trunks of vintage clothes; the bedroom where Jonty slept as a boy. She allowed me to explore and inhabit this house in a way I'm unable to do without her. Pip is always warm and welcoming, a perfect hostess, but Nell made me feel like I belonged.

On the dresser there's a scattering of photographs. Some black and white, some colour, the palette faded to orange tones. My eye rests on an image of the house, a group of people gathered for a picnic on the lawn. I take a closer look. There is Pip, her hair dark like Jonty's, draped over her shoulder in a loose plait. She's wearing flared jeans and one of those cheesecloth, peasant blouses embroidered around the yoke. There are children in this photo, and several other adults, and lots of bottles and half-finished food scattered about. The house behind them is a shock; a tired, decrepit version of the Chimneys I know, with peeling window frames, some broken panes, others replaced with boards, the garden overgrown, neglected. Even the lawn is wild, the long glass flattened by the picnickers and their colourful knitted blankets.

Jonty peers over my shoulder. 'What have you got there?' He groans and points to a little boy with thick dark hair hanging down in front of his eyes. 'That's me.'

'You look naughty.'

'He was naughty.' Pip has come back into the room. 'So, what plans do you have for your retirement?' Jonty freezes. I can smell the tension emanating from him. I could scream at Pip right now. She continues, belligerently. 'This could be an opportunity for you, darling. You're still young enough to change direction, to do something really useful.'

'Thanks.'

'You can choose to take that as a criticism, but you know that is not what was intended. I am suggesting that you could do something you feel passionate about. You don't have the same pressures you had when you took on that job. Local government is safe. A career. And that's all well and good, but now you're free to do as you please.'

'And what might that be?' Jonty's voice is hard, sullen. He sounds like Sam when he's in a mood.

'That's for you to answer. No hurry. You can enjoy exploring. You could start with sailing. The local sailing club runs courses for young people. I heard it's started a residential course for children with behavioural difficulties from Manchester and Liverpool. You could see if it needs any teachers.'

'No, thanks.'

I'm willing her to stop. The more she suggests, the more doors she's closing. With Jonty you need to plant the seed and move on quickly. He'll come back to it when he's ready and make it his own. As if she's read my mind, Pip puts on her glasses and begins to pick through the photographs, her face softened, revisiting memories. 'Don't I look at fright!'

'You could never look a fright.' But she isn't listening to me, she's frowning at the photograph.

'The house looks so sad.'

Jonty scowls. 'Why have you dragged this lot out?'

'A charming young woman dropped in to see me yesterday. She's researching a book about the history of some of the houses on the shores of Windermere. I had such a lovely time with her, reminiscing. She said she might include one or two of these in the book, though I'm not sure I want a permanent record of me or Chimneys looking like this!'

Jonty spreads out the ancient Monopoly board on the table. He doesn't want to allow Pip an opportunity to justify her renovation of the house. There are men in the photograph, but none of them look like Jonty; his father was probably behind the camera.

'Right!' Jonty calls us all to attention. 'Who wants what?' The boot, hat and iron are still part of the collection, but the other missing pieces have been replaced with a little plastic dog, a stone from the garden and a nut from a bolt. We all choose our piece and the photographs and the subject of Chimneys' renovation is skilfully sidestepped. I sip camomile tea from a porcelain cup and marvel at the number of houses Jonty manages to accumulate on his sites. He's a socialist in life, but when it comes to competitive games he's out to win. Sam and I work together to thwart him. I'm aware of how attentive Sam is to me, fetching the camomile tea without being asked, setting aside the purple hazelnut caramels from the selection box for me to enjoy. Pip is clocking it all. Things I used to take for granted have become loaded.

I'm a little foggy from the mix of gin and wine, and getting bored with the game, when I remember the conversation with Fi in the woods. Without thinking, I say to Sam, 'Fi tells me someone from your old school has moved to the high school.'

He drops the dice. 'What's Fi said?'

I hesitate, immediately regretting having brought this up here. 'Nothing. Nothing really.'

'You've been talking about me behind my back?'

I want to say no, but that is precisely what I've been doing.

Jonty is moving Sam's counter around the board. He gives a roar of glee and rubs his hands together. 'Pay up, Sam. You owe me...' He looks down at the card in front of him to work it out.

Pip sips her tea quietly. I don't know what to do.

Jonty looks up and holds his hand out to Sam. 'Two hundred and forty pounds, please!'

Sam's jaw is tight. He doesn't hear Jonty, he's too focused on me. His voice is choked, vulnerable. 'Why are you talking about me behind my back?'

I feel awful, as if I've betrayed him. I say, 'It wasn't like that,' but it sounds feeble. 'I'm sorry. I was just curious. I thought Fi might shed some light…' I tail off, aware that Jonty doesn't know about the truanting. Sam's eyes are huge with alarm, willing me to shut up. 'Sorry. I was just…'

'Well don't! This is nothing to do with you!'

'Hey!' Jonty snaps to attention. 'Watch your tone.'

'Oh fuck off!' Sam shoves back his chair. It topples and lands with a crash as he thunders out of the room.

Jonty leaps to his feet, but Pip's authoritative tone stops him. 'Wait.'

'He can't behave like that! He needs to come back down here and apologise.'

'He will,' Pip says calmly. 'You behaved a lot worse when you were his age.'

As they argue this point, I wonder what to do. Should I follow Sam? I feel responsible for this situation, but when I get up, Pip says, 'Leave him.' It's a command, not a suggestion. 'Let him cool off. He can stay here tonight. I'll see if I can talk to him.'

The drive home is horrible. I feel stung by Pip's tone, and guilty. Jonty is in a pig of a mood, furious with his mother and his son, throwing the car around the bends on the lake road at an alarming speed. He's eventually forced to slow down behind a more careful driver on a particularly winding stretch with too many blind bends to allow him to overtake. I try and calm him down. 'Don't be mad at Sam. It's my fault. I overstepped the line.'

'What line? He's got no right to talk to you that way, or me for that matter.'

Outside the window the lake surface ruffles and shifts, dirty blue on murky grey. I can't explain to Jonty what's worrying me. I'm not sure myself. But something is wrong.

Jonty makes pancakes for breakfast. He's just dishing up when there's a knock at the door. I go to answer it. Fi is outside, her face grim. 'Is Sam in?' Her voice is a shard of slate.

'He's at Pip's. Is everything all right?'

'What did you say to him?'

Jonty appears in the doorway. 'Grub's up! Oh, hello, Fi. Fancy some pancakes?'

I hold up my hand. 'Just a minute.' He catches my look and retreats. 'What's this about, Fi?'

'Why did you have to tell him? *You* were the one asking questions. I should have told you to mind your own business.'

'I'm sorry.' I reach out, but she steps back, her face a grimace.

'He sent me a text…'

'What did he say?' Her face pinches with pain. 'Fi, this is all my fault. I'm really sorry. I didn't realise he'd react that way. I don't understand what's going on with him right now.' She looks ready to cry. 'Look I'll speak to him. He'll be home soon and I'll ask him to call you.'

She refuses to come in. I phone Sam, but there's no answer. I try again, but it goes to voicemail, so I call Pip, who tells me Sam slept in the boathouse and hasn't come in yet. We arrange to pick him up in an hour, but a few minutes later she calls back to say the boathouse is empty and there's no sign of him in the garden or the house. All we can assume is that he's hitched a lift on the lake road. We call Sam's phone again but no reply. Jonty is furious. How dare he just leave without any explanation? But I'm more concerned about his safety. As an hour passes, and then another, I battle against images of drownings, road accidents, malevolent predators, Sam injured and alone, but if I'm honest, what worries me most is that he's run away. There's something happening here that I've missed. That shadowy presence, crouched at the back of my mind is gathering substance.

Chapter 11

The front door slams and Sam races straight up to his room. Jonty follows him. I stay downstairs, my heart banging, frightened by Jonty's masculine rage and Sam's increasing anger. He's been missing for several hours and while I'm relieved to see him, I'm still scared. Whatever is troubling him, it's here with us, now; I can feel it.

There's a lot of shouting. Eventually Jonty comes down with the remains of a bottle of vodka and a grim expression.

'What's going on?'

'He's pissed.'

'Why? Why is he drinking in the middle of the day?'

'I don't suppose this has anything to do with social niceties, Lizzie. He won't be waiting for the sun to be over the yard arm.'

'So he's drinking because he's upset about something?'

'He's seventeen. He's drinking because that's what seventeen-year-olds do.'

'Not like this.'

Jonty rolls his eyes. 'I'll talk to him, but not now, all right?'

And I have to leave it there, because Jonty is the parent and it's his responsibility. I wish I felt more relieved by that.

Later, Jonty cooks a bolognese for dinner. It's Sam's favourite tea, but he doesn't call him down. 'He'll surface when he's hungry and can heat some up for himself.'

I follow his lead, reluctantly. What do I know about teenage boys and alcohol? I'm letting my imagination get the better of me. This isn't a big deal. My brother has always avoided alcohol altogether and my judgement is skewed by my mum. Maybe the best thing is to leave Sam alone and let him learn from his mistakes, but I can't let it go. 'Do you think it could be exam pressure?' This might be why he was truanting. 'He has been studying hard and it's been a bit relentless lately.'

Jonty sighs. 'He's showing off, trying to prove himself the big man, but he's not man enough to apologise.'

'Pip said he apologised last night.'

'Not to me.'

Or it could be the girl.

Jonty brings two steaming plates to the table. We sit opposite one another. Jonty and I have eaten alone many times when Sam's been out, but it feels different tonight. Maybe it's because I know Sam's upstairs and I can feel he's troubled. I wish he would talk to me.

Jonty pours two large glasses of wine.

'Do you think that's a good idea?'

He raises an eyebrow. 'What? We're supposed to stop drinking because he doesn't know when to stop?'

'Maybe we should be setting a better example.'

He picks up his glass and takes a swig. 'To hell with that. I'm pissed off, I've lost my job and I need a drink.'

'That's exactly what I mean—'

He slices through me. 'Lizzie, drop it.'

The silence between us trembles. We've talked about alcohol; he knows my story, but we've agreed that it doesn't need to be an issue between us. Jonty was a big drinker when I met him, he's a sociable guy, but he's not a drunk, never gets out of control or nasty. He's careful drinking around me because he knows it makes me nervous. He can still go out with his mates and drink more than is good for him, returning home a little wobbly, but I don't have to be part of that, and it's nothing like the situation I grew up in.

'Eat.' He nudges a bowl of grated parmesan towards me. 'He's seventeen. He's pushing boundaries. Learning from experience – bad experience. You don't need to read any more into it.'

But I'm not so sure.

Several days have now passed and the tension in the house has become unbearable. Jonty has been putting together a CV on my laptop and getting more and more irritable. He resents having to 'sell' himself after all these years and he's only too aware that there are younger, cheaper, more attractive candidates competing with him. I managed to persuade Sam to phone Pip and apologise for leaving the way he did, but he's still refusing to speak to Jonty and Jonty's only attempt at communication, other than muttering under his breath, is to nag about trivial things Sam's doing wrong. They had a huge row last night over the back gate banging and keeping us awake. Jonty had to go down in his PJs to see to it and made a point of stopping at Sam's room on the way back to bed to berate him for not closing it properly. I'm tiptoeing between them, following Pip's advice and staying out of it, not that my contribution would be worth anything right now. For the most part, Sam remains in his room, appearing only to rummage for snacks and retreat again. He avoids me altogether, slipping in and out of the kitchen without making eye-contact, barely speaking unless it's absolutely necessary.

Something has been broken and I'm entirely responsible. I encroached on Sam's privacy. The trust we'd built has been shattered and I can't bear it. I miss those moments I'd begun to take for granted: the quick chat in the kitchen, or in the hall with him sitting halfway down the stairs as I come in from work, or while he helped load or unload the car. He's angry with me and he has every right to be. I shouldn't have interfered. He's old enough to look after himself.

But I miss him. Even when he's in the room with me, in fact it's worse then, and it's like a physical need. I literally ache for him. I realise now that I used to touch him all the time, without thinking, without it being any kind of problem. Ruffling those soft curls, resting my head on his shoulder when we stood side by side washing up, leaning against him, hip to hip, slipping my arm around his waist and giving him a squeeze. It was easy, natural, warm, but I can't do that now. It's like there's this invisible fence around him, charged with electricity, ready to set off an alarm if I get anywhere close. I think it's worse than it would be if he'd left entirely. I remember a friend telling me about the break-up with her long-term boyfriend, how isolated she'd felt in those final days, sleeping beside someone who didn't love her, his back like a wall in the centre of their bed. Being with someone who doesn't want you can be lonelier than being alone.

When Rebecca calls to suggest a film at the Roxy, Tarnside's slightly shabby but charming art deco cinema, I jump at the opportunity for distraction and arrange to meet her outside. We watch a silly comedy. Rebecca laughs out loud, I can barely muster a smile. I can't get Sam off my mind. As we leave the cinema she links her arm through mine. 'Want to talk about it?'

It's drizzling. I stare at the shimmering reflection of the street lights in the puddles at our feet. Maybe I could talk to Rebecca about this. She might give me a healthy perspective. I suggest the new wine bar and we hurry towards Market Street huddled against the rain.

She insists on getting the drinks and comes to the table with a bottle of New Zealand Sauvignon, clearly expecting us to settle in for the rest of the evening, but I've got a to-do list for tomorrow as long as my arm and can't afford to be hung-over. I'll just have to drink slowly and hope she doesn't notice. I explain that things are difficult at the moment with Sam. She's a good listener, saying very little but paying close attention. When I mention Fi, she moves in closer. 'Is this his girlfriend?'

'No, just a friend. A good friend. Someone he could confide in, until I messed it up. I'm not surprised she's annoyed with me. Me and my big mouth.' I tell her about the girl Fi mentioned.

'It was definitely a girl?'

'What do you mean?'

'Did she say it was a girl?'

'You mean it could be a boy?'

'Possibly.' A twitch of her eyebrow, challenging me.

Sam gay? I consider it briefly, but no. I would have picked

up on that. Wouldn't I? 'No, Fi said "she", I'm sure she did.'

'What did she say about her exactly?'

I hesitate. Maybe this wasn't such a good idea. I've already betrayed Sam once, I don't want to do it again. 'Nothing much. Nothing at all, really.' Which is true. 'It's difficult for Fi. She likes Sam.'

'Likes as in fancies?' I shrug, wishing I'd never said anything. This isn't about Fi, it's about Sam. About Sam and me. We were running smoothly, the two of us. It worked. I remember an image, from a magazine or the TV: the workings of a clock, circular discs of different sizes with little grooves around the perimeter, one rolling against the other, fitting together perfectly. A harmony. That's what we were like, but it's like a bit of grit has got into one of those grooves somehow and is throwing the whole mechanism out of rhythm.

Rebecca is studying me. 'What's wrong?'

I sigh. 'Sam used to trust me. He could talk to me.'

'About girls?'

'Well, no, not really. There haven't been any girls.'

She raises an eyebrow. 'You mean he hasn't mentioned any.'

I pause. She's right. I assumed Sam hadn't had a girlfriend. Now I realise how unlikely that is. But we'd know, surely, if there'd been anyone special? We'd have met her, he'd have said something. Rebecca is watching me, a little smile on her face, and it prickles. She's laughing at me. I wish I'd never started this conversation.

'He's seventeen,' she says, grinning, 'and hot. You think he's never had a girlfriend?'

'Sam's not like that.'

She jerks her head back. 'Like *what*?'

I shrug, feeling my face burn. I realise how this sounds, but Sam's not been interested in girls that way yet. He has Fi. He's probably had the occasional kiss, tested the water, but there hasn't been anyone significant, no one he's wanted to spend time with. I'd know.

Rebecca takes a slug of wine and refills her glass, topping up mine even though it's still almost full. 'Are you sure you're not jealous?'

'No!' This is ridiculous. She doesn't understand. How could she? She's too young, too immature. I was stupid to say anything.

She smiles. She doesn't believe me. I can't explain and I don't want to talk to her about this any more. I'm about to make my excuses when she leans closer and says, 'I'm sorry.' Her hand settles over mine. 'I'm teasing. I get it. You're in a difficult situation. I'm sure he does confide in you about stuff, most stuff, but he's seventeen and maybe he can't tell you about this. What boy tells his mother about his sex life?'

Sex? Is Sam having sex? Maybe. Seventeen. Possibly. Probably. Why am I uncomfortable with that? And as if she's read my mind, Rebecca says, 'You are his stepmother. You're sleeping with his dad. You wouldn't talk to him about that, would you?'

She's right. Of course. He's entitled to his privacy. Things are changing between us because he's turning from a boy into a man, and that's as it should be.

I say, 'I miss him,' without thinking and immediately regret it as Rebecca gives the flicker of a frown. I take a sip of wine and laugh it off. 'Boys, eh? Let's talk about something else!'

Chapter 12

After a tense week, I suggest a family meal. We rarely gather around the table for dinner any more. We've become three independent adults who happen to sleep under the same roof, all submerged in our own lives, our own worries. Sam has been sleeping until lunchtime and then revising in his bedroom late into the night. I know it's revision because I've taken up cups of tea from time to time and seen him working his way through past exam papers. He's taking this seriously. Whatever was bothering him over Easter isn't going to get in the way of his studies.

Jonty has now cleared his desk at work. He's refused any kind of leaving do. If he has any plans, he isn't ready to discuss them with me, and I'm too busy with St George's Day preparations to be much help. There's no opportunity to move on from conflicts, even if we can't resolve them entirely. We used to be a team and that was our strength. Now, I can feel something splintering. I try and pull it back together.

Jonty likes to cook. Sometimes I help, but I am absolutely

not allowed to make suggestions or do anything other than what I've been instructed to do. I get the boring jobs: last-minute shopping for a vital ingredient, hunting out the precise piece of equipment that is required at that moment and appears to have gone missing, or interim washing up. I usually avoid it if I can, but tonight I'm genuinely intending to help. Rebecca calls to suggest meeting at the pub and is a bit put out when I tell her my plan, but this is important. I want the three of us to prepare the meal together, but the phone rings as I tie an apron around my waist. The artist-in-residence I've commissioned to create the banners for this year's Flag Festival wants to know if she can bring someone in to assist. She has another artist in mind, but they aren't local and will need accommodation. I call up the budget on my laptop and look to see what I can do. I'm beginning to regret commissioning this woman. Her work is beautiful but her fee is high, her manner quite aloof and now this. She's got me over a barrel and she knows it. I consider phoning Eve, but I don't need to bother her. Instead, I imagine how she'd deal with it and try and do the same. Cool, efficient. What's important is that the event runs smoothly. I scroll through my document, keeping my eyes on the screen, aware Jonty is laying the table around me, making a lot of unnecessary noise to get the point across. Added to that, Loopy is at the front window, growling and barking at anyone who walks past.

'Food's nearly ready.'

'I'll be two minutes. Why don't you call Sam, see if he can help?'

Jonty slaps a pan on the hob, clatters utensils in the sink. I wince but keep going. 'Sam! Dinner!'

Sam pads reluctantly down the stairs. Loopy throws herself at the window pane, barking wildly. Jonty snaps,

'What's the matter with that bloody dog?' as if I'm somehow responsible. I add the last figures in the appropriate columns. Loopy continues to bark. Jonty strides over, grabs her by the collar and drags her through the kitchen, shoving her out of the back door. She scratches and whines, aware of all the smells coming from the kitchen and the scraps she might be missing, but he ignores her, dishing up in simmering silence. Saving the document, I close the computer lid as Sam distributes the plates around the table. Loopy gives an apologetic yelp outside; Jonty ignores her. I want to let her in, but I don't want to risk annoying Jonty.

When Jonty cooks, he likes to put on a show and wants to be appreciated and the food is always inventive and delicious. I try not to look at the mess surrounding us: the pile of pans, bowls and dishes abandoned on the hob and beside the sink, the chopping boards and knives and food debris that litter every available surface. It's my job to tidy it up. Usually I can count on Sam to help, but that's unlikely given the way things are between us right now. When I cook, I open the fridge, see what needs using and put it together to create something edible. I wash things up as I go along and get a meal on the table with the minimum of fuss, usually with my laptop open, dealing with my inbox at the same time. It's easier all round, but the food is never as good and Jonty needs something to keep him busy. His frustration over the redundancy is so palpable I can almost touch it.

I take a mouthful of tonight's curry. It's mild, sweet and yellow with green chillies and chickpeas. There are spices I don't recognise. 'This is delicious.' I tear off a piece of flatbread, which, Jonty tells us, has been rising on the shelf in the boiler cupboard all afternoon, as if this is something we requested and are failing to appreciate.

He gives a grunt, looks at Sam, waiting for his verdict. 'Well?' But for Sam food is fuel. He shovels it into his mouth like a starving man, barely pausing to chew. I grin at Jonty, willing him to laugh, but he's determined to glower. Outside, Loopy whimpers. Sam gets up from the table and lets her in. Jonty says nothing, but even the dog can sense his mood as she slips under Sam's chair, trying to make herself invisible.

'It's St George's Day a week on Saturday,' I say hopefully, knowing Jonty won't be keen to help, but I'm growing desperate. I've been waking at four in the morning, remembering the rain lashing down last year, the town band huddled under the inadequate gazebo, performing for a handful of hardy souls with umbrellas, and now I've had a text to say one of my volunteer performers has to pull out. 'I need a last-minute damsel in distress for St George to rescue. Any ideas?' Finding someone wouldn't normally be a problem, but St George is played by a local councillor who likes to ham up the role and extend his part. He is truly awful, in a way which has become part of the comedy of the event, but no one wants to perform alongside him, apart from the dragon who is safely anonymous inside a costume. 'You don't fancy putting on a wig and corset do you?' Jonty gives me a withering look. I try Sam. 'Do you think Fi would be up for it?' Sam shrugs as if he couldn't care less. Normally I'd ask Fi myself, but I don't feel I can with the way things are at the moment. 'Could you ask her?' Another shrug, which could mean anything.

I let it go; a problem for another day. If I have to, I'll put the damned wig on and do it myself. I have other things to worry about. 'I was thinking it might be a good idea to do something inside, after the performance. Last year felt a bit flat at the end, the way everyone just disappeared. If we did something in the pub, maybe?'

Jonty takes a slug of wine. I notice the bottle he opened as he started cooking is almost empty. I've had a glass, Sam doesn't drink wine, or not in front of us, at least, which means Jonty's had most of the bottle himself. His response to the pub idea is to say, 'Bit late in the day for that.' I focus on my plate, nudging chickpeas into patterns. 'Which pub?'

I look up, hopefully. 'The Red Lion makes most sense. Right on the square.'

Jonty snorts, mopping up a splash of curry from the table with his bread. 'Good luck with that.' Nigel, the landlord, is notoriously grumpy and reluctant to be involved in anything that requires additional effort on his part. I'm feeling defeated before I've even begun.

'I thought we could have a bit of music. An open mic?'

Jonty empties his glass and lifts the bottle. He glances at me. 'Are you going to have another?'

I shake my head. He hesitates but pours the remains of the bottle into his glass and glances up to catch Sam watching him. There's a moment. Nothing is said, but everything is understood. Jonty takes a belligerent gulp of wine. He takes his time. A challenge for Sam to say something, so he can come back at him. I intervene to shift their attention. 'I'd like to do something to pull everyone together at the end of the festival. I think it would be fun, and it'll give me an opportunity to buy the volunteers a drink to say thank you.' Oh the irony of this! Here I am fretting about Jonty's drinking, and Sam's, while planning to buy alcohol as a reward for my volunteers, some of whom, like Fi, are underage.

Jonty speaks through a mouthful of food. 'Who's paying for these drinks?'

'Me.'

'You're subsidising this event, again?'

What I do with my own money is my business, but I don't need to say anything. Jonty is usually the first to dip into his pocket and buy a round, he's just spoiling for a fight tonight. I sigh, exhausted by this pointless dance. 'I don't subsidise the festivals.'

He raises an eyebrow. 'They're going to pay you then, for your overtime?' He glances at the clock and back at me. I know the time. It's irrelevant. This is Jonty's issue, his anger about his redundancy, nothing to do with my job or my pay. He's touchy because I'm working and he's not. And he's always moody in the run-up to any festival. He likes to spend time with me, and I'm not available. I'm out at meetings, geeing people along, reminding them what they've agreed to do, picking things up and dropping them off, and when I'm home, I may physically be in the room with him, but my head is elsewhere and he can see that. His response to this is to do what he can to get my attention. Sometimes it's nice things like chocolates and flowers. Before the Dickensian Festival last Christmas he bought me a beautiful silk chemise, no doubt in the hope that I'd model it for him that evening, but by the time I got home, frozen to the bone after fourteen hours out in the freezing winter streets, I just about managed a hot bath before I collapsed into bed in flannel pyjamas and bed socks. When Jonty can't be bothered to get my attention in positive ways or feels particularly aggrieved, he teases me or creates dramas about things which at any other time simply would not be important – like the paperwork spread out over the kitchen table, the rolls of bunting, gazebo poles and trestle tables cluttering the hall and stairwell, or financial emergencies which require my attention out of hours.

I decide to ignore him and keep going in the hope that he'll eventually come on board. 'I'll need one or two good acts to top and tail the open mic.' I help myself to a spoonful of yoghurt. 'Any suggestions?'

Jonty glances at Sam. 'She means will *we* do something.' I clamp my teeth together and breathe deeply. This is why I stay away when he drinks with his mates: that all-boys-together thing which drives me nuts. He gives Sam a nudge with his elbow. 'Watch it, or she'll have you playing that guitar of yours for a singalong with all the grannies and farmers' wives.'

This is exactly what I'd been hoping for. Jonty plays guitar and he's got a lovely rich voice. Sam has been teaching himself to play with the help of tutorials on his laptop. I've asked Jonty to take an interest and support him, but as far as I know that hasn't happened. The two of them could play together, but it's not something I can discuss with Jonty in this mood. Added to that, I've just remembered Kay and Nell will be arriving. They're getting the direct train from the airport, something Kay arranged, probably to avoid a long journey with Jonty in the car, but they will need collecting from the station if they've got overnight bags. I'll have to try and fit that on to my list.

'You could ask the school?' Sam says, taking me by surprise. 'Maybe they could get the choir or the school band to do something?'

This isn't quite what I had in mind, but it's a reasonable idea if all else fails. It wouldn't take a lot of organising and would appeal to families. More to the point, Sam is engaging with me again. I beam at him. Jonty, on the other hand, is still sabotaging any attempt to rescue the event. He gives a snort of derision. I stand up to collect the plates. 'Thanks for your support!'

'What? Oh, come on! Where's your sense of humour?' But he knows he's overstepped the mark. 'I'm sure the kids will be fantastic. Get them on. Let's make the place rock!' He grins at Sam but receives no encouragement there. For a moment it's as if they've swapped places and Sam's the parent and Jonty the provocative teenager.

As I head into the kitchen, Sam says, 'You could put an ad up in the pub, for bands? The Crown has those live music nights.'

Another good suggestion and something about Sam's manner, the adult way in which he's presenting himself, causes Jonty to sharpen up. 'If you're going to do that,' he says, 'you'll need someone to set up an amp and all the gear that goes with it.' It's clear that he isn't going to volunteer for this. I remember only too well previous attempts to get sound systems going at community events. A tangle of electrical wires, performers and audience all waiting for a sound to emerge and everyone expecting me to magically work it out. I feel a wave of weary resignation wash over me as I dump the plates in the sink.

'I can help,' Sam says, 'with the sound for Saturday. Fi's dad's got an amp. She knows how it works. And we can ask around. There's this a cappella girl group at school, they're really good. They'd do it.'

'Seriously?' He's rescued me. And he's going to work with Fi. All that horridness is in the past. I wrap my arms around his waist, giving him a big squeeze, and it feels so good to be close to him again, to be back.

But Jonty shakes his head, chuckling to himself. 'You'll learn.'

There is something so mean-spirited about this, so childish, in the face of all the effort I've been making to patch things up, that I snap. 'You know something, Jonty? You could learn a thing or two from this son of yours.'

He starts, eyes wide. He was just grumpy, he hadn't realised how horrible he was being, but I've annoyed him now; I shouldn't have criticised him in front of Sam. 'You think so?' He scowls. 'Well, why not? *He's* the one with the world at his feet. I'm the has-been. What do *I* know?'

Sam reaches across, picks up Jonty's wine and before anyone can say anything, drains it. He looks Jonty directly in the eye, places the empty glass back down in front of him and says, 'Why do you have to be such a dick?'

The silence shivers across the table.

'What did you say?'

'You heard me.'

I can feel my heart racing. Jonty's body is stiff with rage, Sam's face flushed. Their eyes are locked. Jonty leans forward, his face close. Sam remains absolutely still. Jonty's voice is a low hiss, each word delivered slowly, deliberately. 'Don't. You. Ever. Speak to me like that again.'

I know that something has shifted and Jonty feels it too. His entire body trembles with the effort not to lash out. I've never seen him so angry. I've never felt afraid of him before, but in this moment I can see him doing something dreadful, unforgivable.

He picks up the chair and I scream as he hurls it at the wall. The screenprint of the bluebell woods that he bought me for Christmas crashes to the floor, shattering. We stare at the broken glass and then Jonty strides out of the door and into the night.

Chapter 13

Three days later, I'm on my knees in the soggy grass at the park, spreading out banners in order to assess the damage. They take quite a battering each year, flapping about for two weeks, often in wind and heavy rain. Eve suggested I do this months ago and when she asked me about it this morning I had to admit I'd forgotten. I'm not going to cry; tears are pointless and pathetic, but I am wound so tight right now and nothing seems to be going my way. I had to drive down to the warehouse and haul each of these monsters out one at a time, half carrying, half dragging them because they measure five feet by three feet and that's a lot of fabric. I should have asked Jonty to help, but I needed to escape from the pair of them. He and Sam are like two bears circling one another, just waiting for an excuse to attack. I've never felt such physical fear before. I'm no stranger to conflict; things were volatile when I was growing up, but there was only ever my mum to deal with. This masculine rage is something else entirely.

I dropped the bluebell picture off to the framers this morning. I couldn't stand seeing it propped against the side, a constant reminder of that moment of violence. I thought Jonty was going to grab Sam and throw him against the wall and I wanted to stop him, but I was too scared to move, like one of those pointless female characters in an action film. After he slammed out, I gripped the table for support, waiting for things to steady. The room was still reverberating. I said, 'Sam, you can't speak to your dad like that,' but my voice sounded feeble. I was to blame really. I shouldn't have said anything in front of Sam; I should have waited and talked to Jonty later. He felt we were ganging up on him and Sam needed to be told this was not acceptable. It wasn't me and him against Jonty; it doesn't work like that.

Sam's jaw was clamped tight. He'd been defending me and I appreciated that; Jonty had been horrible, but it was wrong. 'He doesn't mean it,' I said quietly. 'That job was his world. It defined him. He's angry, and he can't help himself.'

'He doesn't have to take it out on you.'

'He puts up with a lot from me.'

Sam raised an eyebrow. Pure Jonty in that moment. 'Like what?'

'You know what I can be like when the festivals are in full swing.'

'You're busy. You're tired. You ask for support. You don't attack for no reason.'

I wanted to cry. It was like he was gently dabbing at a tender wound and I was so relieved to have him back. It had been so achingly lonely all week, standing on the outside, waiting to be forgiven, but Pip's warning kept ringing in my ears: *You do realise he's in love with you?*

Sam was watching me, his expression concerned, filled

with... love, of a kind. There was something different about him just then. Something more determined, more masculine. My chest tightened and it was difficult to take more than a shallow breath. I was afraid. Afraid for Sam, for Jonty, for me.

That fear has stayed with me since, lingering like a shadow somewhere in my peripheral vision and creeping into my dreams. What's happening to our family? Because it is a family. Muddled, awkward, disjointed, but a family. Certainly more of a family than I've ever had in my life.

I try and picture my brother at Sam's age. Five years ago Danny was a spotty, geeky swot with a nervous tic. He had a crush on the girl who lived across the street. She was two years older, at beauty college, tall, glamorous and completely out of his league. He used to stand in the front room in his coat, waiting for her to come out of her front door simply to walk down the street at the same time as she did. He didn't have the nerve to speak to her. It was painful to watch, the emotions sincere and torturous for him, but it was a schoolboy crush and it came and went.

Sam cleared the last bits from the table without looking at me and started to load the dishwasher. There was a purpose about him. It was like he'd put on a costume and taken up a role. The role of an adult. But he's not an adult; he's a seventeen-year-old boy. Right then he was a boy who'd crossed the line.

Pip was right to warn me to be careful. This might be a crush, but it's not something I can dismiss. While Danny's passion was safely distant and unattainable, this is potentially dangerous. I'm here, living with Sam, day in, day out. I had to do something.

I followed him into the kitchen with the glasses. He was bent over the dishwasher, arranging the plates. 'Your dad will cool off. We'll talk when he gets back and everything will be fine. Jonty's good at doing sorry. Not good at saying it, but good at doing it.' I laughed, but Sam didn't laugh. I added, gently but firmly, 'You need to apologise to him.'

'No way.'

'You have to show a little more respect. He's your father, not another kid in the playground.'

He straightened up then, face pink. I longed to reach out, to reassure him, but Pip's words held me back.

Be careful.

'I *don't* respect him,' he said, his voice clear and certain. 'He was being a dick. He can't treat you like that. And I'm not a kid!'

The gate outside was banging in the wind again and he opened the back door and went out to close it properly. I'd offended him. I watched him tease the latch into place and waited for him to come back in. He said it again, 'I'm not a kid any more,' but more calmly this time and his voice was lower. His eyes met mine.

I said, 'We need to fix that latch,' because I needed to talk about something ordinary, something that wasn't loaded.

He said, 'There's nothing wrong with the latch, it's just a bit rusty,' but his eyes were demanding a different level of respect. It was like watching him through a distorted mirror: the slightest movement and he shifted from boy to man to boy again.

I didn't mean to belittle him.

It's so difficult to get it right these days. I lose track of who I am, how to be. If I was forty I could nip this in the bud. I'm his step-mother, but the truth is, I'm too young to do that properly and I'm so frightened that if I say the wrong thing I'll lose him again.

I did my best to take control. I told him I knew he meant well, that I understood that he was defending me and I was touched by that. 'But this is between me and your dad, Sam. I'm sorry. I appreciate your support, but it's inappropriate. Your dad and I have a relationship. It's for me to fight my own battles.'

As he turned to head out of the kitchen, I caught his arm; I couldn't bear him to walk away from me hurting. 'Sam, please.' He shook me off. I carried on. 'You meant well. I understand, but it's difficult. You have to let me deal with it.' He didn't move. 'Please?' I hesitated. 'Please, try and make peace with your dad.' He pulled away at this, but I grabbed his arm again. 'I can't do this alone, Sam. I need you. If he's acting like an unreasonable teenager then you need to be the adult. Could you do that for me?'

When he looked at me, his face softened, he was a younger Jonty. Capable. Strong. Loving. He nodded, but should I have asked that of him? I felt grateful, but now I feel guilty, like I've done something wrong.

He and Fi have taken a day off from revision and gone to Bowness to play at being tourists. I'm glad the two of them have sorted things out at least. I had hoped she'd give me a hand with the banners; I dropped some heavy hints, but she didn't offer. She popped round to the house on Wednesday evening and we all leapt at the distraction, but she refused my invitation to stay for tea. I think it's going to be a while before she forgives me. Sam told me she's agreed to be the damsel to St George, but she's doing that for him not me. They're catching the ferry up to Fell Foot Park to do the Treetop Challenge – a series of rope swings and bridges through the trees. It's overcast but dry and a bit of fresh air away from their books is exactly what they both need.

It's a relief to see Sam stretch out a bit. I hadn't realised how tight he'd become, not just the thing with Jonty, but generally. The break from school seems to have done him good. They've gone in my car. I gave Fi my spare set of keys as soon as she passed her test back in February, for when things need picking up or dropping off at short notice and she's available. She knows she's free to use it whenever she needs to, as long as she clears it with me first. Over the last few weeks I've noticed sandwich wrappers in the footwell and she keeps a sleeping bag in the boot, which she says is a good idea in extreme weather, though neither of us ever make long trips and there's not likely to be any snow for the next six months. I suspect she's started to use the car as an emergency bolthole and if that's what works for her I'm not going to interfere. I wish she'd come to the house, I could make her up a bed in the attic where I've got my studio, but she's too proud for that, even when things are good between us, so I keep quiet and pretend I don't know.

It's a cold day, but I should be grateful that it's not raining and I can spread the banners out to get a proper look at them. Several have frayed significantly at the hem and some have rips which need attention. They cover the grass from the manor house down to the tarn edge, forming a sister lake in technicolour, rippling in the breeze. From a distance the imperfections are barely noticeable, but Eve's right, they'll disintegrate slowly if they're not given an overhaul.

I don't have a sewing machine. If I did I wouldn't have the time. If I'd checked the banners when Eve first suggested it I could have asked the resident artist for this year's project to mend them, though I suspect she wouldn't have been too happy. She's apparently working around the clock, along with her friend, who finally agreed to the fee I offered and a room at Jonty's mate's place instead of the fancy B&B. I'm tempted to tell Eve about how I navigated that crisis in order to redeem myself a little, but I know I'm being pathetic.

I sit back on my haunches, feeling helpless and watch a group of children fighting over the zip wire in the adventure playground. A short distance away a father pushes his young child in the bird's-nest swing. A calm, steady rhythm: a memory in the making. I brought Nell and Sam here the first weekend after they arrived. Sam was already too old, really, but Nell persuaded him to climb into the swing with her and they lay back, swaying to and fro, staring at the sky. I thought about joining them, they looked so peaceful and happy, but something stopped me. Not wanting to intrude on what they had together. Not wanting to presume.

I lift the edge of a banner, letting it slide between my fingers. Maybe we should have chosen a more durable fabric? But this shifts and billows so gracefully in the wind. So many decisions to make. So many times I get it wrong or simply don't know. There's always too much to do and I'm not feeling great. Please don't let me be going down with something. There's no one to stand in for me if I'm ill; it's simply not an option.

I hear footsteps approaching and turn to see Jonty and Rebecca walking down from the café. She waves. Jonty's face folds into its familiar lines and he gives a sheepish grin. I haven't seen Rebecca since last week when I tried to talk to her about Sam. She's texted a couple of times, but I've been busy and, if I'm honest, I feel a bit awkward. The conversation about Sam and this new girlfriend left me feeling uncomfortable. Why is she with Jonty?

Jonty looks at the banners and gives a low whistle. 'These need a bit of attention.'

Rebecca smiles at me and I wait for her to explain, but she just keeps smiling. I have a sudden memory from that night at the pub, after we'd been to the cinema. We were sitting close to the fire in The Crown and I was trying to get her off the subject of Sam and his love life. I said something about Jonty being a bit out of sorts and she was surprised.

'Jonty? Grumpy? He always seems so cheerful and easy-going.'

'He is usually...' I hesitated, regretting having started, but she was fixed on me so intently that I had to go on. 'He's been made redundant and I think he's having a bit of a midlife crisis.' I tried to shrug it off, but I could see her frowning, considering what this might actually mean and I didn't want her to misunderstand. 'Not like that. He's not about to buy a motorbike or have an affair with his secretary.' And then I realised what I was saying and I started to laugh, but Rebecca didn't laugh, she just looked puzzled, so I explained. 'It's a cliché? Male midlife crisis – have an affair with someone half your age? I'm Jonty's midlife crisis.' But the explanation killed the joke and though she laughed, I was left with a bad taste in my mouth.

Jonty's looking at me now, all open-faced and trusting. I shouldn't have laughed about him behind his back; it was cruel. He says, 'Rebecca's asked me to give her some sailing lessons. We've just been talking it through.' I'm a little wrong-footed by this. Jonty grins, clearly pleased, his bruised ego recovered a little, but I'm not so sure, though I can't say why. It's a good idea. Jonty loves sailing and he's patient; he'll be a good teacher. I remember Pip suggesting something similar at Easter; it seems a seed was planted after all, but I'm a bit surprised Rebecca didn't mention this to me. Maybe she'd planned to if we'd met up. She must have bumped into Jonty in the café, but it's odd that he didn't say he was intending to be here this morning. Unless she phoned him? I wasn't aware she had his number.

She's watching me and I turn my attention back to the banners, embarrassed. I'm being ridiculous. If she was being secretive, she wouldn't have arranged to meet Jonty here, in the place where I work.

Jonty looks around at the miles of fabric, taking in the scale of the task. 'I know a woman who can sort these for you,' he says, looking at me, his face a question. 'Curtain maker. Retired now, but she's a community-minded sort. Lives down at the priory. Shall I give her a call?'

'Thank you.' It's been a while since Jonty was kind. I stand up, rubbing my damp knees and give him a kiss on the cheek.

Rebecca says, 'Well, I'll leave you two love birds to it. I've got work to do. I'll see you on Saturday, Jonty. You've got my number now, if anything changes or you think of anything else.'

'Will do.'

She throws me a big smile. 'Let's meet up for a drink next week.' A reassuring half wink. She's trying to be a friend and I need a friend right now. I should make more of an effort. Of course she hasn't said anything to Jonty; I'm just being paranoid. She was supportive and I confided in her, that's what friends do.

She's watching me, waiting, then asks gently, 'OK?' I nod. 'Great.' She blows us a kiss and jogs down to the road, easy, light on her feet. I envy her this lightness, the freedom she has. She'll be going to do something creative of her own, while I'm struggling with these banners and the preparations for St George's Day. And when she's at home, she'll be pleasing herself, not tiptoeing around a difficult teenager and trying to keep the peace. She told me she has her own cottage, not in Tarnside itself but just outside, in Seaford, a neighbouring village on the shore of Morecambe Bay. Pip persuaded me to buy a little cottage last year, 'as an investment, darling', and lent me the deposit. It's a skinny little place, hidden in a courtyard behind Fell Rise, which you would never guess was there if you didn't know where to look. You have to turn down a ginnel from the road and go through a gate which no one opens because it looks like it leads into a private garden. My cottage is one of two, tucked away. There's just enough room for a shared bench and some pots, but it's a pretty little suntrap. I let it to Dom, who runs the music shop in town. There's one room on each of the three floors and the kitchen is barely bigger than a cupboard, but it's perfect for a single person. I wish it was empty right now. I wish I could shut myself in there and not have to think about anyone else.

I look at Jonty, feeling suddenly guilty, but his eyes are fixed on Rebecca's pert bottom as she disappears through the gate. He turns to me. 'What?' and shrugs. 'She wants to pay me to teach her what she already knows, who am I to argue?'

'She can sail?'

He nods. 'Been sailing since she was a kid. Sounds like Daddy had a bit of money.'

If Daddy pays the bills, or an allowance, then it would explain how she can both pursue her own creative work and afford a cottage. I tell myself off. It's none of my business how she manages her finances; I'm just jealous. 'Why does she need lessons, if she can sail?'

'Says she's got a bit rusty. Lost her confidence.'

I can see he's not convinced. 'What do you think she wants?'

He smiles. 'Attention.' He puts his arm around me. 'Don't worry. I'll keep it professional.' I'm not worried, but I am puzzled. This is a side of Rebecca I haven't seen before. 'Apparently,' Jonty continues, 'Daddy lived abroad. She didn't see much of him, by the sound of things.' He grins. 'I don't mind playing the game if it gives me a bit of work. And I'm thinking I could do this, you know? I could advertise at the sailing club, other people might be prepared to pay for a bit of one-to-one. I'm going to check out the law, see what qualifications I need, insurance and that.'

I try and remember what Rebecca told me about her family. She has no siblings, but I can't remember anything else. Her family don't seem to be local; she never mentions them. She's been keen to make friends and I've enjoyed that, but this is a step further. If I'd asked her around to dinner to meet Jonty and Sam and she'd mentioned the sailing then, I wouldn't have a problem, but her arranging to meet Jonty alone, without speaking to me, feels sneaky. I know she's lonely, possibly a little desperate for company behind that glamorous exterior, but this is my family; I should choose how close she can come.

She's rattled me. It is possible she's just trying to help, knowing that Jonty needs a distraction. Her idea is more or less what Pip was suggesting at Easter, but if that's the case, it's an extravagant gesture. Expensive for her on her limited income. Maybe Daddy's going to pay.

Jonty's watching me, amused. He smiles and the smile slides into a wink, and I'm reminded of the day we met, following his assistant into his office where he was waiting to interview me, along with Eve and a local councillor. It was all very relaxed; four armchairs around a low table. Jonty got up to make me a coffee, showing off his snazzy machine. He was attentive, relaxed and he put me at my ease immediately. I remember that first smile, I'd never seen a smile like it, his whole face collapses into it, and you can't help smiling back. And those eyes. I looked right into those eyes and I knew something was going to happen between us. He gives me a squeeze and drops a kiss on the top of my head. Rebecca has certainly cheered him up. I haven't seen him this positive for weeks. Hopefully he'll lighten up around Sam.

Chapter 14

Sam drives, his slim fingers gripping the wheel, body tensed, checking the rear-view mirror and the wing mirrors in rotation. I try not to smile. Jonty has shown him the ropes and he's had a little practice up and down the lane that runs through the park, but this is his first proper drive. He wasn't that interested in learning until Fi passed her test, but now the pressure is on. Jonty is out on the lake with Rebecca. He set off with a wry expression and plenty of jokes about a man having to do what a man has to do. She's certainly good for his ego. I was relieved to see him so cheerful.

I drove the car out of town on to the coast road and pulled up to let Sam take over. This is a long, straight, single carriageway that runs along the northern perimeter of Morecambe Bay towards Barrow-in-Furness, perfect for a learner driver. A road of villages and sea views, ice-cream vans and pretty pubs. Rebecca's cottage will be somewhere along here. Sam can take his time and we're not going far, three or four miles to the grounds of the priory.

I'm multi-tasking, as ever: transporting the banners to Maria for mending and giving Sam a driving lesson, or at least some practice, while I take the opportunity to find out a bit more about this girl and what's going on in his world. As far as I'm aware there's been no more drinking. He's relaxed. The break from school is doing him good. I seem to have been forgiven since the night of his row with Jonty, though the two of them are still avoiding one another.

'Indicate left. We're turning in just up there, in front of the sign.'

He's driving at twenty miles an hour and slows to almost walking pace as we approach the turning. Through the passenger window I watch a herd of sheep run across the field as a farmer carries bags of feed from his quad bike to the trough. I can hear their groans of anticipation through the closed windows. Sam turns into the drive. On our right the gold top of the new temple gleams in the weak afternoon sunlight; behind it rise the ancient spires of the original building, like something from a J. K. Rowling story. Maria lives in the cottages that served the priory when it was inhabited by Christian monks, now it's the Buddhists who reside here. We pull up outside a huge Gothic structure complete with stained-glass windows and gargoyles. In the foyer is a giant gold Buddha, but from the outside the priory has barely changed in all the years it's stood here. Sam slides into a wide parking space and turns off the engine with a smile of satisfaction.

We decide to find the cottage first and come back for the banners. The entrance to the courtyard is through a sandstone arch. The cottages have long windows divided into square panes, the woodwork painted in hippy purples, dark greens and dusty pinks, and there are colourful window boxes and plants potted in recycled cans and buckets. An abandoned child's bike and a tangled plastic kite litter the central garden. Some cottages have tables and chairs outside the door. Maria has a wooden bench with arm rests wide enough to hold a plate. There is no bell or door knocker. I rap on the glass.

Maria is soft, round and brown, like a woodland animal. She snuffles a little as she speaks – 'Come in, come in!' – and scurries to and from the kitchen offering tea and lemon cake, trailing scarves, jangling with beaded chains at her neck and wrists. The sewing machine is set up in a corner of the tiny dining room, under a window that looks out on to the garden. I imagine working here, uninterrupted, materials spread out on the floor around me: scraps of fabric, metal and wire, bits and pieces I've found during my morning walks, washed up on the beach or in the woods, paintbrushes in a jar, ideas waiting to be realised. A different life.

Maria pours the tea and looks from me to Sam, beaming. 'You are the image of your dad.' She chuckles. 'You could be Jonty thirty years ago. It's spooky!'

Sam smiles. Maria was at sixth form with Jonty; I wonder if she knows Pip, the earlier version of Pip, bohemian wild child and eccentric. A slice of cake is nudged towards me. I shake my head. I can't stomach cake right now. I think I might have some sort of sickness bug, which is all I need, with festival season well and truly under way. She looks at Sam. 'You need to tell this girl of yours to eat.'

It's as if the moment freezes. Like someone pressing pause on the TV remote. If only I could rewind. Stop. Delete. But the moment continues unrolling, it's just Sam and me who are paused and the longer it goes on the more awful it gets. I can feel him tighten beside me, tension pulsing through him. The panic. The last thing he needs is for me to look at him now.

'I'm not Sam's girl,' I say brightly, as if it's fine, as if we have to deal with this all the time. 'I'm Jonty's partner.'

Maria rolls her eyes. 'Oh Lord! I'm *so* sorry. How tactless of me. I just assumed...' To be fair to her, she does a great job of rescuing the situation, throwing her arms around me, pressing me to her herb-scented bosom. 'Well, well. Jonty, the old charmer.' And she laughs and that laugh saves us. I feel Sam relax beside me. I hear him laugh, but I keep my eyes on the table, on Maria, on the dresser opposite.

We are in a very small room and it's packed with furniture. 'The banners are pretty big,' I say, doubtfully.

Maria tinkles a beaded wrist. 'Not a problem. We can store them in Will's shed. He won't mind.'

We carry the banners in, Sam and I, a few at a time. The shed is tucked against the wall, just inside the arch, so it isn't far to walk. We take one banner into the cottage so that Maria can work on it that evening. I notice she has pots of herbs on her windowsill and colourful bowls and cups. There's a shop in town that stocks similar crockery and I make a mental note to go there for a thank-you present.

When we've finished and said our goodbyes I suggest a walk through the woodland to the beach. Sam falls in beside me. The rhododendrons struggle for the light here, but they put up a good fight. The lower branches are bare and gnarled, the higher ones tangled and muscular, fists of leaves and buds only appearing on the highest levels. In a matter of weeks they'll throw their ruby petals to the air. They're no match for the pruned and preened maidens of colour that inhabit the gardens of the stately homes around Windermere; these are their wilder, more dangerous cousins, but I like them better for that. Someone has flung a length of pink nylon rope over a branch to form a swing. Child's play in the shadows. There's something a little frightening and wonderful about this place. Magic could happen here.

Sam wanders over to the swing and places his foot in the loop at the end of the rope, propelling himself with the other leg in one elegant movement. His limbs are long, his shoulders broadening, but his torso is still slight. I remember the pudgy fifteen-year-old standing in our hall, clutching his sister's hand in his. I remember watching him raid the fridge, shovelling food into his mouth, Jonty peeling extra potatoes, cooking an extra portion of rice, to satisfy his son's increasing appetite as he grew taller and filled out. Sam still wolfs down his meals, but the cheese in the fridge doesn't need replacing every couple of days and the biscuits and snacks remain untouched. He's lost that puppy fat. He's becoming a man.

What was it that made Maria think we were a couple? I run through my behaviour since we arrived, checking myself. Was there anything I said or did that might have suggested something between us? We're easy together, but not intimate. She took the call from Jonty, who might have been organising something for his son's girlfriend, I suppose. To someone who doesn't know us, I'm as likely to be Sam's partner as I am to be Jonty's.

He jumps down from the swing and rubs his hands together, studying his palms, then throws me the rope. As I try to put my foot in the loop I stumble and he grabs my hips to steady me. I'm acutely aware of the pressure of his hands against my body. It's as if there's a heat radiating from them, a red warning sign: *Stop! Stop!* But to wriggle free would be to draw attention to something that's clearly innocent; he's simply helping me on to the swing. Damn Pip and her pronouncements; she's made me self-conscious where once I was easy, she has robbed me of something.

He takes a step back, gripping the rope, pulling it taut, and then lets it go, swinging me like a child and I feel light-headed and silly and absurdly happy. It's a relief to be childish. As I swing between the branches, I imagine remembering this moment years down the line. Where I will be then? Who will I be in relation to an adult Sam? How will he refer to me? There is no label for this relationship we have, but it is significant. It deserves a word, something to identify it to the rest of the world, to give it the status is deserves.

He takes a run, giving me an almighty shove that sends my stomach into my throat and makes me scream in panic. I have to shout for him to stop. Grabbing the rope, he waits for me to climb down, but the world continues to tip backwards and forwards and I stumble into him, so he has to put his arm around me to steady me, and as I glance up I catch Jonty, a younger Jonty and there's an ache inside me, for the Jonty I've missed. But this isn't Jonty, this is Sam, who has his life ahead of him and is his own person and he's looking at me, reading me, the way he does, wondering what it is that's going through my mind. 'Maria's right,' I say. 'You do look like your dad.'

His eyes lock with mine. A moment. Something in his eyes.

I pull away, forcing myself to laugh, brush myself down, brushing it off. We're rescued by a dog hurtling after a rabbit, followed an instant later by a breathless man with a lead. The moment is scattered between the trees and disappears.

'I'll have to tell your dad to bring Loopy down here. She'll enjoy the rabbits.'

Sam laughs. 'Don't think that would go down too well with the Buddhists!'

Jonty now firmly established between us, we meander along the paths between the trees. Someone has built a bridge of stepping stones across a thin trickle of a stream. Sam jumps across and waits for me on the other side. 'What are you going to do when Dad gets old, I mean really old?'

I slip and wobble on the stones trying to keep my balance. Where has this come from? I don't think about stuff like this; live for the day, and all that. Who knows? I could get run over by a bus before then. That's years away. Jonty is fit. He's still young; fifty is the new forty, after all. Pip is approaching eighty and still going strong. Jonty is a long way from being an old man, I don't need to think about that. Yet. 'I'll wheel him out here in his chair with a hip flask and do my knitting while he does the crossword.' But when Jonty is eighty, I'll be about the age Jonty is now. Will I be doing crosswords with an eighty-year-old man?

Before Sam and Nell arrived it wasn't something I felt it necessary to consider. I was free to stay as long as it felt right and to leave when that feeling changed. Those were the unspoken terms on which I moved in with Jonty. I'd been renting a room in a shared house where everyone was arguing over the bills and the housework and I had no space to breathe. Jonty lived alone. We'd started seeing each other and I was sleeping at his place most nights. It made sense to stop paying rent for somewhere I didn't want to be and move in with him. 'No strings,' he'd said. I felt no sense of responsibility and had no idea how long it would last, but we were both happy to go with the flow and it worked. It was easy, comfortable, and that might have continued for a few years, might have gone on longer, I'll never know, because when the kids arrived everything changed.

I became involved. I became part of their lives. I had to take responsibility and there's no going back. I'm knitted to Jonty now through Sam and Nell and I can't walk away.

I don't want to think about the future yet. I'm too young and there's plenty of time. I wonder how Jonty's doing on the lake. I hope they've got a bit more wind in Coniston. He'd left before Sam surfaced this morning. I suspect Sam was waiting for him to go before he came out of his room. With a bit of luck, Jonty will get back in a good mood tonight and the two of them might start to patch things up. 'Your dad's taken Rebecca out on the lake today.'

Sam snaps to attention. 'Rebecca?' He looks alarmed.

I laugh, saying, 'She's asked for some one-to-one lessons,' and raise a sceptical eyebrow, but Sam doesn't laugh, he looks horrified. 'It's all right. For some reason she wants a bit of tuition and you know what your dad's like, can't resist a pretty girl flirting with him.'

Sam's quiet for a moment, staring down at the ground, his trainer making circles in the dirt. 'Sam? Is everything OK?' He kicks hard at a stone, sending it flying into the water. It hits a rock and bounces off. 'I trust your dad. You don't have to worry.' He shrugs, looking up at the trees, his face clouded, the way it has been recently. 'Sam, what's going on?'

He looks at me sharply and frowns. 'What do you mean?'

'I don't know, you just seem out of sorts. Is it something to do with this girl?'

'What girl?' He sounds panicked.

I hesitate. I don't want to remind him about Fi's revelation; the last thing we need is a repeat of Easter Sunday's outburst. 'I'm sorry. It's none of my business. I just worry about you.' He's watching me, his eyes urgent. 'You do know you can talk to me, don't you?' But he turns away and starts to walk towards the beach. I follow. 'Sam?'

'Can we leave it?'

We walk in awkward silence until we reach the edge of the woodland. This thing with the girl might not be as serious as I thought it was. Maybe they've split up. Skirting the rusty kissing gate, no longer attached to any fence, a lonely relic from another era, we pass the red and white sign warning of the dangers of quicksand, and there it is: the opening out, the blue grey of sea and sky and stone; Morecambe Bay in all its quiet glory. We both stop, looking out, taking it in.

I change the subject and talk about Nell as we stroll along the stony beach, and Kay, what we might do with them during their visit. There won't be a lot of time, with the festival occupying most of Saturday, but Kay is taking Nell out of school, to make an early start, so we'll have Friday evening and Sunday morning.

Sam stops suddenly and turns to face me. 'Can you book me a flight to Dublin?'

I try not to let him see my shock. We haven't talked about when he'll go to Ireland, or how long for, but I saw it as some distant point in the future and I realise now that it's only a matter of weeks. 'Your exams don't finish until June. There's plenty of time to organise that.' I'd been assuming he'd stay and relax with us first. Days at Coniston, swimming, sailing, enjoying the early Cumbrian summer before he starts his new life and heads off to Newcastle.

'This weekend. Can we book something for Friday? I can finish at lunchtime on Friday. It's only PE and private study in the afternoon.'

'This Friday?' He nods. His face is anxious. This is important. 'Why? Is something wrong?'

Breathing in, his hands in his pockets, shoulders rising towards his ears, he pulls a face. 'I just...' He looks around him and shudders. 'I need to get away.'

I never expected this. I thought he loved this place, but suddenly he's shrugging it off and desperate to escape.

A slash of pain.

He'll be eighteen in a couple of months. He's becoming a man, his relationship with Jonty is difficult and his relationship with me is apparently becoming a problem too.

His real family are in Ireland.

Something is bothering him, I know it, but he can't, he won't talk to me and I don't want to think about why that is. Kay's his mum. Of course he'll go to her. That's as it should be, though it's worrying that he feels the need to see her so urgently when she'll be over for St George's Day the following weekend. 'I'll see what I can do. It's short notice. It won't be cheap.'

'Please. I'll pay you back.'

'Don't be silly. If you need to go, we'll sort it.'

He calms a little then. Nods. Chews his lip. 'Thanks.' I'm glad that I can do this much at least.

He'll be gone for good soon. I'd assumed that we would be his base while he's at uni, that it would be Tarnside he returns to in his holidays, but maybe not. 'We can sort out your ticket tonight,' I say as brightly as I can manage.

His shoulders drop and his entire body relaxes. This visible relief grazes a raw wound inside me. We sit on the concrete bench in silence. A train makes its way over the viaduct towards Lancaster, beating its rhythm across the sands. A flock of birds takes off and turns, black to silver, a flash of wonder in the air above us. Sam sits, head tilted up; a still beauty. I've grown to love this boy, this half man. There's a softness about him, and a strength; all Jonty's good qualities and some of his own. It's exciting to watch him develop, stretch out, find his place in the world. He needs to leave us. Leave me, and live his life.

And what about us, Jonty and me? How will it be for us when Sam leaves? We've shaped ourselves around him. I don't want to think about what will happen when he's no longer there to fill that space.

Chapter 15

The remainder of the weekend is heavy with rain. I light the woodburner and some candles on the mantelpiece when we get back from the priory, hoping to create a warmer mood in the cottage and draw us all together.

Jonty comes home exhilarated, full of the lake and what a natural sailor Rebecca is and what fun they've had. He takes himself off to rinse and hang out his gear. It's great to feel his positive energy returning. Pip's right, teaching could suit Jonty and give him a purpose, interaction, the status he needs.

I go into the kitchen to cook the pasta and heat the sauce I've prepared for tea. Sliding up behind me, he wraps his arms around my waist, breathing into my ear, 'We should go out on the boat again, me and you.'

'Seriously? After what happened last time?'

'That's because you were inexperienced.'

'Nothing to do with you taking a stupid risk?'

He pulls away, offended. 'Sailing is about risks!' I shake

my head, stirring the sauce. He carries on. 'You should have seen Rebecca today. That girl is fearless.' I grip the wooden spoon. 'She knows how to have a good time. You used to be like that. We used to have a laugh together.' Used to? Does he realise what he's saying? How painful this is? He takes the spoon, oblivious, and tastes the sauce. 'Mmm. Good.'

'Glad to know there's something I can do right.'

A groan. 'Lizzie, don't be like that.'

'Have you arranged to go out again?'

'Next Saturday.'

I drop the subject before it turns into a silly row. I have no reason to be jealous of Rebecca. Jonty's right; she is fun, and if I feel a little dull in comparison, then it's down to me to do something about that.

Sam is upstairs skyping his mum about arrangements for the weekend. He's been restless since we got back, nagging me to book his flight. I check the details with Jonty.

'If that's what he wants.'

'I get the feeling he's running away.'

Jonty is clearing the newspapers and post to make some space on the table, his back to me. He doesn't look up. 'From what?'

I hesitate. 'Me?' I say it because I need him to reassure me. I need him to turn and put those big arms around me and pull me to him and say that's nonsense, that Sam loves me and he's only going to Ireland for a couple of days because he's missing his sister and his mum, but he'll be back. But this is not what happens.

Jonty looks up sharply. 'Why would you say that?'

'I don't know. It's just... lately. The way he's been.'

'With you?'

I shouldn't have said anything. This will just spark up the

hostilities again and I don't want that. 'With both of us.' I turn away, tipping the pasta into a colander, glad of the distraction. 'Can you call Sam? Tell him tea's ready.'

On Tuesday I get in from work after six. Sam shouts 'Hi!' from his room but doesn't appear at the top of the stairs. He went back to school yesterday. I checked in with Mr Wright mid morning and again in the afternoon, just to be sure. Whatever was going on, he seems to have dealt with it. We've booked his flight for Friday and Jonty will drive him to the airport. He'll be back with us on Sunday evening.

Assuming he's in the middle of something, I flick on the kettle so it's ready when he comes down. Jonty will be at the pub with Loopy. It's a routine he established long before I met him. Jonty is at The Red Lion, on the square, at his usual place on the stool at the far end of the bar, every night at six o'clock for an hour. He drinks one pint of XB, his favourite local bitter, and conducts the business of the day, which basically means catching up with his old cronies. I teased him about it when we first met, but I've had to concede that a lot of general business does get conducted at that bar. Contacts are made, favours swapped, news and opportunities shared. Jonty always knows a man (or woman) 'who can', and the pub is where he'll ask the favour or be asked one in return. So the scaffolding tower I needed for the Lantern Festival finale was organised by Pete, who borrowed it from his son who's a rigger for a Manchester theatre company, and the decrepit red Fiesta I drive (and Fi occasionally sleeps in) was written off when Moany Mandy, the hairdresser, got driven into by the postman, but the only thing wrong with it is the door to the boot, which no longer locks, and who would want to steal baskets of fabric scraps and bottles of PVA glue? Countless arts events and projects have been supported by Jonty's regular pint in the pub. I'm glad he's continuing the routine, despite his job having come to an end; it gets him out there, and he might find a bit of work to keep him occupied.

In the back yard our washing droops on the line. Jonty must have taken the hint and finally tackled the overflowing basket on the landing. It looks like there are at least two loads out there and the sky is threatening rain. As the first splashes hit the slate paving stones, I rush outside with the basket.

There are three lines zigzagging across the small yard. As I start at one end, Sam appears in the kitchen and, seeing me, runs out to help, working his way along the line furthest from me. Sporadic splodges of rain begin to splatter the back of my neck. We work quickly. I have mostly jeans and sweatshirts from the dark wash while he's gathering the smalls. As I start on the second line I see that he's stopped and is holding the new fuchsia lace briefs I bought on my shopping spree with Rebecca. I ran out of clean knickers this week and had to resort to my 'fancy pants'. Our eyes meet. He raises an eyebrow. 'This what you wear when you want to get Dad's attention?' And he fingers the fine lace, looking directly at me, as if he's picturing me in those knickers right now. I snatch them from him and shove them in the basket.

As I straighten up, I'm shaking. He hasn't moved. His eyes are on me, accusing, cold. 'Do you want to put them on for me?'

I slap his face.

He jerks back, stunned. I can see the red marks left by my fingers. The cocksure young stud evaporates to a confused boy and he turns and stumbles back into the house.

I collect the rest of the washing, trembling. I should have checked what was hanging on the line. I shouldn't have put him in that position. He was messing about. He was pushing a boundary. He didn't intend it to be serious. I should be more aware, one step ahead. Pip's voice in my head: *Be careful.*

What would she say if she'd witnessed this?

She would say I've been naïve.

I shouldn't have hit him.

I snatch the last things from the line and drop the laundry basket in the kitchen.

That look. His face, red, stinging. And then, a wounded boy. He doesn't know what he's doing. He's lost all sense of what's appropriate. Is it me? Have I blurred the lines?

I go up to his room and knock on the door. He ignores me. 'Sam, we have to talk.' Still no response. I can't leave it like this. Pressing my forehead against the door, I say, 'I'm sorry.' He doesn't answer, but I can feel him listening. 'I embarrassed you. I forgot those knickers were there. I didn't…' Didn't what? I don't understand what it is I'm apologising for. I want this to be over. I want things to go back to how they were, and I know he does too. I have to make this right. 'Sam, I know it was a joke. I overreacted. I'm sorry. It's just a pair of knickers, for God's sake! Can we forget about it?'

He can hear me, but what can he say? We need a bit of space now. He's not going to want to face me. 'I'm going to meet your dad at the pub. I might get us a take-away. Do you fancy a chicken kebab?' I don't wait for an answer. 'Text me if you do and I'll pick one up on the way home. I'll be about half an hour.'

That should give him time to calm down. And if I come back with Jonty and food, the atmosphere will be cheerful and busy and we'll be able to move on. I get up, slip down the stairs, grab my bag and jacket and escape.

Jonty is in his usual place at the bar, deep in conversation with Canoe Man. This is all I need. I try and back out of the door, thinking I'll phone Jonty from the street, but Canoe Man glances up and raises an eyebrow, looking me up and down, taking his time, letting me know he's remembering the lake, my wet T-shirt.

I feel a hand on my shoulder and turn around. 'Lizzie!' It's Rebecca. 'Have you come to join us for a drink?' She grabs my arm and pulls me closer, to hiss in my ear. 'You have to rescue me! That man is a lecherous prick!'

I snort, delighted. 'Tell me about it!' Jonty looks up. That smile. I wish I could wipe out the last half hour. If only I'd come straight here from work, ordered a drink, sat at the bar not knowing anything about what's just happened, then I could simply sink into that smile.

Rebecca pulls me away before I can speak, saying, 'Sorry, guys! Girl talk!' She shoves a glass of white wine towards me. 'Here, take that. I've only had a sip. I'll get us a bottle.'

I want to refuse. I only came to meet Jonty and walk back with him. I should be thinking about dinner. I should be heading back to work things out with Sam.

I pick up her wine and take a long slug. She laughs, signalling to Nigel for a bottle of the same and another glass. Nigel is nodding and smiling and clearly preparing to deliver the bottle to the table. Nigel, who takes orders as and when he feels like it and always behaves like he's doing you an enormous favour by simply allowing you into the pub, is eating out of Rebecca's hand. How does she do it?

Staying in the pub and getting drunk is selfish. It's irresponsible.

Fuck it.

Rebecca says, 'So you've had the pleasure of Matt's attention too?' She is already on first-name terms with Canoe Man. I tell her about the lake. She listens, nodding, unfazed by my wet T-shirt transgression but vehement in her condemnation of Matt's response.

I've finished the first glass of wine by the time the bottle arrives. Nigel makes some sort of comment that's intended to make Rebecca laugh at my expense, but she dismisses him with a quick flash of her smile and leans across the little table conspiratorially. 'So, what's up?'

It's as if she intuitively knows that it's something to do with Sam. And now I've told her about the lake and she hasn't reacted badly or said I was stupid or irresponsible, I feel maybe I can tell her what happened this evening. I have to tell someone and it might be better if that someone wasn't Jonty, not right away.

Her jaw drops as I repeat what Sam said about the knickers, and then she laughs. She actually hoots with laughter. I watch her for a moment. Is it funny? Have I got this all out of proportion? Maybe I'm taking the whole thing far too seriously. I feel myself smiling and then I remember. 'I slapped his face.'

I expect her smile to slip. I expect her to be shocked now, but she keeps smiling and shrugs. 'Good for you!'

I shake my head. 'I shouldn't have done that.'

'You think this is the only time in his life he's going to get a slap from a woman? Better you than someone else.'

'Seriously?'

'Lizzie, that's your problem! You take it all too seriously! You're not his mother. You're not even his stepmother, not really. I mean, look at you, you could be his sister! You could be his girlfriend—'

'No!'

'It's true. I'm not saying that you would ever think like that, but you could be. How old are you?'

'Twenty-seven.'

'Going on forty-seven.'

'Ouch!'

'Oh, come on. Loosen up!' She wriggles closer across the table. 'Admit it. You must have wondered...?'

'No!'

'He's gorgeous. He's a lot like his dad. They've both got that charm. The smile. I'm not saying you'd do anything, but you must have wondered what it would be like? If he was twenty-seven and you were thirty-seven, you wouldn't think twice.'

'No!'

She sits back, shocked. I've overreacted. She wasn't being serious. I apologise. She leans back in. 'No, I'm sorry. This isn't funny for you. I get that.'

'Age has nothing to do with it.' I've made that statement so many times since I got together with Jonty, but this is not about Jonty, it's about Sam. Rebecca is listening, waiting, doing her best to understand, to be a friend. 'It's more complicated than that. It's about trust. Responsibility. I may not be his mother, I may not even be his stepmother, but I do have a responsibility to him. A duty of care.'

'Duty?' She frowns, leans closer. She has a fine line of shimmering green across her eyelid. I would never dare wear a colour like that. 'You worry too much about duty and responsibility. Sam has parents. I don't see Jonty getting worked up about this.'

But Jonty doesn't know and I don't have to tell her this because she reads it in my face. I glance across to the bar. It's gone seven, but Jonty seems unaware of the time. Matt is talking and Jonty is frowning. Is Matt telling him about the lake? But Matt's laughing and he wouldn't be laughing if he was telling that story, would he? Jonty doesn't look angry, but he's not enjoying the conversation. Matt pokes him, as if he's trying to get him to laugh along, and Jonty's smiling, but it isn't his proper smile.

Rebecca is looking at me. 'Why haven't you said anything to Jonty about this stuff with Sam?'

'It's difficult. I don't want to cause trouble between them.' She's irritating me now. I don't want to explain myself; I'm not sure I can. I want to leave. Jonty catches my eye. I look at the clock. He nods. I check my phone. There's a text from Sam: *Yes plse chick kebab x*. I want to go home. I want to get a take-away and sit at home with my family. Jonty is saying his goodbyes. I get up.

Rebecca says, 'We still have half a bottle of wine!'

'Sorry. It's just… I need to sort this out.'

'Are you going to tell him?' Jonty is walking towards us.

'I don't know.'

As he reaches our table Rebecca gives Jonty her full-on smile. 'Hi! How are you?'

'I'm good.' But he doesn't sound good; he sounds deflated.

I take his hand, aware of Matt at the bar, watching us.

I don't want to talk about this in front of Rebecca. 'We'd better get off.'

She's still looking at Jonty. 'I know what will cheer you up.' She winks at me. 'Get Lizzie to model that new pink underwear for you when you get in.'

I'm paralysed by this. What is she doing? I glare a warning at her. She pulls an apologetic face. Thankfully, Jonty shakes it off with a hollow laugh and I usher him out of the door before she can say anything else.

As we head towards the kebab house I ask Jonty what he and Matt were talking about, but all he offers is a dismissive, 'You know Matt.' I want to push him, but the evening ahead is fragile enough as it is and what if Matt did mention the lake? Jonty won't like Matt's innuendo, but he knows he's got nothing to worry about with me.

We're halfway down the street when I feel the chill in the air and realise I've left my jumper in the pub. Jonty goes ahead to place our order while I run back. As I open the door I can see my jumper on the back of the chair where I was sitting, but Rebecca is now up at the bar talking to Matt. I stop dead on the threshold. She sees me and gives a roll of her eyes. I suppose I did leave her in the lurch. I have a moment of panic as I collect my jumper, remembering our conversation about Sam and the knickers, but she wouldn't mention that to Matt; she doesn't like him. I catch her eye as I'm leaving and she pulls an agonised face. She'll wriggle free of him as soon as she's finished her wine.

Sam is waiting for us when we get in. He's stiff, prickly, avoiding my eyes. I'm relentlessly upbeat, bustling into the kitchen and distributing the kebabs on to plates, ordering Sam to get drinks and clear the coffee table in front of the sofa, Jonty to choose something for us to watch. A TV dinner will mean we don't have to face one another or navigate any awkward silences and they both jump on this suggestion, clearly relieved. Regrouping, I think the Americans call it. It sounds like an army term. Something to do with troops after an attack, preparing for the next onslaught, which is just how this feels; the three of us, huddling together, hiding from something I can't explain.

Chapter 16

Jonty stayed late at the pub the following night and came home blurred by drink. It's the kind of drinking I hate. Something's bothering him, but rather than talk about it he's drinking to escape and that's a lonely road that only leads to heartbreak. I know, I grew up there. I don't want that to happen with us.

It must be work, or the lack of it, that's getting him down. I thought the sailing was helping. Maybe a few more pupils would move things forward for him. I thought Rebecca would give him a confidence boost and motivate him, but they've only been out once, maybe I'm expecting too much too soon.

Sam has been avoiding me since the knickers incident. For the most part, he's awkward, embarrassed, and I can understand that, but there are also flashes of anger. He's snappy, aggressive. 'I know what the time is!' when I called up the stairs this morning, stamping down and out of the door, slamming it behind him without so much as a goodbye. This is not the belligerent teenager he was when he first arrived. That was hot indignation, burnt out in a moment, this is cooler, more adult, more threatening. Sam's teenage rage was directed at Jonty, but this cold fury is directed at me.

I take a day off and persuade Jonty to drive out for a proper walk and lunch. It isn't easy to organise this with everything that's going on, but needs must, our family is fragmenting.

The weather is on my side. We're having a good week: powder-blue sky, the odd cartoon white cloud. There are sheep and a few sturdy young lambs decorating the fields, the first fragile buds on skeletal trees. This is my favourite walk: Elterwater to Skelwith Bridge. It's not a proper fell walker's walk, but it's adventurous enough for a city girl like me. A short climb and then undulating countryside with spectacular, perfectly framed views of the Lake District. I like the variety: rolling farmland hemmed by irregular drystone walls sprouting moss and, in warmer months, white and purple flowers, tidy farmhouses spilling geraniums from window boxes, cobbled yards, noisy sheepdogs, ancient woodland, a stretch of river with shiny stepping stones. Jonty thinks it's all a bit prissy – chocolate-box countryside for soft southerners – but it's still beautiful and if we have to put up with the rain and wind for days on end as we go about our routines, why shouldn't we enjoy the clichés the tourists flock to if we get the opportunity?

I have an agenda, of course. I'm hoping the fresh air and exercise will cheer Jonty up and we might be able to talk a bit about his redundancy and what he's going to do next, but really what I want to talk about is Sam. The incident in the bath was awkward, but he wasn't expecting to see me in there, and he couldn't help his reaction. There's probably hormonal stuff going on that makes it difficult for him to control his responses. Things which used to be fine have become a trigger for him, and the knickers incident was an error of judgement. He probably meant it as a joke and couldn't quite carry it off. It would be only natural if he was jealous of my relationship with Jonty. He's exploring the world, playing things out, but his hostility, this anger I can feel, is worrying.

Jonty slips his hand across the back of my waist and into the back pocket of my jeans. I ask, casually, 'Do you think Sam's all right?'

'Apart from being a moody arse?'

'Do you think he's happy?'

Jonty snorts. '*Happy?* I should say so. Seventeen. Everything ahead of him. What's he got to complain about?'

'Why do you think he needs to go to Ireland suddenly?'

Jonty looks at me for a moment, as if he's about to ask me something, but changes his mind. 'How much did that ticket cost in the end?'

'Don't worry, I've sorted it.'

'You shouldn't have to sort it. He's my son. And he needs to learn to plan a bit better instead of springing it on us at the last minute.'

'I think he wants to talk to his mum.'

'He can talk to her on the bloody phone.'

This isn't getting anywhere. When Jonty's in this combative mood he will never see anything from anyone else's point of view. His attitude to his children is infuriating. I remember the first time I saw them, standing in the hall, looking up at me as I came down the stairs: Nell reaching for her brother's hand, Sam's fingers closing around hers, the way he stepped forward a little, instinctively protecting her, watching me, weighing it up. I try not to think about Jonty, throwing his car keys on the side table, avoiding my eyes. I try not to think 'coward', though I called him that later, when the beds had been made and the two of them were settled. As settled as they could be in a house where no welcome had been prepared, in a new life with a father who had done nothing to accommodate them. Jonty's defence had been that it was temporary; as soon as Kay's mother was on her feet she'd be back, but even temporary needs to feel safe and warm.

I was kind and I did what was required and when Nell needed a kiss or a hug, I was there to provide, but I kept a distance. She was not mine to love. She's not mine to miss, she belongs with her mum, but I do miss her. Somewhere between the shopping and washing and cooking and rushing from work to school and home to dance, to swimming, to home again, she crept into my heart and now there's this great big hole. It will pass. It's been nearly two years and it's getting easier, but Sam must feel it too. They were a team. They went through the divorce, Kay leaving, the loss of both their grandparents in quick succession, all those huge emotional events together and now he's alone.

This is a town where people share a history. If you aren't part of that it's difficult to break in. I can do it through work, but in my personal life it's really Jonty and not much else of any substance. Rebecca is the first friend of my own age that I've made here and after what happened last time we met up, I'm having my doubts. She's three or four years younger than me and her immaturity is irritating.

We reach a stile and climb the slate steps over the mossy wall. Loopy sits with her tail wagging, looking at us expectantly. She can't manage the steps. Jonty pulls a vertical wooden slat upwards and reveals a dog-sized hole in the wall that allows her to slip through. Every gate we encounter seems to have a different latch, a different method of getting through. Jonty says it's a trick the farmers play on walkers, forcing the townies to prove themselves. I jump down into the field and wait, but he hesitates on the other side. 'What is it?'

He's frowning at me over the wall. Whatever it is he wants to say requires all his attention. This is too big for walking and talking. My instinct is to turn and run. He says, 'Sam isn't your problem.'

'I didn't mean... I'm just trying to...'

'This isn't working.' I stare at him, part of my brain trying to process the words while the other part frantically rejects them. His face is dark, his eyes are avoiding mine. I'm scared. Too scared to ask him what he means. He must notice because his voice softens, but it's still firm. 'This isn't fair. On you. You should be out enjoying yourself, having fun, hanging out with people your own age.'

'But I'm happy with you.'

'It's different now. With Sam. It's... not that simple.'

What's he saying? The trees are falling towards me. That dark shape in my peripheral vision is clawing its way into focus. This can't be happening.

He takes a deep breath and looks at me. Sad eyes. 'I think it might be better if you were in your own place.'

What? I search his face. The world is contracting around me, the fells, acres of stone walls and metal gates crowding in.

'It's no good – you at the cottage, with Sam.'

He wants me to leave? 'You're finishing with me?' I'm crying, big fat tears, like a child, but I can't help it.

'No. No!' He scrambles over the wall. I wait for his arms to wrap around me, feel the warmth of his chest through his jumper. 'Just until Sam leaves home.'

'Why?'

He steps away, his hands on my shoulders, looking at me. 'Because I should never have put you in this position.'

'What position?'

He tries to find the word, but there is no word. 'You're too young for this responsibility. It isn't fair.'

'I don't mind. I want to do it. I love Sam.'

'I know you do, but that's the problem.' I wait. I can't breathe. 'You care too much, and the worry…You're too young…'

'… to be his mum. But I can be something else. I'm his friend.' He shakes his head, but I carry on. 'It's because I'm not a parent that it works. All this stuff recently, his moods, it's just hormones; it'll settle down, we just need to listen to him. Don't make me go.' My voice is small and fragile. 'I don't want to go.' He pulls me close and I cling tight.

'I thought it would be for the best. I was thinking of you.'

'Well don't. I don't want to be sent away. I love you. Both of you.' I sense him tense, briefly, but he doesn't let go and I feel I've been reprieved, for the time being at least. I can't imagine moving out of the cottage and leaving Sam alone with Jonty, not seeing him every day, no longer part of his life.

Jonty doesn't slide his hand back over my waist as we cross the field but walks alongside me, part of him withdrawn. I snatch a look at his face, the deepening lines across his forehead, something churning away in there and I'm scared. I have always been certain of Jonty. I thought that if either of us were to give up on this relationship it would be me, not him, and I'm not planning on giving up. I took his commitment for granted. Now I'm not so sure. I didn't think he'd be able to consider being without me; not out of arrogance or in the belief that I'm anything special, but because it's easy being with me. I fit. I don't demand anything of him. It suits him. He's fundamentally lazy, Jonty. He loves me, but he also can't be bothered with emotional upheaval and I realise now that, frustrating though this is at times, it's been my safety net. He didn't warn me about the kids moving in because he was scared I'd leave. I meant that much to him, but now he's suggesting I could move out. He could picture that happening. He could make it happen.

We tramp across a muddy field towards the woodland. My boots squelch and the ground sucks at my feet. It's colder than I expected, the chill creeping up my T-shirt, into the small of my back and I regret not bringing an extra layer.

Eventually Jonty says, 'Matt saw you up at Coniston.'

So that's it. Matt whispering things in Jonty's ear, sowing seeds of doubt. The lake. Matt in his canoe, cold eyes fixed on me. 'What did he say?' I feel a little sick.

'Said the two of you were in the lake.' He raises his eyebrows. 'The water must have been bloody freezing.' He's shaking his head now, as if to say we're both mad. Nothing else. A bit of madness. Nothing to be concerned about.

I pull a face. 'We were hot, from the bikes. It was good to cool off.'

He doesn't ask if I had a costume. Does he presume I did? Should I say something? But if I say something I'm making it important and it isn't important. Jonty is easy with nudity. He walks around the house naked without a care in the world and in the warmer months he sleeps naked. I feel the cold up here, so I don't go that far, but since Sam arrived I've been careful. I should tell him what happened, while I have the chance, while he's finding it funny, but he's focused on something else. He says, 'I should have cycled up there with the two of you.'

But I didn't ask him to. I wanted to talk to Sam. I suggested Jonty take the boat out so Sam and I could be alone. 'The sailing did you good.'

He looks at me, deep grooves across his forehead. 'Sam's never wanted to go on a bike ride with me.'

'Have you asked him?'

He's looking at me as if he's trying to work something out. 'He wouldn't come. He'd make an excuse.'

'Ask him. Next time you go.'

He shrugs this off. 'He's revising.'

'A bit of fresh air and exercise might be just what he needs. You won't know if you don't ask.' But Jonty isn't looking for a solution here; he's trying to say something about me and Sam. He can see what we've got and he wants a slice of it, but I've earned this. If Jonty wants a better relationship with his son it's down to him to invest in that. 'Why don't you get Sam involved in the open mic? The two of you could do something together.'

'Perform something, you mean?'

'Why not?'

'He won't want to do that with me.'

'For God's sake, Jonty! You could charm anyone into doing anything if you put your mind to it. It will be nice for Nell, too. She'll love seeing you up there.'

He doesn't respond, but I've said enough. Jonty will come back to this in his own time in his own way. I walk on ahead a few paces. 'Come on, old boy! I'm starving.'

I march him the rest of the way to Skelwith Bridge and

the fancy café where we're going to have lunch. The car park hosts a handful of Audis and BMWs. Pedigree dogs lie beneath the tables on the terrace, their owners huddled in quilted Rab jackets with contrasting zippers and trims in purple and lime, turquoise and pink. City folk escaping to the Lake District. I can tell by the walking boots that sport today's mud and still have immaculate laces. I remember Jonty driving me up to Ambleside to buy my first pair of proper hiking boots when my trainers failed the Cumbrian mud challenge. I almost wept at the price; the most expensive shoes I've ever owned and the ugliest. At weekends and during school holidays this café is peopled by catalogue models on weekend escapes from their metropolitan lives. They spill out on to the riverbank with glossy-haired children and fluffy dogs on patterned leads; today we have their parents and in-laws who have retired here. I can feel Jonty tensing beside me, but the food is good, the shop is doing well, these customers are feeding a local business and I'm in the mood for a plate of interesting salads with a decent cup of coffee.

We find a table outside, overlooking the river. Loopy sniffs at an overweight chocolate Labrador as we pass and then flops under Jonty's chair. I leave them while I go inside to order.

When I come back Jonty is watching a couple at the table next to us. They're about my age and totally loved-up. Eyes locked, chairs pulled close, fingers, thighs touching, brushing. Early days; a midweek break. I remember how that used to feel. I came to the Lake District to do a short-term job for Jonty. Two years out of art school, wanting to escape London, my mother. I'd been hoping for a city job – Newcastle or Edinburgh – but I had to take any opportunity that was offered and get some experience. As far as I was concerned, Tarnside was the middle of nowhere. Sheep, fields, lakes; not my idea of fun. And rain, of course. I'd pictured non-stop rain, but it didn't rain that much and it was far prettier than I'd expected. And quirky. Not a close-your-doors, who-the-hell-are-you, get-off-my-land sort of place, but cautiously welcoming, interesting and interested. All those festivals. Still, I thought it was temporary, a way to get experience quickly and then move on, but I met Jonty. Just like these two here, I fell for him and there was no way I could leave.

I look back at his soft face, the dark eyes and brows, the five-o'clock shadow that is there within an hour or two of shaving, the dimple in his chin. His face is creased into new, unfamiliar lines. When he looks at me his eyes are troubled and I'm desperately trying to think of something distracting, but I can't stop him. He drops it like a grenade on the table between us. 'You should be with someone your own age.'

I stop breathing. Why is he saying this? Is he testing me? 'Don't be daft!' Is it insecurity? Does he need reassurance? 'Where has this come from?'

Jonty looks down at Loopy, petting her head softly, avoiding my eyes. I'm scared now. I've never heard him talk like this. 'What did Matt say to you?'

He shrugs. 'Nothing. He was just having a bit of a dig.'

'Tell me!'

'It's not what he said. But he got me thinking.'

'It's none of his business!'

'Lizzie, listen to me.' He pauses and smiles, but that smile is full of pain. 'You're beautiful. This new look...'

'What new look?'

'Your hair. The make-up.'

'I'm not wearing make-up.' But I know what he means. I've made a bit more of an effort since Rebecca's make-over and I am wearing a bit of eyeliner today. 'I thought you liked it.'

'I do. I do, but...' He sighs. 'You're gorgeous, Lizzie. Young. You could have anyone.'

'I don't want anyone!'

'You could have a family.'

I'm winded. He's slammed right into me without realising what he's done. I lean across the table, as close to him as I can get. '*You* are my family.'

'Kids. You'll want kids.'

I'm struggling to breathe. I want to say that I have Sam and Nell, but I can't. Because I don't. Because it's not my place. Because he clearly doesn't see it that way. And maybe they don't either. I feel something cleave inside me. They are his kids. Not mine. They are a family. Not me.

Chapter 17

I was sick again this morning. Three days in a row. The possibility that I might be pregnant has unfurled slowly, persistently. I have a nagging memory. A two-day conference in Manchester, staying over. Did I take my pill?

It's Friday afternoon. Jonty is driving back from the airport after dropping Sam off and I'm at work, in my little office in the park, with the heater on and my lamp shining a golden circle on my desk, though it's only lunchtime. The world has descended into a thick cloud and gloom. I think I'm pregnant.

In the office next door I can hear Eve singing to herself as she prepares for the weekend. She always does her filing before she leaves, and when she files she sings. I wish I could go next door and sit down and tell her all this, but I can't. Eve wants a family and for some reason she can't have one. The last thing she needs is to hear about my possible, unplanned pregnancy.

Jonty wants me to leave. He wants to end it and I might be pregnant.

I had to talk him round. Sitting in that fancy Lake District café, surrounded by people in holiday spirits, trying to defuse the bomb he'd just dumped on the table between us. I couldn't shout, or cry or cause a scene, all I could do was talk and hope that he'd listen.

I'm clinging to the hope that Jonty loves me and is doing this out of some misguided concern for me, but I suspect it's got more to do with Pip and Matt.

He was calm, firm. 'You need someone who can take care of you,' he said, taking that fatherly tone he sometimes does with me, while behind him the river crashed over rock and stone after a heavy night of rain. A waitress twisted this way and that between the tables collecting dirty cups and plates.

'You take care of me.'

'Not now. I'm just a weight around your neck.'

This I could deal with. 'You've been made redundant and you can, if you want, take early retirement.' He grimaced. 'There's no shame in that. You might enjoy it. You can do anything you want. Sailing, teaching, or not. Money isn't a problem. How many people can say that?' He was about to argue, but I stopped him. 'There's no mortgage left to pay on the cottage. You've got your redundancy money, and your pension if you want to start drawing it. You can borrow against the house to pay Sam's fees if you have to, and he'll get a job. We've got my income—'

'I don't want you supporting me.'

It was all I could do not to reach across the table and shake him. This is when Jonty and I come to blows. When he shows his age with his stupid, outdated attitude. 'I don't have to *support* you. We're independent. We've always agreed that.' The cottage is Jonty's. I live there rent free, but I contribute to food and bills. I have my little place, my investment – my security, if I'm honest, though I'd never say that to Jonty; especially not now. 'It's not financial support that matters, Jonty.' I take his hand. 'It's the emotional support I need from you.' But it was me, not Jonty, who had to provide that for the rest of the afternoon. He cheered up a bit once he'd eaten, but I spent the rest of the day working hard to keep it light, distracting him, telling him daft stories and doing my damnedest to make him laugh.

Jonty effectively snatched my family from me when he suggested I leave and while I managed to persuade him not to kick me out, I don't feel safe any more.

He does not see me as part of the family.

I leave my desk, pulling on my coat and a scarf that got left behind during the Christmas workshops and head out across the grey park to Margaret Thwaite's bench. I sit and watch the settling geese and busy ducks, but there's something melancholy about the shivering reeds, the occasional solitary fish that breaks the surface of the tarn. The park seems abandoned. There's a damp chill to the air and the heavy clouds suggest it's far later than it actually is. It's hard to believe that in a matter of weeks the rowing boats will be pulled out for hire, the ice-cream van will park up and the place will hum with community life through the summer months; this Cumbrian April appears to have no spring, dragging the ragged remnants of winter behind it.

While Jonty dozed in front of the TV last night, I climbed the stairs to Sam's room and tapped on the door. I thought the two of us could talk, or just be, for a while.

'Yup?' He was sitting in the light of his desk lamp, his books spread out in front of him.

'You OK?' I said. He nodded. 'Fancy a cup of tea? Or a beer?'

He shook his head, 'No, thanks,' and glanced back down at his books, but his hands were beneath the desk and he was on his phone, texting or Snapchatting someone, and I felt it as clearly as a door slamming in my face: I was not welcome there.

Jonty's boy. His son. Who am I to him?

The sky is a slate slab. I can feel it pressing down on me.

I think I'm pregnant.

This isn't planned and it isn't good news. Not with things the way they are. How can I talk to Jonty about a baby given the mood he's in? He thinks his career is over, he's talking about me moving out, about me having children with someone else. Does he mean that, or is he saying what he thinks I need to hear, giving me the option to leave?

But I don't want to leave. When Sam decided to come back and live with us we were so happy. It said something; an act of faith in what we'd built together. I thought we were a family; but it seems I was wrong. Jonty doesn't see it that way.

Jonty doesn't want a baby.

It starts to rain and I don't have an umbrella. I pull up my hood. It's that fine rain that is barely visible but soaks through to your bones. Not even Margaret Thwaite can offer me comfort now. There has only been one forlorn figure in the park since I sat down, a dark blue waterproof now standing beneath the sprawling oak tree by the gate waiting for an arthritic terrier to catch up. I hurry past on to the road that leads into the centre of town. There's a chemist on the high street; with a bit of luck there won't be anyone I know in there.

Jonty and I have never discussed children. Kids were not on our radar. I hadn't decided *not* to have children, I just hadn't decided *to* have them, or to consider what that might mean for me and Jonty.

I can't see Jonty with a baby.

Jonty's not the kind of father who stores family photographs on his phone. When he and I first got together, Sam was fourteen, Nell nine. He had them every other weekend, but there were never any plans, no preparation, it was just going with the flow in that lazy way Jonty does. I thought he should do things with them, take them places – the zoo, a water park, the cinema – but he argued that this wasn't real and he didn't want his weekends with them to be like mini holidays. He felt that life should remain as it always was, as far as possible. I'm still not convinced. He can make a good argument, Jonty, to get his point across, but the truth is, he couldn't be bothered. He didn't want to have to do anything, so he didn't organise it. The kids slid in and out of his life without affecting it very much because that was the way he liked it. It had nothing to do with what might be best for them.

I made the decision, very quickly, to stay out of it. I was twenty-four when I moved in. Granted, I wasn't your average twenty-four-year-old; I've been a middle-aged woman since I was a kid. I didn't have the luxury of rebelling, of being immature, reckless, thoughtless. I never got to be a teenager; I always had someone else to consider. It's not a sob story and I don't expect anyone to pity me, I am who I am because of it, but even though I've always been old for my age, I decided I was too young to be stepmum to Jonty's kids, or maybe I'd just had enough, looking out for my brother. They weren't my children; they had two loving parents. I persuaded myself that Jonty's relationship with them wasn't my problem. Every other weekend I made myself scarce, visiting Clare or other friends in different parts of the country, or just taking myself off somewhere alone. I was always gone by the time Sam and Nell arrived and back after they'd left. Jonty's kids were Jonty's responsibility.

Until they moved in.

I approach the counter with the pregnancy kit. The girl is dealing with another customer on the shop floor and tells me she won't be a moment. I put the box down and check my purse as a man approaches and stands to one side of me. I look up.

Canoe Man.

I'm so startled I almost cry out. Matt doesn't smile and I can feel my heart start to race. He's younger than Jonty but older than me, somewhere around forty, with a chiselled face and cold blue eyes. His smile is sticky. Before he can look at the counter, I sweep my arm along it, knocking the pregnancy kit into a basket of bath bombs and rush out of the shop feeling inexplicably dirty and furious.

I hurry towards Fell Rise and the cottage. My boots leave damp prints on the slate floor of the hall. Kicking them off, I run up the stairs two at a time to the bathroom, suddenly desperate for a wee. Sitting on the toilet, my sodden jacket dripping a puddle at my feet, listening to my urine hitting the water, I kick myself for not waiting, or not going to a different chemist. I could be doing the test now. Why did I run? It's none of Matt's business if I'm doing a pregnancy test.

I go downstairs and fill the kettle. I can buy another test.

I hear a whine from outside the back door and realise that Loopy didn't greet me in the hall when I came in. She's outside. The back door is closed but not locked. She must have slipped out this morning and got shut out there by accident. I let her in, expecting her to be cold and bedraggled, but she seems fine. I reach down and touch her coat. It's dry and warm; she can't have been out there long. I run upstairs and check Sam's room, but he's not there and his laptop is on the floor by the bed. I pick up a few dirty cups and take them down to the dishwasher, then I call the school. Sam was in for registration. It's possible he slipped out afterwards, but Mr Wright calls me back to tell me Sam is currently in his English class and has been in school all day. Feeling foolish, I thank him and hang up. Loopy hovers around my feet, looking at me hopefully. Maybe she took shelter in an outbuilding, or found a patch of sunshine. I'm starting to imagine danger where there isn't any. I'm fretting about Sam when I really need to focus on me and Jonty.

Nell was ten when she and Sam arrived. Clutching her brother's hand in the hall, eyes wide, flitting from me to Sam to Jonty, trying to understand what was going on beneath the surface. I must have been frowning. Shocked. She'd been expecting a welcome, not this bewilderment, growing realisation and silent rage. It wasn't her fault, but she was the one that suffered the most in that moment. If I'd known I would have been waiting with egg and chips, the yolk nice and runny the way she likes it, except I didn't know that then. I'd never cooked Nell a meal.

Apparently it was all very last-minute. Kay's mother had been coping with her husband's Parkinson's for some time and everyone thought he would be the one to go first. Her stroke was sudden and harsh. Intensive care. Touch and go.

Kay had to leave immediately. She called and discussed it all with Jonty.

Jonty didn't discuss it with me. He'd kept meaning to, he said later, when the kids were settled upstairs, sharing a room because he'd not thought it through, not grasped that, at fifteen, Sam might be too old to be sharing with his sister. There was only one spare bedroom. The attic space was my makeshift studio: bare floorboards, tins of paint and chunks of driftwood, the only furniture a battered armchair. Jonty, typically, hadn't planned anything. He'd just hoped it would all be over in a few days. He'd meant to tell me.

I wanted to walk out, but I couldn't do that to those kids. I stayed that night because of them. And I stayed the next night because there was more to do and so it went on. The truth was, I didn't trust Jonty to take care of them properly. He didn't understand how lost they were. I was angry, but what I was feeling was not the priority. The last thing those kids needed was another split taking place right under their noses.

I struggle not to get furious now, thinking about it. I marched Jonty out of the house and down to the park, where the kids couldn't hear me. I screamed at him until my throat ached. I shoved him into the tarn in my fury. He stood there, up to his knees, the water soaking up his jeans, literally pulling at his hair, desperate. At any other time it would have been funny. He simply hadn't thought it through. I do believe him. And I understand. I'm not condoning what he did, but I know why he did it. Jonty's a coward when it comes to emotional stuff. He was scared. He cried. I'd never seen Jonty cry before. That great bear of a man, that strong, argumentative, garrulous man who was the life and soul of any party, that confident charmer cried like a boy and told me he was terrified I might leave him. He was turning fifty. He came with baggage. I knew that. Until that day his baggage had been something distant, separate. He'd kept it contained. It wasn't something that affected me. Now there it was. There *they* were. Those two children. Waiting.

Nell was with us for five months. Sunny, hiccuppy, Nell with her crooked front teeth and freckles, pulling faces at me through the window. Nell with her head torch, reading *Harry Potter* under the duvet, eating tomato soup and macaroni for breakfast, attaching Easter bunny ears to Loopy's head and giggling so hard she was nearly sick. Sunshine Nell.

She and Sam both flew out to Dublin together at the end of the summer term, but Sam came back. That hadn't been the plan, but he asked to come home. Home. That word, hearing that word; it made everything worthwhile just to hear him call us 'home'. Cumbria's crags and valleys are in Sam's bones; the lakes and tarns, the shifts in light are echoed in the way he moves. He belongs here in a way that I never will, but it's more than that: he missed us. He missed me.

How can I leave now? How can Jonty even suggest it?

Sam missed me and I missed him.

What would Sam's reaction be to a baby? I want to see his face folding into that smile, that Jonty smile, but what I see is the sneer as he held my pink knickers in his hand. I can't think about that.

I think about Nell. Sweet, innocent Nell. She was excited about seeing her mum but sad to be leaving us, leaving me. She wanted me to go with her to Ireland, but the summer is a busy time at the park, with events and workshops, and I couldn't get away. Or was that an excuse? I could have flown over with her, settled her in. But I got the sense that I'd be intruding. Kay wanted her daughter back. Jonty saw no need to travel with the kids, so it didn't seem appropriate for me to go.

Being busy at work meant I didn't have a lot of time to think, and I was glad of that. I threw myself into everything in order not to have the space to feel too much. After Sam's call, when he told us he was coming back, I took the dog out on my own. I walked for miles, poor Loopy was exhausted, but I couldn't stop, I was afraid to stop, because though Sam was coming home, Nell wasn't.

Nell was easy to love from the beginning. Sam was prickly, hostile, downright rude at times. He was fifteen and justifiably angry, as I had to explain to Jonty over and over again, but we worked through it. Slowly. Nell gave her love so freely, but I had to earn my relationship with Sam, step by painful step. We've built something, he and I, something I can't explain to Mr Wright or Rebecca, something Pip doesn't seem to understand, something without a name but precious all the same. I can't mention a baby to him now. Things are too fragile already.

What would Pip say if I told her I was pregnant? How would she feel about Jonty starting again? Part of me longs to confide in her. I could do with some unsentimental support, but I'm not so sure Pip would be supportive. She'd think me a fool for having got myself into this situation in the first place.

It's half past four. Nell will be home from school by now. Since she got the new phone for her birthday we have texted from time to time, but I prefer to talk if I can. I need to hear her voice. She answers straight away. 'Hello Lizzie! Guess what? Roisin is teaching me to ride! Her pony is very old and grumpy, but we're making the best of it and she says if I'm good and help her with the mucking out she'll see what she can do, which I think means she might be getting another pony, don't you? And if she gets another one I might be able to say it's almost mine, or a little bit mine, at least!'

I know nothing about ponies, but she doesn't need more than the odd exclamation from me to continue on this theme for some time, and I'm happy to listen to her excited chatter, to feel that generous, uninhibited energy and enthusiasm sparkle from the phone. It's like a thirst being quenched in me and I drink her up, but eventually she tells me she has to go and I hang up, feeling her absence like a cold draught. I fell in love with Nell. It was so uncomplicated and so easy, more a sliding into love than a falling, and I didn't realise until she was gone. I should have valued it more. I should have given her more, relished that love more and I ache for her now, but it's too late. It hasn't got easier with time; if anything it's getting worse. I can hardly bear it. And it will be worse with Sam, because I've had him longer and we are knitted together, he and I. This wrench I feel now, letting him go, is nothing compared to what I'm going to feel once he's gone.

I need to go back and buy another pregnancy test, but I can't deal with that now. Another slug of tea and I reach for my coat.

Chapter 18

On Sunday, while Jonty drives down to Manchester to collect Sam, I get a call from Pip asking me over for coffee.

It's a clear day with sunshine and a warm breeze. 'Perfect sailing weather,' Jonty grumbled as he prepared to set off for his four-hour round-trip on the M6. He and Rebecca attempted to sail yesterday, but apparently they spent more time becalmed than they did sailing and he wasn't in the best of moods when he got back. So much for her cheering him up. She called on Friday night to see if I wanted to go out for a drink, but I didn't want to risk saying anything about the pregnancy test. I have a feeling I need to be a little more cautious in what I confide to Rebecca.

Pip has set the table in the garden, beneath a tree. I don't know what type of tree it is, but it has a very thick trunk and sprawling branches that beg to be climbed. I look up through the leafy canopy and wonder if Jonty climbed this tree as a boy.

The coffee is strong and thick, the way I like it. There are delicate lemon biscuits, which I pick at to be polite, but I'm still feeling queasy. Pip is wearing a loose cashmere jumper with a scooped neck. Her hair is twisted up and held in place with an ornate metal clasp. She has painted her fingernails with a nude varnish. Her distorted, clumsy fingers look like they should belong to someone else. She says, 'I want to talk about Sam.' I try not to groan. Now what? 'Kay called me this morning, just after she got back from dropping Sam at the airport.'

'What did she say?'

'She was rather upset. Apparently there was a bit of a scene with her new chap – what's his name? Connor?'

'It is Connor. I've heard Nell mention him.'

'Apparently he's an old school friend she's taken up with again. I'm delighted for her. She deserves a bit of happiness. She's a good woman, Kay.'

I don't know why she's telling me this. I've never thought otherwise. Jonty and Kay split up years ago. There was no one else involved, they just didn't get along any more. Jonty takes his share of responsibility. Once the kids were both in school, Kay went back to college and eventually did a degree through the Open University. She changed. Not in a bad way, from what Jonty says, but she needed to move on. I wait for Pip to tell me something I don't know.

'It appears that Sam behaved badly.'

'What did he do?'

'He said some inappropriate things. She wasn't specific, but they were of a sexual nature, referring to her relationship with Connor.'

I can feel my face burning. Will Pip see it? What has Sam

said? And then I feel a flicker of something else. Relief. It's terrible that Sam has done this, but at least I'm not the only one and now it's out in the open we can discuss it.

'He's done it with me too,' I confide, and I tell Pip about the incident in the bathroom. Her face is serious. She asks me what happened at the lake and is absolutely still as she listens, as if she doesn't want to miss a word. She gives nothing away, processing quietly. I ask her, 'Do you think there's something wrong?' She has three sons. She's been through this with teenage boys. I'm expecting her to talk about testosterone and give me funny anecdotes. I'm hoping she'll make me laugh with stories about Jonty's inappropriate teenage behaviour, but her expression doesn't change. She remains quiet. And the longer the silence continues, the more uneasy I feel. 'What is it?'

Pip sighs. Her eyes meet mine. She looks sad. There is pity there and I want to wriggle away from it, but her eyes pin me to my chair. 'Lizzie...' I don't like the tone of her voice. I don't like where this is going. 'Lizzie, dear, Kay is of the opinion that this has something to do with you.'

I swallow. 'Me?'

'The incident you describe at the lake...'

'It was completely innocent!'

'From your point of view, perhaps.'

'We were cooling off. It was his suggestion!' I stop. She nods. 'I don't mean like that. He wanted me to relax. He was saying that it was no big deal. He doesn't see me like that.'

'But the episode in the bathroom?'

'That was different.' She frowns. I try to explain. 'I don't think that had anything to do with the lake.'

'But he told you it did.'

'Afterwards. After what happened in the bathroom, but when we were at the lake it wasn't like that. It wasn't. Afterwards, he saw it like that, but not at the time.'

She sits back. 'Well, I don't think that makes a lot of difference, whether he thought it at the time or in hindsight.'

'But it does. It does, because at the time I was reading his signals. I have always read his signals. I'm careful. I pay attention. Our relationship has been built on that. If he'd felt at all awkward or embarrassed, if he'd given any indication… But he didn't. He was perfectly happy and relaxed. There was nothing sexual about what happened at the lake.'

'And yet, later…'

'Later. Later he saw it differently.'

'So what happened to change his mind?'

'I don't know.'

We sit in silence. Something must have happened after the lake to make Sam see me differently. Someone must have said something. Was it Matt? He's been talking to Jonty, making jokes, making him doubt himself, us. What if he's said something to Sam? That would explain it. A dirty, leery comment from someone like Matt. Maybe Sam is trying to prove himself in some way, trying to impress Matt. But Sam wouldn't give Matt the time of day. Sam wouldn't want to emulate someone like Matt.

Pip says, 'Apparently Nell was very upset. She was there when Sam said whatever it was he said to Connor and it was rather ugly.' Nell. I can picture her face, the confusion. Poor, innocent Nell. 'Kay now feels, under the circumstances, that it would be better if she and Nell stay in Ireland at the weekend and don't visit Tarnside for a while.'

No! I gulp back the tears. This is too cruel! I haven't seen Nell for months. I have been longing for her. I thought she would ease this ache. I need a dose of her glorious, loving exuberance in my life right now. This is so unfair! I can't go to Ireland. I don't really know Kay or her family, I'm entirely dependent on snatched moments with Nell when she's visiting her father or her grandmother and now even that has been taken away from me. What did I do wrong? Why is this happening to me?

'I'm sorry, Lizzie.'

'I won't let you do this!' I shove back my chair and knock the table. My cup topples over, spewing dark coffee, before rolling over the edge and falling to the grass below.

'Lizzie, calm down. No one is taking Nell away. She lives in Ireland with her mother. She will visit another time, when the dust has settled. You will see her then.'

'I don't want to see her! I want to *be* with her. I want to hold her, to smell her, to, to…' I feel like they're all here, Kay and Jonty, with their arms folded, shaking their heads, blocking Nell so she's unable to see me, to see how much I want to be with her, how much I need her. 'Why Nell? I understand that you're worried about Sam, but Nell? I *love* Sam.' I'm shrieking now and Pip winces, but I can't stop. 'I don't know why he's behaving the way he is and I'm sorry if it's something to do with me, but all I did was go for a swim in my underwear. It was a bad call, I can see that now, but this… this is just cruel!'

Pip sighs. I've embarrassed her. I've embarrassed myself.

The silence trembles in the wake of my outburst. I take a breath to steady myself. 'Are you going to talk to Jonty?'

She frowns. 'You sound anxious.'

I am anxious. She's waiting for me to explain why. It's not the lake, Jonty is fine with what happened at the lake, it's what happened in the bathroom that will be the problem. As for the knickers... But I haven't told Pip about the knickers. She's waiting for an explanation. 'He'll be angry.'

She looks at me carefully. 'Who with?' Sharp as a dart. She understands. Jonty will direct his anger at Sam. He won't be capable of looking at this from the point of view of a parent; he'll see Sam as a rival. All this passes between us in the silence. She nods, slowly. 'It's a problem, knowing Jonty the way we both do. I shall have to think on it. Don't worry, I won't say anything before speaking to you.' She places her hand on mine and gives it a squeeze, but her pity offers me little comfort. I've disappointed her, and right now I think it's this which hurts me most of all.

I phone Clare. I need to talk to someone who knows me. Someone outside the town. Someone who isn't connected to Sam or Jonty and will understand and be discreet. Someone my age. And Clare is a teacher in a London secondary school. She works with teenage boys; she'll be able to help.

She sounds breathless when she answers the phone, giggling. 'Lizzie! Hello!' I can hear people talking in the background, music.

'Where are you?'

'I'm at a private view. A gallery in Whitechapel. A friend of a friend of a friend. Lizzie, you should see some of this stuff! Honestly, I don't know how he's got away with it. You need to get your work out there, sweetheart! You could wipe the floor with this guy.'

She is out in the city, drinking, having a good time with friends. I can't talk to her now; I don't want to ruin her night, but she's alert, tuned into me instantly. 'Lizzie? Are you OK?'

'It's all right, it can wait.'

'No, no. Talk to me. Listen, I'll go outside.'

'Seriously, Clare, I was just phoning to have a moan, but you've cheered me up already. I'll just mix myself a cocktail, put on a CD and pretend I'm there with you!'

I distract her with questions about who she's with, patiently listen to the latest gossip and somehow manage to pull it off. She lets me go, insisting that I come down to London as soon as the Flag Festival is over and spend some time with her.

The silence vibrates around me after I hang up. I try my brother, but he goes straight to voicemail. I even think about calling my mum, but I know that by this time of the day she'll be several drinks in and will just get aggressive towards Pip and Jonty and tell me to move out, or, better still, move back south with her.

Sam's family think I'm a bad influence on him. Kay. Pip. It's only a matter of time before they tell Jonty. Maybe it is true; I am to blame.

I should never have gone in that damned lake.

Chapter 19

Sam barely speaks to me when he gets in but insists he's knackered and drags his suitcase upstairs behind him. Jonty goes straight to the kitchen and grabs a bottle of wine. He's clearly wound up; Kay must have spoken to him. He pours two glasses and sits down at the table. 'Apparently Sam had a go at Connor.'

'How do you mean?'

'Kay wouldn't say exactly.' Jonty takes a swig of wine.

'Did you talk to Sam?'

'I tried, but he as good as told me to mind my own business.'

'And you accepted that?'

'No. Well, not the attitude, but once I managed to get him to drop the smart-arse tone, he told me he'd apologised.'

'Kay didn't say anything else?'

He groans. 'She said plenty. She implied...' He hesitates.

'What?'

'She suggested that the atmosphere here might be a bit...' He gives a weak laugh. 'How did she put it? Loose?'

I feel myself redden and try to swallow the ball in my throat. He frowns at me. 'You OK?'

'Loose?'

He bats it away. 'You know Kay. She's in Ireland. Church every Sunday and God forbid anyone should have a good time.' But his eyes won't meet mine and I know that he's more bothered by this than he's letting on. 'I've been summoned by Pip to discuss the matter. Lunch tomorrow. Can't wait.'

'What are you going to do?'

He shrugs. 'Eat, listen to the lecture.'

'About Sam.'

'What else can I do? I've talked to him. Told him to be a bit more respectful, but he hates the guy, thinks he's a free-loader. You know how boys are with their mums.'

'I don't, actually.'

Jonty watches me for a moment. I can't read his face. 'No teenage boy wants to think his mum's having sex. He'll get over it.'

I sip my wine wondering what Kay meant by 'loose'. There was a time when Jonty and I would have laughed that off, but it's not so easy now. Was she referring to me and Jonty? Or me and Sam?

On Monday I work late and send Sam and Jonty a text to eat without me. I want to spend time with Sam, to talk to him about Nell, about Ireland, but that would mean having to discuss what happened with his mum and Connor and neither of us wants that. Jonty will be in a pig of a mood after his lunch with Pip and I'm in no hurry to find out what she said to him. Besides, I have other things to think about, like the pregnancy test I've bought and shoved to the back of the kitchen drawer where we keep the batteries and matches and things we seldom use. I haven't found the courage to use it yet.

The rain has come and gone in bursts all day. I head out between showers. The pavements reflect the lamplight in yellow puddles. The Red Lion is right on the market square and best placed for anything we might want to do inside on St George's Day, which, given the way the weather has been recently, would be a good idea if we're to prevent a repeat of last year's washout. But Nigel is predictably less than enthusiastic. 'So you want to have this event of yours in my pub?'

I want to remind him that this isn't *my* event; it's a community event, something that will boost the local economy and directly impact on his business, not to mention providing everyone with a bit of fun, but Nigel doesn't do fun. The way he sees it, I'm just another one of those interfering off-comers with big ideas, creating more work for him. 'I'm thinking an open mic session,' I explain as I dig out the money to pay. Everyone likes their five minutes on stage and will drag family and friends along for support. 'I can make sure there's at least one or two local professionals performing, to provide some high-quality entertainment.'

'You paying for that?'

'I'll call in some favours.' I take a slug of wine and immediately regret it. My stomach lurches. 'There could be a lot of people and it will be about this time of the evening. They'll be looking for something to eat.'

He nods towards the restaurant area. 'They can book a table.'

'There's only so many you can accommodate in there, and I was thinking something they can hold in their hand...'

'There's the chippy.'

I suddenly feel exhausted. I seem to be the only one who wants to see this thing happen. I'd get paid the same if I did the bare minimum. I can hear Jonty's voice in my head: *a school parade, a photo opportunity in the square, the mayor saying a few words and everyone goes home.* I make a few suggestions about food, but Nigel cuts across me. 'You got a PA and that, for this open mic thing?'

I want to punch him. I go to take another sip of wine, but the smell makes me gag. I put the glass back down and sigh. 'I'll sort it.'

I can smell dinner when I walk through the door, something rich and meaty. The table is set with candles burning, Jonty's favourite Rat Pack CD is playing in the kitchen and he's sashaying between hob and sink, a pinny wrapped around his waist, singing along in that deep, resonant voice. He smiles when he sees me and holds out his arms, trying to waltz me around the tiny space, and though I'm still in my coat and I'm tired and the smell is making my stomach heave and the drawer with the pregnancy kit scratches for attention like a persistent and irritating rodent, I give in to the dance, because it's a relief after all the rage and gloom and doubt. This is the man I fell in love with. This old-fashioned charmer who is more Bowie's era than Sinatra's but enjoys a bit of romantic nostalgia now and then. I'm so grateful that Pip hasn't got to him, that he's not turned into Nigel, that he's open and cheerful and full of possibility again.

'What's all this in aid of?'

'Thought you deserved a bit of TLC.'

I reach up and pull his face towards me, planting a kiss on his soft mouth. He tastes of garlic. 'Thank you. Where's Sam?'

'Gone to see a film with Fi.' That's good. If he's out with Fi he might be back to his usual self.

Loopy is at the window. She sits up suddenly, tail wagging and slides off the window seat, padding up to the front door just as the doorbell rings. Usually she throws herself at anyone approaching the house. I'm intrigued. Jonty hands me his glass of wine. 'I'll get it. You sit.'

I take a slurp and, hearing the surprise in Jonty's voice, follow him out to the hall. It's Rebecca. Loopy is rubbing herself up against her ankles while Rebecca makes a fuss of her. Seeing me, she holds up a bottle of wine. 'Hi!'

I glance at Jonty. He doesn't look too keen. Normally he would have invited her in by now; he's not the sort to keep people on the doorstep. I'm tired, but I don't want to hurt her feelings. She's watching me, hopefully. 'I felt bad when you left the pub so abruptly last week. You haven't wanted to meet up since. I hope I didn't say anything...' She pauses, watching me. '... to offend you?'

'Of course not.' And I have to invite her in, because I'm frightened of what she might say if I don't.

Seeing the candles, Rebecca says, 'Are you about to eat?'

And Jonty, charming as ever, says, 'Would you like to join us? There's plenty.' I expect her to decline, but she agrees. So much for our romantic meal. She sits down at the table and opens her wine while Jonty dishes up.

She asks, 'Is Sam not eating?'

'He's out.'

'Where?'

'He's gone to see a film with Fi.'

'Fi?' She's watching me, trying to read more into this, the way she did in the pub. I shake my head. She leans in, glancing back to make sure Jonty can't hear. 'Have you told him yet? About the...' She holds up her thumbs and forefingers pinched together as if she's displaying a pair of panties. I glare a warning. I don't want this conversation, not here, not now, not ever.

Jonty brings the food to the table. Rebecca is all smiles and compliments. There's a deep bowl of stroganoff with rice for us to serve ourselves. It looks amazing, but my stomach is lurching. I dish up plenty of rice and the smallest spoon of sauce I can get away with. At least with Rebecca to share, it takes the attention off me.

She asks how things are going at work and I tell them both about Nigel. About the open mic that no one knows about yet because I haven't done any publicity or had time to ask around, about the MC I can't afford to pay, about the PA and speakers I need to borrow and then transport and set up and de-rig again, and about how it seems that no one else wants this event to happen except me and I don't want to do it any more.

Rebecca is sympathetic. 'You need help.'

'Tell me about it.'

'You need a strategy.' Like I don't have strategies. But hey, if Rebecca thinks she can organise my life for me, she can go ahead. She sits up straight, upbeat and infuriating as a fitness instructor. 'Break it down into tasks. First the performers. I can put a notice on my Facebook page about the open mic, and you can ask Sam to do the same and ask friends to share it. Perhaps this Fi will help? You might not have people signing up in advance, but they'll turn up on the night, I'm sure. And we can ask Nigel to put a poster up in the pub.'

'I asked him. He as good as said no.'

She gives me a little smile. 'He'll do it.' And I have to accept, he will do it for her.

Jonty pours another glass of wine. He says, 'Leave the open mic to me. And the transport. Sam said Fi's dad's got a PA. I'll talk to her and sort it out.'

I'm grateful, and I tell him that, but I can't help feeling needled that he didn't offer to help until Rebecca shamed him into it.

We keep a pile of recycled paper held together with a bulldog clip on the table for lists: shopping, jobs that need attention around the house, notes to say we've popped out. Jonty pulls a clean sheet from the bottom of the pad and places it on top, picks up a pen. 'Right, what else needs to be done?' His eyes meet mine. Steady. Certain. He can do this.

'I need people to perform.'

'Rebecca's got that sorted with Facebook and I'll speak to a few people. We could ask Maria, the one who's sorting your banners, she plays the ukulele.' I watch him write down *Van – call Adam*. And *PA – Fi*.

I glance at Rebecca, who's watching Jonty. She turns to me and throws a wink as if everything is just how she planned it. She can manage people, I'll give her that. I carry on. 'Food. People will be hungry and if we don't provide food we'll lose them. I suggested something simple they could eat with one hand. I was thinking nice artisan buns with pulled pork and coleslaw.'

Jonty raises his eyebrows. 'Pulled pork?'

'We had those buns at Kendal Calling last summer.'

'That was Kendal, love. You suggested pulled pork to Nigel?' He roars with laughter. 'Nigel Jackson wouldn't know pulled pork if it jumped up and bit him on the backside!' Rebecca smiles.

'It was just an idea.'

'I'll organise the food,' he says firmly.

'Not cheap and nasty. Not multipack frozen burgers on cotton-wool buns.'

'OK, I get it.'

'And we need an MC.'

'I can do that.' He looks up. 'Unless you can think of anyone else?'

I picture Jonty in front of the microphone. He's used to public speaking. He's introduced events before, he can tell a good story and entertain a table at dinner, why not an audience in a pub? I think he could do this. I'm absurdly grateful to him for offering. I find myself nodding and already I'm feeling better. 'You'd do that for me?' I touch Jonty's face, his lovely, gentle face, the soft flesh around his eyes. 'You'd be all right with that?'

'Yeah. Why not?' He hesitates. 'It's not like I've got anything else to do at the moment.' A brief pause. He glances at Rebecca and flushes. 'I'll just organise everyone to get on and off, introduce them, thank them. Should be fine.'

'I haven't got anything left in the budget.'

He laughs. 'You'll have to find some other way to show me how grateful you are.'

I love this man. This great, loving bear of a man. When he's in a mood like this I feel safe. Cared for. Cherished. I imagine him with a baby in his arms. Our newborn. His face bowed over it, big hands teasing out those miniature fingers.

He could do this. But then I think of Sam and Nell, fifteen and ten, holding hands in the hall, watching me, waiting, uncertain. Jonty is fifty-three; if we have a child now, when that child is fifteen and angry and fighting for their space in the world, Jonty will be in his late sixties. How would that work?

We eat our meal, sharing awful stories about grumpy Nigel and various disasters that have occurred during previous festivals. As I clear the plates, Rebecca asks, 'Is Fi Sam's girlfriend?' I turn back. She's directing her question at Jonty. He shrugs.

I say, 'They're just good friends.' I thought I'd made that clear.

'Does he have a girlfriend?'

She gives me a smile. What is she doing? Is this her way of getting Jonty to talk about Sam? It might help, to approach it through someone else, to open the subject up at least. She got Jonty to take the event seriously and knuckle down. It's worth a shot. 'I think there is a girl, at school.'

'Girlfriend?' Jonty grins. 'Well, well, well. It's about time.' He raises his eyebrows and takes a drink.

'It's about time *what*?' But Jonty just gives a dirty chuckle and I can't help myself. 'Gets his leg over?'

He stops laughing. His eyebrows knit together and I'm aware of Rebecca watching us. 'Lizzie, lighten up, will you?'

'What are you saying? This is your son you're talking about.'

'What's the problem? He's seventeen. That's what seventeen-year-olds do.'

He glances at Rebecca. She avoids his eyes. I watch them. Neither will look at me. 'What's going on?'

Rebecca stands up. 'I should go. The meal was delicious. Thank you.'

'Have you two been talking about this?'

But Rebecca keeps walking towards the hall. I look at Jonty. His face is pink. His eyes are focused on the table. Loopy follows Rebecca out, tail wagging. Loopy is never like this with strangers. She barks when they arrive and then sits, watchful, giving quiet growls of warning to keep them on their toes. 'I'll catch you later in the week!' Rebecca calls breezily as she sees herself out.

Jonty and I sit in silence. I can hear the fan oven cooling, the buzz of the fridge. The CD finished a while ago and no one thought to put another one on.

'Has she been here before?'

Jonty frowns. 'Rebecca?'

'Yes, Rebecca.'

'Not as far as I know. Why?'

'Did you see the way Loopy was with her?'

He shrugs. 'So she's good with dogs.'

'Loopy is never like that with anyone until she's got to know them.'

He's silent, watching me. 'What are you saying?'

But I can't say it out loud. If I say it, I give it substance. 'Have you been talking to Rebecca about me?'

'Not really.'

'What does that mean?'

'She's worried about you.'

'Worried?'

'She thinks it's too much responsibility. She's just looking out for you.'

'So it was *her*. That's why you suggested I move out?' I

thought it was Matt, but all the time it was Rebecca feeding his insecurities.

'Lizzie, you need to back off. Give the boy some space.' He shoves his chair aside and goes into the kitchen to start washing up. I follow him, but he bats me away. 'I've got this.'

I don't want to leave it, I want to challenge him about Rebecca, I want to find out what's really going on here, but I'm scared. That dark figure that's been crouched at the periphery of my thoughts is crawling closer. I don't want to look at it. Jonty thinks I'm bad for Sam. That I need to keep away from him. That I'm responsible for whatever it is that's troubling him. Rebecca thinks it, Kay thinks it, Pip thinks it. I hover, tearing at my lip. 'I just worry about him.'

Jonty looks round sharply. 'Are you sure that's all it is?'

'What do you mean?'

He shakes his head and turns back to the washing up. 'I don't know.' I don't say anything else, because I'm frightened of where this is heading and I don't want to go there.

Chapter 20

The crowd is huge. It's overcast but it isn't raining and everyone is in town. St George has rescued the damsel relatively quickly, thanks to some prodding from the dragon, who is now posing for photographs with lots of delighted children. The town band, huddled beneath the unnecessary gazebo, plays on. Jonty has gone on ahead to the pub with Sam while I wait for the band to complete its final number. I take the mic, thank everyone for their support and invite them to go on to The Red Lion for further entertainment and food. I have no idea what that food is going to be. Jonty got quite cross with me last night when I tried to pin him down about the catering. 'Lizzie! Let it go! I said I would sort it. What's the point of me helping you out if you won't trust me to do it?' He's got a point, but that doesn't stop me worrying. I'm sure I heard him mention hot dogs to Sam and I can't help picturing puce frankfurters in white finger-buns.

After the uncomfortable conversation on Monday night, we've all been madly busy pulling things together to make today a success. Jonty has remained determinedly positive, his phone pressed to his ear constantly, driving here and there, picking things up, dropping them off, barking instructions at Sam, who's been willing and cheerful for the most part. I've kept my distance, not wanting to do anything that would give Jonty or Pip cause for concern. I feel like I'm walking a tightrope with everyone waiting for me to slip. It's awful seeing Sam working so hard to make amends and not being able to respond with any real warmth, but I have to tread carefully.

As I approach I smell a barbecue. There's a Cath Kidston-style floral canopy erected at the entrance to the pub and a trestle table covered in a matching oilcloth. Behind it stands Sam, sporting a crisp white apron, and next to him, commanding people to form an orderly queue, is Pip, looking like a wartime land girl with her hair pulled back in a spotty scarf complete with forties topknot. This is perfect! Sam lifts a sizzling coil of Cumberland sausage. Of course! Why didn't I think of that? Pip holds out a slice of French stick in a gingham napkin, recommending her home-made chilli jelly, making sure everything is presented beautifully. This is so much better than what I'd hoped for. Pip is here. She's helping. She can't be too angry with me if she's agreed to help at my event. I blow her a kiss of gratitude, but she's too busy to notice.

Jonty is inside. A stage area has been cleared to the right of the bar, in front of the vast fireplace. Thankfully the fire hasn't been lit; once people start gathering in here it will get very warm. The mic and speakers are in place and I can see a list of acts scrawled in Jonty's boxy print across a sheet of paper on the mantelpiece.

I can relax, it's all under control. No one is pestering me, there appear to be no crises to avert and everything seems to be going to plan. Jonty, Sam, Pip, our family, are all here, all supporting me, all cheerful. Everything seems perfectly fine. I've been tired, stressed, reading too much into everything. I need to lighten up and enjoy this.

I don't know what to do with myself, so I go to the bar to buy a round. A pint for Jonty, a gin and tonic for Pip. Not wanting to take any chances with Nigel's licence, I order lime and soda for Sam and Fi and the same for myself. Balancing the drinks on a tray, I look around for a place to sit and opt for a long bench near the stage area so Jonty can join us between his MC-ing. As I place his beer on the mantelpiece, he gives me a distracted thumbs-up.

Rebecca, a long-stemmed glass of white wine in her hand, slides into the seat beside me. 'Hi! You don't mind if I join you, do you?'

I hesitate. I do mind. I mind that she's here at all, which isn't kind, but this is my moment and her being here spoils it. She's been talking to Jonty. She's been causing trouble between us. I don't want her sitting here. What if she says something inappropriate to Sam and he finds out I've talked to her and betrayed him again? My face burns with the shame of it. 'There's five of us.' I look doubtfully at the bench.

'Oh, I'm sure one more little one won't make much difference. Are you going to be performing anything?'

I shake my head. I had thought about finding a poem to read, but forgot all about it and I don't know anything off by heart. Judging by Jonty's list, there are enough acts without me having to participate. She nods and smiles, as if she's keeping an exciting secret, but I don't ask what she has planned. I wait for her to say more, but she takes a sip of wine and looks around the room. There are people flowing in, seeking out the tables, filling the space with a lovely warm buzz of expectancy and I'm so glad I persisted with this idea, so glad Jonty came on board, so grateful to this man who is currently greeting people he knows: slaps on backs, handshakes, kisses, lots of laughter. I'm not going to let Rebecca spoil this for me.

Seeing the mayor, with her family, I make my excuses to go and say hello. By the time I return, Rebecca is back at the bar. I sit and enjoy a moment to take it all in. This is why I do the job: this gathering of everyone, this family that's created from a community, the cheerful faces, this sense of possibility. I catch Jonty's eye. He nods, raising his glass and mouthing, *Well done!*

Pip appears first, face flushed, tugging the scarf from her sweaty head. For the first time I notice the papery texture of her skin, the heavy folds of flesh that droop over her eyes. I shuffle up, leaving a gap at the far end of the bench for Jonty. 'You look exhausted.'

'And you look delightful!' I'm wearing some of the make-up Rebecca recommended and the leggings with the net petticoat. Pip gives a little shake of her shoulders. 'What fun!'

Sinking down beside me, she rubs at her swollen knuckles, and seeing my concern insists, 'Nothing that a hot bath won't cure. Is this for me?' She picks up the gin and tonic and takes a sip, looking around. 'What a super event, darling. You should be proud of yourself.'

'It's thanks to Jonty, really.' But Pip isn't listening. She's seen someone she recognises.

'Well I never! There's Louise!' She waves towards the bar and I see Rebecca hesitate. She probably assumes Pip is waving at her and is confused, but then she turns on her full smile and walks towards us. I look at Pip, who is saying,

'Lizzie, darling, this is Louise, the young woman I was telling you about. Who's writing the book about Chimneys?'

Louise?

Rebecca smiles at me, a calm, reassuring smile. 'We know each other, Mrs Mitcham.'

She's been visiting Pip in Windermere?

She sits down. 'Lizzie knows me as Rebecca. Louise is actually my middle name. I use it for my non-fiction writing.'

Before we can say any more, Jonty takes the mic and welcomes everyone, encouraging last-minute orders at the bar as the entertainment is about to start. Pip makes her excuses. 'Forgive me, but I should pay a quick visit to the ladies.' And Rebecca, agreeing that this is a good idea, follows her.

Sam appears a few moments later, jostling cheerfully with Fi, who is forcing the damsel's blonde wig on his head as he tries to squirm away. It's good to see them relaxed with one another again. Sam shuffles in beside me and I give his knee a quick squeeze and lean across to compliment Fi on her performance in the square earlier. She shrugs it off, avoiding eye-contact. I have apologised for what happened, and she and Sam have made it up, but she's not forgiven me yet. I'm surprised; Fi isn't usually one to bear a grudge. I decide to try and catch her alone later and apologise again; I want to put this right.

Glancing at the bar, I catch sight of Rebecca watching us. I thought she was going to the toilet, but it seems she changed her mind. She makes no move to come over. I could call her, make a space, but I don't want to. Pip returns from the bathroom and reclaims her seat.

Jonty is a brilliant MC. I think he surprises himself. The crowd love him. His jokes roll out easily. Sam roars with laughter beside me, cheering his dad on and Jonty beams with pride. He's good at this. He knows who to pick out and how far he can tease them. He's cheeky but just on the right side of respectful towards the mayor, who takes it in good part. I know they've come to blows over arts funding at council meetings before now and he believes she's behind his redundancy, but he's not going to let that spoil the evening. The open mic is fun. There are one or two kids playing instruments or reciting poems, old Mr Lancaster telling one of his ghost stories, the a cappella girls Sam recommended, with their beautiful, haunting voices, Maria, who is a comic sensation with her ukulele, and a few local poets. Jonty thanks each of them and gets them on and off efficiently and then he signals in our direction. I feel Sam getting up beside me. Fi and Pip have to slide out to let him pass. Jonty is leaning into the mic, his voice low and full of portent. 'Now, ladies and gentlemen, if you could put your hands together for… Mitcham and Son.'

The crowd clap. Sam approaches the mic. He picks up his guitar and slings the strap over his neck. He's going to play! He doesn't look up. I can see the flush at the base of his throat rising. His hands are trembling. He strums a few chords. Now Jonty is picking up his guitar. Jonty and Sam! And they're starting to play! And I know this introduction, this song, it's a favourite of Jonty's. He's played it to me in the car and sung along as we've driven out on the winding road to Coniston. An old folky number. I can never remember who sings it, but this is *my* song, the song Jonty sings to me, and now they're both singing it, father and son, together.

I'm stiff in my seat. I can't move. Something inside me is

growing, like a balloon, and I'm frightened it might burst, but I don't want this to stop. I never want this to stop. This room, this community, and the two men I love standing there in front of me, their beautiful voices filling the air; Sam's voice, so soft, almost a whisper, climbing, wrapping itself around Jonty's deeper, darker notes. The two of them. Singing my song.

On it goes. And they're looking right at me, they're singing to me and I can feel people watching and I will burst with this. I will burst.

And suddenly, between verses, I glance towards the bar and I see Rebecca, smiling. There's something knowing about that smile, something private. I scan the crowd. A few people catch my eye and grin. They know that Jonty's singing to me, but Rebecca does not take her eyes off the stage. She doesn't acknowledge me once. It's almost as if she thinks the song is for her. I scan the crowd again, smiling back at friends and neighbours, who all understand what this is about, and then I see Fi, glaring at me. Her face is pinched. She flushes crimson and she turns away.

Sam hesitates mid line. He's looking right at Rebecca and he's stopped singing. His fingers hover for a moment on the strings. I swallow, my throat dry. The moment seems to stretch like elastic that will snap at any moment. Then he turns away, dropping his head, finding the chords, continuing to play while Jonty sings on alone.

Fi is watching me. She knows something. She understands why Sam's upset. Jonty picks up the next verse. Sam's eyes find me. Anxious. They flit to Rebecca and then back to me. There's something wrong here.

Sam continues to accompany Jonty on guitar, but he doesn't

sing another word. The audience assume this is how it's meant to be. It was almost seamless, the way Sam pulled back. But I know. I saw.

Applause. Whistles. I can't move. I should get up and thank them. My boys. They're smiling at me, they're holding their arms out towards me, indicating to the audience that this song was for me and, for a moment, this is all that's important. I get up. I don't know how I get through the crowd, but I reach them, Jonty's face folded into that loving smile. All he's done for me this week. I put my arms around his neck and pull his face to mine and I kiss him, right there, in front of everyone, while the crowd whistles and shrieks and I am so grateful to him right now and so full of love and I will not let her spoil this. I pull away to thank Sam, but he has his back to me, doing something with his guitar and beyond him I see Rebecca, talking urgently to Fi. She catches my eye and her face breaks into a smile so wide and warm I'd almost believe I'd imagined it all, if it wasn't for Fi's stricken face.

Rebecca steers Fi away, into the crowd. I wasn't aware they knew each other. Fi's clearly upset. She's chosen to confide in Rebecca rather than me. That hurts, but at least she's confiding in someone. Maybe that particular song is significant. She has been looking strained recently. Things are probably kicking off at home and she's avoiding me because I know too much. I remember how that used to feel; the shame, wanting to keep things private. It's a question of pride; I mustn't take it personally.

Sam returns to the table while Jonty continues to MC. 'Next up: Rebecca Watts.' Sam stops dead in his tracks. He scans the room. Rebecca is nowhere to be seen. Jonty waits, calls her once more and then moves on to the next act while

Sam slips on to the end of the seat next to Pip, too far away for me to reach him, but I can see him, eyes still searching for her.

Rebecca watching Jonty and Sam singing. Smiling, as if she thought the song was for her. Why would she think that? And Sam's reaction. The shock at seeing her. I remember the day in the priory grounds after we dropped off the banners, Sam's response when I told him Jonty and Rebecca were out sailing together.

I look at Jonty, face flushed and grinning, introducing the next act. Have I missed something? The conversation we had when we were out at Skelwith Bridge the other day, him suggesting I should move out, that he's too old for me. And the other night, when she came over, interrupted our dinner, Loopy, tail wagging, greeting her as if she knew her. Jonty's irritation. He told me she'd been talking to him about me, telling him she's worried about me.

Sam's phone buzzes with an incoming text. I watch him check the message and frown. Before I can speak to him he's up, slipping out through the crowd, away from us.

Chapter 21

Pip is not happy about the song. 'Darling, if you didn't believe me before, you must now. The boy is besotted, and who can blame him.' She looks me up and down. 'You look ravishing.'

'What are you saying?' My voice is harsher than I intended. Pip gives a little shrug. 'You think I dressed like this to entice Sam? Is that it?'

'No, no!' She places a hand on my arm, but I shake her off. I'm tired of feeling like I'm doing something wrong. Sam and I have something. I don't know what that is, I can't define it, but I'm sick of having to apologise for it. If he wants to sing to me, that's his choice and I should be allowed to enjoy that.

'He stopped singing,' I remind her, keeping one eye on the door. It's not like Sam to disappear when there's work to be done. 'It's Jonty's song,' I continue. 'He sings it to me. He will have chosen it and asked Sam to accompany him.'

Sam stopped singing. He stopped singing when he saw Rebecca. Why?

People are gathering their things, putting on their coats and the pub is emptying out. The diehards are heading back to the bar. Jonty has bought us all another drink and is busy winding electrical cables into neat bundles. He's refused to let me help; I'm to entertain Pip while he waits for Fi to find Sam.

Jonty wouldn't cheat on me.

He asked me to move out.

Pip is insistent. 'It was very intense.'

I don't want to listen to this. I look hopefully at Jonty, mouthing, 'Need any help?'

He comes over. 'Everything all right?' he asks, frowning at his mother.

Pip lifts her chin a little defensively. 'Everything is absolutely fine. Lizzie and I were just talking.'

'About Sam?'

'That song...'

Jonty takes a deep breath and leans in close. 'I told you!'

Pip turns her head away.

So I was right. She did talk to Jonty about her concerns, and it looks as if Jonty has defended me. Trickling relief; Jonty is on my side. He loves me. He wouldn't be defending me to Pip like this if something was going on with Rebecca. He straightens up with a nod towards me and then looks about. 'Where the hell is Sam?' He brightens as the door opens. 'Ah! About time!'

Sam strides in, his body clenched, face rigid. He doesn't look at me. Fi follows, slowly, a few paces behind, glowering. I try and catch her eye, but she slips into the seat the other side of Pip and picks up her drink, determined not to look in my direction.

Sam heads straight over to the nearest speaker and yanks

it up. Jonty shouts, 'Steady on!' and leaps forward. 'That's still plugged in!' Sam waits, the speaker in his arms, as Jonty unplugs it and coils the cable. 'What's the matter with you?'

'Nothing.'

'Get that into the car and come back for the other one. Fi? What do you want us to do with this amp?'

'You can leave it here. He can pick it up in the morning.'

'Can you clear that with Nigel, love?'

I follow her up to the bar and place a hand on her shoulder. She tenses and half turns. 'Are you OK, Fi?'

'Yeah, fine.' But her body is stiffened away from me. Something's wrong, but it's clear she isn't going to tell me anything now.

As I turn, Pip raises an eyebrow at Sam, who is carrying the speaker out to the car, furious.

'What's got into him?' snaps Jonty.

Pip hisses, 'Sexual tension,' in my ear and I want to scream. So much for our happy family moment. I pick up a guitar and feed it into its case. When Sam takes the second speaker out, I follow, painfully aware of Pip watching me, but to hell with her. He puts the speaker in the boot.

'What's wrong?'

Sam takes the guitar from me, opens the back passenger door, and slides it inside. 'We might need to do two trips. Or I could walk.'

'Sam?'

He looks at me through his hair.

'Where did you go?'

'It doesn't matter.'

I reach out, but he pulls away. 'Speak to me, love.'

'Just leave it.'

'You seem upset.'

'It's nothing to do with you.'

I wince. He could walk away, but he doesn't. It was all going so well, I don't want it to turn sour now. 'The song was beautiful. Thank you.'

'It was Dad's idea.'

'You have a lovely voice.' He looks down at his feet. 'Why did you stop?'

He doesn't lift his head, but I can see that muscle in his cheek working. 'It's Dad's song. For you. From him. It wasn't… it wasn't for me to sing.'

I want to reassure him, to put my hand on his arm, hold him, but as I step closer he turns and walks away from me, back into the pub.

***

I go up to bed ahead of Jonty and drift off to the sound of him playing the guitar downstairs. I have no idea what time it is when he finally comes up, but the sound of him moving around the bedroom stirs me. I lie with my eyes closed, swimming up from dreams, remembering Jonty and Sam, guitars slung across their chests, singing, performing together, father and son, grinning at me. The three of us; a team. It was meant for me, that song. There's no doubt it was meant for me. I feel this easy warmth surrounding me, cradling me. This is it, this is what happiness is, this man creeping around in the dark so as not to disturb me, fumbling for the edge of the bed, lifting the duvet so carefully and slipping in beside me, the weight of his body next to mine, the smell of citrus from the shower gel he likes, the rise and fall of his breathing. He trusts me. Even Pip with her dangerous misinterpretations cannot shake that trust. And I trust him. Rebecca may be trying to get his attention, she may have an agenda, but Jonty wouldn't do that to me. I reach a hand out and feel for his; big fingers wrapped around mine. Maybe a baby would pull us all closer together. It's not a conventional family, but then it never has been. Maybe it could work.

I turn towards him. He rolls over. I can feel his warm breath on my face. I wait, willing him to touch me. His fingers trace the outline of my hip. I shiver. His body shifts closer. Slow. Tender. Familiar. Home.

Later, as we lie side by side in the dark, I return to memories of the pub. Rebecca watching us from the bar. That expression on her face. Why did she leave so abruptly? Louise?

'Do you believe that all the time Rebecca was interviewing Pip at Chimneys, she didn't realise she was your mother?'

Jonty yawns. 'Why would she lie?'

'Jonty's an unusual name.'

'They were talking about the house; I don't suppose I got a mention.'

I'm not convinced, but I can't see any reason why Rebecca would need to lie. I rest my head on Jonty's chest. 'Why do you think she pulled out of performing tonight?'

'Changed her mind, I guess.'

'Did you see her, watching while you were singing?'

'My eyes were on you, sweetheart.' He kisses the top of my head.

But I can't leave it alone. 'She didn't look happy.' Jonty laughs. I sit up. 'Seriously. She looked... angry.'

'What about?'

'The two of you singing to me.'

Jonty pauses. 'Maybe Sam was singing to her?'

'*What?*'

'Have you looked at her?'

'She's my age!'

Jonty tilts his head a little to one side and studies me.

'What?' I ask, and he shakes his head, but the smile has disappeared. '*What?*'

'Nothing.' But I know what he's thinking. I sound jealous.

Chapter 22

I sleep badly, haunted by dreams of a shadowy figure following me through the streets of Tarnside. It's late, fog grey and there is no one else ahead of me or on the opposite side of the street. I daren't turn around. Slipping down a ginnel and along a hidden access lane, stumbling, feeling with my hands along the stone wall, I cut back on to Fell Rise, towards the cottage, but the street is dark. No street lamps, no lights in any of the windows. I hurry up the hill, but I can't see the cottage. Behind me I hear the footsteps. I run, trip on a loose paving stone and wake, rigid with fear, my heartbeat pounding in my ears. Beside me Jonty sleeps, gentle snores, oblivious. I snuggle into him and he stirs, but then rolls away from me and resettles. I sit up, turn on the bedside light and reach for my book.

Most of Sunday is spent in my pyjamas. Jonty brings me breakfast in bed with the newspaper, cooks a lovely roast and we take Loopy out for a long walk, but I'm still dragging my broken sleep behind me and he's preoccupied. Something is brewing, I can feel it. Sam keeps to his room. When he joins us for dinner, he's cool towards me and barely speaks. Everything was going so well last night and now here we are again.

Jonty insists on doing the washing up but allows me to dry. Sam leaves us to it and goes out. I don't know where and he doesn't offer any information. Something upset him last night. I know it was something to do with Rebecca. Maybe Jonty's right, maybe Sam does fancy her. But where did he disappear to? If he was embarrassed enough to stop singing, he wouldn't have dared to follow her. Maybe it was nothing to do with Rebecca. 'Do you think there might be something going on between Sam and Fi?'

Jonty balances a pan on the draining board. 'I doubt it. Why?'

'When they came in last night, they were both upset about something.'

He shrugs, clearly not interested. 'That a cappella group were really good. I was thinking about arranging a gig for them. If Nigel lets us use the pub, we could sell tickets.'

'What's going on with Rebecca?'

He stops abruptly, a dripping bowl in his hand. 'What do you mean?' His face flushes pink. I meant what did he think was going on for Sam, but now I'm not so sure. It's as if we're on ice that might crack at any moment. Jonty is waiting. The bowl drips into the washing-up water. I'm the one who has to make the next move, but I'm frightened. I search his face for clues, trying to work out why my question was so alarming. What *is* going on with Rebecca? Sam's reaction, that day at the priory when I told him Rebecca was sailing with Jonty, the look on Sam's face when he saw her at the open mic, that was fear. He was afraid. Does he know something?

'Jonty?'

'Lizzie, you have to leave this alone.'

'What? What do I have to leave alone?'

'She's a good-looking woman. He's a horny teenage boy.'

We're back to Sam again. Loopy gives a low growl. The fur along her back is raised. She walks over to the back door and starts to sniff. Jonty says, 'Let her out; she probably needs a wee.'

I open the back door and step outside. The bulb in the outside light has gone so the yard is an inky expanse, grey pooling into black. Loopy hurtles straight out of the gate and down the ginnel. I call her back, but she's gone. 'Jonty!'

He takes his time, wiping his hands on a tea towel as he comes to the door. 'That bloody gate! Why can't anyone shut it properly?'

My heart is bolting. 'There was someone here!'

'It'll be next door.'

'No, Loopy's gone after them.'

Jonty gives a whistle and we hear the responding patter of paws as she trots back down the ginnel, tail wagging. Jonty strokes her head. 'A rat maybe.'

'A rat?' I shudder. He heads back inside with Loopy at his heels, but I stay in the yard. The air is mild and the sky sooty with a few pin-prick stars between the clouds.

When Sam looked up and saw Rebecca last night, he recognised her. The way she was smiling. Something knowing. Familiar. It was Sam she was looking at, not Jonty.

Is Rebecca the 'girl' Sam's been seeing? But if that's the case, she would have said something to me.

The conversation I had with Rebecca in the pub last week, after the knicker incident. *You must have wondered what it would be like?* Has *she* wondered? *Is* there something going on? But she would have said.

Unless it's only just begun. Unless it was after I confided in her at the pub.

I feel a sudden cold deep in my bones.

The questions she was asking about Fi, about other girls; she was digging. I turn back into the kitchen. Jonty is wiping down the surfaces. 'Do you think there's something going on between Sam and Rebecca?'

Jonty sighs. 'For God's sake, Lizzie! First Fi, now Rebecca! Give it a rest!'

'But you said...'

'I said he probably fancies her. You're the one building it into something. What's the matter with you?'

I wish I could tell him.

On Monday I have a terrible headache and feel wiped out, despite my lazy Sunday. I achieve little in the office. It's like wading through sludge. Eve is at a big funding meeting and I'm holding the fort. The phone won't stop ringing, the printer gets jammed, some minor vandalism in the park and kitchen garden over the weekend creates a lot of fuss I could really do without, and I have to postpone my visit to the primary schools that are making flags for the parade.

I get home ready to collapse with a hot meal and a glass of wine, but Jonty is wiping down the kitchen surfaces. 'Did you eat without me?'

'I left a voicemail. I figured you were sorted and made myself some pasta. I can do you some now?'

I glance at the clock. It's nearly nine. I shake my head. 'I'll just have a cup of tea.'

'I'll make it. You sit down.'

The list pad is on the kitchen surface and Jonty has

scrawled *Cherry picker* across it. I slap my hand to my forehead. 'I completely forgot!' A contact of Jonty's has agreed to hang the flags for me on Friday night, in time for the early market shoppers on Saturday morning, but he's waiting for a contract. 'I have to do this now.'

'It can wait.'

Something about his voice. His focus. An urgency. I don't like this. 'OK, just let me go to the loo first.' I rush for the stairs before he can say anything else.

When I come out of the bathroom I hesitate on the landing outside Sam's room, in no hurry to go back downstairs. I don't have the energy for a heavy conversation with Jonty tonight. I knock, but Sam's music is too loud for him to hear me. He's not at his desk when I push open the door but sitting cross-legged on his bed, doing something on his phone. He looks up, startled.

'Mind if I come in?' I walk over to his bed and perch on the end. I feel so tired suddenly, and my stomach groans with hunger. I lower myself back, following the archipelago of damp stains across his ceiling. 'How was your day?'

A non-committal 'OK.'

I close my eyes, feeling my muscles slowly relax, and sink into the mattress. The duvet smells musty. 'You should strip this bed tonight.' He says nothing. 'Have you spoken to Nell lately?'

'Yeah.'

I wait for him to offer something more, but it doesn't come. I sit up. 'How is she?'

He doesn't look at me. 'She's OK.'

He knows what I need to hear; this is cruel. I can't help myself. 'Did she mention me at all?'

He shrugs. 'She said hi.' As if it's something he's offering to placate me. She didn't mention me. She doesn't miss me. I turn away and look out of the window into the night: the sooty outline of rooftops, a smudged moon. Grow up, Lizzie. She's a twelve-year-old girl with a life to live; she's too busy, too happy, to be thinking about you. I try and shake it off. 'I'm starving. Do you fancy fish and chips?'

He sighs and turns slowly to face me. 'You want me to go to the chippy.' It's a statement, not a question. He looks pissed off.

'I never said that.' But if I'm honest, I was hoping he'd offer.

I stand up, suddenly awkward. He used to be happy to chat. He walks over to his desk and starts to sort through a pile of printed handouts. 'I'm sorry.' I sound petulant. 'Sam, what's wrong?'

'Nothing.' He pulls out his chair and sits at his desk with his back to me. I've been dismissed.

Downstairs Jonty is waiting, perched on the chair opposite the sofa, a cup of tea on the low table. 'What is it?'

He waits for me to sit down. I laugh. 'This is all very serious!' But Jonty doesn't smile.

'I think you need to give notice to Dom at your cottage. I think you should contact him tonight.'

Tonight? 'But I thought… You told Pip to mind her own business! It's all been fine. The open mic… Why now?'

'We agreed to wait. You didn't need any more pressure last week.'

'We?'

'Pip and I. Kay was all for you moving out straight away, but we agreed that wasn't fair. You had so much on your plate already. We thought it could wait until after the event. I was hoping to give it another week, until the Flag Festival was launched, but I don't think we can leave it any longer.'

We, we, we. I'm not part of that 'we'. 'That's why you were all helping out?'

'We wanted to support you.'

'So you could hit me with this now?'

'We have to think about Sam.'

'That's all I *have* been thinking about!'

'But it's not your responsibility, Lizzie, it's mine. And Kay's. It's just for a couple of months. Until he's done his exams and left.' His face softens, but he doesn't come any closer to me. 'It could be good for you too? It'll give you some space.'

'I don't want space!'

'You say that now...'

'It's true!'

'How often have you been in that studio lately?'

'It's always like this at this time of year.'

'Lizzie, you're a young woman. You should be out there enjoying yourself.'

'I don't want to enjoy myself.'

His dark eyes hold mine. His voice is low, frayed. 'Why didn't you tell me?' My breath stops in my throat. I can't swallow. 'About Sam, what happened in the bathroom?'

So Pip has told him. I feel myself growing hot. What does he know? The lake, I told him about the lake, he was OK with that, and Pip has told him about the bath, but she doesn't know about anything else. I haven't told Pip about the other stuff. He's waiting for an answer. Why? Why didn't I tell him?

'I didn't think it was important. He was embarrassed. He didn't mean to walk in on me.'

'But you told Pip you were worried about the way he was behaving.'

'Because of what happened in Ireland, with Connor.'

'So why didn't you talk to me?'

The silence gathers around me like a deepening stain. 'I don't know.'

He doesn't look angry, I could deal with anger, he just looks suspicious, and that's worse.

'You can't do this!' It bursts out of me. Someone else's voice, not mine. I'm up on my feet and, inside me, something is gathering, forcing its way, erupting in a stream of words. 'You can't just dump your kids on me and then snatch them back when it suits you! It doesn't work like that! All this time you've not given a damn. As long as it didn't affect you, as long as you could just carry on with your life, you were happy to let me get on with it. Sam loves me! I don't know what's going on with him right now, but I know he loves me. And you know what? I love him. And we can't just turn that off.' Jonty stands up; he's moving towards me, but I pull back. I'm hissing. 'Some little tart starts whispering in your ear and suddenly you decide you want to be a parent? Fuck you! You can't wander back now and say you don't like the relationship I have with your son! I am not going to walk out of his life and give up! No fucking way!'

I storm into the kitchen, with no purpose other than to get some distance. I lean against the counter, trembling. What am I doing here? I thought we were a family, but I'm not part of this family. All this time I've been kidding myself that I belong, that I'm important, that I have a role to play alongside Pip, Kay and Jonty, but they don't need me. They don't want me.

The drawer. The pregnancy test pushed to the back.

And Sam? What about Sam in all this? Does he still love me?

I pull open the drawer. I might as well know the worst.

I can hear Jonty's low voice in Sam's room when I come out of the bathroom. He will be telling him I'm leaving and Sam will probably be relieved to hear it. I'm not welcome here. I run downstairs, grab my coat and slam the door behind me. The street is quiet. Golden lights glow in the windows. Cosy homes with proper families. Where do I go now? I head out to the tarn and Margaret Thwaite's bench, but the park at night is a dark collage of silhouettes and shadows, an alien monochrome world. All the colour and noise and heat has dissolved, leaving a chill quiet broken by slight, unfamiliar sounds. I tense, aware that there are things I cannot see, eyes watching me. I am not welcome here.

I sit on the bench and try to conjure Margaret, but I can't do it. It's as if the world has flipped and this is the underside of everything that was once familiar. All that was light is now dark, all that was warm is cold and all that was kind is cruel.

I am alone.

I scroll through my phone for Clare's number. I don't want to be here right now, but I have nowhere else to go. I need to talk to someone who's on my side, someone I can trust to sympathise and make the right noises and believe in me. Clare takes a while to answer and when she does her voice is slow, heavy, as if she's been asleep.

'It's Lizzie. Are you OK?'

She clears her throat. 'I'm fine. Just a bit knackered after the weekend.' Of course. She's been in Majorca. It will have been one long pool party: drinks on the veranda, watching the sun go down. I feel sick with envy. 'I went straight into work from the airport. Bad idea.'

She's too tired to listen to me moaning now. I let her think I called to ask about the weekend. 'Listen, I'll phone tomorrow, you can fill me in on all the gossip then.' And she agrees, yawning as she hangs up.

I sit looking out at the black gaping hole of the tarn, wanting to be back on the right side, back at the cottage with things the way they used to be, but that's not an option. Instead, I think about Sam, about the 'we' Jonty kept repeating. Jonty, Kay and Pip; they are Sam's family. Not me. He doesn't belong to me. He has his life to get on with and in the meantime I have my own issues to consider. I didn't need to see that thin blue line to know the truth; I'm pregnant. I'm no longer welcome here and I'm pregnant. Now what do I do?

Chapter 23

When Jonty asks me on Tuesday morning if I've done anything about the tenancy agreement, I make excuses, but he's persistent and it's humiliating to cling on like this. Maybe I would be better in my own space? If they don't want me, then to hell with them all.

I go to see Dom straight after work. The cottage looks bleak, spartan. There's an open fire, but the grate is empty. The room is lit by a harsh white bulb, there's a shabby sofa, a veneer coffee table that's seen better days, and little else. It makes me want to cry. Dom isn't too perturbed. He's been thinking about flying out to see his brother in Australia and might take the opportunity to stay over a bit longer. I wish I was flying out for an adventure and not stuck here, pregnant and discarded. If I tell Jonty about the pregnancy, will that change his mind? But I don't want to use that. I don't even know what I want to do about it yet.

On Wednesday evening I have a meeting of the volunteers to go through the plans for this Saturday's Flag Festival launch. I always do my best to make these events fun. We meet in the café in the evening, after it's closed, and I ask Colin, the chef, to leave something for us. He's inventive and generous, using the leftovers from whatever has been the dish of the day to create something simple and tasty. Tonight we have falafel with adventurous combinations of crunchy cauliflower, sweet potato, nuts and seeds, and coleslaw of raw beetroot and carrot, which I wolf down. I'm hungry after weeks of nausea. I do the maths. My last period was early January. I was at the town council meeting and had to pop out to get tampons. The Manchester conference was at the end of January. Saturday, St George's Day, was 23rd April, so that would be three months. Twelve weeks. I could be going for a scan now, passing that little black-and-white image around, basking in my news.

I am so far away from that place right now.

I have to make a decision soon.

I can't think about this now.

Fi is here, thankfully, though still spiky, but we're waiting for Sam. He wasn't at the house when I set off. I haven't seen him since he left for school this morning. I've been careful, aware that Jonty's watching me, afraid that anything I say or do might be misinterpreted, and Sam is keeping his distance, cool with me, as if I've transgressed in some way. I'm worried about him. He's sullen and secretive, there are dark rings beneath his eyes and he looks like he's losing weight. Seeing him struggling and not being able to help is hell. Jonty thinks this is all to do with me, but I know it's more than that. I'm convinced Rebecca is at the heart of this, I just don't know what I can do about it.

I look down at my list and force myself back into work mode. I still have to go and talk to the butcher about his banner. He requested a lamb chop in the design, but the artist, a vegan and not inclined to literal interpretations, designed something more abstract which he's not too happy about. The festival started with a dozen banners, but over the years more and more businesses have come on board, to the point where not having a banner simply looks churlish. This year I have raised additional funds and have encouraged community groups to take part in a procession on Saturday morning, but it's been a real struggle with everything else that's going on. I feel bone weary with it all. Maybe it's time for me to go. What is there in Tarnside for me if I have no family? I came here on a short-term contract; if it wasn't for Jonty I'd have moved on to a city by now. If it hadn't been for the kids, I might be working on dramatic installations with metropolitan galleries, but I chose to stay here, with this family. This town, with its community park, the comfort of the surrounding fells, the crooked, painted cottages, is part of me now. The tarn, Coniston Water, Windermere, all that space and air and light; I don't know that I could live in a city any more.

Fi catches my eye and glances at the clock, pointedly. She's still being frosty with me. We have a bit of time, while people eat, but we should really start going through the list of things that need to be done for Saturday and allocating tasks. I ask her if she knows where Sam is. She shrugs, as if she couldn't give a damn. 'Did he mention the meeting to you today?'

'I haven't spoken to him.'

'Was he in school?' I haven't checked with Mr Wright this week, but if Sam has been skipping school again, Mr Wright would have contacted me.

'He was in, but I didn't speak to him.'

Fi is in Sam's history and BPE class and they see one another in the common room; if they're not speaking, something must have happened on Saturday night. Fi's face is pinched and there's clearly something on her mind, but we can't talk now; there's a lot we need to cover tonight and people are getting restless.

I text Jonty to see if Sam's popped down to the pub. Jonty is hosting a quiz for Nigel tonight and it's possible that Sam has gone down to support him. I'm pleased about the quiz night. Nigel suggested it on Saturday after the open mic. He was all smiles when he saw how busy the pub was (and watched the money going into the till) and was even suggesting that the whole idea had been his in the first place. The quiz is going to be a regular thing. There's no money involved, but it gives Jonty a purpose and allows him the limelight on a regular basis, which he'll enjoy.

Jonty texts back: *Haven't seen him.*

I start the meeting. I'm always so impressed by our volunteers, how willing and professional they are, how much responsibility they're prepared to take. There are more than a dozen here tonight and they range in age from Bill, who is eighty-two and slightly deaf but perfectly fit and enthusiastic, to Fi, the youngest at seventeen.

Sam doesn't turn up. Once everyone's been briefed, Fi takes the stewards off to go through the parade route and issue high-visibility vests and first-aid kits. The rest disappear into the kitchen to wash up but shoo me out, so I nip into the office to write some cheques while I'm waiting to lock up.

Fi comes in to let me know when people have gone. Usually she's fizzing with energy, cracking jokes, buoying everyone up, but tonight she's been grumpy and quite curt, particularly with me. Every time I've caught her eye she's looked away, but now she's hovering in the doorway. I get the feeling she's ready to talk, so I cut to the chase. 'Did something happen between you and Sam on Saturday?'

Her head darts up, face pink. 'Between *us*?'

'No, not that. I didn't mean…' But I did. She knows that I see through her shield: the blue hair, heavy boots and shapeless clothes. If she doesn't attempt to be pretty, no one can accuse her of failing, and yet she is attractive, striking, with deep blue eyes, a wide mouth and lovely skin, and when she's animated she's vibrant. A warrior.

'It's not me you need to worry about!'

The hostility in her voice startles me. 'What do you mean?'

She picks at the torn flesh around her thumb. The skin is raw. 'I saw them. Sam and Rebecca.' Rebecca? Sam and Rebecca? 'On Saturday, after the open mic.'

'What did you see?'

'He had his back to me.' I wait for her to explain, but my imagination is already there, creating a picture in my head. 'Kissing.' She glances up, cheeks alight, her expression a mix of pain and disgust. 'He was kissing her. He had her pinned up against the wall and he was kissing her.'

I don't know what to do with this information. I can't make it settle in my head.

'It's disgusting!' Fi's face is contorted with repulsion. She's hurt. And jealous.

'Fi, I know it's not…' I hesitate, not wanting to humiliate her but wanting her to know that I do understand. 'It's not ideal, but she's not much older than Sam. I don't really like her, to tell you the truth. I thought I did, but there's something about her. She reminds me of girls from school I learned to avoid. She's not the sort of person I'd like him to be with, but—'

'But she's his *teacher*!' A raspberry stain creeps up Fi's neck and covers her face. I stare at her. It's as if the words have landed awkwardly and broken on the floor around me. I stare down at them, pick them up, try and piece the bits back together, but they won't fit.

I stare at Fi, unable to speak.

Teacher.

'She started at the high school in September.' Rebecca is a teacher at the high school? 'She was at Sam's old school. I *told* you about her. When you asked me, at Easter, if there was anything bothering him at school.'

'That was a *teacher*? I thought it was a girl! Another pupil.' A teacher! Rebecca is a teacher. Not a writer. Not a freelance creative, but a teacher at the high school. A sudden image of Sam in the water, the day the boat capsized, the look on his face when he first saw her. That was fear. I thought he was looking beyond me to the boat, the lake, that something else was about to go wrong, but he was looking at her. He recognised her and he panicked. He was afraid. Why did he deny knowing her? Why didn't *she* say she knew him?

The pub. The makeover. The shopping trip. She never once mentioned her connection with Sam. If I'd known she knew him… I remember, with a sudden hot flush of horror, confiding in her about the knickers. *Come on! You must have wondered what it would be like?*

'Fi, are you absolutely certain it was *him* kissing *her*?'

Fi looks at me coldly, her voice low and dark. 'He wasn't like that before.'

'Before what?'

'He told me he didn't like her. He said she was…' She shudders. 'But now…'

'Now she's got him eating out of her hand.'

'You're a fine one to talk.' I feel the words like a barrage of stones.

'Fi?' She looks at me like I'm something soiled. Rebecca was talking to Fi in the pub on the night of the open mic. They know each other. 'What has Rebecca said?' Fear. So cold. I'm alone in a vast open space with no shelter.

'He's changed. He used to be kind, but he's not now. He's…' She shudders, choking back tears. Fumbling in her pocket, she pulls out her phone and starts scrolling through her messages. I assume it's another angry text, but when she taps the screen and hands it to me, it's an image. It takes a while to recognise what it is. The light is blue grey and the picture indistinct. A body. A close-up of a thigh, a dark mass of wiry hair. A penis. She says, 'Did you take this?'

'*Me*?' She stares at me, waiting. 'Fi, what is this?'

'Did you take it?'

'No! Of course not!'

'It's Sam.'

Pip's warning: *Be careful*. 'Fi, where did you get this?'

'He sent it to me.'

'Sam? He wouldn't!'

'Why not? Did you ask him not to?'

'Fi, where is this coming from? I don't understand.'

'Yes you do.' She has no trouble looking at me now and there is such loathing in that look.

'Sam sent you this image?'

'Last night. I messaged him to see if he wanted to meet up. I thought if we could talk… But…'

Sam sent her that image. The walls of trust I've built, brick by brick, crumble to rubble. No. Not Sam, not my Sam. 'Sam wouldn't do this. I know him. *You* know him, Fi. He's not like that.'

'He is now.' She snatches her phone, stuffs it into the pocket of her hoodie and walks out. I do nothing to stop her. I have no room for her anger right now, my head is full of Sam.

Rebecca is a teacher. She was at King James's School. She has known Sam for more than two years, since he was fifteen or even younger. This is why he's never had a girlfriend.

I remember his alarm at the mention of Rebecca's name the day we dropped off the banners at the priory. The outburst at Pip's. The truanting. When did he start skipping school? Mr Wright called me. It was a Friday. I grab my diary and flick back through. I remember I checked in with Mr Wright that following week to make sure Sam was attending again, and they broke up on the Thursday for Easter. He started truanting on Monday 14th March, and there it is, in my diary, for the Saturday before, scrawled across the page: *Coniston?* I was at work, talking to Eve about the weather forecast for the weekend and wrote it in to remind me to mention it to Sam and Jonty that night. Blue skies and sunshine. A Coniston day. It was Sam who suggested we go sailing. Perfect wind, apparently. That was the day we capsized, the day Rebecca sailed up on her board in her sexy wetsuit. She pretended she didn't know him.

He was scared of her.

He didn't go into school on the Monday. He was avoiding her. It was a cry for help. He doesn't want this.

The day at the lake, he was struggling to tell me.

I try not to picture what might be happening. I've read about grooming in the press, but I don't know if this is grooming. It's more complicated than that. The stories I've read were of pathetic male teachers and pretty girls who, in different circumstances, would have been out of their league. These were girls who were looking to break the rules and found an adult who took advantage of that. Or boys. I did read about a boy. I remember a photograph of a cheeky teenager, a chancer looking for his first sexual experience; the photograph alongside was of a drab, shapeless woman with a discontented scowl. But Sam is beautiful. Mature. Self-possessed. Confident. Sam could have any girl he wanted. And Rebecca is not pathetic or unattractive; she could have her pick of men. She doesn't need to do this. If Sam is sending dirty texts to Fi, if he's enjoying the attention, if he's driving this, then this isn't grooming. This is Sam.

I don't know what to do. I can't tell Jonty, he already thinks I'm a problem and this will only add fuel to his fire. I could go to the school, but I have no evidence and Mr Wright will just think I'm hysterical. I could go to the police, but I don't know what's happened, if anything other than a kiss has happened. Is a kiss illegal? I'd need evidence, and if I did show the police that image, they might want to talk to Sam, they might consider him responsible. I can't take the risk.

Fi has the image on her phone. The phone she's just walked out with.

Chapter 24

Jonty's still at the pub when I get back, though the quiz has probably finished. I should talk to him. Jonty is the parent; he'll know what to do. But when I call him to come home, I can tell he's had too much to drink and if I'm honest, I'm relieved. I decide to leave it until the morning when we can discuss things calmly and with a clear head.

He gets up before me and I smell bacon and eggs as I come down in my PJs. I can see he's making enough for all of us, but I don't think I'm going to manage a cooked breakfast this morning.

I'm about to say something when I hear Sam on the stairs. He slides into the kitchen, making the minimum noise, as if by remaining silent he might be missed. The image on Fi's phone is burnt into my memory. I try and blink it away, unable to comprehend how he could do that. Why did he do it? Didn't he realise what the repercussions would be?

He opens the fridge and stares inside it, as if he's waiting for inspiration. His T-shirt clings to the protrusions of his spine. His shoulders have broadened. His forearms are thicker. He was once so familiar to me, but he has another life away from me, relationships I've no part in, feelings and attitudes I'm not privy to. I wonder if I really know him at all.

'What happened to you last night?' I do my best to sound casual. He freezes for a moment. 'The volunteers meeting?'

He slams the fridge door. 'Sorry. Forgot,' as if he doesn't care. A different boy. A stranger in Sam's skin. I feel a sudden surge of anger. How dare he treat me like this! How dare he carry on with Rebecca behind my back. How dare he discard that precious, fragile thing we had and trample it so casually!

Jonty deposits a hot plate in front of me. The smell of the bacon is turning my mouth sour, the eggs look like sick. This is a challenge. He's in a tetchy mood, not just grumpy, more than that, sharper, a little frightening. I'm tensed, waiting for something I can't define. I glance up. 'Sorry. I think I've got some sort of bug. It's going around.'

He looks at me for a moment, as if he's waiting for me to tell him, but I can't speak. This is not a conversation we can have now. He takes my plate without saying a word and scrapes the food straight into the dog bowl. It was good bacon from the butcher, locally sourced; it won't have been cheap. He will have planned this breakfast. I feel wretched. He passes Sam a plate. Sam shakes his head. He doesn't have time for a cooked breakfast if he's going to make it to school.

'Take it!'

Jonty is holding the plate with oven gloves; Sam jerks his hand away with a yelp. 'It's hot!'

Jonty hesitates. He won't have meant it intentionally, but he won't apologise either. 'Don't be soft.'

'You could say sorry.' Sam sucks at his fingers.

I get the milk out of the fridge and stand between them, facing Jonty. 'How did the quiz go last night?'

'Fine.'

'What time did you get in?' As I speak I can feel something against the small of my back and I shift, assuming it's the label of my pyjamas.

Jonty says, 'Why?'

It takes me a moment to realise that it's not the label but something more substantial. I freeze. I can feel something against my flesh. My PJs are a little too big for me and sit on my hips, leaving a gap around the small of my back. Sam is touching me. He's slipped his hand inside the waistband of my pyjama bottoms. I move forward. He follows. I stop. If I do anything now and draw attention to what's happening, Jonty will notice. I wriggle a little, but Sam's hand remains where it is. Jonty is watching me. He's alert. He can sense something.

'I was just asking.'

Sam's fingers are cool against my flesh and moving slowly lower. Everything around me seems to have stilled and Jonty's eyes are flicking from me to Sam, and Sam's fingers are dipping down, hovering now, just above the crease between my buttocks and I am hot, so hot and my stomach is lurching and I have to do something.

I step forward briskly, escaping Sam's hand, push past Jonty and sit down at the table, facing them both. Sam is looking at me, an ugly, unfamiliar smirk distorting his face. I look at Jonty. His eyes are fixed on Sam. And he can see that look.

Sam turns to walk towards the door, but Jonty barks, 'Where do you think you're going?'

'School.'

'I've made you breakfast.'

'I didn't ask for breakfast.'

'What's going on here?'

Sam turns, alerted by something in Jonty's voice.

Jonty straightens his shoulders. 'You want to challenge me? Come on then. Let's see what you're made of.' He sweeps plates and paperwork to one side, clearing a space on the table, and motions to the chair opposite. 'Come on.' He rolls up his sleeve.

I can't believe what I'm seeing. Is he seriously challenging his teenage son to an arm wrestle?

Sam laughs. Jonty grins. It's a joke. He's having a joke. The relief I feel makes me want to slide off my chair and on to the floor. Sam comes back to the table, still laughing it off, but Jonty is determined. He's sitting down. He's bracing himself. Sam is half-hearted; he can't take this seriously. He raises his arm. Jonty shakes his head. 'That won't do. You've got to get yourself behind it.'

Sam laughs again, but Jonty's face turns, all the laughter squeezed out. He sits back, looking Sam up and down, eyes narrowed, as if he's measuring him. There's no warmth in that look. No affection. He glances at me and it's like a slap. And then he's back to Sam again. 'At your age I had a different girl every week.'

Sam shrugs. 'I'm not you.'

'I'm wondering,' says Jonty, warming up to something, 'I'm wondering if it's older women you go for?'

Sam flashes crimson. I can see his chest trembling as he breathes in and tries to maintain his composure. He glances at me and away again. I don't understand what Jonty's doing. I take a breath to speak to him, but he turns on me with such fury and something more, something alien, ugly, almost *distaste*, and I'm left speechless, gasping for breath.

Rebecca with her glossy hair and plastic smile. That image on Fi's phone. Pip: *You do realise he's in love with you?* Sam's hand sliding down my spine.

Jonty pulls his sleeve a little further up his arm and places his elbow on the table, fist clenched. This time Sam follows. Jonty grabs Sam's fist in his own. He's stronger. There's no doubt he'll win. 'Jonty, stop it. There's no need for this.' But neither of them are listening to me. I can't bear it; I have to get up, walk away. Sam holds his own, fuelled by rage. He's close to tears with the effort, the humiliation, the indignation, but he doesn't give in. It takes Jonty more force than he was expecting. There's a moment where they wobble and Jonty almost loses it, but he's bigger, more muscular, and he retrieves the advantage, slamming Sam's arm down on the table with a loud thud. The plates bounce. Sam shoves his chair back and crashes out of the room. I listen to the front door slam.

Jonty gets up, massages his forearm, rolls down his sleeve and looks at me, triumphant.

'What the hell are you doing? Fighting your own son?'

'It was an arm wrestle.'

'Proud of yourself?'

'What's your problem?'

'*My* problem? He's a boy. You're his father. You're supposed to be the mature one. You're supposed to be the one teaching him how to behave. What's got into you? You're fifty-three years old!'

'And he's seventeen.' He nods his head, cold eyes fixed on me. 'There's ten years between the two of you. Ten years. And twenty-six between you and me.' He stops, looking me up and down as if he's stripped me naked.

'What are you saying?'

I remember Sam looking at me in the bath, fingering my knickers, the ugly smirk just now. And I remember how it used to be: my hand resting in the small of his back as we walked under the umbrella from the cinema to the car, standing behind him and resting my chin on his head while laughing over something he was reading in the *Evening Mail*, reaching out to touch him, stroking his arm, rubbing his shoulder. I was being affectionate, but have I crossed a line?

Jonty is watching me. My face is red hot. I know what it looks like. There was a time when I would have laughed this off without a moment of doubt, confident that what exists between me and Sam is innocent, unique, something to be protected, but I'm not sure if that's the case any more.

I know what it looks like, but I can no longer say what it is.

Jonty's eyes are bloodshot and his skin droops around his jaw. He will have stayed at the pub late to drown his troubles last night, making the most of being quiz master, being appreciated, having some sort of status. I can't hold that against him, but he has to know about her. 'I think Sam's in some sort of relationship with Rebecca.'

He rolls his eyes.

'Fi saw them. On Saturday night.'

He dismisses this with a wave of his hand. 'Fi's a jealous kid. She's got a thing for him, it's obvious. What does she think she saw?'

'They were kissing.'

He looks incredulous. 'Sam? And Rebecca?' And then he chuckles. He actually chuckles. 'Well, bloody hell! Randy little sod!'

'Jonty!'

'What?'

'She's his teacher.'

He frowns. 'I thought she was a writer?'

'That's what she told us. But she's a teacher at the high school.'

There's a moment of silence. I let him think through this. All that time with her on the boat and she never mentioned she was a teacher at his son's school. 'This is wrong, Jonty. He's a child.'

'He's nearly eighteen. God, when I think of what I was up to at his age.' But he's still processing, trying to get it to make sense.

'That's not the point. She's a teacher. And he doesn't even like her!'

He frowns at me in a way that makes me itch. 'How do you know he doesn't like her?'

'He told me. He told Fi. She's the teacher who followed him from his old school.'

'*Followed* him?'

I hesitate. Did she follow him? Or was it coincidence? Did Sam say he doesn't like her, or was that Fi's interpretation? Has he actually said he doesn't like Rebecca?

Jonty takes a sip of his coffee and shakes his head. 'He's not a kid any more, Lizzie.' His eyes are sharp. 'You're going to have to get used to that.'

'She has a moral responsibility. He should be able to trust her to behave appropriately.'

'Has she behaved inappropriately?'

I hesitate. 'I don't know exactly. But I don't trust her.'

He gives me that look again, but this isn't about me. 'This is wrong.' He doesn't look convinced. 'If it was a man, if it was a male teacher and this was Nell, would you feel the same?'

He shakes this thought away. 'Nell is twelve!'

'If she was seventeen? And there was a teacher at the school who was... How old would you say Rebecca is? Twenty-four? Twenty-five? Nell. Picture it. Seventeen. He's twenty-five and her teacher.' The smile slides from his face. 'Is that OK?'

'That's different.'

'How is it different?'

But he can't answer that. I'm about to tell him about the sext when he says, 'I think Pip and Kay are right.' He shakes his head. 'Why doesn't he have a girlfriend his own age? Why is he more interested in a woman your age? This isn't healthy, Lizzie. It's messing with his head. We have to stop.'

'Stop?'

'You and me. Here. This.'

'But we're a family.'

He doesn't look at me. 'You can't go on living here. Not with Sam. You need to find a place.'

'I've given Dom notice. I'll be out in four weeks.'

He shakes his head. 'We need to find you something now.'

'You're kicking me out?'

'I'm asking you to leave as soon as possible. For Sam's sake.'

'But why?'

'Because you're the problem, Lizzie. The way you are with him. It's not right.'

'What have I done?'

'You're jealous. You can't accept that he's growing up, that he's interested in girls. It's not healthy. You have to go.'

Chapter 25

I would have walked straight out, to the park, the tarn, but I'm still in my PJs and the rain is hammering outside as if the entire world is furious with me right now. I sit on the bed and look around at this space Jonty and I have shared for almost three years: the original fireplace that looks lovely but can't be used because the chimney's blocked, the ugly flatpack wardrobe and featureless chest of drawers, the low futon with Jonty's pale blue bed linen. My clothes hang in the wardrobe, my hairbrush and make-up sit in a shallow wooden box. There is barely any evidence of me in this room. I can be swept out so easily. I used to think this was my family, my home, my safe place, but I was wrong. This is Jonty's house. Sam's home. Who am I to these people?

There was a morning like this, with the rain pounding outside and the sky so heavy with cloud we had to turn the lights on inside. It was a school day and Jonty must have had an early meeting because I was alone in bed, about to get up and chivvy the kids, when I saw Nell hovering shyly in the doorway. I thought she might be coming down with something. 'What is it, love?'

She gave a little shrug – Pip's shrug, I realise now; that quick twitch of the shoulders, not careless but impish. 'It's so dark and spooky!' She crept up to the bed. 'Can I get in with you?'

I lifted the duvet and she slipped in beside me, her body warm, her silky legs sliding alongside mine. She snuggled into me as I pulled the duvet tight around us, relishing the moment; a gift.

My phone is charging on the chest of drawers. I pick it up, find Kay's number, listen to it ring all the way across the sea in that other house that I can't picture. Kay answers brusquely, clearly in a hurry.

'What is it?' Her voice is sharp, anxious.

I glance at the clock. It's five to nine. 'Sorry, Kay, I didn't realise the time. I was hoping to have a quick chat with Nell...'

'Nell?' she snaps. 'She's gone to school. What's happened?'

'Nothing, I just...'

'Is Sam OK?'

'Sam? Yes, yes, Sam's fine. I'm sorry, I didn't...'

'Jesus, Lizzie! I thought something had happened!'

'No, no, I just... I was missing her.' I hear Kay sucking back the words. She will be rushing to get to work, trying to finish all those last-minute tasks. I can feel a sob gathering in my throat. Blurting 'Sorry,' I hang up.

The house is quiet. I don't know if Jonty's gone out and I don't feel I can go downstairs if he's still there. I get dressed in yesterday's clothes, listening. He's moving about in the hall. Whistling for Loopy, he slams the door behind him as if I'm not here.

I make the bed, Jonty's bed in Jonty's house, where I am no longer welcome.

Rental accommodation isn't easy to find in Tarnside and if it does become available it's snapped up. When you're a landlord, like me, that's great; when you're about to become homeless, like me, it's not so good. There are two possibilities so far: a room in a shared house with a woman in her fifties and her four cats, or a one-bedroomed flat in Barrow.

On Friday afternoon I drive out to Barrow to check in with Lorraine, the constable who's supervising the road closure for the Flag Parade tomorrow. Tarnside police station closed last year and is currently being converted into luxury flats, but sadly none of these are available to rent at the moment, even if they were in my price bracket. I make an appointment to view the Barrow property before I see Lorraine. It's nice enough: neutral decor and furnished, which helps. A leather sofa, Ikea cupboards, a small kitchen and a shower room. I could live there, but Barrow is a world away from Tarnside. It's a working town, dominated by the vast white sheds of the shipyard and the handsome red-brick architecture of what was once a Victorian new town. A peculiar mix of traditional and modern industrial on a spectacular stretch of coastline, it has its own charm, but it's hard enough thinking about moving out of Jonty's house; to leave Tarnside altogether would be unbearable.

I tell the agent I'll think it over and make my way to the police station, where Lorraine is waiting for me. I like Lorraine; she's long and broad like a sturdy plank of wood, with salt-and-pepper hair cut into a practical bob she tucks behind her ears as she leans over the paperwork. A 'can do' woman you can rely on to find a way to make things work. With my job, people like her are a lifeline. She doesn't think what I do is trivial or irritating and doesn't resent the extra work it generates. She doesn't live in Tarnside, but she appreciates the community spirit and believes it should be nurtured. This road closure couldn't have happened without her and I know she's had to do a lot of cajoling to bring her colleagues on board. She's recently raised the money for an arts project I'll run later in the year, working with young people who hang about the park and are 'at risk of offending' – basically, giving them something creative to do so they don't become destructive. She's proactive. There aren't many like her, but when I find them I do my best to hang on to them. I didn't have to come into Barrow this afternoon, all this could have been done over the phone, but it's important to maintain this relationship. Face-to-face contact matters. We deliberately arranged to meet at the end of the day, knowing we'd want to grab a coffee afterwards.

Lorraine takes me to a new café that's opened in the recently renovated Salvation Army building: glass tables and funky plastic chairs amid the cornicing and tiled floors. She suggests a power juice: 'Better for us than coffee.' I'm not so sure, but the waitress brings us two chilled tumblers of a thick green liquid which is surprisingly tasty. Lorraine fills me in on her latest family dramas. She's a single parent with two daughters whose father lives in London and compensates for his absence with extravagant gifts. The latest is a brand-new iPhone for each girl.

'Tilly is fifteen and beside herself with excitement; she's suddenly the cool kid in school and she's on it all the time, messaging her friends. Instagram, Snapchat. I can't prise it off her. But Flo is ten years old. She likes horses and climbing trees and still talks about "playing out" with her friends. What's she going to do with an iPhone? It's too much responsibility. She'll lose it or break it and then she'll feel bad. The man's an idiot!' She gulps her juice, pauses, takes a deep, exaggerated breath and composes herself. 'Sorry. Didn't mean to rant.'

'Go ahead. Rant away. You listen to me enough.'

'Does Sam have an iPhone?'

The image from Fi's phone flashes in my head. 'Not the latest one. It's not that big an issue for him. I think it's different for boys. The PlayStation was the thing with Sam for a while, but he seems to have moved on from that.'

'He'll be focused on his exams now, I guess. What's he planning to do next year?'

I tell her Sam's plans, but all the time that image on Fi's phone is there, hovering. 'I was reading this article in the paper the other day about sexting...'

She rolls her eyes. 'Oh God! Don't get me started. I've given Tilly the lecture, but there's only so much you can do. It's so common now. You'd be horrified. Do you know, we did a project in a local school and a lot of young people just view it as flirting? They don't realise that once they've pressed Send, that image is out there and anybody can get hold of it and do what they want with it and there's no getting it back.'

'Is it illegal to send a sext?'

'Oh yes! It's illegal to take, possess or share "indecent images" of anyone under eighteen, even if you're the person in the picture.'

'So if you receive a text you're breaking the law?'

'Yes.'

'But if you didn't ask for it?'

She holds her hands up and raises her eyebrows. 'It's a really difficult area.'

'So if Tilly received an uninvited sext from a boy, she'd be prosecuted?'

'Well, that gets a bit more complicated. Tilly is fifteen. Technically, anyone under eighteen is considered a minor and that brings a whole other set of issues.'

Sam is still seventeen. So is Fi. They are both minors.

The room is suddenly ice cold.

My stomach is churning. I grip the side of the desk and force my face to play the game. I cannot let her see the effect her words are having. Why did I do this? I was stupid to put myself in this situation. Act calm. Act dispassionate. I'm simply intrigued. This doesn't affect me personally. We're speaking in the abstract, not the particular.

'If you're under eighteen,' she continues, apparently not registering any distress on my part, 'the law sees you as a child. So, if someone has indecent images of a person under eighteen they're technically in possession of an indecent image of a child.'

'Even if they're the same age?'

'It's a criminal offence. Similarly, if you send a sext to a minor, you could be prosecuted and put on the Sex Offender Register.'

Sam could be labelled a sex offender. My stomach lurches. I swallow, but it somersaults, higher this time. My throat contracts. I'm going to be sick. I gulp then stand, scanning the room.

Lorraine is up, on her feet, pointing to the toilet sign. 'That way.'

She waits outside the cubicle as I vomit. I lean over the toilet bowl, my brain whizzing ahead, working out how to play this, what to say.

I emerge, wiping spittle from my face with toilet roll. 'Sorry.'

'Are you OK?'

She turns on the tap and I splash the cold water against my burning face, rinse my mouth, spit. Straightening up, I face her in the mirror. She hands me a paper towel and I dab myself dry. She's watching me, concerned. I have to say something. I decide to expose one secret in order to keep the other. 'I think I might be pregnant.'

She continues to watch me carefully in the mirror. She can tell this isn't straightforward. 'I was sick for six months with Tilly. Day in, day out. Flo wasn't so bad.' Her tone is matter-of-fact. Clinical facts, not bonding. We stand at the sinks, looking at our reflections. There's something comforting about this distance. Side by side, watching an image rather than the real thing. Intimate and yet safe. I can't face her and she doesn't turn to face me. I look down at my hands. They're brown against the white sink. I try to imagine my fingers against the smooth flesh of a baby. I turn my hands palm up to face me, cradling the empty air.

'Do you know what you're going to do?' I look up. Her face is kind. I can't cope with kindness. I blink back tears and then she puts her arms around me and pulls me close and I let myself be held, imagining her embracing her girls like this, feeling the support that seeps from her into me, the care. She says, 'Take your time.'

But I've run out of time.

Chapter 26

The cottage is quiet when I get in. Jonty has gone up to Ambleside to help a friend repaint his holiday let after some emergency building work between bookings. It's a relief to have the place to myself, away from all the brooding hostility for a while. I throw myself down on the battered sofa Jonty and I reupholstered, in a very makeshift fashion, one wet weekend, using a staple gun and yards of fabric left over from one of my community projects. I love this room: the bright, abstract rug that covers most of the floor, the little woodburner, Jonty's prints and paintings on the wall, and the old oak bookcase that came from Chimneys. All this history. It's the stories that make a home, the memories. The flat in Barrow is bare, no memories, but maybe that's what I need? The prospect makes me want to cry.

I head upstairs to the toilet. Sam's bedroom door is closed. I go into the bathroom and push the bolt across. Is he on his phone now, sending more dirty texts? Does he understand what he's doing, the risks? I have to warn him, whatever Jonty and Pip think. I flush the toilet and open the bathroom door, determined to speak to him before I lose my nerve.

Sam is standing on the landing outside his bedroom, naked.

I take a step back. He shrugs and walks towards me. Am I imagining it or is he actually swinging his hips?

'Sam! Get some clothes on!'

'I'm having a shower.'

'Well put something on!'

'Why?'

I turn and run down the stairs, my knees weak, and slip halfway down, landing on my coccyx with a reverberating thump that forces my stomach into my throat. I rest my head against the stairs, my heart banging, my entire body throbbing.

'Are you OK?' His voice is familiar, concerned, but I can't look up, knowing he's still naked, that he did this deliberately. He waited for me to come out of the bathroom and staged the whole thing. Who is this boy? What's happening to him?

I stand, gripping the banister, and make my way down the remaining stairs to the kitchen. I need to think. I need to work out a way to deal with this. Jonty's right; I have to get out of here, I'm in over my head.

I make a cup of tea. It slops over the edges of the cup as I take it to the table. Upstairs I hear the hum of the shower. The cottage feels stuffy, cramped. I open the back door on to the yard and take a cushion from the basket, placing it on the threshold to sit. The sky is streaked with white, gold and pink. This is usually my favourite time of the evening. The Scots call it the gloaming and it's a good word, the right word for me right now; all melancholy and endings.

The peace is shattered, brutally, by an invasion of starlings, their menacing shrieks gathering above me, admonishing, chastising. I have to warn Sam about the risks he's taking. If I leave it any longer, Jonty will be home and the opportunity will have passed. The shower has stopped. I give him time to return to his room and get dressed and then knock. 'Are you decent?'

A sullen 'Yes.'

He's dressed in shorts and T-shirt, sitting cross-legged on the bed with his telephone in his hand. He doesn't put it away and his fingers hover, ready to pick up where he left off. 'What?'

I hesitate and glance at the bed, but remembering what happened last time I sat there, I pull the chair away from his desk and sit on that. I feel a little like an interviewer, but this will have to do. His hostility permeates the air between us.

'Sam, I'm sorry about that day at the lake.'

He smiles that new, horrible, slow smile that makes him unrecognisable. It's a smile that knows things that are better left unknown. What has he been looking at on his computer, his phone? When he looks at me now, what does he see?

'I should have been more careful. I didn't think… I didn't…'

'You knew what you were doing.'

'That's not true!' But I think of Matt, in the canoe, the way my flesh burned with shame. 'It was a mistake. I didn't intend for this…' I don't know what to say, because I'm afraid now. 'I spoke to Fi.' I watch his face for clues, expecting embarrassment, but there's nothing. He waits. 'She says you sent her an image from your phone.'

A flicker of a frown. 'What image?'

'A photograph.'

He shrugs. 'What of?'

'You.'

'Me?'

'At least, I think it's you.'

His head tilts. A silent question, and then the penny drops. His face reddens.

'I need to see your phone.' I hold out my hand.

He hesitates and in that moment he's Sam again. He glances at the screen. He shakes his head. 'No.'

'Fi received an indecent image from your phone.'

'*What?*' He holds the phone away from him as if it's suddenly become toxic and I seize my opportunity, snatching it out of his reach and moving towards the door. 'Hey! What the...?'

'Sam, this is serious. You could be prosecuted and so could she.' Scrolling through the messages. Aware of him moving towards me. Where is it? Quick! I'm turned away from him, my back a shield. Texts. Words. No time to read.

He's behind me now, one arm on my shoulder, the other reaching around. 'Give me my phone!'

'If that image is on here you have to delete it.'

He grips my arm and pulls me around to face him, the phone in the air between us. He's too strong for me. 'There is no image!' Plucking the phone from my hand, he shoves me aside. I wait, holding my breath as he searches. He looks up. 'There's nothing there.'

'You're sure?'

'Yes!' But he doesn't offer me the phone.

'Sam, I saw it. Fi showed it to me.'

'She's lying.'

'I saw it!'

'That doesn't mean it came from my phone.'

I'm beginning to doubt myself now. I didn't check the image came from Sam's phone; I believed what Fi told me.

'Sam, are you in a relationship with Rebecca?'

He stares at me for a moment, as if I have no right to ask such a question. I've offended him. Then he gets up off the bed and slips the phone into his back pocket. 'What is it with you and Fi?'

'Sam, I'm worried about you.'

'Well don't be. Keep your dirty ideas to yourself and leave me alone.'

I call Jonty. 'What time will you be back?'

'We won't be finished here for a few hours yet. We needed to put a coat of damp-proof paint on the gable wall and that needs four hours between coats. It'll be after midnight before I can set off.'

I won't be able to talk to him tonight. I don't like the idea of him behind the wheel when he's this tired. 'Can you stay over and drive back first thing?'

'You'd like that, would you?'

His tone startles me. 'What's that supposed to mean?'

I can hear him breathing down the line. 'I'm sailing tomorrow.'

'But the Flag Parade…'

'Sorry.'

'With Rebecca?'

'Yes.' I let the silence vibrate between us. How can he be meeting Rebecca, after what I've told him? As if he's reading my mind, he says, 'It's a job, Lizzie. I've made a commitment.'

But it's more than that. I don't like him spending time with her. I don't want him to go. I haven't told him about the knickers incident. If she tells him, if he discovers there's more I've kept back, he'll never trust me again.

Tomorrow is a big day with the Flag Parade and launch of

the festival. If Rebecca tells Jonty, I'll just have to deal with that. I need to speak to Fi. I need to make sure that image is deleted from her phone. There is nothing more I can do tonight. I go to bed, doing my best to ignore the snarling voices in my head.

In the morning, I dash downstairs, too late for breakfast, to find Sam in the kitchen, pouring coffee from two cups into a flask. He wraps two rounds of toast in kitchen roll. He's set the table, made breakfast for us both. 'We can take it with us,' he says.

'You're coming?'

He nods. 'If that's OK?'

'Of course!' Sam's back! My Sam. I hesitate for a fraction of a second, but I can't help myself. Throwing my arms around his neck, I squeeze tight. 'Thank you!' Oh, the smell of him! The warmth! I could hold on to him like this for ever. But there is work to be done and Fi to deal with.

As we approach the market square I scan the huddle of volunteers in their high-visibility vests, but Fi isn't there. She's furious, with both of us; she'll probably keep her distance, if she turns up at all. Before I can think about it any more, I'm swamped by seventy children, several attending adults and a highly strung teacher, who has more participants than flags and wants me to do something to fix the situation.

Fi doesn't show up. The Flag Parade goes well enough. The community seem happy. Sam does a great job managing the stewards and generally jollying along the procession, but there is no sign of Fi. I keep thinking about that image on her phone, the hostility in her voice, the way she looked at me before she walked out, what Lorraine said about the implications for Sam. There's a horrible metallic taste in my mouth. I keep looking at Sam. My Sam. Happy, gentle, uncomplicated Sam. He wouldn't kiss Rebecca. Sam at the lake, splashing about in the freezing water. And Sam looking at me in the bath; his hands running along the lace of those knickers. I shove this from my mind. That's not him. He is not that boy.

Though the sun doesn't shine, the rain holds off, but the wind is quite strong and several of the banners get wrapped around their poles, spoiling the effect in places. The drumming band set a good pace, creating a carnival atmosphere, but the incessant banging is irritating and I just want it all to be over. Sam and I fall in behind to scoop up any stragglers on the way to the park, where the procession ends, children scattering to get ice-creams and let off steam in the playground. I try and immerse myself in the event, try not to think about all the litter I'll be clearing up this afternoon. The wind ruffles the surface of the tarn and teases the banners that hang from the main building. Yesterday I filled a wooden trough with sand so the children could sink their poles into it. I made a flag for Nell during one of the workshops, decorated with a turquoise unicorn, and placed it in the trough this morning. Now it's surrounded by thirty others, creating a ripple of colour along the perimeter of the stables. As I take a photograph I wonder if Nell still likes the colour turquoise. She's probably grown out of unicorns. Around me children are laughing, families out together, and I try to give myself up to this, to be grateful for Sam's presence, for his good mood, but there's this bitter taste lingering in my mouth.

I look round and realise that there's someone sitting on Margaret Thwaite's bench. Blue hair, purple boots. Fi. Sam hasn't noticed her and I quickly herd him towards the café, suggesting he offers to help in the kitchen, given the queue for food.

Fi's disgust crawls along the slats of the bench and up my spine. It's getting cold. The tarn is becoming a dark pool reflecting the heavy sky and we may have to run for cover any minute, but I need to hear what she's got to say. Parents call their children in, gathering up picnic blankets and bags.

I turn to face her. 'Do you still have that image on your phone?'

She shakes her head. 'I deleted it.'

This means I have no way of checking the details. 'You're sure it came from his phone?'

'He apologised.'

'Sam?' She nods. 'When?'

'He sent me a text this morning. Said it was a joke. Someone took it while he was asleep. They thought it was funny, but he didn't think it was funny. He said he'd sort it out.'

My throat is clenched. I can barely squeeze out the words. 'Did he say who took it?'

She shakes her head. She's watching me. I can see the doubt. She still thinks it was me. This is Rebecca's meddling. Rebecca has been talking to Fi, just like she's been talking to Jonty. Nasty little seeds of suspicion left to flower.

Fi says, 'I think that image was a message.' She looks right at me. 'Warning me off.'

I turn away. If I say anything I'll sound like I'm making excuses.

The swan that's been nesting on an island of twigs and moss for the last few weeks sits high and proud, protecting her eggs, waiting for her mate to return with food. In the field beyond the park boundary the lambs nudge at their mothers' bellies, searching for teats. I don't know what's going on with Fi, but I know this: Sam did not send that image. Sam is here, with me, helping me. He's back. Whatever is going on, he's chosen to be with me today. I have to hang on to that.

Sam did not send that message. Fi didn't send it. I didn't send it and it wasn't a joke like Sam claims it was meant to be. He knows who sent it, but I don't think he knew that photo was being taken. It wasn't a pose. That was an image taken while he was asleep, while he was vulnerable. Fi's right, that sext was a warning and it came from Rebecca.

I should talk to Jonty about this, but if I mention the sext I have to tell him about the other incidents: the knickers, the touching, the nudity, and he'll want to know why I haven't mentioned anything before. He's suspicious enough of me already. He doesn't think Rebecca's the problem, he thinks I am. Unless I can prove otherwise, I'll only make things worse.

Chapter 27

The rain comes in fat splodges and the last customers at the café hurry off before the downpour. I send Fi home and go back to help Sam clear up. We huddle beneath an old golfing umbrella fished out of the lost-property cupboard and run home. We're laughing, our feet soggy, dripping rain-water into the hall as we fall into the cottage.

Jonty is back, with the TV on, his feet up on the sofa, a glass of wine in his hand. He glances in our direction without smiling. 'Everything go OK?' But there is no interest there. A courtesy question requiring no real answer. The reprieve I've felt today is snatched from me in an instant. He's been with Rebecca.

He looks at Sam. 'The Flag Parade more enticing than sailing then?' Sam glares at him. So Jonty asked Sam to go sailing with him and Rebecca. Whose idea was that? Jonty's or hers? But Sam didn't go, he chose to stay and help me instead. I can't help feeling smug about that.

Sam ignores Jonty and goes straight upstairs. I want to

follow him. There's nothing I'd like more than to hide in his room with him and leave Jonty down here, but that isn't going to help the situation. I glance at the half-empty bottle. There's no point in talking to Jonty now. I consider sitting down, watching the police drama that's unfolding on the screen, but he makes no move to take his feet down from the sofa, so I go into the kitchen and make myself a cup of camomile tea. I'm clearly not welcome. The best thing I can do is go and run a bath and get an early night.

As I soak in the steamy bubbles, door locked, I allow my hands to rest on my belly and imagine the tiny cluster of cells that will be forming. I breathe in so my flesh domes, breaking the surface of the water, and try to imagine it bigger, a baby floating inside. I have no idea what I'm going to do. I have to find out what's going on between Sam and Rebecca. They must be sleeping together. The thought makes me sick. I know I should really talk to Jonty, to work out how we can deal with this, but he doesn't want to talk to me and he chose to spend today with Rebecca. I'm on my own.

Sam doesn't leave the house for the rest of the bank holiday weekend. He stays in his room, telling me he's revising. His exams start in a fortnight. I'm glad to see that whatever is going on hasn't affected his studies, if what he's saying is true. He chose not to go sailing. I'm guessing he's keeping Rebecca at a distance. Maybe he's finished with her. Hopefully.

We are three strangers under the same roof, each moving to our own unhappy rhythm. Sam keeps himself to himself. He and I are both cautious around Jonty. I make the excuse of family activities in the park; they don't really require my supervision, but I need the space and time to think and my office provides the perfect refuge. Sam is back at school on Tuesday and Rebecca will be there, plotting, meddling, twisting. But I'm on to her now. This is my family and I am not going to let her tear us apart.

On Tuesday I discover three banners which were meant to be up in time for the festival launch but got overlooked in all the hurry. I call the high school and suggest we display them at the entrance. They're delighted and I grab my opportunity to take them up towards the end of the school day. I lay the banners across the back seat and put the dog in the boot. Maybe later Sam and I can go for a walk.

I arrive early and manage to find a space in the car park, close to the school buildings. From here I'll be able to see both exits. I deliver the banners to the caretaker and return to the car. As the bell goes and the wave of blue sweatshirts floods out of the doors, Loopy moans in the back, a repeated, high-pitched, impatient plea to get out: all these children and the potential for fussing and petting! She sees Sam before I do and leaps up, trying to scramble over the seat to the front. I wind down the passenger window and am about to call out when he stops to hold open a door, and then I see her: Rebecca. They're talking. He's nodding, she's glancing about. Something has been agreed. As he walks away I see her fingers reach out and briefly touch his hand. A spark, gone in an instant. Something and nothing. If you weren't looking you wouldn't have noticed it. But I was and I did.

She walks across the car park towards a red Mini. Sam heads for the gate. I don't want to attract his attention in front of her, so I wait until she is in her car and has left the car park, by which time Sam is on the street. I drive out, planning to catch up, but I can't see him. The car behind me toots. There are hundreds of young people spilling on to the street and flowing towards the town centre, but Sam isn't one of them. He's tall; he'd be head and shoulders above these kids. Then, as I'm about to give up, I glance in the opposite direction to check the road is clear and I see him. He's walking away from the town centre and taking the first left turn. I flick the indicator and follow.

As I turn the corner I see the red Mini parked in a lay-by further down the street. Driving past, I keep an eye on my rear-view mirror and watch Sam as he approaches Rebecca's car. I pull into a driveway about five hundred yards further on, out of sight, and wait. A few moments later the Mini drives past me and I follow.

They head out to Seaford and park outside a terraced cottage not that different from the one we live in, but this is whitewashed, with plastic windows and a paved front garden. It doesn't have a view of the sea, like I imagined, but is tucked into a side street. I turn right and stop in front of an abandoned pub.

What do I do? I feel I should go and knock on the front door and confront them, but I'm afraid. Not of Sam, but of her. I can see her sneering at me. I can hear her tinkling, little-girl laugh. What if it's innocent? What if he's confiding in her about something? What if he's talking to her about me?

I need help. I wish Jonty was here, but Jonty thinks it's me who's the problem, not her.

You do realise he's in love with you? Pip watching me over her tea cup.

I imagine telling Pip everything. She wouldn't laugh; she'd take it seriously. She loves Sam. She understands; she's a mother, Sam's grandmother. That overrides everything. I have to talk to Pip. I have no idea what she'll say, but she will listen. She'll know what to do.

Pip doesn't answer the door when I arrive at the house. I bang on the window, increasingly frantic, uninvited images of Rebecca and Sam leaping around in my head. I walk around the side, through the gate into the garden and see her down at the water's edge. Yellow kayaks bob past in a surprisingly orderly line. The children wave and Pip raises her arm and waves back.

She turns as I call out to her. 'Darling! What a lovely surprise!' picking up a bulging plastic bag and walking towards me. 'I've been tidying up some of Sam's junk in the boathouse. He's made himself quite at home in there.'

'He's been back?'

'I presume so. You're just in time for tea.'

***

We're sitting on the white sofas in a weak patch of sunlight. I'm babbling. I can't help it. Pip has to ask me to repeat things and clarify them, but she's calm and listens carefully. I tell her what Fi saw outside the pub. I tell her truthfully, even though I want to tell it differently. I want to say it was Rebecca forcing him, but that isn't how it was, and I have to be honest. 'He was kissing her. He was willing.'

Pip frowns at this, her lips a thin line, but she makes no comment. 'Carry on.'

I tell her about the conversation I had with Fi after the truanting. That Rebecca was at Sam's previous school, that she's a teacher. She nods, storing this. I tell her about Sam's behaviour, the way he can be attentive one moment and aggressive the next. I tell her I'm sorry, I'm so sorry, I should have listened to her. If I'd listened to her this might not have happened. She tells me to pull myself together.

I don't tell her about the knickers, the fingers inside my waistband, the nudity. I don't tell her about the image on the phone. I imagine her expression if I did, her fine, colourless hair, translucent skin. I imagine her stricken by it. She is, beneath the tough words and poise, an elderly woman. This is too much for her. She knows enough.

Pip is processing the information I've given her, but she appears more fragile than I expected, less certain. I need to give her something to focus on, something she can actively do. 'I followed them to her house. They're there now.'

She stands up. 'Let's go.'

Chapter 28

My knees are weak as we approach Rebecca's house. I can only take short, shallow breaths and my heart is banging so hard it's echoing in my throat. Pip strides ahead and raps on the door with her knuckles.

Rebecca is dressed in pyjama bottoms and an oversized T-shirt, her hair piled loosely on top of her head, make-up intact. She looks startled.

'Mrs Mitcham. What on earth are you doing here?'

'We need to talk. May we come in?'

Rebecca says, 'Lizzie,' as if we're the best of friends. 'Please, please come in.' Her voice is calm, concerned. She steps back and ushers Pip through the door.

As we enter, I look up the wooden staircase. The bathroom door is open. Beyond that will be two bedrooms. I listen for any evidence of Sam. Nothing. Rebecca indicates the sofa under the window. She sits opposite on a narrow armchair and leans forward, her elbows on her knees. 'You'll have to excuse me, I came straight home and got into my PJs. I wasn't expecting visitors.'

Pip cuts to the chase. 'You told me you were a journalist.'

Rebecca smiles. 'I am.'

'Lizzie tells me you are a teacher at Sam's school.'

Her smile doesn't waver. 'That's right. I also happen to teach. It's a financial necessity for the time being, until I get established.'

Pip is silent, so I speak for her. 'You're Sam's teacher, but you didn't think to mention it?'

Rebecca shrugs. 'I tend to keep my two professional worlds separate. And I teach drama, so Sam isn't technically my student. I didn't realise that Mrs Mitcham was related to Sam. Mitcham is a common enough name.'

'What about me? You befriended me! You spent time with me in the pub, and shopping. I confided in you! But you never thought to tell me you knew Sam?'

The smile slides from her face. She glances at Pip. She fiddles with her hands. 'I was going to tell you, but when you started to talk about Sam, I thought it would be better to listen.' She looks back at Pip, her face folded into apparent concern. 'I was worried about him, you see. Sam has been exhibiting some rather, well, inappropriate behaviour recently…'

I leap in. 'When? How would you know? You said you don't teach him. Why would you be spending time with Sam?'

'We're working on a script together.'

I'm momentarily silenced by this. 'Since when?'

'For some weeks now. Sam is a promising young actor.'

'Sam? Sam's never been interested in acting.'

'He might not have mentioned it.' She looks to Pip. 'I think it's difficult for him, with such a charismatic father. Sam is shy, but he does have talent.'

Pip ignores her. 'You were saying he was behaving inappropriately?'

'Comments. Innuendos. And once or twice he's touched me inappropriately. Nothing sinister, just brushed against me a little suggestively. I thought I might be imagining it at first, but when Lizzie started to talk…' She trails off, as if what she is about to say is too delicate but she will make herself continue anyway, for the good of Sam. 'I was concerned. There were things Lizzie confided to me which I felt… I felt might explain Sam's behaviour.'

'That is not true!'

'Lizzie, calm yourself.' Pip's voice is a stern slap.

'I am so sorry,' Rebecca continues. 'I know this must be distressing for you. I was going to try and talk to Mr Mitcham about it. I have tried…'

'What's with the "Mr Mitcham"? He's Jonty. You call him Jonty. You've been flirting with him ever since you rescued us from the bloody lake. Don't pretend it's all formal now!'

'Lizzie, please.' Pip's voice is weary. 'You are not helping.'

This all sounds so plausible, but it's not true! 'Where's Sam?'

'Sam? I have no idea.'

'I drove to the school to pick him up this afternoon. I saw him walk out of school. I saw you pull into a lay-by and wait for him. I saw him get into your car and I followed you here.' I'm breathless.

She gives a little frown as if she can't quite understand what I'm saying. 'You saw me?'

'You were in your car.'

'Do you think it might have been someone else's car?'

'It was your car!'

'My number plate?'

I hesitate. I didn't look at the number plate. I didn't need to. But this is enough for her. She nods. Patronising. 'There are quite a few red Minis around. I've had complete strangers wave to me before now.' She gives a little smile.

Pip is watching her, glancing at me and then back at Rebecca. She says nothing.

'Sam was in your car. I know he was. I saw…' I hesitate. What did I see? I don't remember. But he was with her, I know it. 'He came here. Where is he?'

She shakes her head. 'I'm really very sorry, but I have no idea.'

Pip stands up. 'Come along, Lizzie.' She looks at Rebecca. 'We are sorry to have bothered you.'

'That's no problem, Mrs Mitcham. I hope you find him. And I'm glad it's out in the open. Perhaps now you could try and have a word with Mr Mitcham?' She looks pointedly at me. 'I'm not sure how much he's been told?'

I can't help myself. 'Sam!' I race up the stairs two at a time before she can stop me and throw open the first door. There's a writing desk under the window, a mattress rolled up in the corner, but no other furniture. The room is dominated by a wall of mirrored wardrobes and my reflection stares back at me, dishevelled, frantic. I back out and shove open the door to the front bedroom. A king-size bed takes up most of the floor space. The sheets are tangled as if it's recently been abandoned. I lift a pillow to my face and sniff something citrusy which might be Sam's shampoo. I throw myself down on the floor and look under the bed, even though I can see it's too low for anyone to squeeze beneath. I straighten up, feeling hot and foolish. She was telling the truth. He's not here.

They're waiting for me at the bottom of the stairs. Pip's face is all disappointment, Rebecca is overflowing with pity. 'I am so sorry.'

'I can smell him.'

Rebecca shakes her head. I sound mad. I can hear it myself.

We drive in silence out of the village and back towards Pip's house, where I've left my car. Her face is impassive as she focuses on the road. 'She's lying,' I say quietly, though I have no proof and I know how weak it sounds. Rebecca has twisted everything.

Pip doesn't answer. I stare out of the passenger window. It starts to rain. She turns on the windscreen wipers. There is a repeated squeak that pierces my head as they sweep one way and then the other. Grey-green fields, sheep with their lambs, huddled against dry-stone walls, hotels with landscaped gardens and regimented topiary. I try and remember what happened, exactly as it happened. I saw Sam approach Rebecca's car. Did I see him get in? I drove past. I was busy checking for somewhere to pull in, not wanting to be seen. Maybe he didn't get in the car. He might simply have stuck his head in the window, exchanged a few words and carried on. But if that was the case, Rebecca would have told us.

We turn and drive up the side of the lake. The sun has been swallowed by clouds. Grey water reflects the sky. I try and work through it out loud. 'I was at your house by half past four. We talked and then we drove back. They had over an hour and a half together. He could have been and gone in that time.' Pip is focused on the road. 'She's grooming him, I know it.'

Pip takes a breath and I'm alert, waiting. 'Lizzie, listen to me. You need to be careful. This woman is highly intelligent. She is charming. She is slick. And you are hysterical.'

'Do you believe me?'

She pulls into the drive. 'We need to speak to Jonty.'

'Jonty thinks I'm the problem.'

Pip switches off the engine and turns to face me. I explain. 'Rebecca's been saying things to him. She goes sailing with him every week. She asked him to give her lessons. I think he liked the attention. He was flattered. He's been feeling so low lately, I didn't begrudge him a little flirtation, if it took his mind off the redundancy. He—'

She holds up her hand. 'Lizzie, stop. Go home. Pour yourself a good deep bath and relax.' She pauses. 'Make sure you lock the door.' It's a warning. 'If Sam is there, don't mention anything. This is a matter for his father and me.'

'I'm so worried about him, Pip.'

'If he is involved with this woman…'

'He is! She's grooming him!'

'… it will take time to extricate him. I know from bitter experience that insisting he does what we believe to be in his best interests is likely to result in the exact opposite behaviour. I will talk to Jonty and we will decide how to proceed.' I open my mouth to speak, but she cuts me off. 'Leave it with me.' It's clear that this is not negotiable.

I can hear Sam's music from his room as I enter the cottage, but he doesn't come down. I don't know if he saw me outside the school. If he was at Rebecca's he might have slipped out of the back door when we pulled up. He might have been hiding in the yard or in a shed. I should have checked out the back.

Jonty is at the table with the local *Evening Mail* open in front of him. He looks up as I come in but doesn't smile. His body language is defeated. I ask, 'What's up?' but as I get closer I see that he's looking at properties to let. I pull back. My voice is serrated. 'Found anything?' I walk straight past him into the kitchen. There's no sign of dinner, so I open the fridge and pull out some tomato passata, an ancient chorizo sausage and an onion. Walking to the bottom of the stairs, feeling Jonty's eyes following every step, I call up to Sam. 'Do you want anything to eat? I'm making pasta.'

'No.'

I long to go up and talk to Sam, to find out if he was there, how much he knows of what's happened, but Jonty's watching me. Pip has made it absolutely clear the family will deal with this together and I'm not included in that family right now.

Pip will talk to Jonty. I'm not sure how much she'll tell him or what his reaction will be. I have a horrible feeling when he hears what happened this afternoon he'll react the same way Rebecca did, assuming I'm jealous, paranoid, not to be trusted, assuming that I have inappropriate feelings for Sam. I don't know if that's what Pip's thinking right now.

I can feel Jonty's eyes on me. I hear him close the paper, get up. He passes me on his way to the front door, takes the dog lead and whistles for Loopy, who leaps from her doze and scrabbles along the tiles of the hall.

'Aren't you going to eat?'

'Not hungry,' and he's gone.

I make pasta for one. When I've finished I wash my plate then sit down with pen and paper and write Nell a letter to accompany her flag. I write about St George's Day, about Loopy and the walk we did at Skelwith Bridge, and Sam and Jonty's song at the open mic. And then I stop, because my brain becomes crowded with other things, things Nell can't know about, things I wish I didn't know. I write a few sentences about the new banners and the Flag Parade on Saturday to explain the gift, but my heart isn't in it any more.

Fi said Sam was kissing Rebecca after the open mic at The Red Lion. *He* was kissing *her*; she wasn't forcing him. He was instigating it. Our relationship has left him confused. He is disturbed and I am responsible.

Chapter 29

I can't sleep. I'm exhausted, but my mind will not switch off. Sam and Rebecca.

He was kissing *her*. He wanted it.

She might have been shocked, fighting him off. It's possible she's attracted to him. He's a beautiful boy. He's not much younger than her. In a year or two they could be in a relationship with no one batting an eyelid. I feel sick at the thought.

I remember Sam in the bathroom, staring at me. *You were coming on to me.*

Is it grooming if he's the one taking the initiative?

Rebecca may be struggling to do the right thing. She may be the victim here as much as Sam. She might be attracted to him but doing her best to maintain a professional distance. Sam might be making that difficult.

I'm worried about that sext. If he did send it, and I have to consider that's possible, he may have sent something similar to Rebecca. If he's sent her indecent images, she might go to the police.

I have to speak to her. If she cares about Sam she won't want this to go any further. If I speak to her, if I get her onside, we can work this out together.

Before the alarm rings, I slip out of bed, grab the clothes I had on yesterday and creep out of the house. I have to get to her before she sets off for school.

She comes to the door in her PJs. Her hair hangs loose and tangled across her shoulders and her face, still puffy from sleep, looks naked and vulnerable without the make-up. She could be seventeen. There's an innocence about her in this stripped-back state that makes me afraid for her. She's a young woman in a dangerous situation. She has no one taking care of her.

She's wary. 'What do you want?'

'I wondered if I could talk to you?'

I'm hoping she'll step back and let me in, but she folds her arms across her chest and blocks the door. 'What about?'

I hesitate. 'I was hoping we could talk about Sam?' She looks me up and down, not budging. I try again. 'I'm worried about him. I think… I'm worried that he may have behaved, that he might…' I swallow, struggling to find the words.

'Might what?'

I look around. An elderly man is watering his garden two doors down. A young woman in vest and shorts runs past, her ponytail bouncing behind her. 'This isn't really a conversation to have in the street.' But she doesn't move and I have no option but to keep going and hope she'll soften. 'I think he has feelings for you. I think he's confused. His relationship with me... He may be acting inappropriately.'

'In what way?'

'You told Pip you were worried.'

'What's been going on between the two of you?'

'Nothing!'

'The knickers? The incident in the bath?'

'You know about that?'

'You told me.'

'I told you about the knickers. I didn't mention the bath. How do you know about the bath?'

She's been talking to Jonty. Which would explain his mood yesterday. Or Sam. Have she and Sam been laughing at me together? She looks me up and down and I feel myself shrinking. 'What has Sam said?'

'He's confided in me. I'm not about to break that confidence.'

Sam, my Sam, has confided in *her*. 'I'm sorry. Has he suggested... I think maybe he's misunderstood, misinterpreted...'

'Really?'

'It's not like that.'

'Not like what?'

'I *love* Sam.' Silence. And in that silence, all the awful accusations echo. 'Not like that!'

'Like what?' Her voice is a blade.

This is not the smiling, cheerful woman I met in the pub and went shopping with. I remember now that she was the one that insisted I buy that underwear, encouraged me to look sexier. That was all part of her plan. It's no coincidence that she met Pip. She's not a writer. She has systematically insinuated herself into our lives. She has developed relationships with each one of us, not together but separately, secretly, divisively. This is not the charming, friendly, flirtatious Rebecca we have all been introduced to. Nor is it the woman Pip and I confronted yesterday. Then she was bemused, apparently innocent, sweet. There is none of that sweetness now.

She takes a deep breath, lifts her head fractionally to look down at me, her nose twitching as if I'm something dirty and unpleasant she's discovered on her doorstep, and says, 'You're worried about Sam, well, so am I. Your outburst the other day, your ugly insinuations, I'm not surprised he's confused. I'm not convinced it's Sam who has the problem with inappropriate behaviour.'

'I don't understand…'

'Oh, I think you do.' I feel like a child. I want to say something, but she's too quick, firing accusations like darts. 'You should know that I spoke to his grandmother last night.'

'Pip?'

'She strikes me as a sensible woman. I thought she was the best person to talk to about my concerns.'

'Concerns?' Swimming in Coniston. Sharing a beer at the lake edge. Is that where it started? Was that the moment I crossed the line? Sam staring at me in the bath. Those bloody knickers! My voice is a dry croak. 'What did Pip say?'

She smiles then and I can feel doors and windows slamming shut. 'I think that's between me and her. I'm sure if she has anything to say to you she'll contact you herself.'

Pip hasn't spoken to me about this. She thinks I've betrayed her. I should have told her everything. She believes I've betrayed Sam. I'm standing alone now, on the outside, looking in at what was once my life.

Chapter 30

I phone Clare, who understands immediately that I need help and time and tells me to get down to London on the next available train. The Flag Festival is underway, I'm owed time off. I throw some things into a bag and head for the station.

I know I'm running away, but I don't have the strength to face the consequences of my stupid errors of judgement right now and no one seems to want me around anyway. I've got lost somehow. I can no longer see clearly. I need to reconnect with the girl I used to be, the person I still am, underneath everything else I've become. Not Jonty's partner, not Sam's whatever it is that I am, just Lizzie.

I call Fi from the station, but she doesn't answer. Her phone goes to voicemail and I leave a rambling message about my visit to Rebecca's this morning. 'Sam's in trouble, Fi. She's dangerous. I need your help. Will you meet me to talk when I get back from London? Please?'

Clare is petite, with rusty curls which were always cropped

and gelled into submission while we were at school but now bubble across her shoulders. She's waving madly from the other side of the barrier, jumping up and down in skinny jeans and T-shirt, her bare feet in canvas pumps. Her skin is dusted gold from the Majorca trip and she looks so young and fresh, like she's just stepped out of the pages of a magazine. I feel horribly self-conscious and sweaty in the sensible waterproof I put on this morning and my heavy boots. It's nearly ten degrees warmer in London than it was when I left Cumbria and I was thinking practical rather than stylish. I'd forgotten that Londoners refuse to bow to wet weather, sidestepping puddles in their smart shoes and dashing between buildings under the cover of designer umbrellas.

Clare throws her arms around me, then pushes me back to take a good look. She frowns at the waterproof.

'I know, I know.'

'Come on, country girl! We'll sort you out. I've got a lovely denim jacket I picked up at the vintage market on Sunday. It will look great on you!' Her energy lifts me immediately.

Clare has a room in a shared house in Streatham. It's a small, neglected Victorian terrace on a bare street with little colour apart from the recycling boxes and the occasional red car. I've been in Cumbria long enough to notice the lack of green. No trees, front gardens paved over for extra parking, no window boxes. When I did I start to crave window boxes?

Clare's room is dominated by a double bed, which we'll share. There's just enough floor space to walk around it and allow for a chest of drawers, which doubles as a dressing table. She has a few things on hangers that dangle from a hook on the back of her door. This is no more than a student room. I feel bad encroaching on Clare's space, but this is how it is in London when you're a young teacher and struggling to make a living. She has shared use of the kitchen, bathroom and lounge, but the couple who sublet the room like to pretend it's just the two of them and Clare prefers to stay out of their way as much as possible. I used to live like this, not that long ago, but already it feels stifling. I've been so lucky to have the run of Jonty's house. But that's no longer my home. I turned down the Barrow flat, but it's only a matter of time before something suitable comes up in Tarnside or Dom moves out. I try to ignore the shift inside my belly. A reminder that things aren't that simple. One problem at a time.

The good thing about London is that you don't have to stay home. There are places to go, things to do, people to meet and as soon as I've dumped my bag, changed into a T-shirt and Clare's denim jacket, we're off to 'this great new bar' in Tooting.

Clare asks about Jonty, and I tell her about his redundancy. She looks worried and I find myself bigging up the sailing and suggesting that he's thinking about starting a business, a consultancy, offering advice and services to organisations in the north-west applying for large grants. It's a job he could do, and the more I talk about it the more appealing the idea becomes, but it isn't Jonty's idea and much as I'd like him to, I can't see him taking it on. If he'd thought of it, he might, but he won't if it comes from me. Something about that makes me feel unbearably sad.

I change the subject before we can get more personal. I want, so much, to confide in Clare about everything, but it's too much. Just thinking about this horrible, sordid mess I need to deal with is too much. Instead, I tell her about St George's Day: Fi as the damsel in distress, the cartoon dragon, the open mic and Jonty and Sam's song. For a moment, I'm in love with my life again, remembering what it is about Tarnside that keeps me there. It might not have the glitter and style and possibilities of London, but it has something else, something quirky and warm and filled with its own magic.

'How old is Sam now?'

'He'll be eighteen in June. Can you believe it!'

'Things settled down a bit?' When Sam first arrived, fifteen and angry, it was Clare I spoke to. She was working in a secondary school and was surrounded by teenage testosterone. When I told her what was going on she would listen patiently before delivering advice. She was always able to look at it from a fresh perspective and show me that, in the grander scheme of things, what was happening was perfectly understandable and nothing to worry about. 'It's a dance,' she said once. 'A dance every teenager takes part in.'

'Not me.'

'You were never a teenager. Take it from me, teenagers get angry, frustrated. They take it out on those closest to them. In your house your mum was the perpetual teenager, so you never got to be one.'

Clare's degree was in psychology, but even before that she was able to see my mother's behaviour for what it was. I've never had to hide from Clare. I wish she didn't live at the opposite end of the country. If she was in Tarnside, or even Kendal or Lancaster, we'd be able to meet up like this more often and I'd be able to tell her things about my life now and ask her advice, but there are so many miles between us and so much time that hasn't been shared. Where to begin? Talking about anything other than superficial things seems impossible.

Clare has tilted her head a little to one side, waiting to

hear more about Sam. 'It's difficult. I don't know who I am to him...' I trail off because I don't know how to tell her, what to tell her. I wish she knew everything, that she'd been there and seen. If she'd met Rebecca she could judge for herself.

'You're his stepmum, I guess?' But she isn't sure. She frowns. 'How does it feel? Do you feel like a mum?'

Beneath the table my hand instinctively moves to my belly. 'I always seem to be the one doing all that stuff. In all my relationships: Danny, my mum, Nell and Sam, even Jonty at times. I feel like everyone's mum.'

'That's what you do. You take care of people. It's learned behaviour, Lizzie. Don't beat yourself up about it.'

'I'm sick of it. Nobody thanks me for it. They expect me to take care of them and when things don't go their way they take it out on me and it's not fair. I'm not responsible for everything. I can't control everything. I don't want to be everyone's mum!'

'Then stop being one.'

I brush my fingers across my belly; an apology to the life unfurling inside. It's not that I don't want to be a mother. It is clear to me, suddenly, now, in this moment: I do want to be a mum. I wasn't expecting it to happen now and it is too soon, really, but I do want it sometime and if this is the time, then maybe I should accept it. I can picture myself with this baby in my arms. I imagine a baby, then a toddler walking with their little hand clasped in mine; I imagine pushing a swing, climbing into that bird's-nest swing at the park with my child and watching the clouds. Mothering a young child is a very different thing from the kind of mothering I've been doing lately. That kind of mothering would be uncomplicated, instinctive, joyous. But with the way things are right now I can't see how this can happen.

'Jonty's asked me to move out.'

'What?' Clare leans in and takes both my hands in hers. 'Why?'

I feel tears stinging my eyes. She squeezes my fingers. 'Listen, I'm going to get us another drink and then you are going to tell me everything. OK?'

I nod, relieved to have someone on my side, an ally who believes in me, who trusts me.

Clare hurries up to the bar. I look around at the other tables, the groups of young people. In Tarnside I know at least half the people in any crowd and those I don't know will know Jonty. Here I'm anonymous. This is a young venue. There's no one over forty as far as I can see, and if there is they do a very good job of hiding it.

Clare slips back into her seat and pushes a tall glass of something pale and fizzy towards me. 'I figured we needed a cocktail.' She glances over her shoulder and back at me. 'That guy at the bar in the tiny T-shirt? I thought it was one of my students for a minute.' She gives a little shudder.

'What's wrong with him?'

'Nothing, but I come all the way out to Tooting to avoid my pupils. I don't want them seeing me…' She hesitates. '… off duty.'

'What if it was him? What if one of your students was here now, what would you do?'

'I'd leave.'

'Without finishing your drink?'

She pauses and grins. 'Well, this drink cost me the best part of a tenner, so I might have to finish it first!'

We laugh for a moment, but I'm intrigued by this. An image of Rebecca at the bar on St George's Day. Sam's flushed face. 'Who would it be more embarrassing for, you or them?'

Clare considers this. 'It depends what I'm doing, I guess. Who's the most pissed! Anyway, enough of that...' She wants to get back to the subject of Jonty, but I need to know more.

'If you lived in a small town, like Tarnside, what would you do? It's not like here; you don't have a dozen other bars a Tube stop away.'

'I'd have to be very careful.'

'Why? You're entitled to a social life. A private life.'

'They're kids. I'm their teacher. It's a persona, a part I have to play. Two-dimensional; clear boundaries. I'm required to be respectable and reliable and I can't allow them to see anything that doesn't fit that persona. If I do, I lose their respect.'

'Seriously? Teachers are allowed to go out for a drink.'

'If I was older, maybe, but I'm too close to them for it to be comfortable. If I want them to take me seriously I have to keep a distance. I have to be seen to be older and wiser. If I want to let my hair down I have to do that somewhere else. It isn't fair on them.' She's different now. Her body language, her expression. Straight-backed, serious. I can picture her in the classroom. No nonsense. Not Clare but Ms Patrick. Not a young woman but a teacher. 'It isn't fair on them if I blur the boundaries,' she says emphatically. 'They don't know where they stand.'

Sam would be safe with Clare.

Sam is not safe with Rebecca.

'What is it, Lizzie?' Her eyes pin me. 'Is something going on with Sam?'

Chapter 31

I get a train out of Euston heading north on Friday morning and text Jonty to let him know what time I'm arriving in Tarnside, hoping we'll be able to sit down and talk before I do anything, but there's no reply.

Usually I love coming back to Tarnside after I've been away. The train from Lancaster chugs across the peninsula through pools of sand and water. Sheep gather on islands of grass. Tarnside station with its Victorian railings and hanging baskets is so charming, but today I feel like dirty litter on this idyllic landscape.

I am not dirty. That's how she wants me to feel, but it isn't true.

It's overcast and sticky as I walk up from the station to the main road. I told Clare everything. It was such a relief. She didn't jump to any conclusions, she didn't judge me, she didn't even say I should have been more careful. The wet T-shirt in the lake was innocent. She understood that. I know she's only heard my point of view, but she believes me when I say it felt OK. It was after that things changed. Sam has changed. He's changed since he became involved with Rebecca. She is grooming him and has possibly been doing so for years, making him misinterpret our relationship.

Clare went straight to her laptop as soon as we got back to her house and googled grooming. We sat side by side on her bed for what seemed like hours, reading all these documents, NSPCC information, parent forums, case studies and psychologists' reports. Eventually she had to go to sleep, but I stayed up into the early hours, preparing myself.

Rebecca is grooming Sam and I have to do something about that.

I reach the main road but do not turn left into the town centre. Instead I turn right and walk up towards the high school.

It's different this time. I initiated this meeting and I'm prepared. I'm wearing my London clothes: a new, pale grey leather jacket with black cigarette pants and statement wedge heels that rap a purposeful beat along the school corridor. I interrupt Mr Wright as he searches for some paperwork for an after-school meeting. I'm lucky to have caught him. He doesn't look up as he speaks or ask me to sit down. He's hoping this will be quick. Outside the window the tarn is an opaque steel plate beneath charcoal clouds.

I've explained that I've come to discuss Sam and this script Rebecca claims he's involved with. 'We feel he should be focusing entirely on his exams right now.' I use the word 'we' as if I've talked this through with Jonty. I'm implying he's fully aware of everything that is going on and we're united on this. 'The last thing Sam needs is any distractions at this point in time.'

Mr Wright looks perplexed. 'As far as I know there is no school production taking place at the moment. We are not in the habit of staging entertainment during an exam period.'

'Apparently this is a script he's developing with Ms Watts?'

He shakes his head, turns his attention to the filing cabinet and yanks open a drawer. 'You'll need to speak to Ms Watts about it.'

'I would rather you did that. As head of year.'

He pauses and looks up. His eyes meet mine. He's an intelligent man and he can read my tone. 'Is there a problem here?'

'I think there might be.'

He stops then and gives me his full attention, sitting down and motioning for me to do the same. He glances at the clock, but I can see that he's resigned to being late. 'Go on.'

'Sam has been behaving out of character recently and is clearly disturbed by something that's going on at school. I believe that's why he was truanting at the end of the spring term. It's nothing to do with his studies, but I think it might have something to do with this additional drama commitment.'

He frowns. 'I didn't think Sam was taking drama A level.'

'He isn't.'

There's a silence. Mr Wright watches me. There are words swarming in the air between us. He proceeds carefully, avoiding them. 'Have you spoken to Sam about this?'

'He doesn't want to talk about it.' I pause and add, 'For some reason,' then pause again for this to register. 'I get the impression that he feels trapped. This is not something he would have chosen to do.'

Mr Wright's head nods up and down. A tiny movement, barely discernible. 'It does seem to me that the most sensible thing would be for you to talk directly to Ms Watts.'

'I've tried. She hasn't been too forthcoming. We would appreciate it if you would speak to her and explain that Sam will no longer be attending any rehearsals.'

We look at one another across the desk. The muscles in his face twitch. I wonder if he has his own suspicions about Rebecca Watts. He's watching me, thinking. I hold his eyes. He gives me a nod. 'Ms Watts is not in school today, she doesn't work on Fridays, but I'll call her. Leave it with me.'

I leave the school just before the final bell rings and make my way down to the crossroads by the station. Fi and Sam often walk home from school together. She turns right here and Sam goes straight into town. I turn right and head around a bend in the road where I can wait, out of sight. It's possible that Fi will go into town, but she usually walks home first to check on her mum and pick up a shopping list. She's brisk, already worrying about what disaster might greet her and I don't have to wait long. She starts as she comes around the corner and sees me.

'Fi, please, could we talk?'

She slows down but doesn't stop walking. I keep pace beside her. 'I know you think I sent that image. I know you're worried about me and Sam, and I understand, I do, but I'm asking you to pause, just for a minute, and think. You know me, Fi. You know how I love Sam. It's not like that. You're right to be worried, because he is in danger. But it's not me. I promise you, it's not me.' She doesn't look at me and she keeps moving, but I can tell she's listening. 'Has Sam ever said anything to suggest that I might…' I can't bring myself to say it. I'm almost frightened to ask. That's the power of

Rebecca; she can make you doubt yourself. 'I promise you, Fi, I'm not that person. Sam's in trouble and he needs us. If you can't believe me, then talk to him. Please. Tell him what you suspect. Talk to Sam.'

I stop, hoping that she'll stop and face me, but she keeps walking. There's nothing more I can do. She believes I'm the predator and if I were in her shoes, I would too. I can't go back to the cottage yet. I need to summon some more courage. I walk down to the tarn and Margaret Thwaite's bench.

As I approach the front door an hour or so later, I feel around in my bag for my keys, but Sam is there, greeting me on the threshold. He's all smiles, pleased to see me, eager even, taking my bag from me and behaving as if I've been away weeks rather than days. The house has been hoovered and all the surfaces are clear. Even the cushions on the sofa have been plumped. There's a vase of wild flowers on the table.

'What's going on?'

'I tidied up.' He stands back, waiting for praise.

'*You* did this?' We laugh. 'What does your room look like?'

He rolls his eyes. 'Don't spoil it.' And it's so good to be back here, to be laughing with him, to be welcome again.

Except I'm not welcome. Jonty wants me to leave. Has Jonty told Sam yet? Or is he leaving that to me? 'Where's your dad?'

'Sailing.'

With her.

I look at Sam. This is not about me, it's about rescuing him and I will do that. I'm not going to let Rebecca hurt him any more.

His smile slides and I can see this is all a front, that he's anxious. 'I'm sorry.'

I hesitate. So he wants to talk. Finally. I ask gently, 'What for?' He reddens. I hate doing this to him, but we can't pussyfoot around any more. Is this an acknowledgement of what's been going on? Is he taking some responsibility?

He sniffs, shoves his hands in his pockets and raises his shoulders to his ears as if he's summoning courage from his feet up. 'I thought you'd gone.' I frown, not sure if I've understood. 'Left us.'

He's close to tears now, fighting and failing to hide them. A frightened little boy inside this great big body. I stretch up to put my arms around his neck, pulling his head down to my shoulder. To hell with Pip and Kay, and Jonty, and Rebecca and Matt, and Fi; this is my boy and he needs me. 'You idiot. I'm not going to leave you!' And I can feel his tears on my neck and the tremble in his chest and I'm so relieved to have him back, to be able to comfort him like this, so absorbed in that relief, that I don't see it coming and, before I realise what's going on, his head has turned and his mouth is on mine and he's trying to kiss me.

I shove him back. 'Sam, no!'

He looks appalled, turns and runs up the stairs.

I'm shaking. I can still taste his mouth on mine. The clumsiness of it. The confusion. Because it is confusion, I can see that now. Everything I've read, talking it through with Clare, remembering all the good stuff, how it was between us, how that grew slowly out of patience and trust. The little boy in him missed me and was scared I'd abandoned him. The young man he's grown into felt he needed to show me how much he cared, to persuade me to stay, and the way he showed that was through an inappropriate kiss, because that's what he's learned – from her.

What is going on between him and Rebecca? What has she been saying to him, feeding him, doing? I've seen her in action, I know how she can take a thread of truth and create tight, uncomfortable knots with it. She's been talking to him about me, suggesting, insinuating, turning something clean and simple into something dark and tortured. The only way to unravel those knots is for Sam and me to start talking. Her power comes from isolating people. She is divisive. Well, we are a package, Sam and I; we need to start pulling together and that begins right here, right now.

I give him a moment to collect himself while I make a pot of tea and then I leave it to brew and go up and knock. He doesn't answer. I hesitate. I could go in, but that doesn't feel right. He has to be allowed a place to hide when he needs one. I must allow this to happen on his terms, when he's ready. I lean back against the door. 'Sam, can we talk?'

Silence.

'I'm sorry if I gave you the wrong signals.' He doesn't speak. We have rewound to the early days, before he could confide in me, a time of simmering confusion that would overflow, scalding us all. Back then I learned not to retaliate but to wait until the anger was spent, to give him the space to come to us.

'Sam, I can't do this on my own. I don't know what's going on. You and me, we were friends. We respected one another. We had something. I thought that something was a good thing, but if you don't, if you think that I, that we, that it isn't…' I don't have the words. 'I'm sorry.'

I wait in silence, listening to the sound of his breathing through the door. I don't know if I can hear it or if I'm imagining it, but I can feel that he's listening. He doesn't move, but I know he can hear me. 'I shouldn't have gone in the lake. I should have locked the bathroom door, I should never have bought those bloody knickers!' I try and make light of it. I take responsibility for it all, because I'm the grown-up here; I have to lead the way. 'It's complicated, you and me. There are no definitions. There's no map. But it's also really simple. I love you. We're family. You're my almost brother. My almost son. My friend. And that works, that can work.'

I listen. He doesn't speak, he doesn't move. I slide down to the floor and sit with my knees raised to my chin. I stay while the light fades outside and I wait. If all I can do is let him know I'm prepared to wait, then that will have to be enough.

Eventually I have to get up. He isn't going to come out if I stay here. 'I'm hungry. Going to make some cheese on toast and watch some mindless telly, if you fancy joining me.'

Sam doesn't come down, but I make enough for two, just in case. Jonty phones as I'm dishing up. He's been sailing all day, up at Ullswater, and has just come off the lake. It will be a couple of hours before he's de-rigged and driven home.

'What made you go all the way up there?'

'Rebecca's idea. Thought it might be nice to try a different lake.'

'Jonty, that woman is dangerous. I don't like this. Don't listen to anything she says, do you hear me?' He doesn't answer. 'Jonty?'

'What do you think she's going to say, Lizzie?'

'I went into the school today, to talk to Mr Wright.'

'You did *what*?'

'Jonty, you have to come home.'

'You went into the school? Without talking to *me*?' He's

angry now. And he's right. I should have talked it through with him first, but I wanted to seize the moment, I had to do something to warn her off.

'I'm sorry. Listen, just come straight home, please?'

'I can't. Matt's driving.' Canoe Man? 'We're stopping at a pub for some food on the way back. I don't know what time it will be.'

Rebecca and Matt? It just gets better and better. I press my forehead against the wall. He tells me he has to go, his tone cool. If this is the mood he's in now, God knows what he'll be like once she's worked on him. And Matt. That's all I need. But there's nothing I can do. The priority now is Sam.

I take both plates into the living room, turn on the TV and call upstairs that food's here if he wants it. Eventually, I hear his bedroom door open, his hesitant footsteps on the stairs, but I don't look up. He slips on to the far end of the sofa. I keep my eyes on the screen as I push his plate towards him. He picks it up and starts to eat. It's a beginning.

I snatch a glance and see that his face is blotchy from crying. I wish I could reach across, but I don't feel that I can touch him. I mustn't touch him. Because I feel guilty. I do feel that I'm to blame somehow. I'm the adult in this relationship and something went wrong on my watch. Something went very wrong.

I want to ask him about Rebecca, but I don't know how. I want to ask him, but I don't want to know the answer.

Chapter 32

I wake in the night, my stomach churning, bile gathering at the back of my throat. I don't need to turn to know Jonty's not in the bed beside me; his body heat is something I notice by its absence. I nudge for him with my foot just in case, but the sheet is cold. He's either very late or has fallen asleep on the sofa. Creeping from the bedroom to the bathroom, I fumble for the bolt we never used to use and slide it across. Then I kneel in front of the toilet bowl and heave.

When I'm done, I splash my face with cold water, over and over. Rinse my mouth, brush my teeth and rinse again. My face in the mirror is grey. I have to talk to Jonty.

I can't talk to Jonty.

I start to cry. Strangled sobs, trying not to make a noise. Helpless. I don't know how long I'm in there. Eventually I pull myself together and wash my face again.

I tiptoe over to the door, slide the bolt back and flick out the light. It takes a while for my eyes to adjust to the dark on the landing. Something moves. A figure. Jonty? Did he hear?

But it's not Jonty. It's Sam standing outside the door, waiting. 'Are you OK?'

'Sorry, I didn't mean to wake you.'

'You didn't.'

He's absolutely still. The air between us prickles with something I can't define. We sat and watched TV together earlier and he eventually took himself off to bed. I didn't ask about Rebecca. He is opening up and he's giving all the signals that I'm the one he'll talk to, but not yet. Things are still fragile between us and I don't want to risk pushing too hard and losing him altogether.

'Gippy stomach,' I say.

A bleep punctuates the quiet. He has his phone in his hand. The screen lights up with a text. He frowns. Is it her? Who else would be texting him in the middle of the night? Has she told him about our visit? My accusations? I hear Pip reprimanding me. *You are hysterical.*

I take a step forward to get back to bed, but he doesn't move and I can't get past him. Maybe he wants to talk now. Both Pip and Jonty have warned me off, but if it's me he chooses to talk to, what then? Better me than no one, surely? 'Do you fancy a cup of hot chocolate?' I couldn't stomach one, but it seems a sufficiently innocent thing to suggest. Childish. Safe.

'Dad's asleep downstairs.'

Jonty will have come home and poured himself a large whisky, then maybe another, then dozed off. He knows I hate it when he does that. We argued about it a few times when I first moved in and I threatened to move back out. He promised me he wouldn't do it again, but tonight he probably didn't give a damn what I'd think. Tonight he'd been talking to Rebecca and Matt.

If we go downstairs we'll wake him and I don't have the stamina to deal with drunken accusations; better to leave it and face the music in the morning. I say goodnight, Sam steps aside and I head back to the bedroom.

Wide awake and unable to get back to sleep, I turn on the bedside lamp, arrange the pillows behind me and take out my book, but I've read just two sentences when Sam knocks on the door. 'Lizzie?'

I can't leave him out there. Whatever Pip says, he clearly wants to talk and I'm not going to turn him away. I'm dressed in an old T-shirt and pyjama bottoms. Jonty is downstairs. I wouldn't even be considering these things if Pip hadn't said what she said, if Rebecca hadn't implied... This is ridiculous. I know I'm not going to do or say anything inappropriate, this is the boy I've been taking care of for the last two years and he needs me.

I throw on a hoodie, open the door and stand back to usher him in, but as I glance at the bed, Pip's warning voice is in my head again. This isn't a good idea. I suggest the attic. It was a junk room when Jonty lived here alone, but after I moved in he put in a space-saver staircase and tidied it up so I would have somewhere to work and make a mess. I follow Sam up the irregular steps from the first-floor landing. We're both whispering, creeping, aware of Jonty snoring below.

There's a full moon shining directly into the skylight, flooding the space with gossamer light. The skylight is huge, the largest Jonty could find, and the effect is dramatic, like a scene from a film. In the daytime you can see out across the higgledy-piggledy slate rooftops of the town. I sometimes drag my chair into the middle of the room to just sit here and think.

Sam picks through the materials I've gathered in baskets under the eaves: driftwood, scraps of metal, fragments and off-cuts of fabrics. There are tins of paint lining one wall. He says, 'Haven't seen you up here much lately.'

'There's been no time. But when the festivals are out of the way I can get back to it.' This magical light, my baskets and tools, the still quiet, make me long to be back here, losing myself to something of my own.

'There's always festivals,' he says, and he's right. But the Flags have been launched and my job is done there. The Comedy Festival is a few weeks away, but that's always far easier to manage because it's a registered charity in its own right, with a strong committee. 'I should be able to make some time next week.'

'Do it.'

Sam's always taken an interest in my work. That's why he started volunteering at the festivals and taking on some of the legwork: distributing flyers and posters, stewarding at events, fetching and carrying and generally doing anything that might save me some time for myself. On the other side of the room there's a single mattress covered with a purple blanket. This was Sam's bed while Nell lived here. She slept in the room downstairs. She liked the idea of sleeping in the attic, but in reality it was too scary for her and she crept down to swap places with Sam. He liked it up here, away from everyone, but once Nell moved out, he moved into the larger room below. He said he didn't want to have to navigate the awkward staircase, but I know he moved out of this room to give it back to me. Sam wants me here, in this house, even if Jonty doesn't and that's some comfort, though it makes no difference to what has to happen. There's no going back now.

His phone bleeps again. He ignores it and sits down on the bare floorboards in the shadowy area beneath the skylight with his arms wrapped around his knees. Not wanting to pressure him, I stand in front of the skylight and look out at the view. It's like a scene from *Peter Pan*, patched roofs and crooked chimneys against a slate sky. We took Sam and Nell to see the film one damp Sunday afternoon at Zeffirelli's in Ambleside. A dinner and pizza deal. It was Nell's favourite place to go for a treat.

Another bleep. And another, almost immediately. She's persistent. I want to grab the phone and scream for her to leave him alone, but Sam doesn't know that I know yet and I have to tread carefully. He swears under his breath and switches off the phone. He's dealing with this, in his own way, and I must not undermine that. I watch the headlights of a car as it snakes its way along a distant country road.

He says, 'Are you pregnant?'

He's guessed. If he's guessed, has Jonty? But Jonty would have said something. I can imagine him grinning, grabbing me and lifting me up in the air with those big arms, roaring with delight, and that image is like a punch in my gut; I can almost feel this child inside me wince because I know, if things hadn't turned the way they have, Jonty would have been delighted with this news. Jonty loves babies, if someone else is doing the caring and he can simply pick them up and play and give them back again. It's when they get older and require more of his adult attention that he struggles.

'I think I might be.' But this isn't true. I'm certain. Why don't I tell him this?

'Dad doesn't know.' A statement of fact, not a question.

I turn around. His face is all dark shadows and hollows. I could sketch him now, in charcoal. What would Pip say about that? Would trying to capture him at this beautiful point in his life, on the cusp of manhood, be deemed inappropriate? Surely there is nothing wrong with admiring the beauty of another human being? Does it automatically mean there's a sexual attraction? I admire other women, I notice. I'm not attracted, I simply appreciate a profile, the long line of a supple limb. I even see beauty in the delicate crepe of Pip's arms. My admiration of Sam is no different from that. He's looking at me, but I can't make out his eyes.

'You won't say anything?'

He shakes his head.

'I don't know what to do.' Jonty would be delighted; why can't I be delighted?

He says nothing. What can he say? He's a seventeen-year-old boy. But he understands that this isn't simple for me and I'm grateful for that.

And that's when we hear Jonty. Stumbling up the stairs and into the bathroom.

Holding our breath, we look at one another through the silver light. What do we do? Maybe he'll just collapse into bed and fall asleep again? He may not notice I'm missing. I can hear him peeing. We haven't got long. Sam glances towards the stairs and looks at me. I nod. I have to wait for him to reach the bottom before I can climb down. Jonty flushes the toilet as Sam descends. Please wash your hands! Please! I hear the tap as I'm navigating my way down the awkward steps, hear water splashing, Jonty moving closer, but my foot slips and I let out a strangled squeal of panic. Sam reaches out to stop me falling just as Jonty opens the bathroom door.

He stops, sways a little as he takes it in. Me in my pyjamas. Sam's hands on my hips. He frowns, struggling to focus.

I straighten up. 'Thanks, Sam. I slipped. It's these socks.' I smile at Jonty. 'Everything OK?'

'What are you doing?'

'We were just having a chat.'

'Up there?'

'We didn't want to disturb you.'

'A chat? In the middle of the night?'

I laugh it off, but Jonty doesn't laugh. He doesn't look well. I move towards him. 'Jonty, what's wrong?'

'Why was *he* up there, with you?' He points a little unsteadily at Sam.

'Jonty, this is Sam.' I place my hand on his chest. 'Come on, this is your son. What's the problem?'

'In the middle of the night.'

'Jonty, listen to yourself. This is silly. Come on. You need to get to bed.'

Jonty staggers and bumps against the doorframe. He looks at Sam and then back at me. He doesn't say anything. We're on the edge of something dangerous. I don't want Jonty to say things he'll later regret. Sam shouldn't see his father like this. If I can get Sam back to his room, I can talk to Jonty. Let him rant if he must, but he'll run out of steam and collapse pretty quickly, judging by the way he's leaning against that doorframe. Tomorrow he won't even remember this.

Jonty swallows. He looks like he's going to vomit. Instead he says, 'You're pregnant.' There is a fissure of such pain through that statement that it makes me ache. Because I should have told him. Because not telling him says something neither of us wants to hear.

Sam groans. Jonty's eyes flick to him and then back to me, pinning me like two nails. 'He knows?'

I can't stop myself glancing at Sam. He looks down at his feet.

Jonty is silent, but the space is full of his rage. It rolls out across the floor to the skirting boards and climbs the walls. I can feel it expanding, pressing in on us. He doesn't shout, but the silence is worse. I try to explain. 'He heard me throwing up tonight.'

But Jonty isn't listening. 'So this is how it is?'

I don't understand. 'How what is?'

'I've been so stupid.' He slaps his own face. 'Stupid.'

'Jonty?'

He leaps at me, hands locked, chest projecting forward as if he's fighting with himself not to hit me. I fall back against the wall and hit the floor. I've never seen such rage, never been the subject of it. I want to crawl away. My body is jerking with fear.

'You dirty, cheating bitch!'

'Dad!' Jonty spins round. Sam is trembling, but he doesn't flinch. 'Stop.'

'What's been going on?'

'Nothing!'

Jonty looks down at me. 'When were you going to tell me?'

'I don't know.'

He looks back at Sam. 'Is it yours?'

Sam's eyes are huge. Like a little boy's.

I beg. 'Jonty, don't. Please. Don't be ridiculous.'

'You think…?' Sam's voice trembles. But indignation strengthens him. 'You think…?' He cannot bring himself to say it. His beautiful face curls into a snarl. 'You sad old fuck.'

Jonty gives in to the rage. His fist arcs through the air, meeting Sam's face. Cheekbone. Left eye. Sam's head snaps back. The smack of bone against bone. The soft squelch of flesh. The spray of blood.

'Jonty! For God's sake!'

Sam clutches his face in his hands and falls to his knees. I crawl towards him. Jonty growls, turns and stumbles down the stairs.

Chapter 33

I bathe Sam's face with a damp flannel. He winces but holds steady as I dab disinfectant on the wound. The flesh is pink and swollen, the eye beginning to close; all that anger is also closing over, curling up inside him, out of sight. I would rather he raged and shouted. Better he berate his father and spend his fury, but he's not like Jonty.

'He'll be so sorry tomorrow.'

Sam says nothing.

Jonty has gone. He was in no state to drive, but he took the keys and I heard the car screech off up the street. He was heading out of town, towards the lakes. Where will he go? I try not to think of him on those narrow roads, blind bends. Let him pull over soon. Let him pull over and sleep it off. 'It was the drink talking. He didn't realise what he was saying, what he was doing. He'll be mortified in the morning.' But how could Jonty think something like that, even drunk, even for a moment? How could he entertain the idea that I would betray him and Sam in that way? I am his stepmum. I may not have that title, but I do that job and I take it seriously. I would never, never… 'It's ridiculous for him to think…' I cannot say the words.

Sam pulls away a little, looking at me through his one good eye. Steady. Pained. He has Jonty's eyes. 'Ridiculous,' he repeats quietly. And all the hurt in that expression tells me that I've wounded him.

He doesn't see it as ridiculous.

This makeshift shelter I've built around us and called a family has no foundations. No support. The earth is trembling and the walls are caving in and I'm standing in the midst of the wreckage, Sam's good eye fixed on me with the same hurt I saw in Jonty's. I've betrayed them both.

I realise I'm still holding the damp flannel in mid air. I lower my hand. Sam turns away.

Not ridiculous.

Not ridiculous, but possible. Painfully possible.

What do I do? What do I say to this half boy, half man who is already so much more of a man than his father could ever be? How do I tell him that it isn't ridiculous, just inappropriate. I love Sam, there's no doubt in my mind about that, but there's nothing sexual in those feelings. This is a child. A vulnerable boy. The feelings I have are warm but not romanticised. I may not be his mother. I may not have changed his nappies and nursed him, but I have washed his dirty underwear, reminded him to change his pyjamas, bought him spot cream and mouthwash and deodorising insoles for his stinking trainers. I have cared for him.

I want to put my arm around him, keep him safe, lead him out into the world and set him free. I may worry about who he ends up with, if they will love him and look out for him, if he'll be happy and realise his potential, I may hope that he comes back, often, and that I continue to matter, but that doesn't mean I want to keep him for myself.

I'd like to say my relationship with Sam is like brother and sister, but my relationship with Danny isn't like this. Maybe, under different circumstances, with a different mother, it might have been. There's something more equal about my relationship with Sam, something that was not a given but had to be earned. He could have rejected me. He was not obliged to depend on me the way Danny was. Sam had a choice. He chose to trust me and we built something together.

Is it broken, that bond we created? Or was it never really there in the first place?

Sam is beautiful, in a way that Danny is not. And that beauty is compelling. I enjoy it. There, I've said it. I like to have a beautiful boy as my friend, as my family. But that doesn't mean I want to have sex with him. I couldn't do that. There is a clear line and it would never occur to me to cross that, not because someone else says it's wrong, but because, for me, it is wrong.

He's confused right now. He isn't sure. That line is not so clear for him. His father has attacked him. His mother has begun a new life that he isn't part of and she's too far away at the moment to help. He needs me and I have to be confident and brave.

'Not ridiculous,' I say. My voice is soft. Not my usual, confident, Lizzie voice, but a girl's voice. A girl who might love a boy. I won't hide this from him. I can't be that girl, but I can let him know that if I could, he would be the one. Of course he would. 'Not ridiculous, but not true.' Because this is a fact. Nothing has happened between us and nothing will. He is my boy. He's confused right now, but I can't be. I'm the adult here, not by much of a margin, which makes it difficult, but there is a margin and I will respect it. I have respected it. I have to lead the way. That's my responsibility. And he may hate me for this, but it has to be done. 'Not ridiculous. But inappropriate.' I place my hand on his forearm. I need to touch him, to reassure him, to know that I can still touch him. He doesn't shrink from me. I look at my fingers against his flesh. Comfort. Love. Not lust. 'What we have is precious, Sam. It matters to me. I would like to protect that.'

The flesh around his cheekbone is beginning to swell and distort his face. He looks down at his feet. I reach for his hand and feel his fingers shift inside mine. And then I pull him towards me, place my palm against the back of his beautiful head and hold him.

We sit like this for some time. And I'm easy with it. It feels right. I'm loving, I'm compassionate, I'm sincere and I am not ashamed. I will not be ashamed of the way I feel about this boy.

We sit side by side on the landing with our knees to our chests. Neither of us wants to be alone. I'm thinking about Jonty, where he might be. I'm trying not to see a tangled wreck in the road.

And then it occurs to me. 'How did Jonty know I'm pregnant? He was downstairs. He couldn't hear us from down there. How could he know? Have you mentioned it to anyone?'

Sam shakes his head. 'I wasn't sure until tonight…' He stops. Something occurs to him. I wait, but he shuts it away and I know then. It's her.

'Does Rebecca know?'

Sam blinks. 'Someone told her.'

Matt. That day in the chemist. Rebecca in the pub, the night I went back for my jumper, sitting talking to Matt.

He frowns. 'But why would she say anything to Dad?'

'To do this. To create a rift between you, between all of us.'

'Why?'

'To isolate you.'

I give him some time to work through this. We're in no hurry. There's nothing that can happen to us now. Jonty believed her. He has assaulted his son and he's lost all faith in me. Things can't get any worse. At least Sam is talking.

His voice is fragile. 'I've done something.'

My stomach trembles. I press a hand against it and will it to settle. This isn't sickness, this is fear. I don't want to know and I have to know.

Sam turns his face away. 'I didn't… I don't know how… It just happened. And I can't stop it.'

I watch the muscle in his cheek twitching. 'What can't you stop?' But he shakes his head and rests his chin on his knees. 'Whatever it is, Sam, we're in this together. OK? Whatever it is, nothing changes us. Here. We're family. We deal with it together.' I can say this now. I believe it. I know it. 'Is this about Rebecca?'

He looks up and nods. He's still so young. His face all pinched and anxious. One big eye, the other swelling, an angry red. I can't believe Jonty did that to his boy. A boy in a man's body.

'Is it her, texting you?'

He sighs. Nods.

I wait. He doesn't speak. I offer a gentle prompt, not too intrusive, not too eager. 'How did it start?'

He seems to relax a little. This part of the story isn't so loaded. 'She was at King James's when I was doing my GCSEs. It was when Nanna… You know, when we moved here.'

So it started then. When he was fifteen and vulnerable. When he needed someone.

'She was like one of us... It was her first job, and... Then she started at the high school this year and that was a bit weird, you know. She was friendly and I didn't want to be rude, but some of the lads, they fancy her, so they started saying stuff, and it was a bit awkward, but I didn't want... She'd helped me before. A bit. She made it sound like... But it was helpful. To have someone. And her parents split up when she was a teenager, so she knew what it felt like.'

'She told you that?'

'She got that I was angry. Like you. She saw it from my point of view.'

Like me.

He begins to rock gently on his sitting bones, hugging his knees, to and fro. I can feel goosepimples up and down my arms. I swallow. Why didn't I pursue this sooner? I knew there was something wrong, but I was so wrapped up in work and Jonty, I didn't follow it up. I didn't give Sam the time he needed. The attention. I hesitate, lower my voice. There is no easy way to ask this. 'Sam, love, has something happened between the two of you?'

He tucks his head right down, burying his face in his knees.

'Sam?' My voice is a whisper now. I'm scared. I have to ask. 'Sam? Have you had sex with Rebecca?'

I watch the back of his head. A nod.

I have to keep going. 'Did you want to?'

He raises his face. Flushed. A frightened child. He shakes his head. 'No.' Then he frowns and turns away. 'Yes. Not at first, but then... I don't know.' He starts to cry.

Chapter 34

I'm aware of a presence in the room; not in the bed, but someone standing in the room. 'Sam?' Is he struggling to sleep? He told me as much as he could bear, as much as I could stand to hear. I thought it best to let him go and come back to it in the morning.

I sit up. There's a figure at the end of the bed. The blind is down, moonlight fingering the perimeter. Not Jonty. As my eyes adjust I can see it's not Sam either, but someone smaller, dressed in dark clothing, female, hair scraped back, and now the contours of her face, the outline of her features. That creepy smile.

Rebecca.

Her voice is slippery, cold. 'Sorry to disappoint.'

My throat is closed, my mouth dried out. 'What are you doing here?' There's something controlled about her and yet out of control. I shiver. 'Sam!' Where is he? A shriek of panic. 'Sam!'

She doesn't move. Watching me. How long has she been

standing there? I feel my gut drop, as if I'm going down in a lift. My body seems to collapse after it, but I'm still sitting upright, facing her. She can't see what I'm feeling. I must not let her see. 'Sam!' I know he won't answer. I can feel it. Like a bad dream that has seeped into reality. 'Sam!'

'He won't hear you.'

'What have you done?'

'Me?' She shakes her head and sits down on the edge of the bed, looking concerned.

'Where is he?'

'He's safe.'

'Why isn't he answering?'

She takes a while to speak. My chest aches from the pounding of my heart. There's something so cool about her. Quietly menacing. In her hand is a small glass jar with a plastic lid. She sees me looking and turns it over in her hand. I hear the rattle of pills inside. She places the jar in my palm and closes my fingers around it with her hand over mine. 'I don't think you meant any harm. You didn't realise what was happening. I understand. I do. He's a beautiful boy and when he looks at you, when he turns that light of his on to you, it's like you're the most important person in the world. And that's irresistible. And he's so like Jonty. All the charm and all the youth. Difficult for you, trapped between them; one too old and one just a little too young. And it's not like he's your son, it's not like you brought him up. He was fifteen, almost a man then. No one could blame you for feeling confused.' She applies a little pressure to my hand and glances down at the jar and then back at me. 'You've crossed a line.'

'No!' I try and pull my hand away, but her grip is firm.

'Not a clear line.' She carries on as if she hasn't heard me. 'But you have crossed it.'

'No! That's you! Not me!'

She does not alter her tone. This low, calm voice continues as if I haven't spoken. 'You were his stepmother. You were supposed to nurture him and support him.'

'I did!'

She shakes her head. She looks genuinely sorry for me. 'Oh, Lizzie. This is destroying you. I wish there was something I could do, because I understand. I do understand how difficult it must have been, living here, being so close, day in, day out, and you were trying so hard to get it right. You love him. I can see that. Of course you do. But you can see what that's done to him. He's in love with you now and there's no going back from that. There's nothing you can do. I can see how you're struggling. It's chewing away at you, the guilt. The day at the lake, the bath, the underwear…'

'You made me buy those knickers!'

'You're right.' She nods. 'I did persuade you to buy them, but I didn't know how you felt about him then. If I'd known… I'm so sorry, Lizzie. Maybe I am responsible, but I was trying to spice things up for you with Jonty; I never thought…' She looks genuinely remorseful. 'It felt good, didn't it? The attention Sam gave you? You enjoyed seeing yourself through his eyes, flirting.'

Was I flirting? Parading in front of him in that outfit, my face painted. I did enjoy it. For a moment.

'I do understand. He's beautiful. And you're not much older than him. And he's so much better suited to you than Jonty is. You work together, anyone can see that. You belong together, and in different circumstances… No one could blame you.'

Be careful. Pip said the boundaries were blurred. *Messy.* She warned me. She could see.

Rebecca squeezes my hand and lets go. I am left holding the jar of pills. 'There's no going back now,' she says quietly. 'What's done is done.' She gives me a soft, sympathetic smile. 'I understand. You love him. That's what matters. You want what's best for him. And you know that the only way he can get through this is with you gone. You do know that, don't you, Lizzie? You can't stay here. If you leave, he will follow you. But you can do the right thing now. For him. This the easiest way. If you love him, if that love is genuine and selfless, you know what you have to do.'

I do love him. I didn't mean to confuse him. I feel a hot tear working its way down the side of my nose. She glances at the jar. 'You can end this painlessly. Just go to sleep and it will all be over, for you and for them. It will hurt him, of course it will, but only for a little while and then he'll be free.'

I run my thumb over the label on the jar, thinking of Sam, my Sam, his face distorted into something ugly, predatory. Sam, my sweet, gentle Sam, sullied because of me.

'With you gone, they'll be safe. Sam will be safe. Nell will be safe.'

'Nell?'

Rebecca tilts her head a little, as if to imply that I do understand really. But Nell? She can't think that I would ever do anything to hurt Nell?

'You can't be trusted, Lizzie. Not after what's happened with Sam.'

Her eyes are fixed on mine. There's a flicker of uncertainty and that's enough, that flicker. She's reading me. She's working me, and she almost had me, but she's taken it too far. Not Nell. Never Nell. I might be worried about my relationship with Sam, about the way other people perceive it, but not Nell. My love for Nell is as pure as the winter snowdrops she picked from the garden the weekend after she arrived. With Sam the boundaries aren't clear and other people can misinterpret, can take this beautiful thing we have and make it dirty, but I know that's not the way it is. I love Sam the way I love Nell. Snowdrop love. Poking up through the winter frost. Fragile flower on a determined stem. A promise. A hope.

I throw the bottle across the floor and try to jump from the bed, but she leaps forward and plunges her fist into my chest.

A crack, lightning pain and she grips my shoulders and smacks my head back against the headboard. I feel my neck click. I scream, but she slaps her hand against my mouth. She's surprisingly strong. I struggle, but she has the advantage, her full weight on top of me. I try to bite, but her palm is flat against my mouth, pushing hard. She straddles my chest and raises the pillow above my face. I reach to grab it, but she pushes it down, crushing my nose. I feel her tip forwards, pressing her chest down, forcing the pillow against my mouth. I can't breathe. I can't breathe. My lungs are pumping, my body jerking. She grips my right arm, nails sinking into my flesh, forcing it down to my side and clamping it beneath her thigh. I lash out with my left arm, grabbing at hair, scratching, but she smacks my flesh and grips it, straddling me entirely. I'm useless. Trapped.

She raises the pillow. I gasp. Sucking in air, my chest groaning under her weight, I turn my head away, but she grabs my hair and yanks me back to face her. 'Stay still or I'll suffocate you!'

I can't fight her from this position. 'What are you going to do? The police will find me. If Sam's been kidnapped, they'll know it's you. Pip will tell them.'

'Pip? She doesn't believe you! She saw you making a fool of yourself. "I can smell him"? Really? Do you have any idea how mad you sounded? She's quite worried about you. About what's going on in that warped head of yours.'

'What did you say to her?'

'I told her that Sam had confided in me about your inappropriate behaviour. That he was scared. That he asked me to help him.'

'She won't believe that. No one will.'

'Are you sure about that? I've only ever behaved reasonably. I've been calm and polite. You're the one making hysterical accusations. No one believes you, not even Jonty.'

Jonty's growing anger. His distaste. She's been feeding his insecurities, whispering doubt in his ear. This has all been planned. 'Why are you doing this to us?'

'You're dangerous.' She believes this. I see it and now I understand. In her reality I'm the predator and she's the innocent and nothing I say will make any difference. She's watching me. A cold flash as she slaps my face. 'You had them both eating out of your hand. All you had to do was click and they jumped. One wasn't enough for you?'

'That's not how it is.'

'Not any more.' She leans back. A slow, narrow smile.

'You can't get away with this!'

'I'll tell them you attacked me in a jealous frenzy. I was simply trying to escape. It was a terrible accident.'

'No!'

Another slap. She presses her face close to mine. Her breath smells sweet and warm. A fine mist of spittle sprays my cheek as she hisses, 'You are going to do exactly as I say. Do you understand?' I blink back tears and nod.

Her eyes are wide, pupils dilated. She's relishing this. Power.

That's what drives her. She wants Sam and I'm standing in the way of that. In order to have him she has to get rid of me. She'll kill me if she has to. I can't stop her. I have to do something. Think. Think!

When my mum wanted a drink she would let nothing stand in her way. I would sometimes hide the alcohol, or her car keys, so she couldn't get out to buy any. She would rage and scream and physically attack me if she had to. I learned to avoid that violence by letting her think she was winning. I'd tell her that she could have the drink, or the keys, as soon as she'd eaten the meal I'd cooked. She would resist, but seeing that there was a way to win, she would eventually agree. She'd stand over the plate, stuffing handfuls of food in her mouth, but she would at least eat something and calm down a little. I would then give her a limited amount to drink. She'd still be drunk, but she would not be passed out on the kitchen floor and needing an ambulance. If I am to get out of here alive, I have to let Rebecca think she's got what she wants.

I sink back into the bed. I tell her I'm sorry. 'I didn't mean to hurt him. You're right. It's you. It's you he wants.' She hesitates, her eyes boring into me, searching for deceit. I keep going. 'I was jealous. I thought I could persuade him – but you're right, it's you. It's always been you, since the first time he saw you and I was jealous. I'm sorry. I'll explain, to Jonty, to Pip. They believe you. If I tell them the truth, it will all be fine. No one needs to get hurt. I'll go. Jonty's asked me to leave. I'm moving out. I'll be gone.'

She didn't know this. She sits back then, as if to take it in, to relish her success for just a moment and that's when I grab my opportunity. I muster all my strength and raise my knees behind her while thrusting my head towards her. My chest bellows with pain. She wobbles, and in that moment I roll, effectively clamping her between my knees and shoulders and throw myself to the side of the bed. Her head narrowly misses the bedside table as we fall. My hip whacks the wooden floor, then my shoulder. She gives a shriek of rage as she tries to wriggle free, but I am bigger and stronger and I roll on top of her, pushing her into the floorboards, ignoring the ripping pain in my chest.

It would be so easy now. I'm sitting astride her, one hand pressed against her neck to keep her face down. I could kill her. She has hurt Sam. She has lied to everyone, persuaded them all that I am the predator. She has torn my family apart.

But I'm not a killer. Under the bed I can see Jonty's belt, the one he thought he'd lost. I reach across, stretching my fingers, and just manage to tease the clasp with my fingertip, edging it across the floor until I can pick it up. I stand, keeping one foot on the small of Rebecca's back, pinning her to the floor. She groans in pain.

'Where's Sam?'

'Somewhere you won't be able to reach him.' She jerks upwards, knocking me off balance, and rolls on to her back, but I manage to steady myself and grip the belt. She raises an eyebrow as if she doesn't believe me. I flick the belt and catch her across her belly. She screams, part pain, part shock and I feel myself flinch with her.

'Next time it's your face. Stay where you are.'

I back out. She doesn't move, but she ripples with fury. I rush into Sam's room. It's empty and watery daylight is pouring through the blind. His bed hasn't been slept in. I walk back. She's attempting to stand, raising herself against the bed. Think. Think.

His phone. The texts. Did she text again? Did she persuade

him to go somewhere? She won't have wanted him to hear what she was doing, to see her in her true colours. She will have persuaded him to meet her somewhere.

She has something in her hand. It's the glass jar. She smacks it hard against the bedside table and it cracks, splinters. She has the cap end in her hand, a jagged weapon.

I need help. I need Jonty. Jonty left in a rage. He was driving towards the lakes. Where would he go?

Pip.

Pip. Chimneys. Pip at the lake shore, carrying a bag of Sam's rubbish up through the garden. *He's made himself quite at home in there.*

The boathouse.

She's stepping up on to the bed, the glass shards pointing towards me. I slam the door between us and run down the stairs, two, three at a time, nearly falling head first, but I grab the banister and right myself by the front door. I can hear her at the top of the stairs. As I reach for my car keys I drop the belt, but there's no time. I yank open the door and run. My car is at the end of the street. I am running, barefoot, with the key fob held out in front of me, unlocking the doors, throwing myself inside, locking myself in. My hands are shaking so badly I can't get the key in the ignition. My entire body is tensed, waiting for her fist to come through the glass, but I manage to get the engine started and jerk out of the parking space and on to the road and I am moving and the street unfolds in front of me, up, towards Windermere, towards Chimneys and Sam.

I swerve off the lake road, through Pip's gates, abandon the car on the pristine lawn, door open, engine running, and run across the damp grass towards the lake, towards the light and the breaking dawn.

Pip opens the door. I scan her body for a message as I draw closer, search the details of her face, but it's still too dark. I keep running, ignoring the searing pain in my hip. I can't stop now, though my chest seems to have collapsed and my lungs have no capacity at all; my legs feel like they're going to run ahead and leave me behind. Pip stands back as I burst past her and through the door. Sam is standing in the middle of the room. I throw myself at him, feeling the solidity of his body against mine, the smell of him, the warmth of him. Thank God! Thank God! His arms are around me. I wince as he squeezes me. My head slots into the small of his neck. He's here. He's safe.

It takes a moment for me to realise that Pip is standing very still, watching us. I turn to face her. Her expression is stern, worried. 'Lizzie, I've spoken to Rebecca.'

'She's lying. Please, Pip. She attacked me. She smashed the jar—'

Pip's hand goes to her chest. She suddenly looks a hundred years old. 'Oh, Lizzie!'

'Pip, it's OK. I escaped.' But Pip is shaking her head and moaning and this woman I thought was indestructible and could cope with anything is crumbling in front of me.

Sam steps towards her, takes her arm. 'What is it?'

She looks at him, swallows and says in the smallest voice I've ever heard, 'Rebecca has been stabbed.'

Chapter 35

There's a police car and an ambulance parked outside the cottage on Fell Rise as we pull up. The front door is open. A man in plain clothes, whose posture and bearing scream police officer, appears on the threshold. As he approaches I recognise Matt, his face a slab of stone.

I get out of the car and walk towards him. I can sense Pip and Sam behind me. Matt's eyes are narrow, watchful. 'I think you'd better step inside.'

Rebecca is perched on the edge of the armchair with one of Jonty's linen kitchen towels pressed to a bloody wound somewhere around her hip. There are vivid red scratch marks down one side of her face and across her collarbone. She looks like she's been attacked by someone vicious, hysterical. Sam gasps when he sees her. I feel Pip stiffen beside me.

Rebecca is looking at Sam, picking at her fingers, trembling, glancing anxiously at me, as if I'm the one to be afraid of. This is a world away from the woman who leapt from the end of my bed and punched me in the chest. This timid-little-girl act is outrageous when less than an hour ago she was hissing in my face. This woman was wild enough to thrust a broken jar into herself, to tear at her own face.

I glance at Sam. He's white with shock. He looks at me, horrified.

'I didn't do this.'

Rebecca glances up at Matt through her eyelashes and that look says, *See? What did I tell you?* And I know that there's nothing I can say that will help me here. She's worked on him. I've played right into her hands. For a stab victim she seems to be in pretty good shape. I'm guessing it's a flesh wound: something dramatic but superficial, like the scratches, but enough to get me into serious trouble.

Matt tells us to sit down, but Sam remains standing in the doorway. He doesn't want to be anywhere near me. Matt closes the door behind him. Pip and I perch on the sofa. You could fit another person between us. Pip is assessing the situation. This doesn't look good for me.

Matt takes Pip's name. 'Mrs Mitcham? You are the mother of Jonty Mitcham, is that right?'

'That is correct.'

'Would you be his next of kin?'

Pip stiffens. Next of kin: three words that conjure sirens, crushed metal.

I struggle to my feet, as if standing would make any difference to this news, as if I can just rush out of here and solve the next problem of the night. 'What's happened?' Let him be alive. Please. Please. Let Jonty be alive.

'It's all right.' Matt holds up his hand. 'There's been an incident.' He hesitates. 'The car is a write-off, but Jonty's fine. A few cuts and bruises. They're keeping him in for a bit.'

'Is that why you're here?' For a moment I think this might

be it. He's delivered his news and will walk out of the door, but of course he can't do that. She won't let him do that.

'I came to notify you of the accident, yes. However, when I arrived I heard shouts from upstairs. Rebecca heard me knocking. She managed to get down the stairs and let me in before she collapsed.' She gives a pathetic whimper as if it's all too much. Matt places a comforting hand on her shoulder. 'It won't be long now. The paramedics are on their way.'

I look at Pip, sitting straight and still, listening, taking it all in, giving nothing away. She thinks I did this.

Matt turns his attention to Sam, who is chewing at his thumbnail and rocking backwards and forwards on his heels. 'That's a pretty nasty black eye you've got there. How did it happen?'

Sam glances at me for the first time since we walked in but looks away again as if scalded. Matt clocks this. 'Well?'

I step in. 'There was a fight—'

'I think we can let Sam speak for himself.'

Sam stares at his feet. 'We had a row.'

'Who had a row?'

'Me and Dad.'

'What was it about?'

Sam shrugs his shoulders, his eyes fixed on the ground.

I can't bear the silence, the accusations in that silence. 'There was an argument. A misunderstanding.' I look at Pip. I'm more concerned about her than Matt. I need her to believe me. 'I got up to go to the bathroom. Sam was awake. We were talking. I was trying to get him to talk about Rebecca, to tell me what's been going on, but Jonty… Jonty misunderstood and—'

Matt interrupts. 'Misunderstood?'

I can feel Pip watching me. I feel dirty. Rebecca is almost smiling. This is all going her way. 'What does this have to do with anything?' I point at Rebecca. 'She attacked me!'

'Rebecca has given me her version of events.' He turns to Pip. 'Mrs Mitcham? Perhaps you could tell me what you know?'

Pip is clear and precise. She got up to use the bathroom and noticed a light on in the boathouse. She went to check and found Sam there. Clearly there had been an incident of some kind as his eye was bruised and swollen, but he didn't want to talk. She decided to let him sleep and to deal with it in the morning. She returned to the house and phoned me. Rebecca answered the phone. She told Pip I'd attacked her, stabbed her—

'I didn't stab her!'

Pip stops. She looks fragile, troubled. She doesn't want to believe this, but the facts are so clear. She continues, her voice measured but frailer now. 'Rebecca warned me that Lizzie was coming for Sam. That's how she put it. She said Lizzie was out of control. I went straight back to the boathouse.' She tells Matt I arrived moments later, at approximately 4.30 a.m.

Matt turns to me. 'Why did you feel it necessary to go to the boathouse?'

'I was worried about Sam. He wasn't in his bed.'

'Are you in the habit of checking on him in the middle of the night?' Rebecca's swollen lip twitches with satisfaction. 'Why didn't you telephone Mrs Mitcham if you were concerned?'

'I needed to see him.'

'Needed?'

'I was worried about him! Worried what she might have done. She's been grooming him. He's in a state of distress.'

Sam keeps his eyes on the floor.

Matt sighs and I feel a door closing. He's made up his mind. I see Rebecca sit back a little in the chair; her shoulders relax. She's won.

'She broke into our bloody house! She attacked me! Why aren't you questioning her?'

Rebecca shakes her head, sadly, as if she's concerned about me. 'You called me, Lizzie.' She looks at Sam: appealing, gentle, apparently innocent. 'I thought she'd caught you leaving to meet me and I panicked. I didn't know what she might do. She's said things to me, about you, about the way she feels about you...'

'That's a lie!'

'I thought she'd done something. Hurt you. I came straight here.'

Sam's scratching at his arms, looking at Rebecca, sweeping over me to Pip. I will him to look me in the eye so I can show him who he can trust.

Matt takes a step towards me. 'Rebecca has made a very serious complaint against you. Given the nature of her injuries, I'm going to have to ask you to accompany me to the station.'

'Me?'

'You do not have to say anything. But it may harm your defence if you do not mention, when questioned, something which you later rely on in court.'

'This is ridiculous!' I've heard these words on television, in films. This can't be real. Matt can't seriously be saying this to me!

'I must stress, before you say anything else, that anything you do say will be recorded.'

'Go ahead!'

'And may, if necessary, be given in evidence.'

'I haven't done anything wrong!'

'Lizzie!' Pip's voice slices between us. 'I suggest you stop. Now. Do as he says.'

'But I'm not the one who needs to be arrested! I'm not the one who broke in and attacked—'

'Lizzie!' Pip's face is a slab of ice. 'Enough.'

She doesn't believe me. She has suspected me all this time. She thinks I'm paranoid, that I'm the reason Sam is disturbed. She, like everyone else, has fallen for Rebecca's charm. I'm utterly alone now.

Chapter 36

We're sitting in a pristine room in the new Barrow police station. The plastic-coated table and four designer chairs wouldn't look out of place in a hotel bar. Matt sits on one side and I sit opposite. I've seen a doctor, who's given me an ice pack and some painkillers for my broken ribs. I didn't want to tell him about the baby, afraid of his reaction, what he'd assume, but he was practical and matter-of-fact and checked the heartbeat and said it all seemed to be fine. They're arranging for a scan. No internal organs have been damaged. It will take up to six weeks for the ribs to heal. I don't want to think about where I might be in six weeks' time.

I feel numb, detached, as if this is a story unfolding on a screen in front of me and I'm simply an observer. I still can't process what's happening to me. I've been arrested. I'm in a police station. I am suspected of abusing Sam and stabbing Rebecca.

Matt has suggested waiting for the solicitor, but I don't want to wait. I've nothing to hide. 'I want to get this over with.'

'I must remind you that you have a right to legal advice before I question you. Anything you say may be given in evidence.'

'Good. I want you to know what happened.'

'You understand that everything you say now will be recorded and may be used…'

'Yes!'

'… in evidence.' He places Sam's phone on the table between us. 'Do you recognise this telephone?'

'I know what this is about.'

'Please answer the question. Do you recognise this telephone?'

'Yes. It's Sam's phone.'

'Are you aware that this telephone has been used to send an indecent image to a Miss Fiona Appleworth?'

'I thought he deleted that image?'

'You were aware of the image?'

I nod, remembering Fi's distress. Her trembling hands. The raw flesh around her fingernail. A nod isn't enough. I'm asked to say it out loud. I do as I'm instructed and wait. He makes me look at the image.

'Sam didn't send that.' Why is it still on the phone? Sam said it wasn't there. But he didn't show me. 'He didn't take that photo. He wouldn't.'

'I've spoken to Sam. He says he did not take the photograph and he did not send it.'

'There you go.'

'Ms Watts says she came to talk to you about this image.'

'She sent it!'

He pauses and waits for silence before continuing. 'Ms Watts says she saw the image on Sam's phone and was concerned.' She's Ms Watts now we're being recorded; he has to sound impartial. 'It is possible that Sam sent this. When a young person is being groomed by an adult they can exhibit inappropriately sexualised behaviour towards other people. Ms Watts is aware that… Fiona… is sweet on Sam. That she would like to have a relationship with him, but Sam has never shown any interest in Fiona other than as a friend. Until this image. Ms Watts suggests that if Sam did take this photograph it might be an indication of his state of mind. A consequence of the abuse he himself has suffered.'

'Sam didn't take that photograph. He would never do that to Fi. Ask Fi, she'll tell you.'

'Did you take the photograph?'

'*Me?* Why would I do that?'

'Could you describe to me the nature of your relationship with Sam?'

'What do you mean?'

'Describe your relationship. As you see it.'

'It's difficult – I mean to describe, not the relationship. The relationship isn't difficult. Well, it wasn't, until…'

'Until what?'

'Until Rebecca started messing with his head.'

'How would you describe your relationship before things changed?'

'I'm like a stepmother, though obviously it's not as simple as that.'

'Why not?'

'You know why not.'

He sits back. He has all the time in the world. I'm the one who wants to get out of here.

'I'm not a stepmother in the typical sense, because I'm not that much older than Sam. It wouldn't work. Our relationship is based on mutual respect. Trust. It's more equal…' He raises an eyebrow at this. 'Not equal really, because I am an adult and I do have the final say, but more like an older sister or a young aunt.'

He nods, replaying in his mind what I've said, dwelling on my choice of words. 'A sister or an aunt.' I'm beginning to think I should have waited for that solicitor. 'Nothing more than that?'

'Absolutely not.'

'You have always behaved appropriately?'

'Yes!'

He looks at me for a long time. We're both remembering the lake. Him in the canoe, me in the wet T-shirt, Sam splashing about in his pants.

'There has never been an occasion where you might have blurred the lines a little? Misjudged things, perhaps?'

'Never.'

He looks disappointed in me. How dare he! I'm not a kid! I was doing nothing wrong. It's his dirty mind! Nothing to do with me and Sam.

'And now?'

'I don't understand.'

'You said things have changed.'

'Only that he's become withdrawn. Not just with me. He skipped school for a bit. He and Jonty… well, you know.'

'Could you clarify what you mean by that?'

'Things are difficult between the two of them at the moment.'

'In what way?'

I hesitate, which doesn't look good, but I'm aware I do need to be careful. 'Jonty's tetchy. With his redundancy. He's feeling his age and he's frustrated. And you haven't helped. You and Rebecca, poisoning his mind.'

'Are you making an allegation against me?' His eyes challenge me, but my issue isn't with him, it's with her. 'Rebecca has been feeding his insecurities. Suggesting that he's too old for me. That Sam and I are...'

'You and Sam are what?'

I don't answer this. He tries again. 'That you and Sam are...?'

'I don't want to say any more until I've spoken with a solicitor.'

He smiles. A flicker. He's enjoying this.

I'm taken back to the cell. The smooth new plaster and crisp finish make me wonder if I'm the first prisoner to inhabit this space. Because that's what I am: a prisoner. They believe I'm a groomer. That I abused Sam. They believe I'm capable of that. They. Matt is a horrible man with a dirty mind and I don't care what he thinks of me. Even though he has the power to keep me here, to persuade people, that means nothing to me. But Jonty... Jonty believes that I'm capable of taking Sam, our Sam, the boy who came to us and blossomed with us, the boy who chose to stay because he felt happy and safe, Jonty believes that I took that boy, that trust we'd built, and turned it into something sordid and ugly. Something unforgivable. Jonty believes this.

And, worse than Jonty, Pip.

Pip's good opinion matters more. Because I respect Pip and I want her to respect me.

I respect Pip. I don't respect Jonty. The significance of this is a solid shape taking form in the room.

I do not respect Jonty.

I try to pinpoint the moment when I lost my respect for Jonty. Dear, loving, easy-going Jonty; the charmer, the lover, the guy who could always look on the bright side. I fell in love with his optimism, the easy peace he provided, the absence of conflict after a life spent in an emotional warzone, but did I ever respect him?

I don't respect him now.

The police officer who brought me back to the cell told me Pip is organising a solicitor for me. I want to think this is because she believes me, but it's more likely that she's doing what she can to protect the family's reputation. She's probably calling in a favour from one of her Windermere friends. Pip has lost faith in me and that's the most devastating truth of all.

I'm expecting a patronising man in an expensive suit, but instead it's a smart woman in her mid thirties who strides into the featureless meeting room with a pile of paperwork under her arm, chestnut waves bouncing around her jawline. She shakes my hand firmly and gives me a broad smile, then sits down at the table and lets me talk.

She has a notebook with a soft pink cover. The pages are covered in small, tight script. When I've told my story she fills me in on what's been going on. There's a positive energy in her voice. She's not afraid of the situation and I take comfort in this, though I realise it has less to do with the gravity of what's going on and more to do with the fact that she deals with horrid scenarios every day.

'The police have searched the house, in particular the bedroom. There appeared to be no sign of a struggle in there.'

'I was in bed. She attacked me in bed.' She nods, impassive. 'She smashed the jar. There was a jar of pills. She was trying to get me to swallow them. She used the jar to stab herself.'

She writes this down. 'I'll look into that.'

'What does *she* say happened?'

'Ms Watts alleges that she received a call from you.'

'I didn't call her. I was asleep, in bed. She must have come in the back door. We leave the back door open sometimes.'

'There is a call registered to her number from your phone at 2.47 a.m.'

I hesitate. 'What time did Pip say I got to Windermere?'

The solicitor sifts through the papers in front of her. 'About four thirty. She couldn't be more precise.'

It's a half-hour drive to Chimneys from Tarnside, which means I left the cottage at about four. I have no idea how long I was fighting with Rebecca, but it wasn't for over an hour.

'She found my phone. I leave it on the table downstairs when I go up to bed. She must have called her number from my phone while I was asleep, before she woke me. But I didn't speak to her. The police can check that, can't they? There will be no content to the call.'

'She says she could hear your panicked breathing and when you wouldn't answer her questions she became concerned and came straight over. The police have confirmed that such a call did take place and the caller is clearly distressed and unable to speak.'

'How convenient. They do know she teaches drama?' She makes a note of this. 'Has she explained why Sam was meeting her at the boathouse?'

She looks back at her notes. 'According to her statement she texted him to say she was worried after she got your call. She asked him to meet her there in order to get him away from any danger.'

I let my head drop to the table. She has an answer for everything. I'm cornered.

We're interrupted by a knock on the door and Matt enters the room. He doesn't look at me but asks the solicitor to step outside for a moment. I'm left alone.

How did it come to this?

Why was that image still on Sam's phone? He lied to me. Why? Did he take that photograph? What will this mean for him?

The door opens and the solicitor steps in, but she doesn't sit down. 'I'm afraid I'm going to have to come back to this later. The social worker has arrived and they are about to interview Sam. Mrs Mitcham is considering legal representation and would like my advice.'

'Has Sam been arrested?'

'Not yet.'

Not yet.

I am taken back to my cell by a stern-faced police officer I haven't seen before. The door closes with a heavy clunk that reverberates along the corridor outside like a giant shiver.

What's happened to us? Can one woman create this much devastation? I'll make my case, but she is so convincing. People listen to her. She lies, but no one can accept that someone so delicate, so apparently sensitive, could lie like that. They don't want to believe it. When the truth is too ugly, people pretend they can't see it. I learned this lesson young, hiding the truth of my life. There are some things you can't tell people, things which are too shameful to share. People like to gossip, but from a distance. They like to talk and speculate, but when it comes to the reality, they don't want to be stained by it.

I am stained. It isn't fair, but it's true. I'm a product of my ugly childhood. Maybe I am to blame for what's happening to Sam. I'm tainted and that beautiful boy, who has done nothing to hurt anybody, who was clean and good and fresh and about to emerge into the world in all his youthful glory, has been tainted by me. They can do what they want with me. I give up. My grief is for him. He doesn't deserve this.

Chapter 37

A uniformed officer opens the door of my cell and steps aside to let Matt enter. Matt is all sharp lines and angles. His face, spiked with stubble, is weathered from year-round outdoor sport. There's a crumb on his lower lip. I could point it out to him, if I cared, but I no longer care about anything. Except Sam.

'Come on.'

I stand up. My legs are unsteady. 'Where are we going?'

'You'll need to sign for your things.' I stare at him. I can't speak. 'You're being released.'

The words hang there. I grasp at them, fruitlessly. Released? He sighs, irritated. I don't understand. 'Have I been bailed?'

He glares at me. He doesn't want to tell me. 'You're being released without charge.'

'You're letting me go? This is it? What's happened? Where's Sam?'

'I'll explain when we get there.'

'Get where?'

But he's turned and is walking out of the door. 'Lisa will take you upstairs.'

'Where's Sam?' But he's gone.

***

Matt reappears as I sign for my belongings at the gleaming desk in the sunlit office. My legs are trembling and I struggle to control my hand. The signature I leave is a wild scribble that bears no resemblance to the one I'm used to.

The world feels unsteady. I am almost weightless; the slightest puff and I'll blow away. He hovers in the doorway, jangling his car keys and leads me across the car park, striding ahead, unlocking the doors from his key fob as he approaches, the car wincing in response. Walking around to the driver's side, he barks, 'Get in.'

I open the passenger door and a sharp pain sears across my chest. Leaning against the car, I catch my breath. The inside is pristine and smells of strawberry air freshener. 'Where are we going?'

'I have some information for Mrs Mitcham and Sam. They've requested we meet at Mrs Mitcham's home in Windermere.'

'Sam? You've let him go?'

He doesn't answer. He's clearly not happy about this. Has Pip pulled some strings? I have a vague memory of her mentioning a police commissioner on one of her committees, but I can't be sure. Matt is tall and straight, his neck stretched long as he feeds the steering wheel through his hands, checking his mirrors, manoeuvring out of a tight space with ease. He is part of this machine now and the signal is clear: I am not to speak.

I lean back against the headrest as we drive out of town. Sam is with Pip, which means he can't be under arrest. I've been released, which must mean I'm no longer under suspicion. Not officially, anyway, though Matt doesn't seem persuaded. I'm going to see Sam, which means I can no longer be assumed to be a threat to him. Though Pip will be there. Is this some sort of confrontation? Have I been summoned to face the music? Will we be discussing my relationship with Sam? There is no way of knowing and Matt is silently fixed on the road ahead, so I give up trying to second-guess and focus on the green tunnel we're passing through. Sam is safe. Winding up the side of the lake, dry-stone walls, glimpses of a mirrored sky between the trees, the lake cruiser chugging reassuringly towards Ambleside. Sam is safe.

Pip explains as she pours the coffee. 'A new witness came forward.'

'Who?'

'Fiona.' I swing round to look at Matt. What has Fi said? Is this some sort of trap? Pip remains focused on serving the coffee. 'As a result, Matthew has had to do a little more investigating. I thought it best that he deliver his conclusions in person, to all of us.'

Matthew. She must know Matt from outside the police force. He's a local man. She will probably know his parents. She may have taught him at some point. There's certainly something about her body language and his that suggests a teacher and pupil. A scowl simmers beneath Matt's features.

His limbs sit stiffly in his dark suit. He looks out of place among the soft colours and textures of this room. His hands grip the porcelain cup, ignoring the handle.

'Sam is on his way,' Pip tells us. 'He's been asleep upstairs.' Sleeping safe in bed in Pip's house. Not in a cell. Not under arrest. I hear his steady footfall across the tiled hall and turn to watch the door. How will he be? Does he want to see me, or is this Pip's idea? Will he avoid me? Recoil?

His head is low, his hair falling in front of his eyes. He glances in my direction with the slightest nod and turns his attention to Pip and Matt. I want, more than anything, to get up and hug him, but I don't know if he wants that; I don't know how he feels about me right now or if I'm even allowed to be near him. And I'm scared, scared that my touch might be enough to sully him, if it hasn't already, and ruin his life. But it's a relief to see him. He looks better as he shakes his hair back. Brighter. The dark rings beneath his eyes are less pronounced, though his bruised eye is now an ugly yellow. His face is puffy from sleep, making him look vulnerable, innocent.

'Ah, Sam.' Pip holds up the coffee pot. 'Would you like a cup?'

Matt shifts in his seat. 'If we could make a start. I've got a meeting back at the station in an hour.'

'Of course.' Pip pours the coffee, taking her time, making no concession for Matt, adding milk from the little jug, passing it to Sam. Finally she sits down and looks at me. 'Fi was outside the cottage the night Rebecca attacked you.'

Attacked me. It's a fact. Pip believes me.

'Apparently she was asleep in your car?'

Sam explains, keeping his eyes on Matt. 'She does that sometimes. When things are difficult at home.'

Pip frowns at me. 'Were you aware of this?'

I nod. 'I didn't know for certain, but I did suspect. She has a spare set of keys.' The silence stretches out between us. I'm painfully aware of Matt in the room, judging me for not contacting social services, but that would have been a betrayal. Fi's situation is complicated.

Sam comes to my defence. 'Fi didn't want anyone to know. Lizzie told her she could sleep at ours any time, but she doesn't want that.' He turns his head a little towards me, but his eyes don't meet mine.

Matt writes something down in his notebook. Pip continues. 'Fi woke up when Jonty left the house, and sometime later she saw Sam leave on his bike.'

Sam adds, 'Rebecca phoned me. She sounded like she was going to do something, hurt herself. She told me she was at the boathouse.'

Pip gives a scornful snort. 'When in fact she was at the end of the street, in her car. Fi saw her get out, walk up to the front window. She looked inside and then carried on up to the ginnel and turned in.'

The back door. The banging gate. Loopy shut outside. 'That wasn't the first time. She's been in the house before.'

Matt looks up from his notebook. 'You make a habit of leaving the back door open?'

'We're at the end of a private-access lane. No one ever goes down there.'

Except Rebecca. Loopy recognised her when she came round that night. That's why she didn't make a fuss. She was used to her. How many times has Rebecca been to the house? Moving through our space, touching our things, picking up clues. I shudder.

Pip has warmed to her story and is eager to fill me in.

'Fiona was curious. She left the car and followed Rebecca around to the back of the house, where she found the door open. Stepping inside, she heard the commotion in the bedroom, but before she could make a decision about what to do, you ran down the stairs and out of the house, followed by Rebecca. Fi remained in the kitchen, not sure what to do. She heard you drive off and then Rebecca returned to the house. Fi stepped back outside where she couldn't be seen.' She turns to Matt. 'Matthew, could you remind me? Did Rebecca appear to have any significant injuries at this point?'

Matt scowls. 'She did not.'

Pip's voice is sickly sweet. 'And what did Fiona say Rebecca did next?'

Matt makes a show of checking his notebook. 'She poured herself a glass of wine and sat down in the living room.'

Pip raises an eyebrow at me. 'She took her time and made herself comfortable while she planned her next move. Fi assumed you'd had to rush off for some sort of emergency and had agreed that Rebecca would remain at the cottage. There was no evidence of any kind of attack. It wasn't until she spoke to Sam that she discovered the allegations made against you. She went straight to the police.'

'So, Matthew, would you like to tell us what Rebecca's response to this new evidence has been?'

I can imagine. Screaming fury. Rebecca does not like to be thwarted. Matt clears this throat. 'Ms Watts has revised her statement. The assault charges have been dropped.' Pip throws me a slow smile, nodding her head as if to say, *Yes, it is true, you are free.* 'So, Matthew, would you like to tell us what you have discovered?'

Matt's voice is a dull monotone. 'In light of the new evidence, we ran a check on Rebecca Watts.'

I glance at Sam. A flicker of a smile. He knows something.

'There was nothing on record. No previous history.' He hesitates and looks at Pip. She knows. She and Sam both know what Matt has come to say. Pip must have been briefed already, but she's made Matt come here to tell us face to face. To tell me. He scowls.

Pip shakes her head, her patience stretched. 'Sam and I had a little chat. And then I went to King James's School to do a bit of investigating myself.' She throws Matt a condescending look. 'Apparently there was a complaint made against Ms Watts by the parents of a pupil.'

'So she's done this before?'

Matt interjects. 'No further action was taken and Ms Watts left the school of her own volition.'

'How come?'

Pip explains. 'I met with Mr Allbright, the head teacher. He remembered Rebecca fondly. A foolish girl who let her feelings get the better of her, apparently.'

'She got away with it?'

'It appears so. Mr Allbright is an older gentleman, rather outdated in some of his attitudes, and, it would appear, with a soft spot for a pretty face. Would you like to continue, Matthew?'

Matt glares at me. This is personal for him. He doesn't like me. Whatever it is he's found out, however innocent I'm proved to be, it won't change his opinion of me. 'We thought, with Sam's statement, it would be wise to bring Ms Watts back in for questioning.'

'And I suppose she denied everything?'

He ignores me. 'I spoke to the pupil concerned.'

'On my insistence,' Pip adds.

Matt continues as if she hasn't spoken. 'It's not clear who initiated the relationship.'

I can't help myself. 'It doesn't matter who initiated it! She's a teacher. It's her responsibility to act appropriately.'

He looks me straight in the eye. 'Yes, well, it's not always that easy to define what's appropriate and what isn't.'

But I don't flinch this time. I don't care if Pip's here. I have nothing to be ashamed of. 'You saw me in a wet T-shirt. Big deal. The only inappropriate thing about that was the way you looked at me!'

Matt's nose twitches, but Pip has her eye on him, he has to behave.

Another pupil. Another vulnerable young person Rebecca has manipulated and sullied. Someone's child. Another family shattered.

'I believe there is more?'

Matt clenches his jaw. Pip tilts her head a little to one side as if to say, *Well?* He grinds his teeth. The words are stuck somewhere, refusing to budge. He sniffs. 'There was also an incident of harassment while she was at university. A younger student.'

Pip sets her cup back down in its saucer. 'It appears there is a pattern.' She turns to me. 'You were right, Lizzie.' She looks back at Matt. 'Perhaps you were a little hasty in your judgement, Matthew?'

He flushes a dark purple beneath his tan. 'I have to deal with the facts as they present themselves. Ms Watts appeared to have been assaulted.'

Pip watches him as if she is waiting for an apology, not

that Matt will oblige, but it's enough to let him know she believes an apology is required.

I glance at Sam. He looks relieved. Looser. Freed.

'What I don't understand is why? She's so attractive. She could have anyone.'

I'm looking at Matt, but it's Pip who answers. 'She's a psychopath.' I laugh, but she's serious. 'You can dress it up more gently, if that feels better. The Americans would call her a sociopath, but it amounts to the same thing. Not all psychopaths are axe-wielding murderers, many never physically hurt anyone. There is research that says as many as one per cent of the population are psychopaths. They're often charming and manipulative and many go on to hold positions of great power and lead a perfectly respectable life. A psychopath doesn't feel empathy the way you and I do, Lizzie, and this means they can lie, blatantly. There is no self-doubt. They will stop at nothing to get what they want. Rebecca was attracted to Sam. I suspect he became considerably more attractive when she met you.'

'Why?'

'Because Sam loves you. Genuinely loves you. And she wanted that.'

I look at Sam. His face is scarlet. Bloody Pip and her theories!

'Psychopaths create their own reality. Rebecca believed she was saving Sam. She persuaded herself that you were the problem and she had to rescue him.'

'So I'm responsible?'

'No.'

'It sounds like it.'

'She has done this before, Lizzie. I've no doubt that having a competitor fuelled her pursuit, but she was already grooming him when she met you.'

'What will happen to her now?'

'She will be referred to a psychiatrist. I don't know what will happen. From what I've read, she's unlikely to learn from this experience any more than she did from her previous encounters. I'm not sure she has the capacity to reflect and change.'

I'm no longer interested in Rebecca; it's Sam I'm concerned about. 'What about the sext?' I look at Matt. 'What's happening about that?'

'The image was sent from Sam's phone.'

'Without his consent!'

'That cannot be proved—'

'But—'

'However, we are allowed to exercise some discretion in these circumstances. We prefer to avoid criminalising young people unnecessarily. The incident has been recorded. Social services, Sam's parents and the school have been notified.'

'But Sam didn't send it!'

Pip intervenes, 'Lizzie. The key thing is, Sam won't be charged.'

Matt nods. 'We've spoken to Fiona and decided that no further action is necessary.'

I sit back and finally allow myself to relax. Sam is safe. He won't be prosecuted or put on the Sex Offender Register. I don't know what will happen to Rebecca, but she won't be able to work in another school after this and Sam is free.

Matt puts his cup down on the table beside the saucer and stands up.

Sam asks the question I've been too scared to voice. 'So what happens now?'

Matt glares at me. 'I fill out a lot of forms.'

Chapter 38

Pip sends Sam out to the boathouse with a bin liner to collect the rubbish and tidy up, while I clear away the coffee paraphernalia. She insists that I don't bend or exert myself and I am feeling the pain in my ribs and hip, so I set the cups and saucers on the work surface. I thank her for arranging the meeting with Matt so that I could be there.

'It's the closest thing you'll get to an apology.'

I take a cloth and wipe the coffee table. Behind me I hear Pip close the door of the dishwasher. She's silent for a moment, but I can sense something. I straighten up and turn to face her.

'I am so sorry I doubted you, Lizzie.' My throat has closed up. I offer a nod of acknowledgement. 'That woman is dangerous.'

We're silent for a moment, the two of us considering all the damage Rebecca has wrought. So much pain with her simple but devastating twists and lies.

'You're pregnant.'

My gut drops. I stare at Pip. Her respect matters to me. I know now that without it I'm pathetic. An outsider. Alone. I nod, picturing the child blossoming inside my belly. Jonty's child. How will we ever get over this?

'How far?'

'Thirteen weeks.'

'Are you going to keep the baby?'

Her tone is gentle. Kind. This sends me reeling. I've dreaded hearing this question spoken out loud. As long as it remained inside my head I could ignore it, which is why I haven't spoken to anyone, but now it's out there, solid and real, the answer is surprisingly clear and the words emerge of their own volition, with no time for me to consider or hesitate. 'Yes. I don't know how. I don't know… but yes.'

I have been thinking it through, churning it over. Of course. I've being doing nothing else for weeks.

Pip hasn't asked about Sam. She doesn't need to ask. That ugly thought doesn't even cross her mind. I swallow back my tears. She nods, as if she knows everything that I might want to say and doesn't need to hear it to understand. 'We had better go and see Jonty.'

We leave Sam at the house and drive in a very different silence from the one I shared with Matt. Where there was hostility there's compassion, where there was suspicion there's trust. Nothing has been said, but I can feel it, an altogether different shape to that which was in the cell with me. Something warmer, more accommodating.

Jonty is sitting up in bed looking sheepish. A naughty boy who knows he's going to have to face the music, with Pip and me, his two mothers, coming to reprimand him. Because that's what I am to Jonty, another mother. Age has nothing to do with it; Jonty is a teenage boy at heart. Charming and for the most part delightful, but he'll always be a naughty child. This is what I fell in love with. I thought I could change him, tame him, but Jonty will never change.

He has no idea what's been going on. As far as he's concerned, he had a bit too much to drink and thumped his son, but, hey, boys' stuff, right? Things sometimes get a bit out of hand. He won't dwell on it. He'll apologise to Sam or do something to show he's sorry without actually saying it. For him it will all be water under the bridge and he'll expect it to be the same for everyone else.

But it isn't the same for me.

He doubted me.

There is a part of him that allowed the image of me and Sam, me *abusing* Sam, to enter his consciousness. It will always be there. He may choose to forget it. He may think it won't come back, but I'm not so sure. I will never be sure.

He doesn't know what's happened since he stumbled out of the house. He'll never really understand what's been going on. In Jonty's world it's a huge fuss over nothing. A crush on a teacher. A bit of drunken jealousy. What's the big deal?

He looks down at my bump that isn't really a bump yet and his face folds into soft creases. Reaching out, he places his hand, oh so gently, on my belly, staking his claim. He looks up at me. 'Is everything OK?'

'They think so. They're organising a scan.'

Joy paints his face. He will love this child. I can see him laying a baby down in a cot and stroking the damp curls on its skull. I can see him lifting a toddler on to his shoulders. I can see him being tender and playful and kind. But a child needs more than that.

He begins by telling me he's sorry, and I nearly lose it then, not my temper but my resolve, because I know what it's cost him to say those words out loud. It makes a difference. I want so much for it to make enough difference to give us another chance, because life with Jonty is easy if you let yourself live the way he does, on the surface of things, not taking responsibility, allowing other people to do that for you. When it was just me and him it was fun and that was enough. But it's not enough now. I place my hand on my belly. It's not enough when there are children involved.

'We're going to be a family,' he whispers. But we were already a family. 'I'll do it better this time.'

Oh, Jonty. True to form: wipe the slate clean, walk away from the mess, start again. It doesn't work like that. 'You haven't asked about Sam.'

His face tightens. All the softness gone. He won't apologise to Sam the way he has to me. There's more pride involved there: Jonty is not about to concede the role of alpha male. He's lost it already, of course, though he doesn't realise.

'When the lads ask how he got that shiner he'll be able to say he put his old man in hospital.' He gives a weak laugh. Even he can hear how feeble this sounds.

Pip shakes her head. 'It's not his physical injuries that are the issue.'

He looks from Pip to me for an explanation and I'm about to speak, to tell him everything that's happened, all I've had to cope with while he's been drunk and hospitalised and incapable, but Pip places a hand on my arm. 'Lizzie, I'll deal with this.'

'Deal with what?'

Pip ignores him. 'When are they letting you out?'

'I'm just waiting for my meds.'

'You'll need a lift.' They've confiscated his licence. He will be prosecuted for drink driving. He'll be needing lifts a lot now. 'We will take you home.' Pip's voice is cool and firm. 'But first there are things to discuss.'

'What things?' Jonty looks alarmed. He assumed the worst was over. For Jonty, everything turns out all right in the end. He makes a mistake, he takes the flak, but he's a nice guy and no one's going to hold it against him for long. But Pip is not amused.

He looks at me. I can't do this any more. All that difficult stuff Jonty likes to dodge is about to break the surface and he's going to have to deal with that alone.

Pip sighs. 'Lizzie, would you see if you can find out what's happening with Jonty's medication while he and I talk?'

I'm relieved to escape. It's cowardly, but I don't have the stamina to deal with any challenges from Jonty right now. I've made mistakes. I should have confided in him, but Pip understands why that was difficult and she won't take any nonsense.

I go in search of a nurse, who tells me Jonty's prescription will be ready shortly. The waiting area has a line of blue chairs positioned in front of a television screen on which a fictional hospital drama is unfolding. I walk out into the corridor where it's quieter and lean my head against the wall.

Where am I going to go now? Living with Jonty is no longer an option. I've allowed myself to drift into a situation which is unsustainable. Jonty's world. Jonty's children. The life I've built in Tarnside is knitted around this family. If I'm no longer part of that, do I still belong? How can I continue to live and work in this small community and not be part of Jonty's life? I'll bump into him all the time, I'll be questioned by friends and neighbours who won't mean any harm but will want to understand. And it will hurt. Him and me. The seeing. The not being together. Because I love him. Because I know he loves me. But that love is not enough.

I have a great job, but there are jobs like it in other parts of the country. If I have no ties I can go anywhere. I could simply pack a bag and fly off somewhere on a one-way ticket. The world is my oyster. Except…

I feel a flutter inside me. A reminder. A protestation? Things are more complicated than that.

Jonty is dressed and waiting with Pip at the end of the bed when I return with his prescription. He looks crumpled – his clothes, his face, his entire body. He knows it all now. Pip's face is taut. She's been merciless. Jonty is chastened. He reaches for my hand, but I can't touch him. Nothing is said. Pip propels him out of the door to the car and I follow quietly behind, waiting for the next instruction, because I have no idea what else to do.

Chapter 39

Sam is waiting for us at Pip's when we pull up. He closes the gate to the road and follows us to the house. We file in, like mourners after a funeral. It's all very peculiar and stilted. Where do we go from here?

Pip goes straight to the drinks cabinet and takes out a bottle of brandy. 'I need a stiff drink.' None of us can join her, though I'm sure Jonty would, given half the chance. He's on medication, I'm pregnant and Sam is underage. She pours a small shot into a tumbler and takes a generous gulp. 'Rebecca has asked to see Sam.'

Sam's face screams horror. 'No!'

Jonty steps forward. 'You haven't agreed?'

Pip lowers herself into an oak captain's chair and places her hands on the arm rests. 'I think it might be helpful.'

Sam shakes his head. 'I don't want to see her.'

Pip sighs. She looks at me. 'I think it might provide some sort of resolution?' It's a question. An image of Rebecca perched on my sofa, her face bruised and bloodied, flashes before me. That look she gave Matt, like an injured, frightened animal, but she wasn't frightened; she knew exactly what she was doing.

I glance at Jonty. He shakes his head.

I don't want to see Rebecca. But if I don't, that image will remain. I'm afraid of her. I fought back, but she returned to challenge me again and though her past has caught up with her, though the law has intervened, I don't feel we're done yet. And if this is how it is for me, how will it be for Sam? He's staring out at the lake, face pinched, that muscle in his cheek quivering. Will he always be afraid of her? 'I think Pip may have a point.'

Sam and Jonty respond in unison. 'No!'

'Sam, listen to me. I'm scared of her too. She's dangerous. But she can only control us if we let her. Can you see that?'

'She's a liar.'

'But if we don't believe her any more, she has no power. We need her to understand that.'

Jonty intervenes. 'He doesn't want to see her. Let the boy make up his own mind.'

Pip stands up. 'I think, Sam, that it's important for you to put this behind you. If you are to do that you need to be honest about what happened and take your share of responsibility.'

'Is anyone listening to me?' Jonty throws his hands in the air.

I look him straight in the eye. 'No.' There is a moment and in that moment he knows it's over between us. He winces and looks away. I turn back to Pip. 'Sam's a minor. *She* abused *him*.'

Pip looks at Sam. He's staring at his feet. 'Sam, it seems to me that you are ashamed of what happened. You shouldn't be.'

Jonty picks up the brandy bottle and unscrews the lid. He

hesitates, the bottle hovering over the glass, and then puts it back down. 'She's a very attractive woman.' He could pass for Sam right now, that fragility, but as he speaks I watch him patch himself back together. A smaller, more fragile man, but he will do this. Jonty is a survivor, in his own way. 'You'd have been a fool not to fall for her, son. She had me wrapped around her little finger.' He hesitates, shrugs, looks abashed. 'I should have known better at my age, but you, you didn't stand a chance.' He sighs, screws the lid back on the bottle and pushes it away. 'She played you. There's no shame in that.'

Pip takes her opportunity. 'I think it would help you if you could tell her it's over, Sam. Take control.'

Sam turns to me. 'Can you be there?'

'Of course.' But I'm scared. I don't know if I can protect him.

Pip is decided. 'We will all be there.'

We meet Rebecca at the police station in a bright meeting room with two rows of low seats, upholstered in royal blue, facing one another. There's a water dispenser on a table under the window and a framed photograph of Sca Fell on the pristine wall. A young police officer sits at the far end, as if she doesn't want to be noticed. Pip and Jonty sit either side of Sam. I take the seat opposite the social worker, where I can watch Sam. This is not about me and Rebecca, this is for Sam. I don't want to be a distraction.

Rebecca enters with Matt. His body language is stiff; controlled and controlling. She has lost her hold on him. He avoids looking at me. Her face is bare of make-up, the scratches have scabbed over. Dressed in jeans and black T-shirt, she looks young and vulnerable. This is the part she will play today: abused victim looking for a rescuer. I should have seen this coming, I could have warned Sam.

She looks at him, eyes big and pleading, brimming with tears, and hesitates, as if she's struggling not to reach out and touch him. Matt places a hand on her shoulder and pushes her down into the chair. She leans forward, her body straining towards Sam and gives a choked whisper of his name.

That muscle in his cheek twitches. His hands, palms down on his thighs, grip his leg as he looks at her. His face is cold. Good boy. You can do this.

Her voice quivers. 'How are you?'

He holds her gaze. 'Fuck off.'

She flinches. 'Don't say that. I love you. And I know you love me.'

He turns his face away.

'They've turned you against me.' She looks at me and hisses. 'She's the one you need to be afraid of! She's the one lying and manipulating and controlling you all!'

I want to grab her and smash her face into the table.

I don't.

I don't need to hurt her. She'll give herself away. I mustn't say a word. I chew my tongue.

She turns back to Sam, her face soft again, appealing. She's back to the mistreated young girl routine. 'Sam, please. Listen to me. I know you love me. You know. We belong together. In a few weeks you'll be eighteen and none of this will matter. We can move away. We can start again. We have to… You can't…' She straightens her back. Looks down. Her hands move.

I'm watching Sam as he watches her and his eyes drop a

fraction, to her belly, and the alarm that begins to register on his face is echoed in Pip and Jonty's as Rebecca slowly smiles. 'Our baby. Something we've created, you and I. You can't leave me now, Sam. It's not just about us any more. We're going to be a family.'

My stomach flips. I gag. No. Please, no! This can't be true. I stand, my legs weak. I can feel everyone's eyes on me. I reach for the plastic cup and place it under the spout. I can't keep it still. The social worker gets up. She fills the cup and hands it to me. My legs won't take me back to the chair. I lean against the wall. Pip's eyes meet mine. The horror is there.

He's bound to her for life. There's no escape now.

Sam. Our golden boy. All that life ahead of him. All that possibility. She has robbed him of that. He'll never be free of her now. Everything he does, every choice he makes, will have to involve her.

Jonty is looking at Rebecca. I watch him lean towards her. He says, 'I don't think so.'

'It's true.'

He shakes his head. 'Can't be.' A flicker of uncertainty crosses her face. Jonty gives a little smile. 'Sorry.'

She turns to Sam. 'It is. You know—'

But Jonty cuts across her. 'Sam can't have children. He's infertile.'

What's going on? Jonty has never told me this. I look at Pip, but she's frowning as if it's news to her too. Sam looks at Jonty, stunned. Rebecca sees this, of course, and waits, but Jonty is ready. He shrugs. 'Sorry, son. Not the best way to find out. Remember you missed starting school? All the other kids had made friends by the time you arrived and it took you a while to settle in?'

He does remember. We watch it register. 'I was too late to sign up for football.'

Pip nods and she looks at me, eyes intense, urging. 'That's right. I remember, Sam had to spend the day at Chimneys because Kay had somewhere she had to be…'

There's something not right about this. Something niggling at me. Jonty would have said. If Sam is infertile, if Jonty knew, he would have said something. Jonty stumbling against the doorframe of the bathroom. *You dirty, cheating bitch!* His fist arcing through the air towards Sam's face. Jonty believed Sam might be the father of my child. He would never have reacted the way he did to Rebecca and Matt's insinuations about my pregnancy if he knew Sam was infertile.

Jonty is focused on Sam. 'You had mumps, mate. Left you firing blanks, I'm afraid.'

Rebecca's face hardens. Jonty stands up. 'Nice try, love. I think we're done here. Sam?'

Sam gets up. He stands looking at Rebecca for some time, as if he's spooling back through what went on between them, rereading it, disentangling himself from her.

She is frowning, trying to work it out, and I see the realisation spread over her face and trickle out across her body. Her fists tighten. 'Wait!' Jonty turns. 'You believed me! When I told you she was pregnant, when I said… You believed that baby was Sam's!'

Sam's voice is low and quiet but solid as stone. 'You bitch.'

She swings round. 'No, no! I was… I was trying to protect you.'

Sam shakes his head; his nose wrinkles as if he's smelt something foul. Jonty ushers Pip out of the room and slips his arm around his son's shoulders to follow.

Rebecca gives an indignant shriek and stamps her foot. 'You lied!'

I step towards the door. 'So did you.'

The police officer stands, but she isn't quick enough. Rebecca gives a roar and leaps at me, teeth bared, nails reaching for my face. I jump aside. She bounces off the doorframe and pounces again, but this time I'm ready and I grab the chair and charge at her, shoving her back, pinning her against the wall. She shrieks, her head swinging from side to side, eyes wild, kicking and hissing, but she can't escape. I feel Matt approaching behind me. Leaning in as close to her as I dare, I hiss into her face, 'It's over.'

Epilogue

I am in my bedroom, in my cottage. Not Jonty's, not the childhood house I had to escape from, not a rented room in somebody else's place, but my home. I'm trying to find something that will fit over my vast belly and look a bit smarter than the jeggings with the stretchy panel and the oversized T-shirt I wear most days. My clothes are on a rail by the window. It's hot and muggy and I don't want to be sweating. I reach for a loose linen dress in a pale grey that I picked up at the car boot sale we host in the park once a week and examine my reflection in the narrow mirror I have propped against the wall. I look like a whale, but at least my skin is clear and tanned and my hair has never been so glossy.

I have a cot ready to assemble in the corner of my bedroom and I'm slowly collecting things I'll need – changing mat, miniature bedding, a plastic baby bath – but it still doesn't seem real. I find it impossible to imagine myself here with a newborn baby. At least it's beginning to look like a home. I'm slowly taking root. I'm due on the tenth of September and Fi will be back from France by then. Eve has asked her to manage the Lantern Festival before she starts at uni. I have no idea how I'm going to cope once the baby is born. Jonty will help. I'm luckier than some.

I step into a pair of Birkenstocks, the only things that will contain my swollen feet these days, and look back at the woman in the mirror, trying to see myself as someone else might see me. Someone who has been talking to Sam about what happened, how it happened.

Rebecca has been charged with assault for her attack on me, but what went on between her and Sam is, according to the solicitor, 'a grey area' and taking longer to sort out. In the meantime, Sam has been attending therapy once a week. His counsellor has asked me to join them today. Last night I dreamt I was being pushed and shoved on to the stage in the town hall by an angry crowd of local people. Matt, and Nigel from the pub, sniggering, Pip looking paper fragile, leaning against Jonty, who couldn't meet my eye, and Eve and Neil Wright watching from a distance, horrified, unable to hide their distaste. I tried to speak, but no sound would come out and I woke to the sound of my own wretched moan.

This will be the first time I've seen Sam in weeks. First there were his exams and then as soon as they were finished he flew to Ireland with Pip. This will be the first time I've been alone with him since the night of Rebecca's attack.

I try not to think about what Sam's said to the counsellor, what she must think of me and some of the things I did that might have made Sam vulnerable. We've arranged that I'll drive him to the appointment. As my cottage is only about five hundred yards from Jonty's front door and my car is parked on the street, I'm assuming I'll call for him.

I'm mentally preparing myself, but as I pick up my keys he knocks on my door.

He's shaking his hair back from those dark eyes, face flushed, shifting his weight from one foot to the other, tapping his slim fingers against his thighs. He seems taller, fuller, more substantial somehow. The sheer closeness of him winds me and I grip the door for support. I immediately assume I'm late, but he reassures me. 'No, no. I was ready so I thought I'd walk round.' He gives a little shrug and all I want to do is lean into him, press my face against his chest and breathe deep, pretending none of this has happened.

I'm flustered, flapping about, talking too much about things that are of no importance, anything not to feel the rawness of this. I'm nervous as a teenager on a first date, which is so inappropriate and the corresponding blush crawls up from my chest to my cheeks.

He has to step aside to let me out of the front door. I ask him if he wants to drive, but he's too agitated to cope with that, so I manoeuvre myself into the driver's seat with some difficulty and wait for him to strap himself in beside me. As I start the engine the radio comes on and I can sense that he's as grateful as I am for something to fill the space between us.

The counsellor is a lovely, gentle woman who introduces herself as Roisin and speaks in a soft, southern Irish accent that conjures pub firesides where old men play fiddles and drink pints of Guinness. She ushers us into a small room with three soft chairs, covered with Indian throws. There's a plant with frilly pink flowers on the table, and a bowl of fruit. Roisin thanks me for coming. 'I know it's important to Sam. He's asked for you to be here today.'

Sam has asked. Not the counsellor. I remember the lake, my wet T-shirt, his comment as I tried to hide my body in the bath: *You were coming on to me.*

Roisin explains how the counselling has been working so far. 'As you know, there is a possibility that this case may go to trial, so we have to be very careful not to contaminate evidence. We are not able to discuss exactly what went on with Rebecca, but we can work on how Sam has been affected by what happened.' I turn to look at Sam as she speaks. He has his head down. 'While we can't talk about specific events, we have been able to discuss how Sam feels.'

It is so difficult not to reach out to him now. I curl my fingers into my palms as Roisin continues.

'One of the things we discussed in the last session was how this has affected Sam's relationships. With his father, his grandmother, and with you.'

I sense Sam tense beside me. Fingers claw in my throat. I keep my eyes fixed on Roisin, but she's looking at Sam, waiting for him to speak and when I turn he's looking at me, that muscle in his cheek shivering, and he says, 'I'm sorry, Lizzie. For what I did. The things I said.'

'It's not your fault. That wasn't you; it was her.'

'It was me,' he says firmly, owning it. 'But she messed with my head. Said things. Twisted them.'

I can see tears forming in his eyes and he's struggling to keep them back. My fingernails dig into my palms. 'She's toxic, Sam. She messed with all our heads. You, me, your dad, even Pip. She had us all fooled.'

He sniffs. Roisin offers us both a tissue. I blow my nose. 'I should have been more careful.'

'No,' he says, 'it wasn't you. You didn't do anything wrong.'

'I was irresponsible, Sam. That day at the lake…' I look

at Roisin. 'I was trying to be... something between a mother and a friend, but I can see that was confusing. The boundaries... it gave her a way in.'

But Roisin shakes her head. 'From what Sam has told me and from what I can see, you have been and continue to be supportive and loving.' She adds, emphatically, 'Maternal.'

She pauses, giving the word time to land.

Maternal.

'You have provided Sam with a positive female role model. He trusts you and you have never betrayed that trust. This has given Sam an anchor. Without it, Rebecca's impact might have been considerably more damaging.'

She's looking at me, nodding, smiling and I'm grasping at these words floating in the air between us. Maternal. Anchor. Trust.

'For Sam's recovery now, his relationship with you is invaluable. He wanted to apologise to you today because he wants to retrieve that relationship and build on it.'

I keep my eyes locked on Roisin's, afraid that if I turn away, the words will float off, but my hand feels for Sam's. I'm waiting to see her frown, for a 'but' or a reprimand, but she keeps smiling. Sam's fingers slip between mine and I feel the gentlest squeeze and in that moment something precious is retrieved.

Pip calls as we leave. She is clipped and to the point. 'Would you mind driving over to Chimneys with Sam? We need to talk. Jonty's here.' Her tone brings me back down to earth with a thud. What Roisin may think of my relationship with Sam is of little consequence if Pip and Jonty still doubt me.

I assume they are anxious about me being alone with Sam, regretting allowing us to travel together unsupervised. It's time to face the music.

It's a beautiful blue and gold day, the lake a perfect mirror of the sky. Families are gathered by the shore with picnics spread out. Children splash about. Boats stitch seams across the surface of the water. I try and picture myself here with a child, but the image is unbearably sad. I don't know if I can stay here. If I can't be with the people I love, if I'm not part of this family, I don't know how I can live this life.

Pip greets us, stiff and straight, her mouth a thin line. Jonty fills one end of the sofa, his face stern, his body dark and glowering against the soft white cushions. They've been talking. They're going to sit me down and insist that the rules be laid out clearly for the future, so there can be no more mistakes. The French doors are open on to the garden. A pair of wooden seats have been positioned on the lawn facing the glimmering lake. I picture Pip and Jonty sitting there before we arrived, preparing what they were going to say and I can't help feeling how ironic it is, after all my attempts to build bridges between them, that it's me and their joint problem with me that has pulled them together.

Sam follows me in, sitting beside me, and I can sense this is a mistake, that he should be on the other side, with them, but I say nothing because I need him here next to me; I can't do this alone. The time has come. They're going to tell me I can't see him again.

Pip lowers herself, straight backed, on to the sofa and takes a breath. 'I have some rather upsetting news.' She glances at Sam and back at me. Her face is creased with worry. I spool back through what's happened today, trying to work out what I might have done to upset her this much. 'I have spoken with the solicitor. It appears that the police are struggling to gather enough evidence to satisfy the Crown Prosecution Service that there is a case to answer with respect to Rebecca and Sam.'

Jonty interrupts. 'She's going to get away with it.'

Pip clicks her tongue, in that way she does with Jonty, and he stiffens. 'Not necessarily.' She pauses. 'But we have to prepare ourselves for the possibility. If it does go to trial, it will be Sam's word against hers.'

'But he was a minor! She was his teacher!'

Jonty is nodding, echoing my frustration. 'But he was seventeen. Old enough, in legal terms, to have consensual sex.'

'Consensual!'

Sam stands up. He moves away from us, hands thrust into his pockets, shoulders hunched. 'She didn't force me.'

'She manipulated you!'

Pip's voice is calm, resigned. 'That's a very difficult thing to prove. And much as we would all like to see justice served, we have to consider the impact a protracted court case could have on Sam.'

We all look at him as he turns to face us. His eyes meet mine and he gives a little nod, as if he's heard my thoughts and understands, but… 'Let her go,' he says, his voice steady, resolved. 'She can't hurt us now.'

Us.

He steps out of the door and we all watch him walk across the lawn towards the lake.

He's right. If we insist on pushing for a prosecution, we remain caught up in this nightmare she created. It isn't just about Sam but all of us and we need to get on with our lives.

Much as that terrifies me, I need to know how it's going to be from now on. And so does Sam.

Pip says, 'If it's any consolation, I can at least make sure she doesn't work in Cumbria again or possibly further afield. I will let it be known that she is not to be trusted around young people.'

'And there's still the assault charge,' Jonty adds, as if this is important. 'She won't get away with what she did to you.'

We watch Sam pick up a stone and crouch low, sending it skimming across the surface of the water. He's been hurt, but he is working his way through this. Rebecca isn't important any more. She was never important.

Pip and Jonty are working up to what they want to say. Now Sam's out of the room they can speak frankly. I'm so tempted to follow Sam. I want to be in the sunshine, looking out across the lake as if none of this had ever happened, but that's not possible. The baby shifts inside me. I picture little fingers unfurling like the fronds of a fern. There's no going back, there's only what happens next and I can't avoid this any longer.

My mouth is paper dry. Pip looks at me, green eyes sharp and I brace myself. Whatever the conditions are that she lays out, I will have to accept them. This is about Sam, not me. She takes a deep breath. 'I would like to make a suggestion. I know you are settled into your cottage and managing perfectly well at the moment, but—'

Jonty interrupts. 'When the baby comes, it's going to be difficult.'

I can't look at his face; the familiar crease around those dark eyes, the gentleness. It would be so easy right now to step back, to let Jonty try and take care of me, but sooner or later I will remember. Some things can never be undone. I shake my head. 'I'm sorry, I can't. It wouldn't work. We've talked about this.'

Jonty shakes his head. 'No, I'm not suggesting you and me—'

Pip snorts. 'Good grief! That would be a disaster. No, no, I'm asking if you would consider moving in here, to Chimneys, when the baby is born. Jonty could bring you here from the hospital and I could help. For as long as you feel that's useful.'

Come back here? With the baby? To this storybook house with its hidden corners and secret spaces? To Pip, who has done this before, who understands?

'Chimneys needs people,' she continues, warming to her theme. 'She needs a family. Looking through those old photographs… I miss the bustle. Chimneys was always bursting with energy and life and possibility. Since Richard…' She stops, swallows, struggling to compose herself. This matters to her. 'It would give me an opportunity to do something positive. To make a difference.'

Pip wants me, the disgraced interloper, the stained offcomer with all her grubby baggage and her unplanned baby, to move in here with her?

'After all those years of patching up and making do…' She looks around the immaculate room, which could be a centre-spread in *Homes and Gardens* magazine. 'But what's it all for? The truth is, Lizzie, I'm lonely rattling around here. I would appreciate the company. Your company. The company of your friends and colleagues – such interesting, creative people with their positive energy – and, of course, the baby.'

'You want a baby in this house?'

She smiles. 'I'm good with babies; it's the teenage boys I find a little difficult.'

We all laugh then, more than we need to. It's a relief to be laughing again. Sam is standing at the water's edge and I'm reminded of the day at Coniston, watching him drinking it in. Let the lake work its magic. It's kind of Pip, and I appreciate the offer, but this is Sam's space and I have to think about what's right for him. As if he's sensed me, he turns and walks back up the lawn towards us. The breeze blows his hair across his face. He's as tall as Jonty now and starting to fill out in the chest, beginning to look like the man he will become.

Pip calls out, 'I'm trying to persuade Lizzie to move in here with the baby.'

He throws me that Jonty smile and nods. 'Good.' He's assuming I'll agree. 'Will you be here by Friday?' That's three days away. 'Nell's coming. You have to be here when Nell comes.'

'Nell? Here?'

Pip nods. 'She's asked specifically if you will be here.'

Nell. Here with us, in this house. Nell running through the room and out on to the lawn, cartwheeling towards the lake. Nell curled up beside me on this sofa, her hand on my growing belly.

'She wants to know if it's going to be a brother or a sister.'

I like the way that sounds. *Brother or sister.* I like hearing Sam say it. This baby will be part of him and Nell, part of Jonty and Pip. I will be connected to these people by a recognisable thread. I can feel it pulling at me already. A family.

Acknowledgements

Thank you to the wonderful team at Head of Zeus. To my editors, Laura Palmer and Madeleine O'Shea for believing in the book and recognising the beauty I was seeking to find, despite a dark story. To Anna Green of Siulen Design for the beautiful cover, to Lucy Ridout, copyeditor extraordinaire, and to the Marketing, Publicity and Sales teams who work so hard to get this book read.

I must thank Wendy Bowker and Frances Wilson at whose creative writing days I dared to believe that this might be something I could do. Thanks also to Barbara Trapido, whose early support and faith have kept me going, to Diana Beaumont, my agent, who has believed in my writing from that very first novel all those years ago. To Alison Hennessey for excellent and generous feedback which greatly improved my first draft. To my writing buddies: first and foremost, Caroline Gilfillan, a continual source of support and encouragement and as essential to my writing life as the air that I breathe. Also to Kirstie Pelling, Beth Broomby, Aga Lesiewicz and all the writers from The Reading Room workshops – one day we will write the perfect synopsis! Thanks to those early readers: Ola Bayford, Melanie Gifford, Jan Heffernan and the infinitely patient Anna McCullough, who has listened to me go over and over the story of this novel during countless dog walks. Finally, thanks to Jo Ball for her left-field suggestion, which provided me with a dramatic and engaging first chapter.

For research I am grateful to James Bailey, who is a far better man than his fictional counterpart! I shall make sure there's a much nicer policeman in the next novel. Also thanks to Marett Troostwyk, for advice regarding the behaviour of vulnerable young people, and to Dr Nicola Graham-Kevan, Reader in Psychology of Aggression, University of Central Lancashire, who took the time to read and offered fascinating insights into psychopathy. Finally, thanks to Joe and Louie Sherno for that Mitcham smile, and my family, for their never-ending support and continuing patience.

[illegible] the [illegible] Reading Room workshops—one [illegible] Thanks to those early [illegible] Jan Heffernan and the [illegible] who has listened to me [illegible] novel during countless dog [illegible] for the left-field suggestion [illegible] and engaging first chapter [illegible] to James Bailey, who is a far [illegible] I shall make sure [illegible] next novel. Also thanks [illegible] regarding the behaviour [illegible] and to Dr Nicola Graham-[illegible] aggression, University of [illegible] the time to read and offered [illegible] Finally, thanks to Joe [illegible] smile, and my family, for [illegible] continuing patience.